S. J. Bolton was born in Lancashire. *Awakening* is her second novel. Her spellbinding début, *Sacrifice*, is also published by Corgi Books and her new novel, *Blood Harvest* is out soon. She lives near Oxford with her husband and young son.

For more information about the author and her books, visit her web

CRITIC͟ ͟ON

'Splendidly crafted, deeply disturbing'   *The Times*

'A chilling, mesmerising thriller'   TESS GERRITSEN

'Grabs from the very beginning and holds on tight'
Literary Review

'A dazzling début in thriller-writing: fast paced, gripping and full of atmosphere'   *Classic FM*

'S.J. Bolton is one to watch'   SIMON BECKETT

'There is enough forensic pathology, both animal and human, to keep fans of Patricia Cornwell happy . . . remarkable'   *Birmingham Post*

'This eerie tale had me so hooked I was reading it through the night'   *Peterborough Evening Telegraph*

'An intense, fast paced thriller'   *Crimesquad.com*

'A bone-chilling, spellbinding tale'   *Scots Magazine*

www.rbooks.co.uk

AWAKENING

'S. J. Bolton has elevated herself to the High Priestess of English Rural Gothic. If she carries on like this she will have worshippers in their millions'   *The Times*

'Bolton goes for the gothic with gusto here ... a powerful cocktail of creepiness'   *Time Out*

'Assured and original. *Sacrifice* was good: *Awakening* is even better'   SIMON BECKETT

'Full marks ... Bolton racks up the tension in preparation for a nail-biting finale'   *Yorkshire Post*

'A tour de force – totally grips from beginning to end'
JENNI MURRAY

'Devilishly clever ... a terrifying climax ... a classy, fast-moving and gripping thriller ... You wouldn't want to miss it!'   *Lancashire Evening Post*

'An original and atmospheric chiller'   *Daily Mail*

Also by S. J. Bolton
and published by Corgi Books

SACRIFICE

Awakening

S. J. Bolton

CORGI BOOKS

TRANSWORLD PUBLISHERS
61–63 Uxbridge Road, London W5 5SA
A Random House Group Company
www.rbooks.co.uk

AWAKENING
A CORGI BOOK: 9780552159784

First published in Great Britain
in 2009 by Bantam Press
an imprint of Transworld Publishers
Corgi edition published 2010

Addresses for Random House Group Ltd companies outside the UK
can be found at: www.randomhouse.co.uk
The Random House Group Ltd Reg. No. 954009

The Random House Group Limited supports The Forest Stewardship
Council (FSC), the leading international forest certification organisation.
All our titles that are printed on Greenpeace approved FSC certified paper
carry the FSC logo. Our paper procurement policy can be found at
www.rbooks.co.uk/environment

Typeset in 11/14.5pt Sabon by
Falcon Oast Graphic Art Ltd.
Printed in the UK by CPI Cox & Wyman, Reading, RG1 8EX.

2 4 6 8 10 9 7 5 3 1

For my mother, who is nothing like Clara's,
except in the extent to which she is loved; for my
father, who gave his daughters their dreams and
the courage to chase them;
and for Vincent, who is our rock.

'Look before you leap, for snakes among
sweet flowers do creep.'

Proverb

Prologue

THE DARKEST HOUR I'VE EVER KNOWN BEGAN LAST Thursday, a heartbeat before the sun came up. It was going to be a beautiful morning, I remember thinking, as I left the house; soft and close, bursting with whispered promises, as only a daybreak in early summer can be. The air was still cool but an iridescence on the horizon warned of baking heat to come. Birds were singing as though every note might be their last and even the insects had risen early. Making the most of the early-morning bounty, swallows dived all around me, close enough to make me blink.

As I approached the drive leading to Matt's house the fragrance of wild camomile swirled up from the verge. His favourite scent. I stood there for a moment, staring at the gravel track that disappeared around laurel bushes, kicking my feet to stir up the scent and thinking that camomile smelled of ripe apples and of the first hint of wood-smoke on an autumn breeze. And I couldn't help but wonder what it might be like to walk up the drive, steal into the house and wake the man by rubbing camomile on his pillow.

I carried on walking.

When I reached the top of Carters Lane I saw the door to Violet's cottage was slightly open; which it shouldn't have been, not at this hour. I drew closer and stood on the threshold, looking at the peeling paint-work, the darkness of the hall beyond. She was probably an early riser, old people usually are; but at the sight of that open doorway, something began to tense inside me.

The doorstep was damp. Someone with wet shoes had stood here minutes earlier. It didn't necessarily mean anything; it could easily be coincidence, but none of the reassurances I could summon up seemed to soothe away a growing sense of disquiet. I pushed at the door. It opened a further six inches and hit an obstacle.

'Violet?' I called. No reply. The silent house waited to see what I would do next. I pushed the door again. It moved a few more inches, revealing a damp trail on the floor. I squeezed round it and stepped into the hall.

The sack behind the door was hessian, with a string-tie pulling the opening tight. It looked like the sandbags the Environment Agency produces when floods are imminent. But I didn't think this sack had sand inside. It wasn't heavy enough, for one thing. Nor did it have the solid, regular shape of a sandbag, especially a damp one. And this one wasn't damp, it was soaking.

'Violet,' I called again. If Violet could hear me she wasn't letting on.

The door at the end of the hallway was open and I

could see the room beyond was empty. There was no sign of Violet's dog, Bennie.

And that's the point at which I stepped from anxiety to fear. Because a dog, even one that's elderly and far from well, won't normally allow someone to enter its house without a response of some sort. Violet could still be asleep; she might not have heard me call. Bennie would have heard.

Knowing it was the last thing in the world I wanted to do, I turned and bent down beside the sack. Wet, solid, but not sand; definitely not sand. I pulled out the small penknife I keep in my pocket, cut through the string and allowed the sack to fall open. Then I took hold of the bottom corners and tipped the damp, dead contents on to the worn linoleum of Violet's hall floor.

Bennie, looking even smaller than he had in life, lay before me. I didn't need to touch him to know that he was dead, but I bent and stroked his coarse fur even so. There were a few shallow wounds around his face and neck where he'd injured himself, scrambling to be free as he'd sunk deeper into whatever pond or river he'd been flung. But the sack still wasn't empty. I moved my fingers and something else fell out. Terribly injured, its body badly mauled and just about torn apart in places, the snake convulsed once before falling still.

For a moment I thought I'd be sick. I sank down on to the cold floor, knowing I had to find Violet, but unable to summon up the courage. And the strangest thought was going through my head.

Because it seemed that something was missing. I was remembering history lessons from school, when we'd

11

studied Ancient Rome and hung on the teacher's every word as he'd entertained us with stories of Roman justice, torture and executions. One particular mode of death had caught our imagination: the convicted prisoner – who, I think now, must have committed just the worst sort of crime – was tied into a sack with a dog, a snake and something else; was it an ape – or some sort of farmyard animal? And then flung into the river Tiber. Most of the class had laughed. It was all so long ago, after all, and there was a touch of the comic about that particular collection of animals. Even I could see that. But I'd never really thought before what it must be like to be tied up in a sack with an animal – any animal – and flung into water. You would fight – frenziedly, hysterically – there'd be teeth and claws everywhere and water flooding into your lungs. And the pain would be beyond . . .

I had to find Violet.

I made my way along the hall and through the living room. A door at the far end led to the stairs. I found a light-switch and flicked it on. It wasn't a long flight of stairs but climbing it seemed to take for ever.

There were two open doors at the top. To the left, a small room: twin beds, dresser, fireplace, and a window looking out over woodland. I took a deep breath and turned to the right.

Part One

Part One

1

Six days earlier

HOW DID IT ALL BEGIN? WELL, I SUPPOSE IT WOULD be the day I rescued a newborn baby from a poisonous snake, heard the news of my mother's death and encountered my first ghost. Thinking about it, I could even pinpoint the time. A few minutes before six on a Friday morning and my quiet, orderly life went into meltdown.

Seven minutes to six. I'd run hard. Panting, dripping with sweat, I found my key and pushed open the back door. The moment I did so my young charges started screeching.

Rubbing a towel across the back of my neck I crossed the kitchen, lifted the lid of the incubator and looked down. There were three of them, hardly more than a handful apiece, hungry, grumpy balls of feathery fluff. Barn-owl chicks: two weeks old and orphaned just days after birth when their mother hit a large truck. A local birdwatcher had seen the dead owl and knew where to find the nest. He'd brought the chicks to the wildlife hospital where I'm the resident veterinary surgeon. They'd been close to death, cold and starving.

They'd been starving ever since. I took a tray from the fridge, found a pair of tweezers and dangled a tiny, dead mouse into the incubator. It didn't last long. The chicks were thriving but, worryingly, getting far too used to me. Hand-rearing wild birds is tricky. Without some sort of human intervention, orphaned chicks will die; at the same time, they mustn't become dependent on humans. In a couple more weeks I was hoping to introduce them to avian foster-parents who would teach them the skills they needed to hunt and feed themselves. Until then I had to be careful. It was probably time to move them to an enclosed nesting box and start using a barn-owl-shaped glove puppet at mealtimes.

Three minutes to six. I was heading upstairs for a shower when the phone rang, and I braced myself to be called in to deal with yet another roe deer run over on the A35.

'Miss Benning? Is that Miss Benning, the vet?' A young woman's voice. A very distressed young woman's voice.

'Yes, speaking,' I answered, wondering if I was going to get my shower after all.

'It's Lynsey Huston here. I live just up the road from you. Number 2. There's a snake in my baby's cot. I don't know what to do. I don't know what the hell to do.' Her voice was rising with every word; she seemed verging on hysteria.

'Are you sure?' Silly question, I know, but be fair,

a snake in a cot isn't something you see every day.

'Of course I'm sure. I'm looking at it now. What the hell do I do?'

She was too loud.

'Stay quiet and don't make any sudden movements.' I, on the other hand, was moving fast, out of the house, grabbing my car keys as I went, bleeping open the boot, reaching inside. 'Do you think it's bitten her?' I asked. Surprising myself, I remembered that the baby was a girl. I'd seen pink balloons outside the house a few weeks ago.

'I don't know. She looks like she's asleep. Oh God, what if she's not asleep?'

'Is her colour normal? Can you see her breathing?' I grabbed a couple of things from the back of the car and set off up the hill. I could see the Hustons' house, a sweet, whitewashed cottage at the top of the lane. The family was new to the village, had only lived there a few weeks, but I thought I could picture the mother, about my age, tallish, with shoulder-length fair hair. She and I had never spoken before.

'Yes, I think so; yes, she's pink. Can you come? Please say you can come.'

'I'm nearly there. The important thing is not to frighten the snake. Don't do anything to alarm it.' I pushed open the gate and ran up the path to the front door. It was locked. I ran round the back. The phone I was carrying was too far from its base station and began to beep at me. I switched it off and pushed at the back door.

I was inside a brightly coloured, modern kitchen. For

17

a house with a newborn baby it seemed remarkably tidy and clean. I put the phone down on the table and walked along the hall in the direction of the voice I could hear gabbling upstairs. As I approached the stairs I noticed damp patches and traces of mud on the otherwise spotless tiled floor. A familiar sound caught my attention. Glancing to the right I saw an incubator of newborn chicks in a small utility room. The family kept chickens.

'I'm in the house,' I called out softly. When I reached the top of the stairs I saw a scared, white face peering at me from behind a door at the far end of the corridor. The woman beckoned and I walked towards her. She stepped back and allowed me into the room.

I was in a small, pink and cream bedroom tucked under the eaves. Supporting beams stood out dark against the white plaster of the walls. Pink fabric, printed with fairies and toadstools, lined the small, deep-set window. Stuffed animals, mainly pink, were everywhere I looked. Against the longest wall stood the crib, a baby princess's cradle from a fairy tale: all cream lace and pink flounces. I stepped closer, still nourishing the hope that had sprung up when I answered the phone, that the snake would be a toy one, a practical joke played on the mother by an older child.

The baby, tiny and perfect, panted softly in a white baby-gro embroidered with pink rabbits. Her mouth was slightly open, I could see the perfect raised pores above her upper lip, long dark eyelashes and the faint traces of a milk rash on her cheeks. Her fists were clenched and her arms thrown above her head in the classic newborn-baby sleeping pose. She looked absolutely fine.

Apart from the fact that she was sharing her bed with a venomous snake that would strike the moment she moved.

2

SURPRISINGLY, GIVEN THE ROW THE MOTHER HAD BEEN making, the snake appeared to be sleeping too. It lay, half curled up, half stretched out, across the baby's chest, enjoying the warmth of the infant's body, slowly raising its own body temperature to match hers. It was about fourteen inches long and, I guessed, would have a circumference of about three and a half inches at its widest point. Not a young snake.

With my arrival, the mother had quietened down, but still looked ready to lose it any time.

'I thought it was probably a grass snake,' she said in a theatrical whisper, 'but I couldn't be sure. They can be dark grey, can't they?'

I was pulling on my gloves, made of toughened leather and reaching past the elbows; they protect my arms from the bites of larger mammals, badgers, foxes and the like. I hadn't used them to handle a snake before.

'It isn't a grass snake. I need you to stay where you are and be calm. Don't make any sudden movements or noises.'

'Oh shit, it's not an adder, is it? That man, last week, on the high street, it was an adder that bit him. They say he's really ill.'

I moved closer. I hadn't heard about anyone being bitten, but the news didn't concern me particularly. 'He'll be fine,' I began. 'An adder bite won't . . .' I stopped. I'd been about to say an adder bite wouldn't kill a healthy adult, which would have been extremely tactless in the circumstances. The last person to die of an adder bite in the UK had been a five-year-old child. A newborn baby bitten by an adult adder might not live until we got her to hospital.

'Quiet now, please.'

'What should I do? Should I phone an ambulance?'

She wasn't capable of quiet. I had to get her out of the room.

'Yes, but do it downstairs, do it quietly. Tell them the situation and say your baby may need medical assistance immediately. They'll need to be prepared to resuscitate a young infant.'

Reluctantly, she left the room, and I moved forward. My legs were having trouble doing what I asked of them and inside the thick gloves my hands were shaking. It felt like a long time since I'd been scared of an animal. I'd been in cages with tigers and filed elephants' toenails. I'd given sedatives to badgers crazed with pain and helped a buffalo give birth. I'd experienced excitement, exhilaration, many times; I'd had several attacks of nerves, but I'd rarely felt fear.

I was very frightened, though, for the innocent little tot just feet away from me, dreaming her safe baby

21

dreams of milk and cuddles. Because the predator on her chest, leaching away her warmth like a parasite, had phenomenal killing power. Snake venom is a complex substance, designed to immobilize, kill and then aid digestion of prey. If this tiny creature were bitten, within minutes the anti-coagulants in the adder's venom would prevent her blood from clotting and she would continue to bleed from the wound. She'd feel immense pain; the shock of it alone might kill her. After a while, proteolytic enzymes would start to break down her body tissues and she'd suffer internal haemorrhaging. Eventually her flesh would swell, her skin turn blue, purple, even black.

And all this with just one bite. Just one lightning-charged strike and her brief existence could be over. Even if she survived she'd be badly scarred.

Well, not if I had anything to do with it.

I took a deep breath to steady myself. The snake was still asleep but the baby – oh no, no, no – was waking up. She murmured, stretched, wriggled. If she was any-thing like my nieces had been as babies, the moment of waking would be the instant she realized she was starving. She'd open her mouth and wail for her mother. Kick her legs and throw her arms around. The adder would panic. It would defend itself. Time had run out. Even then I didn't move.

I'd never touched a wild British snake. I wasn't even sure I'd seen an adder before, but there was no doubt what I was looking at. Grass snakes are long, slender snakes with oval-shaped heads. This snake was shorter, squatter, with the distinctive zigzag down its dark-grey skin and the V for viper on its forehead.

The baby mewed; the snake woke.

It rose up and looked around, tongue flickering, sensing a threat but unsure where it was coming from. There was a sudden noise outside. Lynsey was back. I reached for the snake. It spun round, struck at me and we grabbed each other.

As the adder fastened its fangs into the leather of my glove I took hold of it close to the head with my other hand and lifted it up and away from the crib. Lynsey gave an inarticulate cry and ran – faster than the adder's strike, it seemed to me – for her baby's cot. She grabbed the child and began to mutter mummy nonsense as I kicked open the lid of the animal-transporter box I'd brought from my car and dropped the snake into it. It took a bit of persuasion for it to let go of my glove, but a gentle squeeze behind the head did it. I closed the box, locked it and pulled the gloves off. My right wrist had two tiny indentations where the snake had grabbed me, but the skin wasn't broken. I turned back to Lynsey and her daughter. Tears were pouring down the mother's face.

'We need to get her undressed,' I said. 'I'm sure she's fine but we need to check.'

I steered them both to the changing table and, when Lynsey seemed incapable of functioning, took the baby gently from her and laid her down. I took off the baby-gro, vest and nappy, hardly able to believe the softness of her pearl-like skin.

Furious that her normal routine of snuggles and all the milk she could drink was being withheld, the baby's

23

arms and legs shot in every direction and her face turned puce as she yelled for breakfast. I took hold of her wrists and stretched out her arms, then the same thing with her legs. I turned her over and examined her back, her plump bottom, the nape of her neck. Everything perfect.

I picked her up and reluctantly (how surprising, I've never been fond of babies) handed her back to her mother. Lynsey grasped her like she was a missing part of her own body and tugged open her blouse.

After a few minutes, during which Lynsey didn't seem capable of talking and I had nothing to say, I heard footsteps downstairs and a male voice. Bracing myself (meeting strangers for the first time is always an ordeal), I picked up the snake's box and went down to meet the ambulance crew. Carefully avoiding eye contact, I explained what had happened, grabbed my phone and called goodbye to Lynsey and her daughter.

Only as I was walking home did I realize I hadn't asked the baby's name and that I would probably never now get the chance. Pearl, I decided I would call her, because she had skin like a soft-pink pearl.

The owl chicks, ever hopeful, started up again when I opened the front door. They were probably making less noise than both the house phone and my mobile but the difference was marginal. I glanced at the house phone still in my hand. Work. Then at my mobile on the kitchen table. Also work. Hobson's choice.

'Clara, we've got badgers.' It was Harriet, my veterinary nurse and receptionist. 'Badly injured. Coming in now. How quickly can you get here?'

'Badgers? Plural?'

'Three of them. Hardly alive. Found this morning in a warehouse just outside Lyme. They've been badly mauled.'

I sighed and looked at the clock. It was 7.20 a.m. and I'd already gone head to head with a poisonous snake and spoken to three more people than I normally do all morning. Now I had to deal with a particularly nasty case of badger-baiting.

About two miles on to the A35 I pulled off the road. There's an area of heathland there, an adder's natural home. I walked a hundred yards in and let the snake out of the box. It disappeared in seconds.

3

ONE OF THE BADGERS WAS A PREGNANT SOW THAT gave birth fifteen minutes after arriving at the hospital. A few seconds later she was dead. The three tiny cubs, hardly bigger than mice, were whisked off to intensive care.

The more badly injured of the two remaining adults was a young boar. He had serious lacerations across his abdomen, bite marks covering both his front claws, half his snout was missing and I really didn't like the look of one of his front legs.

'Bastards,' said Craig, the senior nurse, beside me. I couldn't argue.

Badger-baiting was outlawed in the UK in 1835 but continues to this day as one of our most cruel, illegal blood sports. For some unfathomable reason, it's even enjoyed something of a renaissance in the south-west in recent years. The rules of engagement are pretty simple: you take one healthy, adult badger, deliberately harmed in advance to slow him down, and put him in a confined space with several dogs. Then you place bets on how long the badger will last.

At one time, fights typically took place in setts, the badgers' underground homes, but these days the animals are more often chased from their setts by terriers and transported in secret to specially dug pits. Open countryside, particularly if it offers shelter in the form of old farm buildings, is a popular choice of location, but evidence of badger-baiting has been found close to towns, on industrial estates or in abandoned warehouses.

Should a badger ever win, he gets clubbed to death. Finding three survivors was extremely unusual, and I could only imagine the fight had been interrupted and the perpetrators forced to flee.

Our badger was already in a strong, close-meshed steel cage, so I wouldn't have to worry about handling him. Badgers are extremely strong, entirely un-predictable and frequently aggressive. They also have exceptionally powerful jaws. You do not – ever – want to get bitten by a badger. Over the next hour, I would try to get him stable, treat the worst of his injuries and load him up with pain relief. After that, it was up to him.

Craig lowered the ceiling of the cage until the badger was immobile and I could inject a mix of medetomidine, ketamine and butorphanol into his hind-leg muscle. It was a pretty effective cocktail of anaesthetics and painkillers, but the anaesthetic would need topping up by inhalation throughout the procedure. That would be Craig's job. When I judged it safe, I opened the cage and Craig and I lifted him on to the operating table.

He'd lost a lot of blood. It took me a minute or two to find a vein, but after that I soon had him hooked up to a drip. I gave him an injection of methyl-prednisolone to treat his shock and one of amoxicillin to help fight infection.

'Any hope of catching the gang?' I asked, as I began cleaning the wounds around his snout, relieved to see the muscular damage wasn't too bad. Some of the pelt was hanging loose. I would try to reattach it.

'Not much,' said Craig, his voice muffled by the mask he was wearing. Bovine TB is a common problem in the south-west. Not all badgers are infected but, when treating them, we have to assume they may be. 'They've got a van registration number and they've tracked it as far as Exeter, but their vehicles are nearly always stolen, aren't they?'

I nodded. These were organized gangs. They made a lot of money from their illegal gatherings. They knew how to protect themselves.

The lacerations on the abdomen weren't as serious as I'd first feared, but in late spring fly-strike on open wounds can be a problem. I rinsed with disinfectant and insecticide. Once the wounds were clean, I could suture them quickly.

'Police found a dead dog at the site,' said Craig. 'Staffordshire bull terrier. Some poor kid's pet.'

I'd heard that tremor in Craig's voice before. He could cope with the sickest, most badly injured animal but found it hard to deal with deliberate cruelty. 'How do you do it, Clara? How do you stay so calm?' he'd asked me once, tears streaming down his face as we'd euthanized a young fawn whose eyes had been gouged out by a gang of teenagers. He and the rest of the staff thought me cold. But how could I tell them that human cruelty never surprised me. I'd been dealing with it every day for as long as I could remember.

The door opened and Harriet appeared. I saw the look on her face and braced myself to hear that the other badger was dead.

'Clara, you need to take a phone call,' she said, hovering in the doorway.

I shook my head and held up gloved hands, covered in blood and bristles. 'I'll be done in an hour,' I said and turned back to my patient.

'Clara, it's your father. You really need to take this.'

I looked at her again, realized what her watery eyes and scared look really meant. Not a badger, then. It wasn't the badger that had died.

I unhooked my mask and pulled off a glove. Pressing the receiver to my ear, I listened to what my father had to say, then told him I'd call him later. He was still talking when I pressed the tiny button that cut him off and handed the phone back to Harriet.

'I'm pretty certain the right front humerus is broken,' I said. 'If he survives the night, I'll have a look at it in the morning. An intramedullary pin might work.'

Harriet was still in the room, ostensibly cleaning the phone with disinfectant. Out of the corner of my eye I caught her giving Craig a look.

'Everything OK?' he asked me. I nodded my head slowly and got on with my stitching. I forced myself to concentrate, knowing Harriet was mouthing words

29

to Craig and that he was struggling to lip-read. He was no longer looking at the badger's head, and it takes a lot to break his concentration. I glanced up.

'I think he's waking up,' I said. Craig looked down, mind back on the job.

'Clara, you should go. Be with your family,' tried Harriet.

'When I'm done,' I said, without looking up. 'Can you make sure blood samples get sent to DEFRA? And how are the cubs doing?'

She shrugged, gave one last look at Craig and left the room.

I passed by the nursery on the way to collect the other badger. The three orphaned cubs were huddled in an incubator. They'd taken some milk – a special version of infant formula we use on newborn mammals – and were doing as well as could be expected. They lay together, huddled for warmth, panting and mewling. Tiny, scared, motherless.

Rather like me.

4

THE LITTLE ORDER OF ST FRANCIS, WHERE I'VE worked for nearly five years, was founded by Catholic monks in the late nineteenth century to treat sick and injured wild animals. These days a charitable trust keeps it going: we get donations from all over the world, hundreds of people are our 'Friends' in return for an annual subscription and the visitor centre attracts thousands every year. We will treat any British wild animal – mammal, reptile, bird, amphibian – no matter how small or how badly injured. Only when an animal is in so much pain that to treat it would be cruelly to prolong its suffering do we put it down. Some people accuse us of being ridiculously sentimental, of squandering charitable goodwill that could go to more deserving causes. Personally, I think people should be free to choose for themselves the object of their charity and that all lives, even tiny, secretive, short ones, have a value and a purpose.

The third badger was not so badly injured. It took me just over forty minutes to do as much as I could, then I sent him away for rest and observation. When we'd finished, Harriet was waiting for me again, and I braced myself to run her gauntlet of motherly concern. She was going to make me take a break, serve me hot sweet coffee, force me to talk and, with any luck, break down and cry on her shoulder. Harriet had known me for five years. You'd think she'd know better by now.

I set off towards the nursery, and Harriet had to tag along behind, almost trotting to keep up.

'Clara, there's someone waiting for you in reception. One of the doctors from the Dorset County. He's been here nearly an hour. I told him you were busy and that – well, that it wasn't a good time – but he said it was important. Something about a snake.'

I stopped dead in the corridor and Harriet walked into the back of me. The baby I'd rescued that morning would have gone to the Dorset County Hospital in Dorchester for observation. If the doctor wanted to talk to me urgently, if he was actually here, the adder must have bitten her after all. How could I have missed it? I turned back and was in reception seconds later. A young man in jeans and a sweater jumped up when he saw me. A large shoulder-bag sat by the side of his chair. He strode across, hand held out to take mine. We'd never met before but he seemed in no doubt I was the woman he wanted. Someone had warned him about how I look.

'Miss Benning? Thanks for seeing me. I'm Harry Richards. I'm an ITU consultant at the Dorset. I'd really appreciate the chance to ask your advice about something.'

'Is it about the baby?' I couldn't remember the name

of the family. 'The baby who was admitted this morning?'

'No.' He looked puzzled. 'What baby? I've come about John Allington.'

'Oh,' I said. I didn't know a John Allington. Behind us, Harriet was pretending to shuffle papers.

'I'm very sorry to tell you this,' Dr Richards continued, 'but I'm afraid Mr Allington died this morning.'

'Oh, I see.' Still no nearer.

'I'm sorry. I hope he wasn't a close friend of yours.'

'No,' I said, wondering how long this could go on. As he hadn't come to tell me about the baby, I'd lost interest.

'Sally Johnson suggested I get in touch with you. She said you know a lot about snakes.'

Enough was enough. 'I'm sorry, but I think there's been some mistake. I don't know these people and I really have to . . .'

'You are Clara Benning, the vet here?' He sounded cross, which made two of us.

'Yes. And this is a very busy morning for us . . .'

'Sally Johnson is one of the district nurses attached to the hospital. She told me you and she live in the same village. The village Mr Allington lived in. She says she's your next-door neighbour.'

OK, massive slice of humble pie on the menu. Of course my next-door neighbour was a district nurse; I saw her in her uniform quite often. I think I'd even known her name was Sally. When I'd first moved in she'd popped round a few times, refusing to be put off by the ever chillier welcomes on my part. In the end, I'd just stopped answering the door.

Behind Dr Richards, Harriet had given up all pretence of working. A door opened behind us and a woman and toddler came in. The tiny boy was carrying a shoe-box. 'Birdie,' he explained, marching up to the counter. Another casualty.

'I'm sorry,' I said to Dr Richards. 'It's just been one of those mornings. Look, I have to do a round of the outside enclosures now. Why don't you come with me? We can talk on the way.'

Richards nodded, turned to pick up his bag and then followed me through the reception doors and into the gift shop.

'You're familiar with what happened to Mr Allington?' he asked as we nodded to Holly at the desk and walked outside.

I didn't answer immediately. Then I had it. Lynsey had mentioned someone on the high street being bitten by an adder. That must have been John Allington. And he'd died?

'He was bitten, wasn't he?' I said. 'By an adder.'

'Five days ago. I really need to speak to someone with some knowledge of snake bites and their effects.'

We were in the part of the hospital where we keep hedgehogs, wild rabbits and ducks in low-fenced enclosures. It's popular with children, and we passed a couple of tots with their parents peering into the tiny hutches.

'Surely you've spoken to the poisons centre?' I asked.

The UK National Poisons Information Service should be a doctor's first port of call when dealing with any case of poisoning. They have a number of regional centres and are well set up to offer advice over the phone and on their website, 'Tox-Base'.

'Of course. I was in touch with them as soon as he was admitted and they guided me through his treatment. But no one there is an expert on snake bites. The advice they can give me is very general. There just isn't a need for that sort of specialism in the UK.'

'I understand.' He was right. The last recorded fatality due to snake bite in the UK, the five-year-old child, happened thirty years ago. Since then, probably fewer than twenty patients suffering from snake bite had been referred to hospital.

'So, can you help?' Dr Richards was saying.

'Well,' I said, stalling for time. I wasn't sure whether I could. I wasn't even sure if I wanted to. 'In my second year at university I chose an elective in exotic and wild animals,' I said, in the end. 'I did my summer work experience in Chester and Bristol zoos and, for one reason or another, spent a lot of time with the reptiles.'

I broke off to exchange a few words with the keeper who looked after our small-animal enclosures. All patients were doing well, she told me, and the doctor and I crossed a small bridge and arrived at the lake.

'After my final year I was one of the assistant vets at Chester for a few months, then I spent a year in Australia helping on a reptile research project,' I said, when I realized Dr Richards was waiting for me to continue. 'I also volunteer occasionally at the reptile re-homing centre in Bristol. But for the last five years I've worked here. We don't see many reptiles, I'm afraid.'

We stopped to watch the waterfowl on the lake. It

was more crowded than usual but at this time of year we often get perfectly healthy specimens dropping by for a quick visit. Dr Richards was watching a moorhen splashing around in the reeds.

'The truth is, Clara,' he said, when I'd run through my reptilian resumé, 'nobody at the hospital knows I'm here.'

I said nothing. The moorhen climbed out of the water and shook its feathers.

'I'm sure you know it's highly unusual for a healthy adult, even one of Mr Allington's age, to die from an adder bite,' said Dr Richards. 'As soon as he was admitted we sent samples of his blood off to the bio-chemistry lab. We had the snake that supposedly bit him but, even so, we had to know exactly what we were deal-ing with. We got the results back a couple of days ago.'

'And?'

'There was adder venom in his blood, no doubt about it.'

'And you say the snake was found,' I said, beginning to wonder where all this was going. 'That it's been identified as an adder?'

Richards reached into his shoulder-bag and withdrew a sealed, clear wallet. Inside it was a small snake which I judged to have been dead for several days. 'It was in the garden close by Mr Allington when his gardener found him,' said Richards. 'He'd managed to kill it before he lost consciousness.'

I took the wallet from the doctor and held it up to get a better look at its contents. 'He was brought in un-conscious?' I repeated.

'Yes, but that was a result of his head injury. We think he fell and banged his head, possibly when he started to feel ill. And to cap it all off, he landed in his pond, which is pretty deep by all accounts. Luckily, his head stayed clear of the water. Although as things turned out . . .'

'Yes, quite,' I muttered, handing back the wallet and wondering if I was beginning to share Dr Richards' unease about his patient's death. 'So did he regain consciousness?'

'He did. But it didn't help much. He couldn't really remember anything and was barely lucid at the end. He suffered from extreme vomiting, shortness of breath, lost all control of his limbs and had a high fever.'

'Adder venom is more potent in the spring,' I said. 'When they come out of hibernation. Were there any other underlying conditions? Heart condition? Respiratory disease?'

'None. He was sixty-nine but in very good health for a man of his age.'

'People who are allergic to wasp and bee stings can sometimes react badly to adder venom. Could that have been the problem?'

'The poisons centre suggested that. But none of his symptoms suggested an allergic reaction. Just severe poisoning.'

'Can I ask how you treated him?' I asked. In spite of myself, I'd become interested.

'When he first came in we cleaned the bite site and gave him an anti-tetanus shot. Then I phoned the poisons centre. They told me to keep a close eye on him, to monitor his pulse, his blood pressure and his respiration at fifteen-minute intervals. We weren't too concerned at that point.'

'But he deteriorated?'

'Quickly. We started to see a lot of swelling, not just around the bite site. He was in a huge amount of pain, so I gave him analgesia; also anti-emetics to try and control the vomiting. We gave him a colloid infusion, anti-histamines and adrenaline.'

'What about anti-venom?'

'The poisons centre biked some down. European Viper Venom Antiserum. It seemed to cause an initial improvement but the next day his blood pressure fell and we started to see cardiac arrhythmias. By day three he was suffering seizures. Day four brought acute pancreatitis and renal failure. He spent his last ten hours in a coma.'

I gave Dr Richards the moment of silence the situation seemed to call for.

'That's pretty dreadful. I'm sorry,' I said, after a while. 'But what do you need from me?'

I sat at my desk in the lab, staring down at the papers Harry Richards had left behind. A chemical analysis of a dead man's blood. Every couple of seconds I glanced up and checked the information on the computer screen in front of me. Scattered around the desk were several of my old college textbooks. I looked at the blood-test results again. They weren't going to tell me anything I didn't know already. I picked up the phone.

'It's Clara Benning,' I said, when I got through to

Harry Richards. 'The snake is definitely *Vipera berus*. In other words, a common British adder. And I can't disagree with what your lab found. The venom is also from an adder.'

'Right, then.' He paused for a moment, realizing, as I'd known he would, that I had more to say. 'Is there anything else?'

'Just one snake was found? Is it possible there were more?'

Silence for a while. 'This is the first mention I've heard of others. I suppose there could have been but . . .' He stopped.

'When you examined him, how many bite marks did you see?'

He thought again. I heard a rustling of paper.

'Just one. Two indentations where the fangs punctured the skin. I'm looking at photographs. I can show them to you. Why, what have you found?'

'Not sure yet,' I said. 'Can I hang on to these results and the snake for a couple of days? There's someone else I'd like to ask.'

'So what do I tell the coroner?'

'Tell him tests are still being carried out. I can get back to you on Monday.'

Dr Richards and I wished each other good morning and I started to get up. I had a huge amount to do. Then I sat down again, thinking. Two incidents involving venomous snakes. In the same week. Even the same village. I sighed and picked up the phone again.

'Roger,' I said when I was connected, 'what are you doing tomorrow morning?'

5

'NOT ANOTHER SNAKE!'

I jumped. Harriet had crept up behind me and was staring over my shoulder. She took a closer look. 'Not sure there's much we can do for that one.' Then she leaned towards me, put a hand on my shoulder. I resisted the urge to stiffen; she meant well. 'Clara, are you sure you're OK?' she said. 'I know we're busy, but we can manage if you want to get away.'

I turned round. She was very close, her face not more than six inches from mine, but Harriet was used to me. She didn't flinch.

'What do you mean, "Not another snake"? How many snakes have we got?'

'None in residence,' she said. 'We just seem to have had a rush on them lately.'

'I haven't seen any.'

'Well, you wouldn't have. They were either dead or perfectly OK, just tangled up in netting. Once we got them loose we let them go. They'll all be on the system.'

I pushed my chair so that it slid sideways along the

desk. Every animal arriving at the hospital is recorded in our admissions log. I scanned down the list. That day was the third Friday in May. At the beginning of the week someone had found a grass snake tangled in the netting covering their pond. Harriet and one of the other nurses had cut the nylon net away, checked the snake, found it completely unharmed and set it loose. I checked who'd brought it in. A man from my village.

The previous week, a dog owner had brought in an adder that his animal had caught and savaged while out walking. It had been dead on arrival. I wondered how the dog was. Any snake cornered will put up a fight. The dog owner lived in my village.

The third incident hadn't resulted in an animal appearing at the centre. Someone had called in a panic to say they had an adder in their kitchen. Craig had gone to investigate and discovered that the snake was a smooth snake, similar to the adder in appearance but perfectly harmless. He'd encouraged it out of the house. My village.

It didn't necessarily mean anything. The previous year we'd had a long, hot summer; it was perfectly feasible that a greater than average number of snakes had been born. And so far we'd had an unusually warm spring. All hibernating snakes would be awake and active. It was probably nothing to worry about. Sooner or later natural balance would be restored.

And that's what I told myself – several times – as I drove home.

*   *   *

I'd intended to leave early, but it had just been one of those days. No sooner had we got the badgers stabilized than a young muntjac, badly injured by a speeding car, was brought in. By the time I'd stitched him up, three orphaned fox cubs were waiting for my attention. Despite all my best intentions, it was approaching seven o'clock by the time I turned into my lane.

People in my front garden.

The short, narrow lane curves round to the right, so that the house at the bottom, mine, is tucked away and can hardly be seen until you're practically upon it. I was pulling into my drive when I saw them – one on my doorstep, two loitering in the garden and the fourth leaning over the wall talking to my neighbour, Sally, the district nurse.

I parked the car but didn't move, in the faint hope that they'd just wanted a sneaky look round my property and would slink off now that I'd arrived. I just had to take my time.

When I looked up they were all waiting for me to get out of the car, wondering why I hadn't moved. Fighting a temptation to run round the back, I collected my bags, got out of the car and walked towards the group, making myself look at them and not at the ground. The oldest of the four – they were all men – came towards me with his hand held out. He was tall with thick white hair. I judged him to be in his late fifties.

'Miss Benning? So sorry about this, but we've been hoping you'd come back in time. I'm Phillip Hopwood, from The Elms, top of the high street. You know Daniel, I'm sure.'

I didn't know Daniel from Adam, but Daniel grabbed my hand in both of his. 'I can't tell you how grateful I am,' he said. He was tall and dark-haired, a pleasant-looking man in his early thirties. 'Lynsey's been beside herself all day. I can't think what we would have done without you.'

'Doesn't bear thinking about,' agreed man number three, now standing slightly behind me, making me think – ridiculous, I know, they were all perfectly friendly – that I was being deliberately surrounded, that I was back in the playground. I half turned. He was young but largely bald. Thick stubble on his chin. 'Any idea how the thing got into the bedroom?' he continued.

Daniel shook his head and ran one hand up through his hair. 'God knows,' he said. 'There were windows open but . . . we were wondering if the chicks might have attracted it. Snakes eat baby birds, don't they?'

'How is she?' I asked him, surprising myself. I hadn't planned on talking until it was unavoidable.

'Oh fine, absolutely fine. Lynsey's the wreck. Jumpy as a cricket. Won't let Sophia out of her sight.'

'Can't say I blame her,' said the man who had been talking to Sally. 'Linda would be the same. Can't bear the things.'

'Yes, well,' said the tall man with white hair. 'Time's running on. Perhaps we can explain to Miss Benning . . .'

' 'Course. Go ahead, Phillip.'

'Miss Benning – Clara, is it? – people are concerned. We've all heard about John Allington . . . terrible business . . . and, as for the incident this morning . . . well, thank God you were there.'

'It was no problem, really,' I said, because they seemed to be expecting me to respond. 'I didn't know John Allington but I'm very sorry . . .' I felt my hand tightening on the bag I carried. The snake that had killed John Allington was closer than they knew.

'Yes, yes . . . Thing is, Clara, I've spoken to the local police station, but they say it's not a matter for them. So, we're all getting together tonight to see what can be done about it. Several heads better than one and all that.'

'We'd really appreciate it if you could join us,' said Daniel. 'In ten minutes. At Clive Ventry's house. The old manor.'

I opened my mouth to explain that there'd been a death in the family, that I had phone calls to make, that I really didn't want to spend the evening I'd lost my mother with a load of strangers and what did they – honestly, for heaven's sake – think they were going to do about a sudden increase in the local snake population; and found I couldn't think of the words.

'I'll walk down with you,' offered District Nurse Sally, as if I wasn't capable of finding my way to the manor without help.

'Thanks, but I've got some calls to make. I'll be there as soon as I can.' I squeezed past them and unlocked my front door. They were still watching me, still opening their mouths to speak to me, when I closed the door and shut them out.

* * *

I hadn't realized my answer machine had so many lights, or that they could flicker on and off quite so demandingly. Seven or eight of them were flashing. I flicked the Play switch and went into the kitchen, wondering if I had time to make and drink tea, whether I had anything I could eat quickly.

'Hello, Clarey, it's Dad. Call when you can.'

I opened the fridge and found mineral water. I didn't bother with a glass. Just drank like I'd emerged from a month in the desert.

'Clara, it's Vanessa. I've tried you at work but they said something about an emergency. I expect you'll be home soon, anyway. Call me when you get in.'

I looked at what food I had in the fridge: salad, fruit, cold chicken, cottage cheese. What I wanted was fish and chips, the greasier the better; or a cheeseburger; or mass-produced pizza, dripping with mozzarella and cheap pepperoni. Was this how my grief was to manifest itself, then? In an unprecedented craving for junk food?

'Vanessa again. I can't seem to get through on your mobile either. It would be really good if you called, Clara.'

'Oh, Miss Benning, it's Lynsey Huston from up the lane. I just wanted to say that Sophia is fine. We were discharged about half an hour ago and have just arrived home. Thank you so much for everything you . . .'

Lynsey talked until the machine cut her off.

'Dad again, darling. I'll try later. Hope you're OK.'

'Clara, this is so typical of you. Do you have any idea how much there is to do up here? And what is the point

45

of having a mobile phone if you never answer it? If, for once in your life, you can bring yourself to think of someone other than yourself, could you please give me a call? If it's not too much bloody trouble!'

Twenty minutes later I was out again, already late for the meeting. I couldn't bring myself to hurry, though, as I walked up Bourne Lane.

Including my own, there are seven houses in the lane, built at varying times over the last two hundred years. Down the western side runs a narrow, stone-lined watercourse, one of several diversions of the river Liffin. The Liffin has its source higher up in the Downs, then flows over the chalk for a few miles before splitting into several smaller streams, many of which wend their way through the village and then join the river Yerty a further half-mile downhill.

These little watercourses are one of the distinguishing features of the village: they run down the sides of streets, flow in and out of the village pond, ford their way across roads, disappear under houses, only to re-appear again as a spring in someone's garden. Most large properties here boast streams, ponds, waterfalls – even a lake and a pebble beach in one case. The aquatic nature of the village could certainly go some way towards explaining a thriving grass-snake population. Adders, of course, were another matter. Heathland was their natural home.

I reached the top of the lane and turned to walk down towards the main part of the village. I still hadn't called Dad. I had no idea what I would say to him. Nor had I called Vanessa. I knew only too well what I'd probably end up saying to her.

I walked down the hill, listening to the stream as it bubbled its way over pebbles and noticed another house had a SOLD notice on it; the fourth I'd seen in the last few weeks. Yet no one ever seemed to move into these houses. The SOLD signs would disappear, but the houses remained empty.

For the last four years I've lived here, in this quiet, half-forgotten village on the Devon/Dorset border, where we have a Dorset postcode but a topography that is all Devon. About thirty minutes inland from Lyme Regis, you turn off the B road and head downhill along a single-track road that leads only to this village.

We have no passing traffic. We'd be a safe place for families; except the risk of being cut off in winter deters a lot of people with young children. We're just a little too far from the main towns to be a commuter area so we don't attract the young professionals. Old folks complain about the damp and move out to be nearer the amenities that great age seems to crave. Young people leave as soon as they can and rarely come back. And this slow but steady exodus is being encouraged. Every couple of weeks I get letters from a local property company interested in buying my house. I suspect my neighbours get them too. Mine go straight in the bin.

Because I like it here. I like the quiet; the old, beautiful houses; the fact that I so rarely see my neighbours. I love the vegetation that cloaks everything, softening the hard lines and muffling sound. I think we must have the most fertile soil in England. Our older trees reach massive heights; even the younger, smaller ones have formed dense green canopies over most of the lanes. Gardens flourish, brimming over with colour, while stray plants burst from beneath walls and neglected gutters, even from loose mortar between bricks.

I'd reached the village green. At this point, three roads lead to an area that contains the small village pond, a stone bridge over the river, a patch of daisy-studded grass and the war memorial.

Crossing the bridge, which is just wide enough to take a small car, a sudden splashing made me jump. Thinking immediately of otters, I stepped down to the water's edge and peered underneath the bridge. The Little Order was involved in a project to re-introduce otters to this part of the county, and we were always on the look-out for signs of success.

We'd had a long, wet winter and the river levels were all much higher than normal. It could have been debris rubbing against the side of the bridge that I'd heard. I crouched down and waited, just to be sure. Under the peak of the bridge, the light couldn't reach the stonework and I was staring at black shadows. I waited, keeping my eyes on the water-line, hoping for the tell-tale gleam of tiny, bright eyes.

Something gave a low, guttural cough.

Jumping up quickly, I almost fell over. I looked round but there was no one in sight. In any case, the noise had come from under the bridge. Not wanting to go too close this time, I crouched again. It could have been a fox, even a domestic dog. Except it had sounded distinctly human. Nothing under the bridge but shadows; and a glance at my watch told me I was now twenty minutes late.

Oh, what had I let myself in for? I could just picture it. One or two sensible types trying unsuccessfully to keep everyone calm. They might have persuaded a constable from the nearest police station to join them, and he'd be explaining to an increasingly agitated room why the Dorset Constabulary couldn't provide extra manpower to run snake patrols.

Everyone would have a snake story and insist upon telling it. And I, heaven help me, had been appointed the local snake expert. They'd want to know why there were so many snakes around, why John Allington had died, what the proper authorities (whoever they might be) were going to do about it, how they could keep their children safe. They'd all have something to say and none of them would listen to reason. Well, I had no answers for them and I wasn't going to waste my time. I walked back over the bridge, meaning to turn for home, brace myself and phone Dad.

'Clara, there you are! I was just coming to get you.' District Nurse Sally was standing across the green, sounding out of breath. 'They're waiting for you before they start.'

Resigned to the inevitable, I followed Sally across the grass and into Church Lane, one of the three roads leading into the green. We walked downhill a few yards and turned right into a small, yew-tree-lined cul-de-sac, one I never went down because it led only to the large Tudor manor house at the end. Sally and I walked through a stone archway and across a cobbled courtyard. The house surrounded us, the main wing directly ahead. Sally pulled open the heavy wooden door and ushered me inside.

We were in a large hall, gleaming with dark panels. A minstrels' gallery ran the length of one wall, and an ornate staircase led down from it. Out of the corner of my eye I thought I saw a tall figure dressed in black disappear behind an upstairs door.

Several stairs up stood Phillip Hopwood and, beside him, a tall, powerfully built man. I guessed he was the house's owner and our local celebrity: Clive Ventry, self-made millionaire and round-the-world yachtsman. Ventry's head was turned from me as though he too had been watching the figure on the gallery. And yet I was sure I'd heard he lived alone. Did he have staff? He turned back and I saw that he was in his late forties, maybe just fifty, with thick dark hair, heavy-lidded eyes and a slightly hooked nose.

There must have been over thirty other people in the hall, most of them men. They were all standing, talking loudly, but they stopped when they heard the door close and turned to face me. Thirty people, staring at me: a situation I'd spent my entire life trying to avoid.

Phillip waved from his vantage point on the stairs and beckoned me forward. The last thing I wanted was to be raised above the crowd for all to see but Sally pushed from behind and the folk around the stairs parted to let us through. Phillip leaned down towards me, took my hand and pulled me up until I was on the step below his. I was going no further.

'Miss Benning,' he said, when he'd given up trying to tug me higher. 'Thanks for coming.'

There was movement and scuffling noises as chairs were dragged away from the table and people sat down. Others gathered behind them, leaning on chair backs, some standing against the panelled walls. Clive Ventry nodded at me but didn't speak. Then he glanced again towards the gallery.

Around the furthest corner of a large, wooden refectory table sat a group of five older people. In spite of the warm evening, the three women were huddled into winter coats. One of them wore a red woollen hat and clutched a small terrier on her lap. The two men looked sullen, as though here against their better judgement. One of them was staring nervously at the table top. The other, slightly better dressed, glared round the room.

'As I was saying . . .' A stocky, sandy-haired man had remained standing at the foot of the table, facing the stairs. 'They deal with this all the time in the States. We just need to get ourselves organized.'

Behind me, Phillip puffed out a loud breath.

The sandy-haired man took his hands out of his pockets and, as his eyes fixed on me, his lips curled in a sneer. 'In Kansas, New Mexico, Texas, Oklahoma, Alabama and Georgia . . .' He ticked the states off on his fingers as he recited them. I realized what was coming. I knew what, among other things, those particular states were famous for. 'And in several other states as well,' he continued, 'they have a serious rattlesnake problem.'

Out of the corner of my eye I saw a glance of understanding pass between the two old men, and I thought perhaps the woman in the red hat clutched her dog a little tighter. Around the rest of the room, eyes were fixed on the speaker. And his remained on me.

'People working in the fields, young children playing,' he said, 'they get bitten all the time. Often they can't get to a hospital or there isn't enough antidote available and they die. Maybe they lose an arm or a leg. Millions of dollars' worth of livestock are lost every year due to rattlesnake bites. Snakes move into houses, make their nests in basements, in attics; creep around the house at night looking for food. Just like they're doing here.'

I felt myself give a deep sigh and didn't try to hide it. What he was saying was about one-fifth truth and four-fifths arrant nonsense. Occasionally, people in the States were accidently bitten by rattlesnakes, but most reached hospital before any serious effects had a chance to set in. The majority of rattlesnake bites, though, were a result of stupidity or bravado on the part of the human involved. Even then, treatment was usually successful. There was no documented evidence I'd seen that the snakes were colonizing human dwellings. Rattlesnakes, like most reptiles, avoid human contact whenever they can.

'So, in the spring months,' continued the man, who seemed grimly fascinated by me, 'they hold rattlesnake round-ups. They gather the snakes up and they put them down, humanely. It's a legitimate cull, authorized by the state authorities, and it keeps the population under control. It also provides the venom that the antidote is made from.'

He was beginning to make me angry. And it wasn't just his staring. There is nothing remotely humane about a rattlesnake round-up. The snakes are driven out of dens by gasoline or other toxic chemicals, crammed into unhygienic containers and transported, without food or water, to the round-up events. Most don't survive the journey. The ones that do are used in dare-devil stunts – which usually result in far more bites than would ever occur if the snakes were left to themselves. At the end of it all, the surviving snakes are decapitated or clubbed to death. It's a cruel, stupid spectacle and one that causes huge environmental damage every year.

'And you're proposing we have a round-up here, Mr Keech?' asked Clive Ventry, speaking for the first time. He had an accent that I couldn't quite place. Then I remembered he was South African.

'Starting tonight,' said Keech. 'Round 'em up, put 'em down.' I looked round the hall: to see unwavering attention, nodding heads, an unseemly gleam in a few eyes. It's never far from the surface, is it, our willingness to mistreat those weaker than ourselves? Given a legitimate reason to be cruel, how often do we jump at it?

'What do you think, Clara?' asked Phillip, startling me.

I made myself look directly at Keech. I'd had enough of his gawping. 'I'd be very concerned,' I said, 'if I thought there was the remotest chance of you catching any.'

His eyes narrowed. He must have been ten feet away, but he seemed to lean towards me. If anything, his gaze deepened. 'Oh, I'll catch them,' he said, and it sounded like a threat.

'Rattlesnakes are big snakes,' I said, hoping my voice didn't sound as shaky as it felt. 'They live in easy-to-spot dens and burrows.' By this time my heart was beating so fast I suspect those close to me could see a pulse in my neck. Confrontation is something I avoid at all costs. 'They're relatively easy to find and catch,' I went on. 'Albeit extremely dangerous. Our snakes are much smaller. They hide away, their dens aren't easy to find. Most people in this country have never seen a native snake.'

There was a murmur around the hall. I thought I heard someone questioning what village I lived in.

'More to the point . . .' I began. (I was forcing myself to keep my eyes on Keech, even though the derision I could see as his eyes raked over my face made me want to run for cover. He was the sort of man who saw no earthly use in unattractive women.) 'There are no federal or international laws protecting the rattlesnake,' I continued. 'People in America, unfortunately, are free to do what they like. That isn't the case here. It's against the law to kill or injure a wild British snake. What you're suggesting is illegal.'

'Tell that to John Allington's family!' someone called out.

'She's absolutely right,' said a voice from the doorway. Silence fell, and all heads turned to face the newcomer. He was a slim man of around average height, maybe an inch or two taller. He had very short, dark hair and wore black-rimmed, oblong spectacles. I

54

guessed he'd be in his late thirties, maybe a little older. He had pleasant, regular features that didn't quite tick the handsome box. There was nothing unusual or remarkable about him at all; except that his appearance had calmed the mood of the meeting, if only super-ficially, sending the undercurrent of violence scurrying further beneath the surface.

'I'll let you have a copy of the Wildlife and Countryside Act, Allan,' continued the man at the door. He had an air of authority about him and I wondered if he were from the Environment Agency or perhaps DEFRA, the Department for Environment, Food and Rural Affairs. In which case, I'd gladly step down and let him get on with it. He seemed to be a man people listened to; I was just someone they liked to gawp at.

'That's all very well, Matt,' countered Allan Keech, turning away from me for the first time since I'd entered the room. 'But we do have a problem. My girlfriend's scared to go into the garden.'

The newcomer by the door, Matt, glanced briefly at Allan and then looked back at me. His gaze didn't falter. He held my eyes steadily.

'We do seem a bit overrun, Miss Benning,' he said. 'Can you offer any explanation?'

'Probably just a freaky trick of nature,' I said, wondering if I was right to play down the situation. The number of snake incidents over the past few days had puzzled me too, but the last thing I wanted to do was feed the panic I sensed growing around me. 'We've had a warm spring,' I finished. 'There'll be a lot of food around.'

'What feeds on adders?' asked Matt, immediately. Around the hall, everyone was quiet, listening to Matt and me. I could see eyes flicking between us.

'Larger birds of prey,' I said. 'Owls in particular. Also larger mammals, like foxes or badgers.'

'So we increase the owl population and the problem's solved?'

'It would be nice to see more owls,' I said, wishing someone else would join in. 'But they tend to manage their own breeding programmes.'

Across the hall someone laughed.

'Actually,' I went on, sensing a lightening of the atmosphere, 'more food will encourage the owl population to increase. Chicks that might otherwise die of starvation will find enough to eat and stick around. Same with young foxes. Sooner or later, the problem should sort itself out.'

'But in the meantime,' said an overweight man in a tweed coat, 'we have poisonous snakes coming into our homes. What are we supposed to do while we wait for the young owls and foxes to grow up?'

'How sure are we that John Allington died from an adder bite?' asked Matt, ignoring the interruption. 'The hospital said they'd been in touch with you.'

It occurred to me that he might be a doctor. 'Well, I think there are still tests being carried out but, yes, I believe it has been confirmed as an adder.' An adder that was, at that very moment, in my fridge at home.

'But from what I understand, he could have had some underlying medical condition making him more susceptible to the poison?'

I nodded. 'The only people normally at risk from adder venom are very young children and those susceptible to anaphylactic shock.'

'OK,' said Matt, with an air of someone determined to draw proceedings to a close. 'What I'd like to suggest is that we all calm down. We wait for the coroner's report on John but we don't jump to any conclusions until we know exactly what he died of.'

Several people tried to interrupt. He raised his voice.

'In the meantime, we take extra care. We don't leave downstairs windows open. We don't walk our dogs through long grass and, if children are playing in gardens, we make them wear wellies and thick jeans. Anything else, Miss Benning?'

I shook my head. He was a solicitor: that air of authority, his ease at speaking in public, the respect in which he was obviously held.

'Now, I've had a long day, and I think we should leave Clive to his supper. Good night, everyone.'

He left the hall and I found myself almost shaking with relief. What must it be like, I wondered, to have that sort of confidence, the ability to calm people just by the tone of your voice and a few well-chosen words? Phillip Hopwood stepped down beside me. He'd visibly relaxed. At the bottom of the steps, Sally was smiling. People were leaving. Allan Keech had gone into a corner with a group of the younger men. They were talking eagerly about something, and I wondered if the snake round-up idea had been as effectively quashed as I'd hoped.

'Come back for a drink, Clara?' said Sally.

I shook my head. 'No, thank you. I've got some work to finish.'

'I'll walk with you,' she said, either not seeing or ignoring my dropped head and rounded shoulders, the way I've always, since being a child, shrugged off unwanted attention. We left the hall and set off back along the yew-tree-lined lane.

'I've been meaning to have a chat with you,' said Sally, who wasn't going to be put off by any lack of communication on my part. 'I play in a band, you see. Just five of us: bass guitar, rhythm guitar, drums, saxophone and vocals. We've been together about five years.'

'Oh?' I said, wondering what on earth had prompted Sally to share details of her life with me.

'And we're losing our vocalist in a few weeks. She's moving up north and I was wondering whether . . .'

I walked on.

'Thing is,' said Sally, 'I know you sing.'

I stopped walking and turned to look at her. 'I don't sing.'

'I hear you,' she said, smiling at me. 'All the time. Through the window.'

'It'll be taped music,' I said, wondering if my cottage was a listed building and whether I'd be allowed to fit double-glazing.

'Clara, I can tell the difference between taped music and someone who's singing live and unaccompanied. You have a beautiful voice.'

Over Sally's shoulder I could see Allan and his friends leaving the arched gatehouse that led into the manor's courtyard. Sally had her back to the house. So she didn't see them notice us and stop moving. She didn't see them gather in a huddle, listening intently to what Allan was saying, staring all the while at us – well, mainly at me. I made myself ignore them and concentrate on Sally. She was a little older than I am, maybe early thirties, with short hair dyed a bright shade of red. Her skin was olive and her eyes a hazel-brown. What had she been saying? Something about my music being too loud.

'I'm sorry, I had no idea I was disturbing you.' I wondered who else could hear me; who else had been listening when I'd thought I was completely alone.

'Don't be daft. How do you feel about trying out for the band?'

How did I feel about it? Like I'd rather slice off my own arm. But Sally was being nice. She was paying me a compliment. Over her shoulder the gang of men started moving again. I wanted to be away before they reached us.

'I don't think so . . . really. Thank you, but . . .'

'Will you think about it? I could just introduce you to the others. No pressure.'

'OK,' I said, because it seemed the easiest way to end the ridiculous conversation and get away. 'I think I might go for a run now. Good night.'

I turned away from her and started jogging, heading away from home, knowing she'd think me rude but simply unable to take any more. Too many people, too much talk, far too much attention on me. I'd had it with human contact. I was slithering away, through the undergrowth, away from the noise and vibrations, seeking solitude and safety.

I was wearing neither running clothes nor proper trainers but I didn't care. Picking up speed, I ran across the green and down Carters Lane before turning into a single-track lane that led to the lowest point of the village accessible by car. Villagers called this 'the Bottom Lane'. Whether it had ever had a real name I didn't know. The Bottom Lane led only to one empty house.

I ran on, past the old house, without looking at it, down the narrow, hazel-lined track that led through the beech woods and out of the village. I ran through the woods and across the farmland that lay below them. I reached the river Yerty and still kept running. Not till the light was noticeably fading from the sky did I begin to retrace my footsteps and head for home.

By this time I was tired. I'd been out running that morning before my adventure with the adder and I'd barely eaten during the day. My chest was tight, beads of moisture were dripping off my temples and both arms and legs were starting to tremble. I should have slowed down and walked the rest of the way. Maybe if I had, things would have turned out differently.

It had been a warm, wet spring, bringing nearly twice the average amount of rainfall for this time of year, and the narrow, steep track that took me back to the village didn't drain too well. Pools of thick, black mud lay in wait for the next few hundred yards. On both sides the hedge thickened and grew taller, as hawthorns, sycamores and young oaks joined the hazel trees. The larger specimens met overhead, forming a canopy of pale green and blotting out what little light was left in the day. Which is why I didn't see the sharp flint amidst a scatter of smaller stones. My foot hit the ground, the rock shifted, my ankle twisted beneath me and I went down hard.

For a second all I could think about was pain, burning across my ankle and foot. Then I pushed myself up and limped forward a couple of paces. I was at the gate of the Witcher property. I leaned against it, waiting for the pain in my foot to subside and my breathing to return to normal.

The Witcher house was old. Three hundred years ago, maybe earlier, it had been built as four 'two-up, two-down' labourers' cottages, to house workers on the nearby Ashlyne Estate. Some time over the years, dividing walls had been knocked down and the four cottages had become one sizeable house. It had been empty for months now.

The once-beautiful garden hadn't been touched since the previous summer, but nature is wonderfully tenacious and, even with no one to care for it, the garden was coming back to life. From among the apple trees the soft tantalizing sweetness of tiny lilies drifted towards me. I shut my eyes, trying to ignore my throbbing ankle. After a few seconds I was breathing normally again and the pain had become a dull ache. Probably just a sprain. I opened my eyes again. And saw Walter Witcher looking at me from a first-floor window.

Utterly impossible.

And yet there he was, at the upstairs window, third from the left. Walter: slight form, wispy grey hair, pale eyes, saggy, loose jowls and the stubby remnants of a white beard. And you know what? I felt my arm bending at the elbow, my hand getting ready to wave.

Because Walter, for some reason I could never quite fathom, had been the only person in the village with whom I felt anywhere close to comfortable. Maybe I sensed that he, too, avoided his own kind whenever possible. Certainly he had no more desire for idle chit-chat than I had, but he was always polite. I chose the times of my early-morning and late-evening runs to minimize the possibility of human contact and yet I never minded coming across Walter.

He'd been such a sweet, gentle man. Once, he'd brought an injured rabbit into the hospital. It had become caught in netting in his garden. I'd fixed the rabbit, and the two of us set him loose by the river two weeks later.

Walter had always looked me straight in the eyes.

When I got home from work the night after we'd released the rabbit, I'd found a dozen pink dahlias on my doorstep. There'd been no note, but I knew perfectly well in which garden pink dahlias grew. I was standing by it now, would have been able to see the green shoots had I been able to lower my head, but of course I couldn't. I couldn't take my eyes off the face at the window; that of a man who'd died eight months ago.

A shout behind made me jump and turn. I looked back and the window was empty. The face ... Walter ... was gone.

I checked the other windows. All empty. A large, heavy padlock held a chain in place around the gate. The gate was tall, roughly six feet, with spikes on top. It could probably be scaled, but not easily and certainly not by a man in his late seventies. The hedge on either side of it was high and thick.

From that distance the door of the house seemed solid enough. The downstairs windows were all boarded up. There was no sign that anyone might have entered the house. Least of all Walter.

Another shout. A woman's voice, calling for her dog. I knew the couple by sight. A widowed lady in her mid-fifties and a high-spirited lurcher called Scruffy. I was tempted to step into the opposite hedge, to wait in the field until they passed, but I knew Scruffy wouldn't be fooled. She'd sniff me out like a truffle hound, I'd be discovered skulking in the hedge and my reputation for oddness would take a giant leap forward.

One last look at the upper windows – empty – and I started walking up the path. Scruffy and her owner came into view and the dog sped towards me. Too good-mannered to jump without encouragement she stared up at me. I bent down, took hold of her head and scratched her ears. Encouraged enough, she stood up on her hind legs, giving me both forelegs to hold. In this position, she was almost my height.

'Scruffy, leave her alone!'

'She's OK,' I muttered, looking at Scruffy's hairy, good-natured face, thinking how sweetly non-judgemental dogs were and how nice it would be to live in a world of just animals.

'Scruffy, down. Come here.' Scruffy's collar was grasped and she was yanked away.

'Hello, Clara. Lovely clear even— Are you OK?'

I nodded and made myself look up. The woman's eyes were green, her hair blonde streaked with grey. I wasn't sure I'd ever really looked at her before. My eyes fell.

'I'm fine,' I managed. 'Took a tumble. I'll be fine.'

I muttered goodbye to the mud at my feet and walked on. I hadn't – couldn't have – seen Walter. It had been a late-evening trick of the light, that my brain, shocked by sudden pain, had misinterpreted.

I turned into Carters Lane. Another four hundred yards and I was at the village green. Daisies, just starting to close their petals, littered the grass like fallen stars.

I had another five hundred painful yards up the hill to go. I struggled on, remembering the morning I'd heard about Walter's death.

His wife, Edeline, had been out waiting for me; had refused to settle for my curt, quick nod and had stepped out on to the track, flagging me down as you might a passing car. My heart had sunk. Edeline always seemed to take a grim pleasure in looking at me, to be fascinated by me, the way small boys are by dead animals. I avoided her whenever I could.

'Walter's left us,' she'd drawled, and for a second I thought she meant he'd just upped and left her after fifty years of marriage. Heaven knows I wouldn't have blamed him.

'Him parsed on in t'night,' she'd gone on. 'Ar wassnd there. No one ud take me.'

64

I already knew that Walter had been admitted to hospital two or three weeks earlier, suffering from pneumonia, brought on by damp conditions and poor sanitation in the ancient cottage. I'd told her, truthfully, that I was very sorry.

As I was speaking, I'd seen Edeline's eyes leave mine and wander to the left side of my face. I was used to people doing that, but most at least tried to be polite, to disguise what they were doing. Edeline never could. I'd asked if there was anything I could do, anywhere I could take her, but she said people were coming from the hospital that morning and that they'd promised to take care of everything.

The following morning, and for weeks after, she'd been waiting for me at the garden gate, and I'd resigned myself to listening patiently while she brought me up to date with Walter's decision to leave his body to medical science, on the service at the hospital that was just for family, on her plans for a memorial stone in the village churchyard.

I'd never liked Edeline, and I liked her less and less as the days went on, but every morning after Walter's death I forced myself to stop, to look interested and to listen to her for a few minutes; telling myself she was lonely, probably had been for a long time. As far as I knew she never left the house. She was grieving and scared and I – I of all people – should be able to deal with that for a few minutes a day.

As it turned out, I didn't have to deal with it for very long. After just three months Edeline followed her husband into the hereafter. She hadn't left her body to medical science. I doubt Edeline had ever given away anything in her life and she wasn't about to start in death.

I reached the corner of Bourne Lane and caught a scent of roses on the air; a rich, musky perfume from one of the older varieties. The bush sprawled decadently over the wall that rimmed the corner property, its dark-pink blooms tumbling almost to the ground. I bent closer. It was the scent of my mother. She'd made her own perfume, lining stone jars with salted fresh rose petals until the essential oils seeped from them. The scent had followed her round the house, clinging to fabrics, hovering in sunshine-streaked dust, lying in wait for us. Mum! Mum's been here. Not too long ago. Follow the trail, track her down.

I gasped out loud, suddenly fighting for breath, with an almost overwhelming urge to scream like a small, frightened child. And it hit me, like a blow around the head, it finally hit me.

My mother was dead.

For a moment I thought I was choking. That I would never breathe normally again. That my life was to end, here and now, at the corner of my street, a lonely, terrified little girl screaming for her mother.

Then the pain faded and I was breathing again. I was still alive, still here, still able to move, speak, live. But she was not.

I stumbled down the lane, unlocked the front door and ran to the phone. I lifted the receiver and dialled the number.

'Daddy,' I gasped, when I heard the familiar voice at the other end, 'it's me.'

I spoke to my father for a very long time but can't remember anything that was said. After we'd wished each other good night, I sat at the open window in my dark bedroom, not thinking exactly, just sitting.

Until the screaming began.

6

FOR WHAT FELT LIKE AGES BUT COULD ONLY HAVE been seconds I wasn't capable of moving. The threat was one I couldn't even begin to quantify. So I just sat there, letting my body take over, draw itself up, shift to fast, shallow breaths, move into full alert.

My second reaction – I admit – was to hide. To close my windows, lock my door, keep the lights off and hunker down. But those were children screaming. I stood up and stuck my head out of the window, trying to trace the sound. But the back of my house overlooks mainly fields and woodland.

I ran downstairs, wincing at my still-sore ankle, pulled on boots and opened the front door. Lights were flickering on in upstairs windows, but the yelling wasn't coming from the houses of any of my immediate neighbours. I set off up the lane.

As I reached the top, Daniel Huston appeared in the doorway of his cottage, pulling a sweatshirt over his head.

'It's the Poulsons,' he said, when he saw me. 'The longhouse.'

I followed him round the corner and a few yards down the hill just as the door to the corner house opened and the family, almost literally, fell out into the street. The mother carried a small sobbing child, not more than two years old, on one arm. With the other she dragged along a boy of about seven who was screaming hysterically. A much older man seemed barely able to walk. He leaned on a younger man who stumbled along at his side, clutching his own arm. All five looked as if they were in serious shock. The mother's eyes fixed on mine.

'They're everywhere!' she yelled. 'Over the whole house. Nick's been bitten.'

The younger man swayed. Daniel muttered a curse and ran forward. Getting between the two men, he slid his arms under their shoulders.

'Come on,' he said, 'let's get you to our house. We can call an ambulance from there.'

Other people were arriving, including Sally from next door. She shot a quick, frightened look at me and then joined Daniel, helping him walk the Poulson family away.

'What the hell is it?' demanded a middle-aged, bearded man who I thought might live in my street.

'Nick's been bitten,' said another man, whom I remembered from the meeting as one of Allan Keech's friends. 'I'm not sure what's happened to Ernest. Hit his head, I think someone said.'

'Shall I call the police?' said the man with him. 'Give us your mobile, Steve.'

'I think I should get Allan,' said Steve. He stayed where he was, looking at me. They were all looking at me.

The front door to the Poulsons' house was still open. There were lights on inside. I crossed the narrow footbridge that led to their door and stood on the threshold. It was a traditional Dorset longhouse, large and linear. Before me I could see a large entrance hall that stretched the width of the house. There were damp patches on the wooden floorboards and traces of weed scattered about. They bothered me, although I wasn't sure why.

I stepped inside and pushed the door not quite closed behind me.

The walls were yellow, and a large mirror hung opposite the door. I caught sight of my reflection and turned quickly away. Behind the almost-closed front door I could hear the soft whisperings of the men, who couldn't quite pluck up the courage to join me.

I was not alone in the Dorset longhouse. All around the room, the creatures watched me with their round, black pupils, their slender bodies swaying to and fro, tracking my movements, their tiny tongues working overtime, flickering in and out, tasting the air, tasting me. Foe or food? They weren't sure.

Walking carefully, I crossed to the open kitchen door. For a second I stood there, watching a long, graceful body glide along the groove of a cupboard, flowing like water around its curves. Another hung from the light-shade in the centre of the ceiling. I looked all around, counting, checking positions, then walked back through the hall to the sitting room. A slender, dark tail disappeared behind a sofa. A tightly wrapped coil slept, oblivious, on an armchair. Something was making its way slowly up the curtain cord.

I'd seen enough. I went back through the hall and opened the front door a little more. Four pairs of human eyes looked back at me, and I saw another man jogging up the hill. One I thought I recognized.

'They're grass snakes,' I said. 'There's a lot of them and I can understand why the family were scared, but they're all perfectly harmless.'

They looked at each other, still wary, unsure whether they could trust me.

'Nick's been bitten,' said Daniel, who'd reappeared. 'He's in a lot of pain. We've called an ambulance.'

'They will bite if they're threatened,' I said. 'Most snakes will. But they're not venomous. Nick might be sore for a few days but he'll be fine.'

'But how the hell did they get in there?' asked Steve. 'Mandy said there were hundreds of them.'

'Well, at least a dozen,' I admitted. 'And I don't know how they got in there. I'm going to roun— gather them up now.'

I could feel the tension lessening in the group. 'What can we do?' asked one of them.

'Get me something to put them in,' I said. 'Buckets with lids would be best. Empty pillowcases will do. My house is open. If someone can run down, you'll find car keys by the front door and some plastic carry-boxes in the boot of my car.' I turned to Steve, making him look me in the eye. 'After that, no one comes in here unless they're bringing me stuff I need, and no one is to touch a snake.' He looked back at me, and I knew he was still undecided.

I turned to go back inside. I'd seen a bucket in the kitchen. The sooner I got started the sooner I'd finish.

Five minutes later the kitchen was filled with the acrid smell of distressed grass snake. They emit a foul substance from their rear end when threatened. It's harmless but deeply unpleasant. They were also, for their size, putting up a pretty good fight, and twice I'd narrowly avoided being bitten. I wasn't standing for any nonsense, though, and I'd put four of them in the bucket. From what I could tell, they were all healthy, young specimens, possibly born earlier that spring, or maybe just a year old.

I heard voices, footsteps, then the front door opening.

'I'll watch the door. Sorry, guys, can't stand snakes.'

'Wussy!' Whoever was doing the mocking was over-emphasizing the *s* sound to make hissing noises. They were being too loud. Men – how quickly fear turns into bravado. This scared bunch had become a gang of boys all set for adventure.

'She's in here.'

I turned round to face them. Four men: my bearded neighbour, Keech's friend Steve, Daniel Huston and a newcomer – the quietly spoken, dark-haired man – Matt – from the meeting. Several carried buckets, Daniel had the carry-boxes from my car, Steve had a pile of pillowcases over his arm. In fairness to them, they'd done exactly what I'd asked and they'd wasted no time.

'What the hell is that smell?'

'Pissed-off grass snake,' said Matt. His eyes met mine. Behind the glasses they were a soft grey.

'I'll be fine now, thanks,' I muttered as I turned to carry on. After a second I realized nobody was moving.

'I'll work better if the house is quiet,' I said, turning back to them once again. 'You should leave it to me now.'

'It's OK, we'll help,' offered the man with the beard.

Oh, was I to be allowed no peace? It was the middle of the night, we were surrounded by snakes, and I still couldn't get people to leave me alone. I shook my head.

'I can't let you get involved,' I said. 'If one of you gets hurt, I could be liable.'

'No, you couldn't,' said Matt.

I found myself staring at cool grey eyes.

'There is no contractual relationship between you and us,' he went on. 'And you owe us no duty of care. We're here under our own volition. We've listened to your advice and decline to take it. The Poulsons are our friends and we want to help.'

Silence. Oh, he was a lawyer all right. For a second I was tempted to leave them to it. But the message behind those oblong glasses was clear. I wasn't going to win. I could make myself look stupid by storming out. Or I could get on with the job.

'Anybody handled snakes before?' I asked. Four heads shook.

'OK, the important thing to remember is that they can't hurt you,' I said. 'So try very hard not to hurt them. Distract them with one hand, take them with the

73

other. Don't take too long, you'll just stress them out. Pick them up firmly but gently and put them in a bucket. No more than about four together. When the buckets are full, put them outside. That chap out there will watch them?'

Several nods, mutters of agreement.

'And he shouldn't let anyone else in,' I added, fearing the arrival of Allan Keech and his mob, all set for a bit of grass-snake sport.

'OK,' said Daniel, 'let's get this over with.'

'I'll do upstairs,' I said.

I took some pillowcases and crossed the hall. As I climbed the spiral staircase I sensed someone behind me, but it wasn't until I turned the bend that I realized it was Matt.

'Hold up,' he said and reached up through the staircase, past my right leg. 'Gotcha,' he said. With a grin he held up a small, dark-grey snake with elegant white markings, one I hadn't spotted. I held an open pillowcase towards him and he dropped it inside.

'Do you know how the family are?' I was surprised to find myself asking as we reached the top of the stairs. I had no desire to chat, just get the job done and get home.

'There's another one.' He reached past, over my shoulder. He'd showered within the last half-hour. I could smell shampoo and the hair at the back of his head was still damp. I wondered what he'd been doing at 3 a.m. to necessitate a shower. He lunged and pushed against me, forcing me to step backwards.

'Sorry,' he muttered as he straightened up. He'd

missed it. 'Slippy little suckers, aren't they? Mandy and the kids are upset but otherwise fine. Ernest's probably in the worst shape. Got a nasty bump on the head. Nick's highly embarrassed he made such a fuss over a grass snake.'

I stood at the top of the stairs, looking round. We were in a long, narrow corridor that ran the length of the house. I could count five doors opening off it, most of them open. What worried me, though, was the timber framing of the house and, most especially, the fact that the upper floor was open to the roof. The old timbers and the ill-fitting plasterboard that divided the rooms from each other were riddled with small holes and gaps. Snakes could roam at will around the upstairs of the house and catching them was not going to be easy.

'I'm Matt Hoare, by the way, I don't think we've met. I'd offer my hand but I've got a snake in it. Oh, Christ, I think I've killed it.'

I looked down. Matt Hoare had captured a monster of a snake, relatively speaking. Nearly five feet long and thick around the middle. It lay slumped in his hand, motionless, its mouth wide open, blue-grey tongue protruding.

'I hardly touched it,' he protested, looking horrified.

I held out the pillowcase. 'It's fine,' I said. 'Grass snakes often feign death when they're threatened.'

He looked down, incredulously, at the snake in his hand. 'You mean this thing's lying doggo?'

I nodded and gave the pillowcase a small shake. Matt took the hint and lowered the still-flaccid snake into the white cotton bag. Once released, it began to move again.

'Well, I'll be . . .' He shook his head and then looked back up at me. 'It's Clara, isn't it?' he said. 'Our gardens back on to each other. I hear you singing sometimes. What shall we do, start in the master bedroom, work our way back?'

He set off to the left and I followed, wondering how he knew where the master bedroom was and – for heaven's sake – what did these people think I was, the village minstrel? Listed building or not, I was getting double-glazing.

'And yes, Slippery Sam, I'm having you.' He leapt towards the bed, grabbed the coiled creature that lay on it and held it out towards me.

'Come on, Clara, I'm winning three–nil at the moment.'

'I caught four downstairs. Are you sure you haven't done this before?' The ease with which Matt was picking up and handling the snakes was something I'd never seen before in a layman. Snakes are pretty intimidating creatures if you're not used to them.

'Never, but my father was a river-man. I worked with him on school holidays. When you've handled fully grown eels, grass snakes are a doddle.'

I decided to take his word for it and concentrated on getting my own tally up. Five snakes later, we'd rifled through cupboards and turned out drawers, climbed on to wardrobes and remade the bed. It felt like an intrusion of the family's privacy but, on balance, I guessed they'd thank us. Finally, we declared the master bedroom and en-suite bathroom snake-free. We closed the door and moved towards the next room.

'OK, I feel I've earned my spurs now,' said Matt. 'I can ask a question. How did so many snakes – what have we got now, eight from just the stairs and one room? – how did so many get into the house?'

It was a good question. 'I don't know,' I admitted. 'Grass snakes do get together in groups to mate. And it is round about this time of year. They come out of hibernation and . . .' I paused. I really wasn't comfortable discussing the facts of life, even reptilian life, with a stranger.

'Party?' suggested Matt. I was looking at the floorboards, but I could tell, just from the tone of his voice, that he was smiling.

'Maybe they were heading for one of the streams and just got lost,' I said, making myself glance up. 'One of them came in through an open doorway and the rest just followed.'

He paused on the threshold of the next room. 'Ever heard of this sort of thing happening before?'

I shook my head. 'Never.'

He looked at me for a moment, as though about to ask another question, then walked into the room. I followed. We were in a boy's bedroom: untidy, brightly coloured, full of toys and *Marvel Comic* posters. Several drawers were open and clothes were bursting out of them. We would have to walk over bits of Lego and the contents of a dressing-up box.

Two young snakes, probably not more than seven or eight months old, were coiling round each other on the window ledge, and I walked towards them. Although I studied reptiles in college, even considered a career working with them, lizards, rather than snakes, had been my favourites. These two, though, were really quite cute. They were each about eighteen inches long and slender as pencils. They were the colour of young beech leaves, with bright black eyes and tiny, active tongues.

'Oh-ho, a big one,' said Matt behind me. 'You are for the pillowcase, my friend.'

I will never know what made me turn round at precisely that moment. I'd already decided Matt did not need me keeping an eye on him. But turn round I did. Just in time to see the snake he was about to take hold of. I gasped; nothing came out. I tried again, forcing sound through a throat that felt horribly constricted.

'Don't touch that!'

Puzzled, but a long way from being alarmed, Matt turned to me. 'What . . . what's wrong?'

The snake rose up, looked around lazily and then focused on the man in front of him. We both watched it as I was frantically trying to remember what I'd learned years ago about scale patterns and head shapes. There were distinctive orange markings down the snake's back. But colouring could be confusing; one could never rely upon colour.

'Step back,' I said. 'A big step. Very slowly.'

Matt did as I asked. The snake swayed, rose higher and watched him.

'Again. Another step. Keep it slow.'

He stepped back again. 'What the hell is it? What . . .'

'Don't talk.' My own voice would barely work. 'Keep coming back.'

The snake swayed backwards and froze. It was a classic strike pose. I was holding my breath. I was two paces from the door, Matt a little further into the room. He took another backwards stride, and I put a hand on his shoulder, tugging him towards me. I pulled us both into the doorway and pushed him behind me. I had not once taken my eyes off the snake.

Nor had it off us. As we'd backed away it had relaxed, but it was still watchful. I judged it to be a little over a metre long. A snake can strike faster than the human eye can follow but only up to half its length. We were safe for the moment but, if it started to move, we had to be on the other side of the door within seconds. Matt was close behind me. I could feel his breath on my neck.

'I take it that's not a grass snake,' he said.

7

THE SNAKE AND I WERE HOLDING EYE CONTACT, AND I was beginning to wonder if there was something in the old stories about snakes having the power to mesmerize. 'No,' I said, 'that isn't a grass snake.'

'What, then? It doesn't look like an adder.'

'Get the others out of here. Don't let them touch anything else. If you can close windows and doors, that'd be good, but don't go near any more snakes. The man who was bitten – make sure he gets to hospital straight away. He needs to be under constant observation. Then get me an empty carry-box. And a weapon of some kind – hammer, axe – something like that. Be as quick as you can.'

'But what . . .'

'Just do it!'

He was gone. I heard him cross the corridor, feet pounding on the bare wooden floors, running downstairs, shouting to the other three men. I heard them questioning, even arguing, and then all of them left the house. The front door slammed shut and the house was silent.

The sudden flurry of noise had disturbed the snake. It moved, heading for the refuge of the open wardrobe. If it went inside I could trap it, wait until help and proper equipment arrived. Oh, please let it go inside.

The snake didn't go inside the wardrobe but instead started to glide up the door, the carvings on the old oak making it an easy task. Reaching the top, its body shimmered and disappeared over the rim.

OK, I had to stay calm. The snake on top of the wardrobe had to be caught or, failing that, killed. And I had to do that knowing there could be others in the room, or elsewhere in the house. I felt sick, realizing the danger I'd put those men in. I should never have let them stay in the house.

Right, think. Was this really something I could handle alone? But how soon could help get to me? The nearest zoo was miles away and it was the middle of the night.

I heard footsteps running lightly up the stairs and felt an overwhelming sense of relief. Which was not the least disturbing thing to happen to me that night. I, who had never relied on a man my whole adult life, who was so used to being in charge, was going mushy at the first sign of real danger.

Matt crossed the landing quietly, and I risked taking my eyes off the wardrobe for a second to look at him. He had the carry-box, a large wood-chopping axe and a wide-eyed look on his face. It could have been a pretty alarming sight. Except, given the choice between an axe-yielding madman and what was on top of the wardrobe, most days I'd take my chances with the axe.

'Get back here, now,' he whispered, gesturing me to join him in the doorway. I shook my head.

'I'm not arguing,' he said, so softly I could barely hear. I found myself backing towards him.

'What is that thing?' he said, instinctively keeping his voice low.

'I'm not sure,' I replied, because I wasn't. Not 100 per cent. 'It's a little on the small side but . . .'

He said nothing. Just looked at me.

'I think it's a taipan,' I admitted.

'A what?' He looked disappointed; he'd expected me to say cobra, pit viper, rattlesnake – one of the better-known dangerous snakes.

'A taipan,' I repeated. 'They're from Australia.'

'And they're bad?'

I nodded. 'They're the most dangerous snakes in the world.'

He took hold of my arm and pulled me out of the room, on to the landing. 'Right, we're out of here. The police are on their way. They can deal with it.'

I resisted. I'm quite strong when I need to be.

'Absolutely not. If you can get a herpetologist with experience of venomous snakes out here in the next half-hour, then go ahead. Believe me, I have no desire to go back into that room. But to ask young policemen who've never handled a snake in their lives before to try and catch it is just asking for several of them to get killed.'

He screwed up his face in disbelief. He thought I was exaggerating, being hysterical, like any other woman

82

confronted with a scary snake. I had to make him understand.

'Taipans can be very aggressive snakes. They're fast and strong. Each one of them has enough venom to kill a whole battalion of policemen. People die within hours of being bitten, and I really doubt the Dorset County Hospital carries the right sort of anti-venom.'

'So we close down the house and we wait for experts. We get your herp— What do you call them?'

'Herpetologists. But look at this house. It must be four hundred years old. There are gaps and holes everywhere. The snake will escape. And believe me, you do not want one of those things roaming the village.'

I could see him thinking about it. I stood there, watching him, feeling angry that he'd just waltzed in and taken charge, purely on the strength of being a man and (by this stage I was sure of it) a lawyer. At the same time, half of me was hoping he'd hold out and refuse to let me back in the bedroom. It's surprising how the prospect of a rapid and painful death can make you value what little you do have in life.

'OK, what's the plan? I'm not saying I'm going to agree to it. Just that I want to hear it.'

'We need to catch it quickly,' I managed. 'We may have to kill it, but I think catching it might be marginally less dangerous.'

'How do we do that exactly?'

'It's on top of the wardrobe,' I said. 'If you're OK to help, first thing we have to do is knock it off. Then we use the axe as a grab-stick. If you feign attacking it with the wooden end, it should bite on to it. I can then take

83

hold of it round the neck and it'll be safe. We can drop it into the box.'

'Christ!' He looked round, noticing the ventilation gaps beneath windows, holes in wooden beams, an open skylight in the roof. 'You're right, it can escape. Are you sure you can do this?'

Now that it came to it, I was far from sure. I nodded. 'Let's go.'

I turned back to the door. First thing was to check the snake was still where we'd left it.

'Hold on.'

I turned. Matt was shrugging off his brown leather jacket. He held it out to me. 'Put this on,' he ordered.

I was wearing a fine-knit cotton sweater. No protection at all from a taipan bite. Even so I shook my head. 'You're the one it'll be aiming for. You need it.'

'I'll get something of Nick's. Now put it on, and the gloves, and stay there.'

I put my arms in the sleeves of Matt's jacket and pulled it over my shoulders. He wasn't a big man, but it certainly felt huge on me. It was thick, strong leather – it would help. It was also still warm from his body. So don't ask me why I started shivering the moment I put it on. The gloves I found in the pockets were useless, and I dropped them against the wall. Too late to run home for my own. I stood in the doorway, watching for movement in the room and wondering if I was doing the right thing, whether there was any possible alternative. Waiting for expert help was the only really sensible course of action, but there was a real danger of the taipan escaping. And the police would get here first.

They might not listen to me, might try and catch the snake themselves. At least I fully understood what I was facing. I turned to see Matt coming back, wearing a green quilted coat. His right arm looked huge, and several inches of towel were visible below the cuff of the sleeve. He didn't hesitate but walked into the room and looked all round. Then he pulled the duvet off the bed and threw it out into the corridor.

'Check it,' he said. I did. Nothing there.

Once I'd shaken my head at him he stepped on to the bed and peered forward to see the wardrobe top. I moved in, scanning the room, left to right, up and down, watching for any hint of movement.

'It's still there,' he said. 'It's coiled up but it's watching me.'

'We need it on the floor,' I said, knowing it wouldn't be that easy. 'I can't get hold of it up there.'

'I'm going to knock it off into the corner. Can you be ready?'

I slipped past him. There was an eighteen-inch gap between the end of the wardrobe and the wall. Miraculously, given the state of the rest of the room, it was clear of young boy's debris. If Matt managed to knock the snake into it, we'd stand a good chance. On the other hand, a cornered snake is the most dangerous kind of all.

'I'm ready,' I said, knowing I'd never be ready for what was about to happen.

Holding the blade with both hands, Matt swept the handle of the axe across the top of the wardrobe. The snake reared up with a defensive cry. Startled, Matt stepped back and wobbled on the soft mattress. He swiped again at the snake and managed to dislodge it, just as he fell backwards. The snake tumbled over the edge of the wardrobe, twisted itself round in mid-air and fell on the bed, where Matt lay half sprawled.

'Move!' I yelled at him.

Matt rolled over the side of the bed and jumped to his feet. The snake lunged towards him. Matt staggered back and came up against the window. He'd dropped the axe.

I bent down, my hands connected with something and I hurled it at the snake. It was a child's Darth Vader mask. It hit the snake squarely on the back of the head. The taipan swayed and turned. Faced with two threats, coming at it from opposite ends of the room, it was unsure. Then it decided. It was coming for me.

I threw something else – a football annual – and as it landed uselessly in a crumpled heap, I realized I'd made a terrible mistake; one that was about to cost me my life. I was aware of Matt moving forward, bending down, but could look at nothing but the glossy, gunmetal-grey scales and amber eyes of the creature bearing down on me. It reared up. I took a breath to scream.

Then Matt hit it against the side of the head with the axe handle. The taipan turned and struck, sinking its fangs into the wood. I shot forward and, without pausing to think, or I'd never have been able to do it, grabbed it with both hands round its neck. The taipan released its hold on the handle and struggled to be free, but I had it tight. Matt dropped the axe and reached for the carry-box. He knocked off the lid, grabbed the taipan's tail and pushed the lower part of the snake into the box. I shoved the head in, holding it in place, and Matt got the lid ready to drop down. The snake stopped moving.

Matt and I stared at each other.

'Where the hell are the gloves?' he demanded.

The gloves he'd offered me earlier had been huge on my hands. They might have offered some protection but they'd have completely removed any dexterity.

'This is the tricky bit,' I said. 'Once I let go, he'll probably strike. And he'll move faster than me.'

'And again, I ask, where the bloody hell are the gloves?'

Beneath my hands the snake's body was trembling. 'They were too big,' I said. 'I wouldn't have been able to do anything with them on.'

'Great.'

'Guess I have a taipan by the tail,' I said.

He glared at me. 'It's not remotely funny.'

'Give me that T-shirt,' I said, thinking, *Humour, since when do I do humour?*

Matt looked round and found the crumpled piece of soft cotton I was indicating. He held it out and I risked taking one hand off the snake. I could just about still hold it but probably not for long. I took the T-shirt, scrunched it into a ball and pushed it down on the taipan's head to pin it to the bottom of the cage.

I looked up at Matt. There was no need to speak. He knew exactly what I was about to do, what he had to do. Faster than I'd ever moved in my life before, I pulled away my left hand. Matt dropped the lid on the box and I locked it. The taipan was safe, with a Spider-Man T-shirt for company.

Moving as one, Matt and I sank to the floor and sat looking at each other over the lid of the box. Neither of us, it seemed, had the energy to move.

'What now?' he said at last.

'We look for the others,' I replied.

He closed his eyes and sank back, full length, on the bedroom carpet. And I did something I'd never have dreamed I'd do in such a situation. I laughed.

There were no more taipans in the Poulsons' house. Five minutes after we captured the snake, four police officers arrived, all of whom seemed to know Matt Hoare very well, and then we resumed our search. We found a few more grass snakes and one adder – dead. A young constable found it in the grandfather's bedroom and called me in. I'd already given strict instructions that nobody but me was to touch any snakes, and the police had been happy to agree.

The adder was at the foot of a single bed. Its head had been crushed. It was the only snake we found that night that had been harmed in any way.

'One of the family must have done this,' I said, knowing a dead snake could hardly have found its own way into the house. 'This could have been what bit the father.'

'This is old Dr Amblin's room, though,' said the young policeman, who was no longer looking at the snake but at the side of my face. I turned away and,

88

without speaking again, we searched the rest of the bedroom.

Definitely a room belonging to an elderly man. Plain, dark furnishings, clothes brushes and combs on the dresser, shaving equipment in the tiny en-suite bathroom. On the pillow was a mark that looked like a bloodstain. And something formed a small bump under the covers. Bristling under the constable's stare, I moved forward. Close enough to touch, I paused for a second. Was the lump moving? I didn't think so, but . . .

'Let me take the other side,' said the policeman, moving round. At the same time, with a small amount of hesitation on both sides, we took hold of the sheet.

'One, two, three,' the constable counted, and we whisked the sheet back. The young policeman laughed. I didn't.

'He's a bit long in the tooth for soft toys, wouldn't you say?' he said.

'Probably the little boy's,' I said, looking down at the small stuffed monkey we'd uncovered.

'I think we're done in here,' said the PC. I followed him out, thinking, why, of all the soft toys I'd seen in the house, would it be a small, brown stuffed monkey hidden in the grandfather's bed? A snake and a monkey. Now, why was that bothering me?

8

ANOTHER HOUR, A FEW MORE GRASS SNAKES AND we were pretty certain the house was clear. I told the sergeant in charge it should really be checked again before the family could be allowed back, but I was happy it could be left for the remainder of the night.

Then I found myself driving across country with a car full of snakes.

Once the house was snake-free I'd wanted nothing more than to get back home and leave the police to it. The previous day had been pretty eventful and I hadn't even been in bed yet, let alone had any sleep. But the sergeant had pointed out that the snakes had to be taken somewhere, it would be too insensitive to release them in the village and where better than the local wildlife hospital? I argued for a while, but my heart wasn't really in it. I could see his point. I'd gone for my car and then the constable who'd found the adder helped me load up the thirty-nine snakes, all safely housed in buckets, pillowcases and large Tupperware boxes.

I hadn't seen the taipan, or the man who'd helped me catch it, for some time. I figured one had gone home, the other was safe in police custody. It was half past four in the morning and starting to get light. Then Matt appeared, walking up the lane, talking quietly to the sergeant and carrying the taipan's box. They saw me and came over.

'So,' said Matt, holding up the box. 'What do we do with the Devil from Down Under?'

Without a pressing and immediate task in hand, I found it difficult to look at him. I concentrated on squeezing the various snake containers into the boot of my car.

'I'm taking the other snakes to the Little Order. That's the wildlife hospital where I work,' I said. 'I'll double-check they really are grass snakes and, if they're healthy, they can all be released.' I focused on the taipan's box; easier to look at that than at Matt.

'I'm not qualified to deal with that one, I'm afraid,' I went on, addressing the sergeant this time. Funnily enough, it was easier to look at him too. 'You probably should get confirmation that he really is a taipan. If he is, you might be able to track down where he came from. Then find somewhere to take him. One of the zoos might have him. London's probably your best bet. Or a private collector.'

'Private collector?' said Matt. 'You're kidding me. People keep these things as pets?'

I walked round to the door of my car and spoke over my shoulder, again aiming at the sergeant.

'In Australia they do. Although it's not something I'd

ever recommend. I've not heard of one being kept in Britain, but it's possible.'

'We're hoping you'll take it, miss,' said the sergeant, allowed to get a word in at last. 'Until a safer home can be found.'

I shook my head. 'The hospital isn't set up to deal with venomous snakes. I can't ask my staff to take that risk.' Even before I finished speaking, I realized I knew somewhere that was perfectly able to deal with dangerous reptiles, that had people who could identify the snake and find the best possible home for it. And that I'd been planning to go and see them later that day anyway. Both men stared at me for a second and then Matt nodded.

'OK,' he said. 'I'll keep it. What do I feed it on?'

'Put it in the boot,' I sighed. 'I'll take it to some people I know.'

I opened the driver door and caught the sergeant turning away to hide a grin. Matt walked round to the passenger side and climbed in, taipan box on his lap.

'What are you doing?' I asked.

'Coming with you.'

No! Enough! I wanted to be on my own. 'What on earth for?'

'It's nearly five in the morning and you look exhausted. I'm not leaving you to deal with a dangerous snake by yourself.'

'It's perfectly safe. It's in a box.' I looked round to find the sergeant, wondering if he might back me up. He was already walking back to the Poulsons' house.

'You look a bit shaky,' said Matt. 'Do you want me to drive?'

I started the engine, thinking what – in the name of all that's reasonable – did I have to do? I worked with wild animals. I lived at the end of the quietest street in the most remote village I could find. I made a point of not knowing the names of my neighbours. I did my shopping by mail order. What exactly did I have to do to be left alone?

'Besides,' he said, as we headed out of the village. 'You're still wearing my jacket.'

I resolved to say nothing more on the six-mile drive to the Little Order. When it comes to being silent, to freezing out another person, I have mastered the art, believe me. I can go away, to a place in my head, where I'm so far removed from the world that I don't even hear voices talking directly to me. When I have to, I can just fade away.

We drove up the narrow, steep hill that leads out of the village. It twists and turns continually, making concentration essential, even in the daytime. Beech, oak and sycamore trees meet overhead, forming a dense black tunnel of foliage. Stray branches scraped against the side of the car and bats, confused by the headlights, fluttered close before zipping away again.

'Deadliest snake in the world, huh?' said Matt, sounding a whole lot clearer than he should have, given that I was zoning him out. 'How come I've never heard of it?' he went on.

I told myself I was concentrating on the road.

'I've heard of pythons, boas, vipers . . . rattlesnakes, of course. But not taipans. If they're that dangerous, how come everyone hasn't heard of them?'

It was impossible. This man was not going to be ignored.

'They were discovered relatively recently,' I said. 'Round about the middle of the twentieth century. Even today, they're not commonly seen. Which, trust me, is a good thing.'

'But why are they so dangerous? Mambas. Black mambas. I've heard of those. Are they dangerous?'

I sighed. 'OK, when it comes to venomous snakes, there are the big three: the black mamba in Africa, the cobra in most of Asia and the taipan. Herpetologists will argue for hours about which is the deadliest and, frankly, you can make a case for each of them. All are large, strong and fast.'

'This one isn't big,' he interrupted.

'That one's very young. Taipans can grow to over three metres,' I said.

'Blimey. So go on – big, strong and fast. What else?'

Nearly five in the morning and I was giving a reptile lecture to a man I'd just met. What had happened to my quiet life? But he was staring directly at me, waiting for me to go on.

'All three species are notoriously aggressive when attacked,' I said. 'They all do something called repeat striking. They strike, release, then strike again. It means a great deal of venom can be injected into the victim. Each one of them has venom that is complex and highly toxic. A victim that doesn't get treatment will die – horribly – within hours. And, by reptilian standards, all three species are pretty intelligent, which, given their lethal capabilities, does tend to make one a little uncomfortable in their company.'

'If I had a brain, I'd be dangerous?'

'Exactly.'

'So which gets your vote?'

'The taipan.' I didn't even need to think about it. 'Every time.'

'You've seen them before?'

I nodded. 'I worked in Australia for a while. I was studying lizards, but I came across snakes too. I met people who'd survived taipan bites. I heard about a lot more who didn't.'

Matt fell silent. The conversation could easily have ended there.

'There are two species of taipan,' I found myself saying. 'The coastal and the inland. A single coastal taipan bite is thought toxic enough to kill twenty-seven people.'

'Christ. And we've got one of those?'

'No. I think that's an inland taipan. I seem to remember they have orange markings. Our friend in there has a faint orange stripe down its back.'

'Small mercies, huh? So, how many people can the inland variety kill with one bite?'

'Sixty-two.' I risked a glance out of the corner of my eye. Matt's face was deadpan.

'Can I put it on the back seat?' he said at last.

I couldn't help it, I started to laugh again. After a second he joined in.

'Did the police say what they're planning to do?' I asked when the laughter had died away and the silence was starting to feel uncomfortable.

Matt glanced at me, seemed about to speak then

changed his mind. 'They'll make enquiries about the taipan in the morning,' he said after a few moments. 'See if one's been reported missing.'

'And the grass snakes?'

He shrugged. 'Well, they can hardly bang 'em up and charge 'em with trespass. They've already dusted for fingerprints but, with a large family and lots of visitors coming and going, it might be difficult to spot anything. There were no obvious signs of a break-in.'

I'd already decided I'd done more than enough talking for one night, or I might have asked him how he knew so much about police business. We weren't far from work and I drove on. I was keeping my eyes firmly on the road but could feel him watching me. He was on my left side. I should have let him drive after all.

'What do you think?' he asked. 'Another freaky trick of nature?'

I thought for a moment. One snake entering a house was unusual but hardly unheard of. Several dozen, including one non-native, was a different matter entirely.

'Difficult to see how that many snakes could get into a house without help,' I said after a moment.

'Quite so,' Matt agreed. 'I'm wondering if our local vandals might be to blame. Maybe they got bored with cutting telephone wires and breaking windows.'

I nodded, but I was remembering the damp patches I'd seen on the floor of the Dorset longhouse, of the traces of mud. I'd seen the same thing at the Huston house when I'd rescued baby Sophia from the adder. And capturing and handling several dozen snakes, including a couple of venomous ones, suggested a considerable amount of skill. Not what you expect in your average graffiti-spraying vandal. Should I say anything? I was already more involved than I wanted to be.

'And that meeting at Clive Ventry's house could have given them the idea,' I found myself saying instead. 'Suddenly, everyone's scared of snakes.'

'Well, if they weren't before, they will be now,' agreed Matt.

Silence fell again. We'd reached the main road, empty at this time of the morning. In the east, the black of the night sky was melting away, turning silver; the vast, empty heathlands of Devon were appearing before us. A sudden ringing sound made me jump.

'That'll be for me,' said Matt, making no move to find and answer his phone. The ringing continued.

'I'd help myself but I'm not sure I know you that well,' he said. 'Inside pocket, left-hand side.'

Of course, I was wearing his jacket. He leaned over and held the steering wheel with his right hand, holding it steady for me. I could smell his skin, his hair, the coffee he'd drunk in the last hour.

Shrinking away, I fumbled inside his jacket until I found the phone and held it out. He leaned back in his own seat and I reclaimed the wheel, hugely relieved that, for a few minutes, his attention would no longer be on me. The other party to the conversation was doing most of the talking and Matt responded in a few monosyllables. After five minutes, he rang off.

'That was the Dorset County,' he said, putting the phone in the pocket of his shirt. 'Nick's doing fine. He's sore around the bite site, but there's no unusual swelling, his breathing's OK and his temperature's normal. He's showing none of the symptoms that John Allington had. They'll keep a very close eye on him, but no one seems unduly worried.'

'What about the rest of the family?' I asked, thinking of the dead adder I'd seen in the grandfather's bedroom.

'Old Dr Amblin has a mild concussion. Seems he banged his head in the confusion. Mandy and the kids are fine. They're all being kept in but none of them has been bitten at all.'

'Well, that's a relief.'

'Absolutely. But there's anti-venom available for most snake bites these days, isn't there?'

'European Viper Venom Antiserum is readily available. And we keep ViperaTAb at the hospital. Maybe I should bring some home with me.'

'What about this little fella?' asked Matt, indicating the box on his lap.

'There's an anti-venom for taipan bites,' I told him, 'but the snakes are found in very remote parts of Australia. So the anti-venom is kept in those parts. You'd have to locate some, get it flown to a major city and then on to London. Then couriered out here. It would take too long.'

He was silent for a moment.

'So, if one of us had been bitten tonight, the chances are nothing could have been done?' he asked at last.

I didn't reply, but he was right.

9

BY DAYBREAK, THE GRASS SNAKES WERE SAFELY housed in the wildlife hospital. Come Monday morning, if they looked healthy enough, they'd be released back into the wild. I'd promised to do it several miles from the village. Before we left, I took a small box of ViperaTAb from the fridge. I would keep it at home for a couple of weeks. Just in case.

The Devil from Down Under, as Matt seemed determined the taipan be called, was still with me. I dropped Matt off at his house, returned his jacket and thanked him for his help. I had a quick shower in my own cottage, checked the bruising on my bad ankle, ate breakfast, climbed back into the car and started driving.

The Aeolus Trust, on the outskirts of Bristol, is a reptile re-homing centre. Run by volunteers, it's a registered charity that takes in former pets such as snakes, lizards and turtles that have been injured, abandoned, or just grown too big for their owners to manage. It provides medical treatment if necessary; then finds suitable homes for as many as possible.

I'd heard about the work and people of Aeolus – unsung heroes of the veterinary world – during my first term at vet school and since then I'd helped out as often as I could. Help was something they were always grateful to receive, because there never seemed quite enough of it to deal with everything they had thrown at them. Deliberate cruelty or just ignorant neglect, reptiles always seem to get more than their fair share.

One year I'd been working the late shift in the run-up to Christmas when a Bearded Dragon, a popular lizard native to Australia, had been brought in with some of the worst burns I'd ever seen. Its owners, well meaning but totally ignorant of their new pet's needs, had put it in the airing cupboard for warmth. The creature had become trapped between the lagging and the hot-water tank. By the time the owners found him, his body was so severely burned it had melted on to the tank.

That had been the worst case I'd encountered, but far from the only one. Working at Aeolus over the years, I'd seen terrible suffering that could have been avoided easily by reading a book or two, checking a few internet sites, talking to the local pet shop.

The reception area seemed busier than normal for a Saturday and I wondered if word had got round about the centre's latest arrival. Few reptile aficionados will miss a chance to see the world's most venomous land snake.

The door to Roger Tennant's office opened before I could reach it, and he strode over to meet me. I'd known Roger a long time; he lectured to my year at Edinburgh and his enthusiasm had been one of the factors in my choosing to study reptiles. He kissed me on both cheeks, as he always does. He means well but I wish he wouldn't; I really don't like people touching my face. Instead of taking me into his office, he ushered me along the corridor and into one of the examination rooms.

It was a room I'd been in many times before; two examination tables in the centre and a wide stainless-steel counter round the walls. Head-high cupboards ran the length of the room. The surfaces were spotless, instruments gleamed, cages stood awaiting new residents. It was a perfectly ordinary veterinary examination room, if a little on the large side, the type I worked in every day of the week. Apart, of course, from the tall, scruffy man who was lying (full length and apparently fast asleep) on the larger of the two examination tables.

'Wake up, Sean, she's here,' said Roger. With old-fashioned courtesy, Roger had taken the taipan's box from me, even though it wasn't remotely heavy. Seeing nothing unusual in having a sleeping tramp in his examination room, Roger carried the box over to the spare table and put it down. I could see his fingers were itching to open it, but he glanced over at his unconscious visitor. As I watched, the man's eyes opened. He blinked twice, glanced around and sat up.

I never stare at people, never. I know only too well how excruciatingly uncomfortable it can be having people gawp at you. But the minute this man opened his eyes I knew exactly who he was; and in real life his appearance was even more remarkable.

In his mid- to late-thirties, he was Caucasian: his face, head shape, eyes – a bright hazel green – told me that, but he was so deeply sun-tanned he could have passed for a native of north Africa. His hair was long and black, falling in dreadlocks to past his shoulders. He was tall, maybe an inch or two over six foot, and very lean. He was wearing jeans that were dirty and torn, a faded blue-checked shirt, a leather jacket that bore a dozen battle scars and boots that looked as though he'd trekked through fifty miles of jungle in them; which, as I was to find out shortly, he just had.

'Clara, this is Sean North,' said Roger. 'You may have . . .'

Heard of him? Of course I had. Who in the reptile world hadn't? And this, of course, was the real reason for the crowd in reception. Sean North was probably the world's best known herpetologist. He was an Englishman, honorary curator of reptiles at a couple of our bigger zoos but rarely ever in the country. He travelled the planet, usually with a television crew, seeking out the rarest and – typically – most dangerous reptiles to study and film. Venomous snakes were his speciality, but I'd seen some mesmerizing coverage of him with monitors, crocodiles and chameleons. His films were astonishing: his ability to find the shyest creatures was legendary, and his courage handling dangerous specimens simply awe-inspiring. He seemed to have no fear, risking his life over and over again, in some of the most hostile environments on earth. He was a genius. He was also, as one of my colleagues once put it, a complete nutter.

He was holding out his hand to me. Unable to think of anything to say, I took it. It was dry from too much sun; pitted and scarred from bites and scratches.

'Sorry,' he said, stifling a yawn. 'Long flight.'

'Sean got in this morning,' said Roger. 'I knew he was due back today from Indonesia, so I left a message on his mobile and he came straight up. I couldn't think of anyone better.'

Neither could I. I just wished I wasn't finding his physical presence so intimidating.

Completely awake now, North was lifting the taipan's box, testing its weight, gently rocking it and listening to the sounds coming from inside. Then he put it down on the table and released the locks. Roger, who'd been very close, took a step back. Glancing round, I saw several faces watching us from the corridor window. North lifted the lid to create a gap of a little over an inch. I was holding my breath. What if it was something completely harmless? What kind of an idiot was I going to look if Sean North – Sean North, for heaven's sake – had been dragged, exhausted and jet-lagged, all the way to Bristol to look at a harmless escaped pet?

'It's a baby,' beamed North. 'Got a hook, Rog?'

Roger passed him a snake hook and, showing a complete disregard for a taipan's ability to spring, North lifted the lid clean off and reached in with the hook. He pulled it out, the snake safely captured around the neck.

'Wow,' whistled Roger, coming a step closer. 'Isn't he a beauty?'

In daylight, and in safe hands that weren't mine, the snake was beautiful. He gleamed a colour too dark to be silver, too bright to be gunmetal, and the beaten copper stripe shone along his full length. His eyes were like living topaz, the round black pupil so much more appealing than the elliptic stripe of some species. North was holding his tail, stretching him out. At North's request, Roger found a measuring stick.

'Snout/vent length 102 centimetres,' he said. 'Total length 117 centimetres. And, I'd say, definitely an elapid. Look at the shields on the head.'

Elapids are a family of venomous snakes found in tropical and sub-tropical regions, including the Indian Ocean and the Pacific. They have long, slender bodies, smooth scales and a coffin-shaped head covered by larger, shield-like scales. All have hollow, fixed fangs and venom glands in the rear of the upper jaw. I started to thank my lucky stars that Roger, at least, shared my opinion that the snake was an elapid. Whatever else it turned out to be, an elapid has no place in a Dorset child's bedroom.

'It's a taipan all right,' said North. His eyes flicked towards me then back to the snake. 'You did well to spot it.'

'I worked in Australia for a time,' I said, hugely relieved at having recovered my ability to speak. 'I've seen them before.'

'It's not Australian,' said North. 'It's Papuan.'

'There are taipans in Papua New Guinea?' said Roger. I hadn't known that either.

North nodded. 'Yup, separate subspecies. Actually far more of a problem there,' he said. 'It's rare to see a taipan in Australia, but in southern PNG they cause around twenty-five fatalities every year.' He turned to me. 'Any idea where it came from?'

I shook my head. Just before I'd dropped him off earlier that morning, Matt had taken another phone call, this time from the police. 'The police are checking everyone in the area who has a licence to keep reptiles,' I said, 'but no one's reported anything missing.'

'Very unlikely they will,' said Roger. 'There can't be many taipans being kept legally in this country, if any. I just can't see the local authorities granting licences. Do any British zoos have taipans, Sean?'

'London's had four for a few years now; only one on display though,' said North. 'Not sure about the others. Bristol possibly; don't think Chester has. I can soon check, but if there'd been an escape, I think we'd know about it already.'

'You said it was a baby,' I said to North. 'Any idea exactly how old?'

North held the snake up higher, looked at it carefully, got Roger to measure its circumference. 'They grow quickly in their first year,' he said. 'It could be four months old, possibly five. Probably brought here as an egg, then hatched inside somewhere, in warm conditions.' North was confirming what I'd already guessed. There is a thriving illegal trade in venomous snakes which, ironically, the lowering of trade

restrictions across Europe has done a great deal to pro-
mote. Dangerous snakes are being brought into Britain
all the time and sold on the black market. But to
transport a live taipan all the way from Australia – or
Papua New Guinea – would be incredibly risky.
Smuggling eggs, on the other hand, was a far easier
proposition.

'OK, let's have you back,' said North, talking to the
snake. He carried it across to the counter, where a
transparent-sided box was waiting. He dropped the tail
end in, lowered the hook, released the snake and
secured the lid. Remembering my fumbling attempts
with the Spider-Man T-shirt the night before, I had to
admire the ease with which he handled the creature.
North turned round to face me.

'You caught this by yourself last night?' I felt myself
blushing, my eyes dropping to the snake box, even
though there was nothing much to see. The taipan had
curled itself up, as though bored with all the fuss.

'Well, I had someone helping,' I managed. 'He was
pretty competent,' I added, wanting to be fair to Matt.
'I couldn't have done it without him.'

'How, exactly, did you catch it?' asked North.

I gave a condensed version of the snake's capture,
glossing over my terror, the fumbling around, the close
shave.

'Sounds the sort of thing you would have done at her
age,' said Roger.

'What's worrying you?' asked North, who hadn't
stopped looking at me. I felt a pang of disappointment
that this man, whom I admired so much, should be

106

fixated on a facial deformity. I'd expected someone like him to be above such things, somehow.

'Can I ask you something else?' I asked. He nodded.

I explained the circumstances in which the taipan had been captured, the adder I'd seen in baby Sophia's cot and my neighbour, John Allington, dying the day before from an adder bite.

'Sounds like a lot of snake activity for Dorset,' drawled North.

I turned to the bag I'd left by the door and, reaching in, pulled out the papers Harry Richards had left with me the day before and the clear, plastic wallet.

'This is an adder, right?' I said, holding up the wallet.

North looked at it and wrinkled his nose. 'Yup,' he said. 'Got bitten by one of these suckers when I was fourteen. At a county show. Hurt like the blazes.'

'Don't tell me, you didn't even go to hospital,' said Roger.

'Who'd have taken care of the other three I had with me?' said North, who was looking at me again. I held out the papers and he took them from me.

'It's a haematology report,' I began, as North turned and bent over the counter, where the light was better. 'The blood was taken from John Allington, the man I mentioned who was bitten by an adder.' North didn't look up. 'This adder,' I added, indicating the snake in the wallet.

'It seemed to me,' I went on, 'that the blood sample in the report definitely contains adder venom, just as the haematologist concludes, but what they don't mention is that the concentration is just far too high. I remembered a study of adder bites being done in Sweden a few years ago so I looked it up on the net. The highest concentration of venom they recorded was 64µg/L. And that was taken from a very young child, with a much smaller body mass than my neighbour would have.'

'Whereas here we have over 200µg/L,' replied North.

'Exactly,' I said. 'I couldn't see how a single adder could inject that much venom.' I left the question hanging. North stood up, allowing Roger to check the report too. Roger looked at it for a few seconds, then muttered something about finding some books and left the room.

Alone with Sean North, my immediate instinct was to escape. Coffee! I could offer to get him coffee.

'Can we get coffee somewhere?' he asked. 'I feel in need of a caffeine shot.'

'Of course, yes, I'll bring you some.' At the door I stopped. I hadn't asked him how he took it. But he was right behind me. He reached out, pulled the door open and allowed me to lead the way along the corridor and into the staff kitchen. I have a very sensitive nose, people who work outdoors a lot often have, and in the confines of the kitchen I could smell him. But it wasn't the smell I'd have expected from a man whose clothes didn't seem to have been washed in weeks. Sean North smelled of rain on tropical plants, of tree bark and warm animal skin. I concentrated on filling the kettle, finding milk in the fridge. There'd be no need to talk.

'Roger tells me you know more about Antipodean lizards than anyone he's ever met but you work with hedgehogs and rabbits,' he said. A nod of the head without looking round would have been the simplest response, the one I'd normally employ, but I didn't like the faint note of derision in his voice.

'Also badgers, foxes, deer of various kinds, just about every species of British bird and, increasingly these days, snakes,' I replied.

If he realized he'd annoyed me, he didn't care. 'Still seems an odd sort of choice for a reptile specialist. Wouldn't you rather be with one of the big zoos?'

What is it with some people? What makes them feel when they meet a perfect stranger they can probe into their private business? Of course I'd been asked that question before and, usually, I mutter something about there being very few openings for zoo vets. Sean North, of course, would spot that big lie immediately. Which might be why I chose that moment to tell the truth. I turned round, looked him full in the face.

'I did for a while. I worked at Chester. I just got a little tired of feeling like one of the exhibits myself.' I took my own coffee and left the room, letting the door swing shut behind me and not really caring if it slammed in his face.

Great, I thought, as I walked back along the corridor. *On top of everything else, I've just offended probably the most influential person in my profession.* Was it really any wonder I chose to work with hedgehogs and rabbits? They didn't have impertinent, well-meaning owners, visitors didn't come in their thousands to gawp at them. Working with wild animals was the easiest way of ensuring that I did not, normally, encounter people. Because look how badly I handled it when I did.

Back in the examination room, Roger had books spread all around the table. He was flicking from papers to book in the exact way I had the previous day. I hoped he'd come to a rather more meaningful conclusion. A few seconds later, it looked like I was going to be disappointed.

'It's viper venom, I'm sure of it,' he said. 'It's got none of the characteristics you'd expect in Elapidae. That was the first thing I checked, in case this was a taipan bite, but it isn't. It's also quite distinctive from Colubrids. And there's no way it can be from Hydrophidae.'

Roger was doing exactly what I'd done: ticking off the species. Just about every venomous snake in the world belongs to the Xenophidia super-family, which divides into five families: Achrochordidae, the non-venomous file snakes; Colubridae, a mostly non-venomous family but including some rear-fanged snakes; and Atractaspididae, a small, difficult-to-classify group which I knew very little about. The two families containing the most dangerously venomous snakes are Elapidae, including mambas, cobras, sea snakes and, of course, the taipans, and Viperidae, including vipers, pit vipers and rattlesnakes.

'Look, Sean,' he said. North was perched on the stainless-steel counter, swallowing back coffee as if it weren't nearly scalding hot. He didn't move. 'I'm pretty certain it's not from a pit viper, it has some characteristics in common with rattlesnake venom but . . .'

'Save it, Rog,' said North. 'The haematologist was spot-on. It's from a northern cross adder. I've seen loads of the stuff.'

Northern, European, common or cross adder, different names for the same creature: *Vipera berus*. But . . .

'The common adder doesn't produce venom with the sort of concentration you see in that sample,' I said, forgetting I was annoyed with him.

'No, it doesn't,' he agreed. 'I'm glad you're speaking to me again, by the way.'

Roger glanced quickly from North to me and back to North again. 'So we're talking about . . .'

'Either a very large, mutant adder with venom strength comparable to about ten ordinary snakes, which, frankly, is a little unlikely, or multiple bites from more than one snake,' said North.

'I thought of that,' I said. 'I made a point of asking. There was only one bite.'

'Adders have been known to bite with one fang. The other bites might have been missed. Or just mistaken for large bruises.'

I hadn't thought of that, but he was right. A viper's fangs are at the front of its mouth on a short maxillary bone that can rotate back and forth. When not in use the fangs fold back against the roof of the mouth into a membranous sheath. The left and right fangs can be rotated together or independently. I felt a surge of excitement. That had to be the answer. Of course, it left us with the unappealing possibility that a dozen or so adders had found their way into John Allington's garden and, simultaneously, attacked him. Now that *would* be a freaky trick of nature.

At that moment my mobile started ringing. I excused

myself and went out into the corridor to take the call. What I heard did nothing to cheer me up. I argued for two minutes, using the now-tired excuses that I really didn't know enough to be of help, there were other people far better qualified. Then I gave in and agreed to set off immediately. I rang off and went back to join the two men.

'Roger, something's come up, I'm going to have to go,' I said, as both men turned to me. 'What about the taipan? Can I leave it here?'

'Of course,' said Roger, frowning at me. 'I'm not sure how successful we'll be finding a home but we can certainly keep it in the short term.'

'I'll take it,' said North. We both looked at him.

'I've got a trip planned to PNG in the autumn,' he said. 'If it's healthy and I can clear it with the authorities, I can take it home. In the meantime, it's probably safer with me than anywhere else.'

'Well, that's certainly true, but are you sure?' said Roger, sounding worried. 'It sounds like a terrible imposition.'

'No worries, mate,' replied North, but he was looking at me. 'Anything up?'

I really hadn't intended to say anything. It was not their problem, it wasn't even my problem but . . .

'That was the Dorset County Hospital,' I said. 'The man who was bitten last night, by what I thought was a grass snake . . .'

'Yes, what's happened?' asked Roger. North was frowning.

'He's taken a turn for the worse.'

10

I WAS DRIVING FASTER THAN WAS REALLY SAFE, especially given my lack of sleep the previous night, but there was no sign of Sean North's Land Rover in front. He'd insisted on coming with me to see Nick Poulson in hospital – not remotely out of his way, he'd said, he lived in Lyme Regis – but he'd driven off at a speed I didn't dare match.

I slowed down as I neared my exit, wondering what lay ahead of me, what condition I'd find Nick Poulson in. Technically, grass snakes do have venom glands. But they lack the mechanism to inject venom into their bite victims. I really didn't think it possible that Nick could be ill as a result of a grass-snake bite. Neither did Roger or Sean North. We reasoned there had to be something else wrong with him.

Or it hadn't been a grass snake that had bitten him after all.

When I pulled into the car park at the Dorset County Hospital, North's Land Rover was parked near the entrance in a space reserved for disabled drivers. I parked, legally, and got out of the car, hoping he'd gone in before me, maybe even sorted it out already, and I could just quietly slink away. More in hope than expectation, I peered through the grimiest window I'd ever seen on a vehicle that was actually on the road. North was fast asleep. An arm's length away and keeping my eyes in the opposite direction, I rapped on the window. A second later I heard the car door open.

'What kept you?' he asked, unfolding his body from the seat.

'Been here nearly an hour,' I snapped. 'Waiting for you to wake up.' I walked ahead of him into the hospital, stopped at the reception desk to find out where Nick Poulson was and then summoned the lift. As the doors closed, North leaned back against the rear wall with his eyes shut. I wondered if he was about to fall asleep again; if he did, I might just leave him where he was.

The doors opened and so did his eyes. We walked the length of the corridor and at the nurses' station found Harry Richards, the consultant who'd just sought my advice for the second time. He looked as if he'd had even less sleep than I had in the last few days, but he seemed genuinely pleased to see me, and positively delighted when I introduced Sean North. He told us that Nick Poulson had seemed fine at first but had deteriorated during the night. Blood tests were being carried out, but the results weren't expected back for an hour or so. After what had happened to John Allington, Dr Richards was seriously concerned about his new patient.

* * *

Nick Poulson was lying in bed. His skin was clammy, his colour high and his eyes a little too bright. His breathing was fast and shallow and he looked decidedly uncomfortable.

'How you doing, mate?' asked North.

Nick stared at him, while Dr Richards made the introductions. Then Nick looked at me. 'I heard you found a poisonous snake in my house, last night,' he said. 'Something from Australia?'

'Papua New Guinea,' I muttered.

'The thing that bit me wasn't a grass snake, I'm sure of it. It was black, about four feet long . . .'

People always suppose grass snakes are green, and a lot of them are. But they can also be various shades of brown, grey and black. A four-foot-long black snake could easily have been a grass snake. On the other hand . . .

'What are his symptoms?' asked North.

Dr Richards didn't need to check Nick's notes. 'Headache, nausea and vomiting, diarrhoea, stomach cramps and fever,' he recited. 'He seemed OK for the first four or five hours, but he's been getting worse since first thing this morning.'

'Can I see the wound?' asked North.

Dr Richards took Nick's arm and loosened the adhesive tape that was holding the dressing in place. He pulled back the gauze. The bite was swollen and inflamed. It glowed a bright red, and I thought I could see pus around the wound. It didn't look good. I glanced up, caught Dr Richards' eyes. He didn't look too good either.

115

'Has it been bleeding since you came in?' asked North.

Nick looked at Richards. 'No,' replied the medic.

'Let me see your gums,' said North to Nick.

'My what?'

'Your gums, mate. Open your mouth.'

Another look between patient and doctor, and then Nick opened his mouth. North leaned forward, muttered a low, 'Excuse me,' and took hold of Nick's upper lip. He pulled it up to give a clear view of the gums, looked all round the upper part of the mouth and then did the same thing with the lower one.

'Any problems breathing?'

Nick shook his head.

'Have you taken a piss since you came in?' North asked next.

Nick nodded, clearly wondering what sort of madman we'd set loose on him.

'What colour was it?'

'Oh, for God's sake!'

'This is important, mate. Was it normal? Straw-coloured, yellow, whatever? Or was it reddish-brown?'

'Normal,' muttered Nick, his eyes flicking from the doctor to me. As if either of us had any explanation to offer.

'Can you move your arms and legs? If you had to, could you walk?'

In response, Nick Poulson pulled back his covers, swung his legs over the side of the bed and rose up. He wasn't too steady, but he made it across the room then turned to face us.

'Congratulations, mate, you weren't bitten by a taipan,' said North, looking pleased with himself.

'How can you be so sure?' asked Dr Richards.

'. . . the hell do you know?' demanded Nick at the same time.

'Taipan venom is particularly nasty because it contains both a neurotoxin and an anti-coagulant,' said North, folding his arms and leaning back against the wall. 'The neurotoxin binds to the neuro-muscular junctions and stops them functioning. Most victims not treated with anti-venom suffer respiratory paralysis within four to six hours of being bitten. The anti-coagulant would cause continual bleeding from the bite wound and from the gums. Internal haemorrhaging is a problem, especially in the brain. You'd have suffered convulsions, probably slipped into a coma. Oh, and the poison eats away at muscle tissue. Your piss would turn reddish-brown as your muscles deteriorated and passed through your kidneys.'

North paused for breath, giving us a chance to interrupt him. Nobody did. After a split second he went on.

'What I'm really saying, mate, in a very long-winded fashion, is that I know you weren't bitten by a taipan because you're still alive.'

Nick Poulson's colour drained before our eyes. He walked back to the bed and sank down on it. Nobody spoke for what felt like a very long time. Then North turned to me.

'And while I'm on the subject, love, next time you come across one of those buggers, don't pick it up.'

I didn't reply. But I was far from arguing. I looked at Nick Poulson's bed and realized how close I'd come to being in it. Or on a trolley in the morgue.

'So what the hell *is* wrong with me?' said Nick.

North stood away from the wall and took a step closer to the bed. He bent to look once more at Nick's wound.

'I'd say you got infected,' he replied. 'Most grass snakes carry salmonella. A few days on antibiotics should sort you out.'

I hadn't realized I'd been holding my breath.

'Well, I certainly hope you're right,' said Dr Richards, who was looking as thankful as I felt. 'We're expecting the bloods back any time now. Infections, we can deal with.'

We left Nick Poulson – not nearly as pleased as you'd expect at hearing he wasn't going to die just yet – and, on Dr Richards' invitation, went to his office on the next floor up. Over coffee, which North and I both drank like we were dying of thirst, I explained the conclusions we'd all come to back at Aeolus: that whilst the venom in John Allington's blood was definitely from a common adder, its concentration appeared too high to have come from a single snake. Dr Richards dug out several photographs of John Allington's wound, taken shortly after admittance, two days later and post-mortem. Sean North then explained his theory about other, less noticeable, bite marks.

'There might not have been the obvious two fang marks, maybe a series of smaller scratches from the teeth and just one larger puncture wound. You'd expect local swelling, maybe some discoloration.'

Richards shook his head. 'Nothing that I spotted. But, to be honest, I didn't think about multiple bites. I was too busy trying to treat the one I could see.'

North was staring at one of the photographs. 'Come and look at this, Clara,' he said. Instead of handing me the photograph, he beckoned me over, so that I was forced to lean over the back of his chair.

'Anything strike you?' he asked.

I reached out and took hold of the photo. He released it, and I walked over to the window. There was plenty of light in the room, I just didn't feel comfortable being so close to him. I'd decided there was something slightly reptilian about Sean North. He had a way of watching intently, as though he were sizing you up, before . . . before what? . . . pouncing, striking . . . What was it, I asked myself (when I should have been examining the photograph), that I expected Sean North to do? Knowing he was staring at me again, I forced myself to concentrate.

The photograph was of a man's neck, shot from only a few inches away. It must have been taken immediately after Allington's admittance, because the swelling around the wound was minimal. I could see the pores of his skin, the stubble of a beard on his chin and the wiry grey hairs on the back of his neck. Two puncture wounds, red and with a little surrounding blood, were evident just above his collarbone.

'What do you think?' asked North, and I couldn't help feeling he was testing me. I was tempted to say, no, nothing was striking me, and hand the photograph back but . . .

'Do you have a measurement for the distance between the two puncture marks?' I asked Harry Richards, deliberately ignoring North.

Richards shuffled through his notes for a few seconds, then looked up. 'Eighteen millimetres,' he answered. 'Why, what . . .'

There was nothing for it but to look at North. His eyebrows were raised, as if he were my science teacher or something. And why on earth was I so pathetically anxious to impress him?

'Seems a bit on the small side,' I ventured, although the truth was I really wasn't that sure about the adder's anatomy. It just didn't seem a terribly wide bite mark for what can be a pretty chunky snake.

'The big-snake theory doesn't seem to be going anywhere fast,' agreed North.

'I don't quite . . .' said Dr Richards.

North turned to him. 'I assume there's going to be a coroner's post-mortem?'

Richards nodded. 'Almost certainly,' he agreed.

'Ask the pathologist to examine that wound carefully and compare it with what's known about adder bites,' continued North. 'He should also check the body for other bites. His blood needs to be . . .'

'Can you take a look?' asked Richards.

'Me?' said North. He shook his head. 'Not remotely qualified, mate.'

I had a moment of satisfaction at realizing that the big, macho man wasn't keen on the idea of viewing a dead body. Then realized that, if North refused, I might be next on the list.

'I'm not comfortable with any of this,' said Richards. 'To be honest, my colleagues don't particularly agree with me. The fact that the snake has been identified as an adder and the venom confirmed as adder venom is enough for them. But John Allington was my patient, and I need to give as much information as I can to the coroner. At the moment, I'm just not happy.' He waited a while, for one of us to answer him. 'And you two don't seem to be either,' he added, when neither of us did.

'I'm not happy about the head wound the patient suffered,' he continued, 'or about the fact that Mr Allington managed to kill the snake but still wasn't able to phone for help. Nor am I particularly comfortable about the family that were brought in last night or the young baby that was in here yesterday. From what I understand, she'd have been bitten too, if you hadn't been there, Miss Benning.'

'I'll have a look,' I said. Then I turned to North. 'Although, frankly, my experience of snake bites is negligible.'

For a second, North glared back, then I could see the tiniest smile just starting to crack lines along his cheeks. 'OK, OK,' he said, shaking his head. 'Christ, I'm beginning to wish I'd stayed in the jungle.'

11

I'D NEVER SEEN A HUMAN CORPSE BEFORE, AND ALL I could think of in the lift down to the hospital morgue was that Mum had died the same morning as John Allington. Mum was being kept in cold storage somewhere. Mum's body would probably be in exactly the same condition as the one I was about to see. And I couldn't get out of my head the weirdest idea that the body-bag would be unzipped and it would be Mum's face staring out at me.

All the way down I was rehearsing the line that would get me out of it after all: 'I'm sorry, but my mother died this week,' I'd say. 'I'm really not up to this right now.' They'd understand, of course, but I'd have to face a whole gambit of questions – when? how? why? They'd have another reason to feel sorry for me.

The words didn't come out and, faster than I could have expected, we were at the door of the morgue. We went through, and Richards led us past the small waiting area for relatives of the deceased and into another room. A large window took up most of one wall.

Through it we could see the brightly lit examination room beyond. I stood there thinking, *What if I faint, what if I throw up? He's going to think me such an idiot.*

'Need a jacket?' said North quietly in my ear. I shook my head and took a step away from him before he could see me shiver again. It wasn't even that cold.

Harry Richards excused himself and left us. After a second we saw him enter the examination room, talking to one of the morgue staff. The lab assistant glanced over at North and me, standing in the window. He crossed the room to a phone, spoke into it for a few seconds and nodded at Dr Richards. He disappeared just as North turned to face me.

'Clara, this might not be very pretty,' he said. 'There's no need for you to get involved. Why don't you wait for us outside?'

It was a perfectly reasonable suggestion. I was neither a doctor nor a herpetologist and, were I a sensible woman, I'd probably have agreed immediately.

'You look a bit green yourself, Mr North,' I said. 'Maybe you should sit this one out.'

North shrugged and turned back to the window, just as two lab technicians pushed a trolley through the large double doors. They stopped, not two feet from our window, unzipped the black body-bag and lifted out the cadaver that lay inside. And, prepared for the worst though I was, I couldn't help the small cry slipping out of my lips.

The last five days of John Allington's life had not been easy, and I really hoped that the painkillers he'd been given had been strong and that he'd known very little about what had been happening to his body.

Because his body had begun to die some time before his heart stopped beating.

The last time I did any reading on the subject, there were twenty known types of toxic enzymes found in snake venom, each with its own special function. Some are there to paralyse prey; others exist to break the body tissues down and aid the snake's digestive process. The venom of each species will typically contain between six and twelve of these toxins: its own unique cocktail of death. The adder is a viperine snake, and its venom is haemotoxic (it poisons the blood), necrotizing (causes tissue death) and anti-coagulant (prevents blood from clotting).

All of these had had time to get to work on John Allington. The area around the bite site, just above his collarbone, had only minimal swelling, but both arms and his left leg had swollen horribly. One common complication of snake bite is acute compartment syndrome, when swelling occurs within a muscle compartment, causing a limb to enlarge. A fasciotomy, a surgical procedure involving opening the fascial compartments to relieve pressure, had been performed on Allington's right arm. Two deep cuts, one on each side of the limb, ran from just below the shoulder to his elbow. He'd died before the swelling had gone down, and the wound still gaped open, the muscle bulging out of mottled, purple skin.

I took a step closer to the window, curious to see the man who'd been my neighbour for several years. He had been almost seventy, with dark-grey hair receding at the temples and thin on the top of his head. He was six foot, maybe six one, in height and must have been muscular as a younger man.

He might have been a complete stranger; nothing about him looked remotely familiar. Twenty-four hours after death, the skin on his face was a lemon-yellow colour, giving him the appearance of a waxwork. His mouth was stretched wide as if he were still, even then, trying for one last breath; and the corneas of his still-open eyes were dull and chalky.

Sean North's hand dropped on to my shoulder. I turned and realized he was looking at a large monitoring screen in the corner of the room. Harry Richards, carrying a small hand-held camera, was walking round the table, and the images he was filming were being relayed on to the screen in our room. The technology allowed North and me, as well as Dr Richards, to check the undamaged parts of Allington's flesh for other bite marks.

The necrosis, fortunately for Allington while he was still alive, and for we who had to examine his body, had been contained within the right arm. Elsewhere, the flesh, while considerably swollen, was otherwise unmarked. There were several bruises, but we could see no sign of skin lacerations. Small bites might have healed, of course, in the few days he'd been in hospital. But then, small bites wouldn't result in envenomation. For that to take place, a fang had to make a deep puncture into the tissue. If John Allington had had other serious bites, they'd still be here for us to see.

Except there weren't any. After a few minutes the

body was turned, and Dr Richards resumed his slow walk around the trolley. After twenty minutes we were as sure as it was possible to be that John Allington had suffered no other bites.

'We don't seem to be getting anywhere,' said Harry Richards, with no attempt to hide his disappointment.

'Oh, I don't know,' replied North. 'Can you go back to the wound on his neck, please? Clara, come here a sec.'

Wondering when, exactly, I'd given North permission to treat me as an assistant, I allowed him to lead me closer to the screen. The camera in Harry Richards' hand was pointed at the bite wound on John Allington's neck. North stood back to let me get closer to the screen.

'Tell me what you see,' he instructed.

I looked. I could see two puncture wounds, each roughly four millimetres in diameter, just under twenty millimetres apart, lying just above the collarbone. 'I'm sorry,' I said, 'but . . .'

'Does that camera have a magnifying facility?' called North.

After a second or so, the image doubled in size.

'Think about how a viper strikes,' North prompted. 'Tell me what you know.'

I thought about it. Some snakes, cobras for example, have relatively short fangs that are fixed in position. Vipers' fangs are much longer. They work on a hinge, springing into place when needed and then resting, horizontally in the jaw, when not being used.

'They have long fangs,' I said. 'The wounds would be deep.'

'Which these are, of course. Go on . . .'

'They're a strike-and-release snake,' I said. 'They give one very powerful bite, using the lower jaws to drive the fangs deeper into the prey, and then they let go.'

'How many teeth do they have on the lower jaw?'

'Two rows, typically.'

'So if the lower jaw is an essential part of the bite mechanism, would you expect to see marks from the lower teeth?'

I looked up at him, forgetting that I was annoyed, then back at the wound.

'Yes,' I said. 'Yes, I would.'

Harry Richards was holding the camera steady but sending frequent glances in our direction. Even the two morgue attendants looked interested by this stage.

'There's nothing there,' said Richards. 'No tooth-marks below the wounds at all.'

North ignored him. 'What about upper teeth?' he said to me.

'Vipers have fewer than most snakes,' I said, struggling to remember the reading I'd done when I'd been working with snakes. 'They have the gap to allow the fangs to fold up.'

'Diastema,' prompted North.

'But still teeth there. Two rows, I think.'

'See any toothmarks?'

I shook my head.

By this stage I was standing on tiptoe to get closer to the screen. North put his hand on my shoulder to steady me.

'Look at those punctures,' he said. 'Think about how the fangs enter the target . . .'

I looked. What was it, exactly, he wanted me to see?

'Think about how they leave the target . . .'

Of course! 'The skin would be torn. Just slightly, as the fangs are pulled out. There'd be a ripping, the wounds wouldn't be regular, you'd be able to judge the angle at which the snake struck.'

'See anything?'

I looked at North, at the screen, at North again. He was smiling at me. I found myself smiling back.

'No,' I said. 'They're perfect.'

'OK, being very patient here, guys,' interrupted Richards. 'Anyone want to tell me what's going on?'

North stepped back but kept his hand on my shoulder. Strangely, I no longer minded.

'Your patient in there died by poisoning from adder venom,' he said.

'Yes,' said Richards, impatiently. 'We know that . . .'

'Which is interesting. Given that he wasn't bitten by a snake.'

12

'YOU'RE SAYING SOMEONE INJECTED ADDER venom into John Allington?' We were heading away from the morgue. Richards sounded incredulous. In all fairness, I could hardly blame him. 'Is such a thing even remotely possible?' he continued.

'Easiest thing in the world if the victim is unconscious,' North replied. 'John Allington took a blow to the head, from what I understand?'

'He fell,' said Richards.

'Are you sure?' said North.

No answer.

'Anyone with experience of snakes could milk an adder of its venom,' continued North. 'Milk several – around six might do it – and you'd have the sort of concentrations Clara spotted in John Allington's blood.'

'And you can just inject it into someone?' said Richards. 'Using – what – a hypodermic syringe? That's possible?'

North shrugged. 'Never done it myself, but I don't see

why not,' he said. 'In our friend's case, I'd say it was injected pretty deep into the tissue. There was very little swelling around the bite site itself – that's the first thing that made me suspicious – and then I'd guess whoever it was took a sharp, thin instrument, something like a small screwdriver, and made those two puncture wounds to disguise the needle mark.'

Richards had stopped walking. He looked at North. 'Blow to the head, you say?' he repeated.

North frowned. 'Well, let's just say a head injury. Cause unknown.'

'What's the matter?' I asked.

Richards looked from North to me.

'Nick Poulson's father-in-law was admitted last night as well,' he said. 'The whole family was, actually, but the mother and children were discharged first thing this morning.'

North and I waited.

'The old man was suffering from mild concussion,' said Richards after a moment. 'He'd banged his head on something.'

'There was blood on his pillow,' I said. 'And the police found a dead adder in his room.'

We stood there, in the middle of the corridor, as staff and visitors made their way around us. Nobody, it seemed, could think of anything to say. Had Ernest Amblin been in line to suffer the same death as John Allington? In the end, I was the one to break the silence.

'I think you need to speak to the police,' I said to Richards.

He started to nod.

'Hang on a sec,' interrupted North. 'We don't want half southern England getting hysterical about snakes. Why don't we just see if this chap will talk to us before we start panicking? He wasn't actually bitten by the adder, was he?'

'No, but . . .'

'What do you think? Will he be up for visitors?'

Ernest Amblin wasn't just willing to see us, he was eager. North and I waited for just a few seconds at the nurses' station before Harry Richards beckoned us forward. As we crossed the small ward to his bed by the window, the elderly man pushed himself up in bed, and I realized I'd seen him at Clive Ventry's house the previous evening. He'd been one of five elderly people sitting around the table corner.

'That snake you found,' he said, when we were still feet away. 'The venomous one. Have you managed to identify it?' He was looking directly at me; talking only to me.

I stole a glance at North as Dr Richards stepped forward and raised the bedhead to support Dr Amblin. North nodded at me to continue as Richards tried, in vain, to persuade Amblin to lean back.

'We think it's a taipan,' I said, turning back to Dr Amblin. 'They're found in the southern hemisphere, in Australia and Papua New Guinea. But we're pretty certain it isn't what bit your son-in-law—'

'Yes, yes,' interrupted Amblin. 'Are you sure, though? About it being from the southern hemisphere? It can't have come from anywhere else?'

'Like where?' asked North.

'Oh, I'm sorry,' said Richards. 'Dr Amblin, this is . . .'

'Like Africa,' snapped Amblin. 'Or . . .' his eyes were flicking from North to me, completely ignoring his doctor, '. . . or North America? Could it? Could it have come from North America?'

Unsure what to say, I looked at North again.

'No,' he said, without taking his eyes off Amblin. 'Taipans have never been found outside Australasia. And the only elapid in North America is the coral snake. They're very distinctive, with brightly coloured stripes. It isn't one of those.'

Amblin seemed to shrink down on to his bed. 'Thank you,' he muttered, and his eyes fell to the folded sheet around his waist. Only then did I have time to look at him properly. He was a well-preserved man in his mid-seventies; lots of thick, steel-grey hair; brown eyes behind heavy spectacles. A large square dressing covered the wound on his left temple.

'Dr Amblin, we found an adder in your bedroom last night,' I said. 'Did you kill it?'

He looked back at me for a split second, then dropped his eyes again. He started to shake his head, then grimaced. 'No,' he said, as his hand went up to touch his wound. 'I didn't see an adder.' Eyes back up. 'If I'd been bitten, would I know about it?'

'Oh yes,' said North.

Seemingly reassured, Amblin settled down again. 'I'm not sure that paracetamol you gave me is really doing the trick, Dr Richards,' he said, without lifting his eyes. 'Could you find me anything a bit stronger? I really would like to get some sleep.'

'I'll see what I can do,' replied Richards, walking round the bed to face his patient. 'Can you tell us how you hurt your head?'

Amblin closed his eyes before opening them again to focus on nothing in particular. 'I'm afraid not,' he said at last. 'I don't think I was properly awake. I'd been dreaming. Bad dreams. Someone from a long . . . Then I heard Nick shouting at the children to wake up. I don't remember much else until we were outside. I must have fallen on the stairs or something.'

Dr Richards announced that his patient needed to rest. North and I took the hint and prepared to leave. The doctor walked us to the door of the ward but didn't tell us what he was thinking, just thanked us and sped away.

'There was blood on Dr Amblin's pillow,' I said, as we waited for an elevator. 'Why would it be there if he hit his head on the stairs?'

'Shaving cut?' suggested North. 'Or maybe he remembers more than he's telling us. I'm not sure this lift is working.'

We set off to look for stairs. 'And if he didn't kill the adder, who did?' I said as we set off down. North didn't reply. We reached the bottom of the stairs and made for the main exit. At the A&E reception area I stopped walking.

'It makes no sense,' I said, forcing North to stop too. 'Why would anyone go to all the trouble of milking adders and injecting their venom into people when they have a taipan at their disposal? Death is pretty much guaranteed from a taipan bite.'

The Accident and Emergency department was busy. People were noticing us. Starting to stare at me.

'But much harder to pass off as a natural death than an adder bite on an elderly chap,' said North. 'What were the chances of Richards smelling a rat, getting in touch with you and then you meeting me this morning? I'd say someone got very unlucky. Hi! How're you doing?'

To my alarm, a small crowd had gathered round us. But nobody was paying any attention to me at all. It was Sean North they were interested in. I'd forgotten he appeared on national television on a regular basis. And was the sort of person you didn't forget in a hurry.

Slowly, stopping to shake hands and sign scraps of paper, North made his way out of the hospital, and I followed. At the doors, we left his fans behind.

'Why would anyone want to kill two elderly men?' I asked, to myself more than North, as we crossed the car park.

North smiled down at me. 'That's a question for the police,' he said. 'I'm a reptile man, not a detective. It's been a real pleasure, Clara. Gotta run.'

13

THE CHURCH BELLS WERE RINGING A QUARTER AFTER eleven when I arrived. It wasn't easy to park, even on a Sunday, but eventually I managed it and walked back along the busy high street to what is generally considered one of the finest Norman churches in the country. Its huge rectangular tower soared above me, blotting out the late-morning sunshine as I walked through the gate and up the church path. In the south porch, I tucked the owl chicks' cage beneath the wooden bench. I'd be away from home most of the day; I'd had no choice but to bring them.

Even through the thick yew doors I could hear the voice of the archdeacon. I knew from experience what a racket the old doors could make when opened, and how every head in the congregation would turn to look at the interloper, but I'd learned a trick over the years. I pushed the door gently forward until I felt resistance and slid the catch upwards as far as it would go. Then I pulled the door back an inch and lowered the catch. Pushing gently, I swung the door open, and it made not a sound. Only George, the elderly churchwarden, saw me come in and slip into an empty pew right at the very back. And the archdeacon himself, of course, who misses very little, even when he's leading prayers.

The service was drawing to an end. George scuttled over with prayer and hymn books and I managed to smile at him. He pressed my hand, and his eyes filled with tears. I looked quickly away. The vicar announced the final hymn, and the congregation, just a second or two behind the choir, rose to its feet.

Over the last few decades, Church of England congregations have been in rapid decline. Not the case in my home town. The church was usually full for the weekly Sunday service, and today was no exception. The voices of the twenty-strong choir burst upwards, and the congregation joined in with varying degrees of talent but consistent enthusiasm. Everyone but me. Normally, I enjoy congregational singing, feeling my voice spreading out from me like a warm wave of sound. That morning, though, I hadn't the heart for it.

The service finished, and the vicar bade us all go in peace and serve the Lord; the congregation responded in time-honoured fashion and started to drift away. It took a long time, as it always does. Everyone wanted their handshake and their two minutes of attention from the vicar and, especially, the archdeacon. Over the years, I'd watched him become a master of the personal greeting: the brief but entirely individual chat and the warm, gentle dismissal. No one ever felt less than perfectly welcome.

I sat, half hidden behind an immense stone column, my eyes cast down. Eventually, the last few stragglers had passed through the nave, and I got up. In the porch, I waited in line until the two clergymen had bidden farewell to the last of their flock. The vicar saw me, patted my shoulder briefly and hurried away. I held out my own hand for the archdeacon. He waited a second or two before taking it, and I had time to notice that he looked a little thinner than when I'd last seen him, that his hair seemed a bit unkempt and that there was decidedly less of it. There were dry patches of skin around his forehead; his eyes, it seemed, had lost just a fraction of their colour. But when he took my hand it felt as soft and warm and strong as it always had. I saw his need of me and was glad I'd come home.

'Hi, Dad,' I said. It was just about all I could manage.

We walked, arm in arm, back along the high street, to the house I'd called home for most of my life. We'd arrived here nearly thirty years ago, the Benning family: Dad, the church's brightest rising star, at forty-three one of the youngest clergymen ever to be appointed arch-deacon; his wife, Marion, nearly twenty years younger, already dissatisfied with rural, clerical life; Vanessa, the elder daughter, a precocious five-year-old; and me, a nine-month-old baby. We'd expected to be here a decade at most, before Dad was made a bishop and we moved, ever onwards and upwards. It hadn't happened. First up, there'd been me to deal with. By the time ten years had gone by, Mum was fighting a losing battle with alcoholism and serious depression and no longer considered bishop's wife material.

'Vanessa's mob is here,' said Dad, as we turned into the gate. 'I think there's lunch planned.' It was a gentle warning, but unnecessary. I'd seen Vanessa, her husband Adrian and their two daughters in church and had sunk a little lower in my seat as they left.

'But how did the tie-pin get into the little boy's bedroom?' asked ten-year-old Jessica.

'Very good question,' I replied, pushing some green beans around my plate. I could never eat very much of Vanessa's food. There was nothing wrong with the way she cooked, it was just . . . well . . . something in my stomach seemed to tighten whenever I was around my elder sister. 'The only thing I can think of is that it escaped from someone who probably shouldn't have had it in the first place,' I said.

'Or was set loose when the owner realized it was too much to handle,' interrupted Adrian, my brother-in-law.

'Well, that's also possible,' I agreed. 'And it certainly wouldn't be the first time.' At Aeolus, we'd been called out more than once to recapture exotic snakes from parkland, open countryside, even domestic gardens. Snakes that seemed cute as infants had a habit of growing very big and strong.

'But what about all the grass snakes?' prompted Jessica.

I gave up trying to put more food into my mouth and laid my knife and fork down together. Out of the corner of my eye, I saw Vanessa glare at me. And heard Dad give a soft, quiet sigh. I was beginning to wish I hadn't mentioned the whole snake business, but conversation around the lunch table had been difficult, even more than normal.

'Allegedly, grass snakes swarm,' I said, not wanting to

get into any of the other, more sinister theories. 'I've never seen it, but I know of people who have. Dozens of them just move together. It's possible the taipan came across a swarm and just fancied the company. It's a very young snake. Or maybe it saw them as dinner.'

'What would have happened to the baby if the adder had bitten her?' asked eight-year-old Abigail.

'Abigail, this is not the time,' warned her mother, and for once I was happy to go along with Vanessa.

'Think you have a practical joker in your village?' asked Adrian. 'You've had a few problems with vandalism, haven't you? Could be someone's idea of a lark.'

'Someone died,' I said, more abruptly than I meant to. 'It isn't really that funny.'

'Exactly,' said Vanessa, as Adrian reached out to top up Dad's glass and refill his own. Vanessa and I never drink. 'And I think we need to talk about Friday. Has Andrew confirmed, Daddy?'

Andrew Tremain was Bishop of Winchester, Dad's boss and a long-standing family friend. He would have been asked, as a matter of course, to conduct Mum's funeral. My father replied that Andrew would be delighted to take the service, and Vanessa began to announce her funeral plans to the rest of us. I watched Dad nodding agreement to her suggestions for flowers, hymns and readings and allowed myself to drift away. It made no difference to me whether Mum's flowers were roses, lilies or buttercups and daisies. Mum was gone. And with her, it seemed, had fled my last chance to come to terms with what she'd allowed to happen. I'd waited so many years for the right moment to confront my mother about how totally she'd destroyed my life. Now, I'd never be able to hear her say sorry. Nor would I ever tell her how totally and completely she'd been the centre of my world.

'Global warming,' said my brother-in-law, who probably hadn't been paying much attention to Vanessa either. 'Got a lot to answer for. What have we had? The hottest April since records began, with May looking set to follow. And now the population's exploded. Things are swarming around all over the place.'

'What are you talking about?' I asked.

'Snakes,' he said, looking at me and blinking hard. 'I thought we all were.'

'Auntie Clara?'

'Yes, Stringbean?' I'd survived lunch. My youngest niece and I were sitting in the shade of the apple trees at the bottom of Dad's walled garden, giving the owl chicks their lunch. Every so often a breeze shook the trees and a confetti shower of late blossom drifted around us like a fragrant snowstorm. Through the wide, wrought-iron gate we could see a flock of swans sailing past on the river.

'My waist measures seventeen and a half inches,' my niece replied indignantly. She bent forward, gingerly holding a dead mouse in a pair of tweezers. Abigail declared her intention to be a vet like Auntie Clara at every opportunity – I suspect she already knew how much it annoyed her mother – but she was struggling a bit with the whole food-chain business.

140

'Sorry – Broadbean,' I corrected, watching the breeze lifting the curls around her face. Abigail's hair is a rich glossy brown like mine, and she wears it long. Just as I do.

'Can I ask you something?'

'Yep.'

'Mummy says I shouldn't.'

I made her wait for a few seconds. 'Well then, it really depends on the extent to which you have confidence in your own judgement, and how that compares to the trust you place in your mother's wisdom,' I said eventually.

'So can I?' repeated Abigail, without a second's reflection.

I was bending over the cage. She couldn't see me smile. 'Yes, you can. I won't tell.'

'I saw on the news about face transplants. And I was wondering if you could have one.'

The chicks were calming down a little. I reached out, picked one of them up, and laid it gently on Abigail's outstretched hand. In just over a week, they'd be introduced to their foster parents and all human contact would cease. I figured a few seconds in a little girl's hands wouldn't hurt. 'I don't mind how you look,' Abigail said hurriedly, her eight-year-old brain already processing the possibility that Mummy might, after all, have had the sounder judgement. 'It's just, I thought it might be nicer for you . . .' Her voice trailed away.

'Well, it would be,' I said, slowly, because I really hadn't prepared myself for this one. 'But it's not something that can work for me just yet, I'm afraid.'

'Why not?'

'Well, I've had a quick look into it,' I said, wondering if hours poring over every internet and magazine article I could find counted as 'a quick look'. 'You know, with any transplant, there's always the risk of the body rejecting the transplanted organ and of it having to be removed, don't you?'

'Ye—es,' she replied.

'So transplants aren't usually done unless they're considered absolutely necessary.'

'But the man on the news had been—'

'Yes, he had,' I interrupted, taking the chick from her and gently putting it back in the cage. 'But his face was very badly damaged. Much worse than mine. He couldn't eat or speak. And it was still a very risky procedure. He'll have to take high-dose steroids and immune suppressants for the rest of his life to prevent his new face being rejected. Those drugs carry a high risk of cancer and kidney failure, and even then they may not work. His body could still reject the transplant.'

'What would happen then?'

I didn't like to think about what would happen then. The new face would blacken, eventually just slough away.

'They'd have to take it off again. He'd be worse off than before.'

Abigail squeezed my hand tight. 'You shouldn't do it,' she said.

'No,' I agreed. 'I shouldn't.'

I stood, picked up the owl cage, and Abigail and I walked back to the house.

14

I SPRANG UPRIGHT. THE BEDCLOTHES FELL AWAY AS I knelt on the bed, not daring to move, staring down into the shadows where a large and extremely dangerous snake was coiled. Trembling, I reached for the bedside light and flicked it on. Nothing there. I'd been dreaming.

OK, deep breath. If *I* was getting this jumpy about snakes, how on earth would the rest of the village be coping? Just beginning to feel stupid, I looked at the clock. Almost 3 a.m., which meant the alarm was about to go off anyway. It was feeding time.

I got up, still tired. I'd arrived home late the previous evening. Dad had asked me to stay the night, but I'd muttered something about dangerously ill patients at work. The glass on the bedside table needed refilling, so I picked it up. As I walked through the door I reached automatically for my robe, then changed my mind. The air was sticky, the night unseasonably warm. Longing for the days when feeding the young owls would no longer be my responsibility, I crossed the wide gallery-landing that doubles as a study.

Someone had been in here. Things had been moved.

My keyboard is always a hand's span from the edge of my desk, but that night it was hardly more than an inch away. And it wasn't straight. My paper tray had been moved too. It was just a fraction further to the left of the desk than it normally is.

I crossed the landing, pushed open the door of the spare room and flicked on the light. Nothing out of place that I could see. Maybe, with everything that had been going on, I'd been less tidy than normal. I set off down the stairs. The chicks were creating seriously as I pulled open the door that led to my small kitchen. It was a clear night and soft light was finding its way through the kitchen window, reflecting off the white-washed walls.

So there was no mistaking the dark figure of an elderly man standing beside the kitchen table looking down at my owl chicks. The glass fell from my hand and smashed on the tiled floor. The intruder took no notice of me, didn't appear to have heard the glass break; just reached into the cage. Frozen to the spot, I watched him pick up one of the birds. He brought the chick up to his face, seemed to be sniffing it and, for a second, I thought he was going to eat it.

Until that point, I think I'd been more shocked than scared. But realization was beginning to set in. There was a man in my house in the middle of the night. It was late May and he probably wasn't Santa Claus.

I started to walk backwards. The man put the owl down and bent over the cage. I could hear him muttering and grunting to himself but could make out none of the words; I wasn't even sure he was speaking English. Misjudging the distance I'd moved, I came up sharp against the curtained window of my dining room. A thin beam of light shone through the room and on to the kitchen table. The man saw it and looked up. The moonlight fell on his face and he was no longer just an indistinct figure. I could see him almost clearly. And my fear became outright terror. I was looking at a dead man.

And he was coming straight for me. Crossing the wooden floor, only yards away. I turned and fled before I'd even worked out where to run. Useless to head for the front door – it would be locked, I'd never open it in time and the stench of him had caught me already, was wrapping itself around me, getting ready to take hold. Leaping for the stairs, I made it up four, and then my legs were pulled from under me. I went down hard and it hurt like hell. And something cold and wet had taken hold of my left ankle. I was being dragged down. Frantically, I reached out and caught hold of a balustrade. Then I kicked back hard with my free leg. I felt my foot make contact with damp fabric. I took a deep breath. I was going to scream – the only thing for it, really: scream the bloody place down.

Somehow, I'd turned. He loomed above me. Little more than a stinking, dark shadow in the stairway, staring down at me. But not at my face. My fall and the struggle had made my full-length nightdress tangle around my hips. He was looking down at my bare legs. One of which he was still holding tight. And with his other hand he reached down.

And then something that felt nothing like a human hand, but like something fashioned from slime and decayed bone, was stroking my calf, travelling upwards, and his eyes were moving . . .

The terrifying sound broke through the night. Harsh, primitive, piercing cries. My own. Over and over again I screamed. And maybe something else. Another voice? From far away? And then everything was dark. And silent. I'd stopped screaming. I found the courage to kick out again. Nothing there. I opened my eyes. I was alone on the stairs. Hardly daring to move, I shot frantic, terrified glances left and right. Behind me. Where had he gone?

He'd been right above me, pawing at me, his eyes raking over me. The smell of him still hovered: heavy, cloying. But he wasn't there any more.

I blinked away tears. And found myself sitting up, staring all round. He was absolutely nowhere in sight. Even the smell was fading. I glanced down, at the damp patch on my lower calf where he'd held me, but even as I watched, the moisture evaporated away in the warm night air. Not a trace left.

Telling myself that I didn't believe in ghosts, that I had never believed in ghosts, that it couldn't have been . . . I forced myself to stand up and stagger across the dining room. Knowing I might have seconds before he attacked again, I grabbed the phone. I hardly dared lower my eyes to look at it but somehow managed to dial 999 and ask for the police.

As I waited to be connected it was all I could do to stay still. Where was he? He hadn't just vanished into thin air. People don't do that. He couldn't have got past me on the stairs, the front door was double deadlocked, I could see it from where I stood, and I would surely have heard the back door if he'd gone out that way. He was still in the house.

Unable to keep my voice from trembling, I explained my situation to the officer who answered the call. I was a little, but not much, reassured by his promise to have someone with me within twenty minutes. A lot can happen in twenty minutes.

I couldn't just stay where I was, clutching the phone. I risked crossing half the dining room.

What on earth was wrong with the chicks? I'd never heard them make such a din. Had he hurt them? I stepped into the kitchen, just far enough to be able to glance into the cage.

The chicks weren't hungry – they were terrified. A grass snake, nearly three feet long, was in the cage with them. As I watched, hardly able to believe my eyes, it reared up and sprang, grasping a chick at the throat. I didn't think. I grabbed the snake, squeezing hard on its neck, and it let the chick go. I pulled it out of the cage, ignoring its frantic thrashing around, and, with one hand, unlocked and opened the back door.

I am never rough, inconsiderate, or in any way unkind to animals. But I'd had enough: I was overtired, unhappier than I think I'd ever been and very seriously scared. Worst of all, for the first time in as long as I could remember, I felt totally out of control. Which is probably why I chose that moment to do something completely unprecedented: I vented my rage on an animal. I hurled the snake as far from me as I could. It sailed up, twisting through the air, and landed in some shrubs at the far end of the garden. I felt a second's stab of guilt before a sudden noise, close behind, made me jump and turn. To see a dark figure coming towards me.

I took a step back, my foot twisted and I fell, scrambling backwards as the figure came closer. The night had clouded over, and the back of my house is always much darker than the street side. The trees surrounding the garden are high and dense. The black shape stood over me, and it was all I could see. I opened my mouth, but the screams were all used up. Nothing but a pitiful whimper came out.

'Clara, it's me. Matt Hoare. What the hell's going on?'

And the dark figure became a man I knew. I could only really see his eyes as light from the house reflected off them, but the outline of his body was familiar. And so was his smell. Shampoo and clean skin. Fresh coffee. I think I whimpered again. He crouched, reached out a hand which I somehow managed to take, and pulled me to my feet.

'I heard you screaming. I leapt over the fence and thought I heard someone running round the front of your house. I figured it was probably you, but there was no one in the lane. What the hell's the matter?'

A sound came from behind me. Probably nothing more than a night-bird landing on a bush, but I jumped like a scalded cat and sprang away from him.

'Clara!'

I had to get a hold of myself. But I wasn't really there,

in that dark garden, with Matt. I was spinning away, to a dark place inside my head . . .

'Come on, deep breaths. Let's get you inside.'

An arm was around my waist. I was being pushed gently back towards the house. And something about the chill under my feet and the warmth of Matt's arm brought me back to myself. My attacker had gone. The noise in the lane Matt had heard had been him running away.

'I'm OK,' I managed, as we stepped over the threshold into my brightly lit kitchen. 'I've had a break-in. There was a burglar. He touched me. I . . .'

I couldn't go on. I was suddenly acutely aware of what I must look like. Matt stared at me for a second, his eyes dropping from my face, moving downwards. He coloured, turned away from me and left the room. Alone, I felt panic rearing its head again, but he was back in seconds, carrying a thick, quilted coat that always hangs by the front door.

'Put this on,' he said, before turning away while I did so. As quickly as I could with shaking fingers, I pulled the coat round me and fastened each of the eight toggles. It fell down to below my knees, covering me almost completely. It didn't feel like nearly enough.

'Have you called the police?' Matt asked, over his shoulder. In spite of the coat, he still couldn't bring himself to look at me.

I nodded, even though he couldn't see me. 'They told me twenty minutes.'

He walked to the kettle and filled it. He pressed the on switch, then glanced back. 'You should sit down,' he said.

I was still standing, stupidly, in the middle of the kitchen floor. I made myself turn, walk to the table and pull out a chair. I sat, pulling the coat a little closer and wishing it were floor-length. Then I looked up quickly and caught him staring at my feet, the only part of me still visible. Our eyes met. And I wanted to sink down and hide beneath the table.

'Ready to tell me what happened?'

Forcing myself to concentrate, I explained about getting up to feed the chicks, seeing the intruder, trying to run and being caught. The kitchen light was reflecting off the glass in Matt's spectacles, and I couldn't see his eyes properly. I had no idea what he was thinking but, as I got to the part where the burglar had grabbed hold of me, I could see his shoulders tensing.

'Did you get a look at his face?' he asked.

I shook my head. 'Not really,' I said. 'It was dark and I was panicking.'

'Look like anyone you know?'

I dropped my eyes to the table. Could I really tell him I'd just seen a dead man? That the corpse of someone I once knew had taken hold of me? I shook my head.

The kettle was boiling. Matt turned away again and began opening cupboards, reaching for tea bags, pouring water. He started spooning sugar into mugs. He hadn't asked me whether I take it. I don't, of course, but it hardly seemed important. I couldn't look at him any longer, even with his back turned towards me. I dropped my eyes to the table again.

I'd just been attacked, in my own home, by a man who couldn't possibly exist. And yet, what I felt that night, waiting for Matt, who was taking an inordinately long time, even for a man, to make tea, wasn't anything like shock at what had just happened, or terror of what might lie round the corner. It was embarrassment. And – yes, no other word for it really – I felt a deep sense of shame.

I have a secret, you see. That I would never, in a million years, have expected anyone else to discover. I spend ridiculous amounts of money on lingerie and nightwear. Silk, satin, chiffon, lace – I love the feel of the fabrics against my skin, the softness as they slide over my head and shimmy down my body.

I spend very little on other clothes. What, after all, would be the point? But when it comes to underwear, I am the fussiest, most fastidious shopper there is. I get it all by mail order, of course. I could never buy such things in a shop, see the amused, pitying looks on the faces of shop assistants. And I spend beyond reason, hoarding my treasures in drawers lined with scented paper.

But now, in the space of a few minutes, two men had learned my secret. Matt Hoare had seen the green silk, sheer as a dragonfly's wings, that clung to – and revealed – every inch of me. As had the man whose hand had felt like damp moss growing over the bones of a corpse. And so I sat there, staring down at the tabletop, and at the tiles below my chair, wondering how I'd ever be able to raise my head and look Matt in the eyes again.

There were damp patches on the floor. Small puddles around the table. Either Matt or I could have made them; the lawn outside was damp with dew. But had we also brought in the delicate thread of weed that had wrapped itself around the table leg? It was a plant that grows most commonly in rivers.

I heard a chair being dragged across the floor and sensed Matt sitting down at the table facing me.

'How's the Devil from—'

'In very safe hands,' I snapped, without looking up. Strange, scarred and very unpredictable hands, but as safe as we could ask, in the circumstances.

'Is it true that if you kill a king cobra, its mate will hunt you down and kill you?' asked Matt.

I looked up. 'What?'

'Drink up, you're shivering. Something I read. If you kill a king cobra, you need to watch out because its mate will seek revenge.'

I picked up my cup, swallowed too much and burned my tongue.

'So is it true?'

Pain was bringing tears to my eyes. 'Of course it's not true.'

'Shame, I thought it quite romantic.' And then he sat there, just looking at me. I dropped my eyes again but could feel his stare. Then I heard a low, muffled sound and sat upright again.

'What was that?' I asked.

Matt looked puzzled. 'What was what?'

'I heard something.'

I stood up and crossed the room. I have a very small cellar, hardly more than a cupboard, beneath the kitchen. It isn't big enough even for me to stand upright, but it's useful for storage. I reached the door and stood listening. Another sound: low, guttural, halfway

152

between a grunt and a mutter. I turned back to Matt in horror and, at the look on my face, he stood up. I half ran across the dining room to the front door. It was still locked and bolted. I'd unlocked the back door myself not minutes earlier. There had been no way out. The intruder was still in the house.

I raced back into the kitchen just as Matt moved away from the table. The sound of his chair scraping back against the floor was loud but, beneath it, I heard a third movement. There was definitely someone in the cellar. I never normally keep the cellar door locked – why would I? – but there was a bolt at the top of the door. I reached up and slid it in place.

Matt was next to me. I leaned close to the cellar door. Then stood sharply upright again.

'He's in there,' I whispered. 'He's in the cellar. I can smell him.'

Matt copied my movements and sniffed loudly.

'Can't smell anything,' he said, shaking his head. 'Are you sure?'

'Totally,' I said. 'He smells dreadful. It was over the whole house earlier. He smells like a male tramp.'

'Really?' he asked, and I sensed he wasn't taking me too seriously.

'Male tramps smell of stale sweat and urine,' I said, keeping my voice low. 'If you get close enough, you'll smell alcohol – pretty nasty stuff usually – and they often vomit while they're asleep. They root through rubbish bins for food, and that smell will cling to them. And quite often they soil their clothes. You can smell faeces.'

153

'How do you know so much about Eau de Vagrant?'

'A lot of our patients are brought in by people sleeping rough,' I said, moving backwards away from the door. 'I think we should go outside.'

Matt looked at me for a while. Then he leaned towards the door and took another exaggerated sniff. 'Still can't smell anything.'

His complete lack of concern made me want to scream at him. 'You shower in the evenings,' I said. 'You wash your hair most nights. You drink coffee rather than tea but you had a glass of red wine this evening. You've been petting your dog in the last hour and I think you just cleaned up after her.'

'You're telling me I smell of dog shit?'

'I wish you'd move away from that door. He's in there and that bolt isn't strong.'

Matt glanced at the bolt on the door and then back at me. 'If he's still in there,' he said, 'who did I chase up the lane?'

I had no answer for that one. And while I was thinking about it, Matt was reaching up for the bolt.

'No!' Suddenly I was right beside him, my hand reaching up to stop his. 'No. Don't even think about it. Leave it for the police.'

'Clara, there's something . . .'

At that moment, there was a knock on the back door and a large shape appeared outside. Matt moved before I did and opened the door. He received a startled-sounding 'Oh, good evening, sir,' and then ushered three policemen into my house, for all the world as though he lived in it himself.

The police listened to my story politely, but when I told them I was convinced the burglar was in the cellar their attitude changed, becoming tense, more alert. One of them, the most senior of the three, looked at Matt.

'And Miss Benning called you, sir?'

Matt shook his head. 'No, I was up anyway. My dog's very young. She needed to go outside.'

'And did you see the man in Miss Benning's house?'

'Afraid not. I heard her screaming. And movement of some sort round the front. I banged on the back door but it was locked. I ran round the front but, before I got to the door, I thought I heard footsteps. I went about halfway up the lane and I could hear scuffling. I didn't actually see anything.'

'Lot of badgers around at the moment.'

'True. I had one in my garden the other night,' agreed Matt.

'I don't care what you chased up the lane,' I snapped. 'The man who attacked me could not have left the house. Both doors were locked until I opened the back door.' I pointed at the cellar. 'He's in there.'

Matt looked at me for a second and sighed. 'Right, well, now that back-up's arrived, I'd better take a look. Cover me, won't you, Sergeant?'

And with that, he reached up, unbolted the door and took hold of the handle. *Cover me, Sergeant!* I grabbed his arm before he could pull the door towards him.

'What do you think you're doing? You're behaving like a cheap extra in a Spaghetti Western. There are three police officers behind you. Get out of the way and let them deal with it.'

'Clara . . .'

Over Matt's shoulder I saw the two constables exchange a glance. The sergeant couldn't hide his smirk. Matt lifted my hand from his arm.

'Clara, I'm touched, but . . .'

'What do I have to do to make you take this seriously? There is a man in that cellar who attacked me. You might find it hard to believe anyone would want to, but I promise you he did, and if you open that door you are likely to get seriously hurt.' I could feel tears stinging the backs of my eyes. I wasn't thinking straight. All I knew was I really didn't want Matt to go into that cellar.

'Actually, miss . . .' began the sergeant.

I had no idea how it had happened but by this time I was holding tight to both Matt's hands.

'I'm really not impressed by stupid heroics, so if you can't be sensible, go home, and let the professionals deal with it.'

There was a snort behind us from one of the officers.

'Clara, shut up,' said Matt quietly.

A sudden thought hit me. All three police officers looked as though they were thoroughly enjoying themselves. Matt raised his hands, still imprisoned within mine. I took a step back, with a horrible feeling I'd just made the biggest fool of myself ever. Free to move again, Matt reached for the back pocket of his jeans. He pulled out a small black leather wallet.

Oh no.

He opened the wallet with one hand to reveal an identity card. It took just a few seconds to read it, to check that the small, passport-sized photograph really was the man facing me.

'Dorset Constabulary?' I said, as though the writing on the card hadn't been perfectly clear. *You idiot, Clara!*

'Yup.'

'Assistant Chief Constable?' *Well, of course he's with the police. How else would he have known them all? Why else would they all treat him with such deference?* I'd never felt so stupid in my life before. I could have kicked myself. No, that wouldn't be nearly enough. I could have stamped hard on my own foot right there and then.

'Guilty as charged,' he said. 'Now, I could let three of my men investigate the intruder in the cellar while I stand up here holding hands with you, but I really don't think I'd ever hear the last of it. Constable Atkins, would you stay with Miss Benning, please?'

Constable Atkins strode to my side whilst Matt opened the cellar door, leaned inside and switched on the light. Barking out a warning, he began descending the steps. The sergeant and the other constable followed. Atkins and I stood where we were, listening to the sounds of the three men moving around in the cellar. After a few minutes Matt reappeared in the doorway, stepped out into the kitchen and gestured me to follow him. Once in the next room, he turned to face me. There was an expression on his face I'd never seen before.

'Clara,' he said, 'your cellar's empty.'

15

'WE'VE CHECKED EVERYWHERE,' SAID MATT. 'There's nowhere anyone could be hiding.' I stared at him. I'd been sure. I'd heard him moving around.

'He must have got out another way. Maybe through a window,' he went on. 'That could well have been him I heard running up the lane.'

I shook my head. 'He was in the cellar.' Even as I said it, I realized how stupidly stubborn I must sound.

'Are you happy for the officers to look round? Check for any windows open? Any other signs of a break-in?'

I nodded, and the three policemen started searching the house. I waited for a few minutes, then couldn't bear it any longer. I walked through to the kitchen and pulled open the cellar door.

'Hang on a minute!' Matt was behind me. I got to the bottom and stood looking round, as though I might see something two police officers and their assistant chief constable had missed.

The walls were stone: damp in places, one of the

streams flowed very close by; dry and crumbling in others. There were stacks of plastic boxes, an old built-in cupboard that I use for storing tools, and shelves of veterinary supplies. There's also an upright freezer. No hiding places. No way out. Except . . .

Built into the low ceiling of the cellar is an ancient trap-door. In the days before central heating it would have been used to allow coal to be poured in from the lane above. It was hinged along one side, had deadbolts on two further sides and a padlock on the remaining one. Above it, at street level, was a large and very heavy flower planter. I walked over and took a good grip on the old iron of one of the bolts.

'We tried that,' began Matt. I pulled hard, but the bolt was rusted over and wasn't moving. Matt crossed the room, stooping to avoid the low ceiling, and took my hands away. He put his own in their place and tugged several times. Then he tried the other bolt and the padlock. The trap-door wasn't moving.

'You could have heard a rat,' he said. 'Water rat, most likely. They're quite common in the village.'

'I guess,' I admitted, although I knew a rat couldn't have made the noise I'd heard.

'Come on,' he said. We went back upstairs.

The police stayed another ten minutes, found no sign at all of forced entry and then, promising to send a fingerprint expert the next day, they left. They'd been polite, which I suspect was entirely down to Matt's presence. I'd been certain, though, that they didn't believe me. Matt could only confirm he'd heard my screaming and scuffling sounds which might, or might

159

not, have been running footsteps. Other than my word, there were no signs of an intruder at all. Even the snake had gone.

I said good night to Matt, then locked all the doors, double-checked the windows and fed the chicks. The injured one wasn't too bad. A few swipes of antiseptic, and I was happy for him to sleep it off. I went upstairs, found an old pair of thick flannel pyjamas and got back into bed.

Sleep was a long time in coming. And when it did arrive it was restless, filled with dreams and shivery half-wakings. Towards dawn I had the recurring dream that I most dread.

I am in a hall of mirrors. Everywhere I turn I see reflections of myself. As the dream goes on, the reflections become more and more distorted. No longer is it just my face that's scarred, but the rest of me as well. That night the dream was worse than normal. Every mirror was draped in green silk. As I ran through the hall, desperate to find the way out, something was tugging the silk off the mirrors just as I got to them. The mirrors started falling; each one I touched tumbled to the ground, crashing around me. And then I wasn't in the hall of mirrors any more, I was in my own kitchen. Swathes of green silk blocked my way out and whatever was trapped in my cellar was banging hard on the door.

The bolt was trembling in its casing and the wood around it was beginning to splinter. I had to get out of the house. Except I couldn't move. I was on the floor and, in the way that only happens in dreams,

160

trying in vain to crawl towards the back door.

I sprang awake, drenched in sweat, to find I hadn't been dreaming the banging at all. Someone was hammering on my back door. I climbed out of bed, pulling off my pyjamas and tugging on a tracksuit. I had little doubt my early-morning visitor was Matt Hoare, hoping to catch me once again in something completely hilarious and have another story to share down the pub. *Pathetic cow,* they'd be muttering over their pints; *as if anyone who wasn't actually blind would . . .*

I peered out of the window, but Matt was shielded by the porch roof and I couldn't see him. I went down, determined that I wasn't even going to let him in.

'For pity's sake, you lot, shut up,' I snapped at the chicks. I turned the key and opened the door just a few inches, to see Sally from next door.

'Meals on wheels,' she chirped at me.

I didn't reply. But I did notice the tray she was carrying. And the smell wafting from it.

'I wanted to make sure you're OK,' she went on. 'And yes, I am desperately curious about last night.'

Still, I said nothing.

'You can't have two police cars parked in your lane at 3 a.m. and not have half the village know about it,' she went on. 'I'm just the only one brazen enough to come round. And I make the best bacon sandwiches.'

That's what I could smell. Bacon. And coffee.

'I'm about to go for a run,' I said, out of habit.

'You're three hours late for your run,' she replied.

I turned to the kitchen clock. It was almost nine.

161

'And, frankly, you don't look up to charging round the countryside right now.'

Realizing she was right, I backed into the room. I didn't ask her in, but she assumed an invitation anyway and followed me.

'I should get dressed,' I said. 'I need to get to work.'

'You need to cut yourself some slack. Come on, sit down and eat.'

I realized Sally was probably a master at dealing with difficult patients and that I wasn't likely to win this one. Besides, I was starving, and did it really matter if, for once in my life, I was late for work?

Sally poured two mugs of coffee and pushed a white floury roll filled with the better part of a pig towards me. I hadn't eaten white bread in years and I rarely touch red meat. I had no idea how amazing a bacon sandwich could taste.

'Thank you,' I said, slightly embarrassed, when I came up for air.

'Welcome,' she said. 'So, come on. Share. Were there any wriggly, slimy things involved? And just how brave and capable was the delectable Matt?'

'Just the one wriggly thing,' I said, deciding I was going nowhere near her last question. 'And snakes aren't slimy. The smooth-scaled ones feel like silk.' Now, why had I said that? Silk was the very last thing I wanted to be discussing.

'I'll take your word for it. But you had a break-in? Someone was in your house? What the hell is wrong with those birds?'

I gave her a condensed version of the night before.

She pushed another sandwich in my direction – I wasn't arguing – and then got up to feed the chicks for me.

'So,' she said, after a minute or two. 'Someone's breaking into houses in the village and leaving snakes behind. Why would they do that?'

'We don't know for certain they are,' I said, knowing all the while that she was absolutely right.

'Oh, don't give me that,' she snapped back at me. 'How often do you hear of a snake in a house? Almost never. But suddenly they're more common than house mice. And that's without some rather exotic species cropping up.'

I watched her offering dead rodents to eagerly waiting beaks.

'There's an undesirable element in the village at the moment,' said Sally, looking thoughtful. 'I've had rotten eggs thrown at my door in the last couple of weeks,' she went on. 'The Rushtons and the Poulsons complain about kids banging on front doors and running away. Mind you, breaking into houses seems a different league somehow.'

I, too, had seen windows broken around the village. My own dustbin had been emptied across my drive a couple of times, but I hadn't let it bother me. Sally was right, though. Breaking and entering was another matter entirely. And that had not been a teenager who had taken hold of me last night.

Sally, meanwhile, was still feeding the chicks. She was rather competent, given that she probably didn't feed orphaned birds too frequently. I wondered how often she fed semi-orphaned neighbours.

'The police didn't believe me,' I said at last. 'They think I made it up.'

She gave me a strange look. 'Why would you do that?'

'Why do people invent crimes? For attention, I suppose.'

'For someone who spends most of her life avoiding attention, that would be a bit out of character, wouldn't it? Here you go, my sweetheart.'

Shocked at how easily she'd seen through me, I couldn't answer her. She finished with the chicks and came back to join me at the table. Sitting, she picked up her coffee mug, cradling it in her hands.

'Did Matt believe you?'

I thought about that one for a second. 'I really don't know,' I said in the end.

'I was talking to Harry Richards yesterday,' she said, surprising me for a second. I'd forgotten she knew Dr Richards, that it had been she who had told him about my so-called reptile expertise. 'He told me – in the strictest confidence, of course – about your visit on Saturday. And about you and your snake friend. I've seen him on TV, by the way. Weird-looking guy.'

'Yes,' I agreed. 'He is.'

'So if the two of you were right, if John was murdered, then whoever broke into your house last night could have been . . .'

She paused, possibly for dramatic effect. I said nothing. But the shudder caught me unawares and I had no way of stopping it.

'I'm sorry, I didn't mean to scare you.'

'I'm not scared,' I lied. 'The injected-snake-venom theory was Sean North's, not mine,' I went on, when it was clear she didn't believe me. 'I can't argue with the facts he cited, but the idea of someone using a snake as a murder weapon still seems pretty far-fetched. And even if someone did kill John Allington, why would they try to kill the Huston baby, or the Poulsons?'

Sally wasn't smiling any more. 'I don't know,' she said. 'But for someone to risk killing a newborn baby, not to mention two young children, they'd have to be pretty disturbed, wouldn't they?'

I thought about it. Breaking into people's houses and leaving dangerous snakes behind was the action of a disturbed mind, no two ways about it. But I was even more uncomfortable with the way people seemed to be turning to me for answers. I was a wildlife vet. Whatever was going on, it really wasn't my responsibility.

'Well, the police will look into it,' I said. 'If there's anything to find, they'll find it.'

'I'm not sure they will,' said Sally, getting up and rinsing out the mugs.

'Sorry?'

She looked back over her shoulder. 'Harry Richards was pretty pissed off when I spoke to him. Otherwise I'm not sure he'd have told me as much as he did. He's told the police about what you and Sean North said, but they don't seem to be taking it very seriously. Sean North's a pretty unconventional character by all accounts, and I'm not sure they think him all that reliable. They've had some run-ins with him in the past, apparently – snakes escaping from his house, that sort of thing.'

The food I'd just eaten was starting to feel very heavy in my stomach. 'And after last night, they probably won't consider me too reliable either.'

'We'll have to see what the coroner says, I guess. But the unofficial feedback is that he thinks your theory about venom concentration is highly subjective. He's done a bit of reading up himself. Apparently, un-expected deaths following envenomation aren't unheard of. And John Allington *was* nearly seventy.'

'I see,' I said, wondering why the bacon sandwiches were knotting themselves up inside me. I hadn't wanted to get involved. 'Sally, can I ask you something?'

'Fire away.'

'Do you remember the Witchers? Edeline and Walter?'

'Of course,' she said, frowning at the sudden change of subject but going along with it. 'I tried to visit them several times. I really didn't like the conditions they seemed to be living in. But I never got past the front door.'

'I remember Edeline's funeral, last November, but not Walter's. I wondered if you knew whether it had taken place somewhere else. Maybe at the hospital.'

'He died last autumn, didn't he?'

I nodded. 'Some time in September, I think.'

'I can't immediately . . . wasn't there something about his body going to medical science?'

'Yes. But I'd have expected a service of some sort, wouldn't you?'

166

Sally leaned back against the sink. 'Clara, what's this about?' she asked, as I should have known she would.

I really hadn't wanted to get into this. But Sally was going nowhere in a hurry.

'Last night,' I began, thinking my reputation for being odd was about to increase to the power ten, 'the police asked me if I recognized the man in the house.'

'And did you?'

'I said no. I said it had been dark, he was gone in a split second and I really couldn't be sure.'

Sally wasn't stupid. 'But that wasn't strictly true?' she prompted.

I shook my head. It hadn't been true at all; I'd recognized the intruder immediately. 'I think it was Walter,' I said in a small voice, bracing myself for Sally to make her excuses and leave, suggesting on her way out that I might want to make an appointment at the local surgery soon, just to have a chat. She said nothing. And that wasn't surprise on her face. Neither did it appear to be concern for my mental health. She looked as though she might actually believe me.

'Why are you not surprised?' I asked, wondering why being taken seriously wasn't making me feel any better.

She seemed to shake herself. 'Oh, I am,' she assured me. 'Just not . . . totally.'

'You've seen him too?'

'No, no. It's just that, there's been talk, at the surgery.'

'What sort of talk?'

'Daft talk. Just kids really. There's a gang that hangs around down the lower part of the village, near the old church and the Witcher house. We suspect they're responsible for most of the problems we've been having, so we keep an eye on them. One or two of them have gone home to their parents with strange stories. You know what it's like when houses are empty for any length of time. They always get a reputation for being haunted and . . .'

'They've seen Walter?'

Sally looked uncomfortable. 'Seen Walter's ghost is what they said.'

The sun must have moved behind a cloud at that moment, because the light in my kitchen seemed to grow just fractionally dimmer.

'That was no ghost I saw last night,' I said, wondering who I was trying to convince. He'd touched me. With a hand that felt dead. 'He left damp footprints behind,' I went on quickly. 'Not to mention a snake.'

'But if it was Walter, then . . . wow!'

'Exactly.'

'Did you get your locks changed when you moved in?'

I shook my head, realizing how foolish I'd been. Anyone could have keys to my house.

'Might be a good idea,' she offered. I nodded my head. Suddenly, it seemed like a very good idea.

16

IDROPPED THE LAND ROVER INTO SECOND GEAR, BUT the ground was swampy, the wheels were starting to spin and I really didn't think we were going to get much further. In any event, the river was only a hundred yards away. We could walk. I reversed back a couple of yards and switched off the engine.

It was mid-morning on Monday, and there were three of us: Craig, my head nurse, Simon, a twenty-year-old student on a work-experience placement, and me. We'd received a call that morning from the local area office of the Environment Agency. A mute swan had been reported trapped in the river just below the village.

Getting out of the car, we climbed into chest-high waders, none of us relishing the task ahead. Mute swans are large birds and, with young to guard (highly probable at this time of year), can be vicious. Capturing an injured swan is never easy.

I was carrying my bag, a swan hook and a large cage. Craig and Simon between them carried a dinghy that had been specially designed for shallow, fast-flowing watercourses. It was light to carry, for which we were frequently thankful.

We reached the edge of the river, the one all the streams running through the village feed. Fortunately, the dog walker who'd spotted the swan had been able to give us an Ordnance Survey reference and we were confident we'd find it quickly. We fanned out, Simon walking upstream, Craig going in the opposite direction. I stayed where I was, looking across to the other bank, where the land started to rise, gently at first and then more steeply. I could see thick coverage of trees and bushes and, through them, almost at the top of the incline and just over a quarter of a mile away as the crow would fly, the thatched roof of what I was sure must be the Witcher house. I'd never seen it from this angle before.

'It's here,' called Simon. Craig and I picked up the dinghy and carried it the twenty yards or so to where Simon was standing. The trapped bird on the opposite bank could barely be seen amidst nettles, cow parsley and ground elder.

'He's on an island,' said Simon, pointing a little way upstream. 'Look, you can see where the river forks off just up there. There must be a very small backwater running behind it.'

Simon held the dinghy steady while Craig and I climbed on board. Then he joined us, and the two men (determined to be chivalrous, at least until the danger-ous work began) paddled us to the opposite bank. A good ten yards upstream of the swan we climbed out.

The cob, or male, mute swan can weigh up to ten

kilograms with a two-and-a-half-metre wingspan. They will defend – aggressively and relentlessly – any perceived attacks on their nest. As we neared the swan it raised both wings and the feathers along its back. Its head swooped lower in the water as it prepared to charge us. It's an intimidating procedure, very effective in scaring off a rival male or predators. When we were only a couple of yards away, I looked at Craig.

'What do you think?' I asked. 'Hook or hand?' The preferred way of catching a swan is by hand, every time. A hook might allow you to get a hold on the swan's neck, but then his wings will flap around furiously and you'll struggle to get a firmer hold.

Craig was watching the swan. 'He won't be that tame,' he said after a second. 'Not living out here in Hazard County.'

I couldn't disagree. A swan living on a busy river, frequently visited and fed by people, would be relatively friendly and easy to catch without a hook. This one probably didn't see people from one month to the next.

'I'm going to give it a go by hand first,' I announced. Behind me, I sensed Craig and Simon share a look.

'Ready?' I asked Craig sharply.

I stepped into the water and approached the swan. When I was just out of range I threw a handful of bread pieces that I'd had ready in my pocket. Unable to resist, probably very hungry, the swan reached his head forward and started eating. I allowed him to finish and then threw some more, moving closer. On the bank, Craig was closing in too. When I was close enough, I stepped forward, grabbed the swan round the neck with my right hand and scooped the bird up, pinning both wings against my body. He struggled briefly, twisting his head towards me, but I had him firm. After a few seconds he settled down.

'Nice one!' muttered Craig, who then slid into the water beside me. The cob began wriggling again, still distressed, but a swan held in this way is pretty much incapacitated. What you do not want to do, of course, is release the head, or you might find yourself missing an eye. Simon now moved forward and crouched low on the bank.

'Fishing wire,' he said, 'wrapped several times around his right leg, and caught up in some tree roots. Leg is bleeding. Possibly broken, but it's hard to tell. Oh, and there's what looks like a hook sticking out of him.' He pressed the wire cutters around the line and cut the swan free.

Back on the bank, Simon held out the cage and we lowered the swan into it. We'd take him back to the hospital, take blood samples to test for lead poisoning, treat his injuries and then release him, exactly here, in a day or so.

There wasn't room for all of us and the swan in the dinghy so Simon and Craig rowed back with the cage. I wanted to see if Simon had been right, if I was standing on an island. I walked a few yards, navigated my way round some bushes and small hazel trees, and discovered that he was. The backwater I was looking at was little more than two yards wide. Willows met over the mid-stream point, creating a dark, slow-moving tunnel of water. Algae and foam gathered amongst tree roots. I could see rat holes on the opposite bank, before the land began its steep climb towards the village.

Behind me I could hear Simon and Craig bantering as they reached the home bank. I began to follow the backwater downstream, curious to see how long the island was.

I walked about twenty-five yards. The undergrowth on the opposite bank had grown thicker and taller. I could barely see the hill beyond it. I walked carefully, wary of tripping, keeping a sharp look-out for traces of otter habitation. This quiet spot was as perfect a place as any to spot them.

There was something not quite right in the flow of the backwater.

Up to the point at which I was standing, it had been slow-moving, held back by decades of accumulated silt, overgrown tree roots, rotting vegetation. But the water I was looking at was flowing swiftly. And almost seemed to be coming from a different direction. Not three yards away from me, on the opposite bank, some willow trees draped their branches low in the water. It was impossible to see behind them. But, coming from beneath the trailing fronds, the water was flowing in a decidedly south-easterly direction, whereas the backwater itself flowed easterly. I took a step down off the bank, meaning to test the depth of the channel, see if I could wade across.

A hissing, flapping mass of white feathers leapt at me from beneath the bank. I'd found the swan's nest; and its angry mate. I scrambled back up to hear Simon calling my name, and walked back to where he was waiting to row me across.

Towards the end of the morning, I'd been changing the dressing on a young hare with a badly lacerated leg when Harriet appeared at the window of the treatment room, holding the telephone receiver and gesticulating frantically in the way that is particularly Harriet, when she means that I really have to come and take the call, absolutely without fail, and, by the way, did she mention that it was urgent?

Shaking my head and gesturing towards the patient on the operating table, I was bemused to see her leave the window only to appear again in the doorway, cross the room to the whiteboard on the far wall, grab a pen and, without putting down the phone, write SEAN NORTH in capital letters followed by several exclamation marks. Harriet isn't good with technology and has never mastered the mute button on the phone. Any of us could teach her in a minute, but we quite enjoy her antics. Normally, I use being in theatre as an excuse to avoid speaking to anyone, but that day I found myself reaching out for the phone.

'Am I disturbing life-saving work on a hedgehog?' North drawled in his distinctive not-quite-British but not-quite-anywhere-else-either accent.

'Four-week-old leveret,' I replied waspishly. 'What can I do for you?' Out of the corner of my eye, I could see Harriet hovering.

'Thought you'd like an update. I've spoken to the reptile curators at just about all the big zoos. I've also emailed all the main suppliers and private collectors. No one is owning up to having a taipan gone AWOL.'

'Why am I not surprised?'

'Right. Anyway, if anyone's interested, I think the police need to be checking overland routes and ferries coming into the north-east coast. Maybe private yachts. The airports all have pretty good facilities for spotting illegal imports, so I'd be amazed if it arrived by plane. My guess is that it came overland through Asia and Russia and into the UK via Eastern Europe. Maybe even Scandinavia.'

'Have you told the police?'

'I'm not exactly flavour of the month down at my local nick. Every time there's a snake on the loose in West Dorset, I'm to blame. I thought I'd let you tell them.'

'Thanks,' I replied, wondering why I was being so grumpy. He was only trying to help. Except, could he not have found someone else to tell?

'The taipan is female, by the way. And grouchy as they come.'

Harriet was still close by. 'I'll give you back to Harriet now,' I said. 'I think she'd like your autograph.' I handed the phone over and got back to work.

17

IT RAINED FOR THE REST OF MONDAY, AND BY EVENING the air was rich with earthy perfumes. Swifts darted around the car as I approached Bourne Lane. It's a tight turning and I always slow down as I approach it, which was lucky on this occasion – because a woman appeared to be kneeling in the middle of the road.

She must have heard my engine, but she didn't look up. She was elderly and deeply intent upon something in the road before her. I pulled up and switched off the engine. She was muttering to a small dog that lay, panting and in obvious distress, in the road beside her. I jumped out of the car. She saw me coming and reached towards me.

'Oh, look at my dog,' she said, in the strained, dry voice of the very old. She must have been in her eighties. 'Look at my poor little Bennie,' she went on. 'He can't get up.'

I crouched down beside her. Poor little Bennie was also elderly, a rough-haired Border terrier. He looked extremely ill: his eyes were dull and unfocused, his skin waxy and his breathing much too shallow.

'Has he been hurt?' I asked. 'Did a car hit him?'

'No,' replied the woman. 'He just collapsed. He stopped walking and fell over. I can't lift him.'

Borders are tiny dogs, but the woman looked very frail.

'Let's get him home,' I said, getting to my feet. 'I can have a proper look at him there. Can you stand up?' As I spoke I bent down and took hold of the woman gently under the arms. Despite the warm evening she was wearing a thick overcoat and a red wool hat. I'd seen her before, somewhere. I remembered the red hat, just not the occasion.

She gave a quiet moan, but I didn't think she was hurt: just old and stiff and sore. I walked her to the car, not easy because she really didn't want to leave her dog for a second, but at last I had her safely inside. Then I went back to the dog. His lead was still attached to his collar. I picked it up and wrapped it gently around his jaw in a temporary muzzle.

'What are you doing? Be careful,' called the woman, leaning precariously out of the car door.

'I won't hurt him, I'm a vet,' I called back. 'I need to pick him up safely, then we can take him home.' I scooped one hand under Bennie's shoulder and slid the other under his pelvis. He wriggled and tried to snap at me but the lead held firm. He weighed nothing and I carried him to the car and settled him on the woman's lap. She started muttering to him again, and it was all I could do to get her attention and make her tell me her name – Violet Buckler – and where she lived. I drove the few hundred yards to her cottage in Carters Lane.

Carrying Bennie, I followed Violet into her house – and back in time. We were in a long, narrow corridor, with peeling linoleum on the floor and flock wallpaper that was stained with damp. We passed a closed door and then Violet opened another at the end of the hall. I followed her into an old-fashioned room that doubled as a kitchen and sitting room. Along the rear wall, to one side of the back door, stood a Belfast sink with a stained, flower-patterned curtain beneath it. On the other side of the door was an electric cooker that must have been older than I am. One of the rings had been removed, leaving a gaping hole, in which the debris of years had collected and blackened. A Formica-covered dresser displayed a collection of mismatched crockery, much of it chipped or scratched. Elsewhere in the room were two easy chairs, neither of which I would happily have sat upon, a fold-up table tucked away against one wall, and a much-chewed plastic dog basket.

Kneeling, I put Bennie down on a threadbare rug in front of an electric fire. Muttering that he needed to be warm, I switched it on and then turned back to Violet. Not in a much better state than her dog, from what I could judge. She was visibly trembling, and I wondered if she might be going into shock. The dog I could deal with; distressed elderly neighbours were more difficult.

'Mrs Buckler, you should sit down,' I said, jumping up. 'I'll make you a cup of tea, but I should probably look at Bennie first. Are you OK for the moment?' She didn't answer me, seemed not to notice my unfastening her coat, easing her into one of the armchairs. The

178

electric fire wasn't powerful, and the room still felt decidedly chilly. I didn't attempt to remove either her coat or hat. Where had I seen that hat before?

'Do you think I should phone for a vet?' she asked, her eyes not leaving the dog for a moment. 'There's a vet in Honiton I saw once, just after Jim died, but he was so expensive.'

'I'm a vet,' I repeated, kneeling down again and opening my bag. I turned back to her and forced a smile. 'I don't charge neighbours.'

'A vet, you say,' said Violet. 'It's difficult to get to one of the vets in town. They stopped the bus service.'

'Are you happy for me to look at him?'

Her eyes started to moisten. 'Would you, dear?' she managed.

I turned away from her and concentrated upon my patient. He lay, panting, in front of the fire. I didn't like the dullness of his eyes, or the clammy feel of his skin. It took me a few seconds to find his pulse. Very weak. I held each of his paws. All cold.

'How old is he, Violet?'

'Oh, I can't remember too well. Four, maybe five.'

I hid a smile. Bennie was twelve if he was a day. I reached out and stroked him, running my hands across his back and stomach, down each leg. His abdomen was distended but, elsewhere, he was a skinny dog.

Bennie started to cough again.

'How long has he been coughing?' I tried.

Violet stared at me, confused, as though I were a form teacher who'd just asked a challenging and not entirely fair question.

'He had a cough last week,' she said, eventually. 'I gave him some of my buttercup syrup.'

I took out my stethoscope and listened to Bennie's heart for a few seconds. It had a very distinct murmur.

'How's his appetite?' I asked.

'Oh, he loves his food, does Bennie. Always has a healthy appetite.'

I looked again at the dog in front of me. Apart from the swelling around his belly, he was skin and bone. I might as well be asking my questions of the dog, for all I could rely on the answers. Besides, I was pretty certain I knew what was wrong with him. And that I really ought to bring up the subject of euthanasia. Except I didn't think I could do it. This was not my field at all. After just ten minutes in Violet's company, I knew the dog meant everything to her. It was all so very different from treating a sick fox.

'What would I do without my Bennie?' muttered Violet, as though she'd been reading my thoughts.

What indeed? But I couldn't help feeling she was going to find out very soon. Bennie, I was fairly certain, was suffering from chronic heart failure. If heart disease is found in time, it can be treated with drug therapy. Bennie, though, was just too old and had been ill for too long.

'Violet, he needs to rest now. Tomorrow I can give him an injection of something called frusemide. It's a diuretic.' Blank look from Violet. 'It'll get rid of a lot of the fluid that's trapped in his body and help his heart beat,' I tried again. 'There's a chance he'll improve. If not . . .'

I wasn't sure how much she was taking in, and I couldn't help feeling the worst danger for Bennie was that, come the next morning, Violet would have forgotten his attack and try to take him out walking again.

I pushed myself to my feet. A glance at my watch told me I still had time for the run I'd missed that morning.

And yet, how could I leave Violet, fretting and shivering in her overcoat and hat? I offered to make tea and she jumped so eagerly at the suggestion I knew I was going nowhere.

Violet's kitchen had a walk-in pantry, but its wooden shelves were dusty and all but empty. I found a pack of tea bags, a small bag of sugar and a cardboard packet of milk that didn't look too fresh. She seemed to survive on a diet of tinned food. I wondered when, if ever, she ate fresh food and where she'd get it from anyway. The village has one shop, which doubles as a post office; it sells bread, milk, eggs and butter, but everything else is dried, packet or tinned. Violet, with no car and no local bus service available, would be unable to leave the village. She must be without family, or they'd never leave her in this neglected state, dependent upon a dog and the occasional pity of strangers.

As I handed over the mug I remembered where I'd seen her before. Three evenings ago, she'd been one of the attendees at the village meeting. She'd sat with four others, each as elderly as she; one of whom, I knew now, had been Ernest Amblin. They'd said nothing, but had listened intently.

'Violet, can I ask you something?'

She leaned forward, looking suddenly more alert.

181

'I've been trying to remember when Walter Witcher died,' I went on. 'Walter who lived in the house at the bottom of the village. The one that used to be four cottages.'

Something in Violet's face changed; her eyes shifted away from me and dropped to the floor.

'Four cottages,' she almost hissed. 'We wondered why they bothered knocking them through. It wasn't as though we didn't all know what was going on.'

'I'm sorry?'

'They were bad boys, they were. Bold, bad boys. All except Walter.' She looked at me again, with her watery blue eyes. 'We all felt very sorry for Walter,' she went on. 'He used to grow dahlias, beautiful things, every colour you could think of. I admired them once when he was working in his garden and then, next morning, on my doorstep was a great bunch of them. Kind man.'

'Yes, he was. Violet, do you remember when he died?'

'Walter died?' Her face crinkled with distress.

It was hopeless. Violet could barely remember what had happened an hour ago. I nodded. 'Some months ago. I can't remember the funeral. I wondered if . . .'

'Harry died. Harry got drunk one night. He was always getting drunk. He was walking home along the railway line – not long after he came back – and got hit by a train.'

Who on earth was Harry? Violet's husband? But hadn't she said his name was Jim?

'I remember Edeline's funeral,' I tried again. 'Last November, wasn't it?' Thinking about Edeline's death still brought a pang of guilt. She'd died alone in her house, of heart failure brought on by chronic pneumonia, and had been dead for four days before the postman had alerted social services. And people talk about small villages being caring places. I looked around me, saw little sign of anyone caring for Violet. Was she fated to go the same way as Edeline?

'Edeline.' Violet was shaking her head, and I waited for her to go on. It was clear from her pursed lips that she hadn't thought much of Edeline.

'Bold as brass, she was, with her tight dresses and her bosoms on show for all to see.' Violet leaned forward, as though there were others around who could overhear us. 'Ronnie Gates was postmaster in those days, used to deliver early and get his rounds out of the way. Said he never knew which cottage she would come out of on a morning. Even Archie, and him in the church.'

Archie? Harry? Violet was rambling. And talk of the past was upsetting her. I tried to interrupt but she was on a roll.

'Standing up and spouting in church doesn't make you a good man,' she said. 'He was a – what do you call it? – lay preacher. Used to take services while we were without a vicar. Until he left too. Went to America, they said. In 1958, it was, the year Jim and I got wed. We had to go to the next parish, what with the church being destroyed and all.'

The conversation was racing ahead of me. But mention of the church caught my attention. 'The church had a serious fire, didn't it? At least, I've always assumed it did,' I said. I run past it sometimes. You can still see the charred beams. 'Is that when it happened, in 1958?'

183

Violet was shaking her head. 'It's no good asking me about that night, dear. I never really knew what happened. People who were there didn't talk about it. Even Ruby, and she was my best friend.' She stopped and yawned. I stood up.

'Violet, I'll let you get . . .'

'And they say the snakes all died. Couldn't survive the cold winter.'

I hadn't heard her properly. I had snakes on the brain, that's all.

'When we heard about John and the baby, we thought, oh no, not again.'

I took a step closer, waited and then sat back down again. 'Violet, what did you say?' I asked, as gently as I could. 'About snakes?'

Violet looked back at me but couldn't seem to focus on my face. Then she gave a huge sigh and her eyes closed.

'Violet,' I said, leaning towards her, touching her gently on one arm. She sighed again, without opening her eyes. I could see her breathing, softly but steadily, and realized she'd fallen asleep. I stood up and moved quietly away. I was just opening the door that led to the hallway when her voice startled me.

'My dear, what happened to your face?'

I turned. Violet's eyes were open again, and she was looking directly at me.

'An accident,' I said, after a while. 'A long time ago. I was only a baby.'

She sighed and shook her head. 'And you so pretty as well.'

I stared back. Nobody had ever described me as pretty before. It was a joke, wasn't it? Except Violet wasn't laughing. Neither was I. Nobody was laughing.

'It's what's inside that counts, dear,' she said as her eyes slowly closed again.

I walked down the dark corridor and let myself out of the house, allowing the door to lock itself behind me. 'That's what I tell myself,' I whispered, as I stood there on her doorstep.

18

I'VE ALWAYS RATHER LIKED CHURCHYARDS, ESPECIALLY the older ones. I like the haphazard arrangement of old headstones, sprinkled like pebbles among the grass. I like to read the carved tributes, think about lives lived well, of people dying, in their eighth and ninth decades, survived by children, grandchildren, even great-grandchildren, to be sadly missed and fondly remembered.

Oh, I know a churchyard will have its fair share of sad stories too, that there will always be those taken before their time by accident or sickness. Generally, though, I'm comforted by the signs of love scattered over these places like litter: the urns with dried flower stalks, the fading plastic toys, the Christmas baubles that appear in midwinter.

Given my father's profession, I spent a fair amount of my childhood visiting churches, and I always preferred to be outside, staring up at the yew and elder trees that run around the periphery, enjoying the wildflowers that grow in such profusion: the violets and primroses in early spring, followed by bluebells and foxgloves as the weather gets warmer. And especially the tiny, shy forget-me-nots that grow so frequently, and so appropriately, in churchyards, like the sweet souls of those gone from us but still in our hearts. I think the forget-me-not is my favourite of all English flowers. Mum and Vanessa, more interested in the stained glass and wood carvings on the inside, always shook their heads and called me Contrary Clara. But for once, I genuinely wasn't trying to stake an easy claim to individuality: I just happen to like churchyards.

So why didn't I like this one?

I must run past the old village church of St Birinus several times a week, but I'd never pushed open the iron gate and gone inside the high stone wall before. Now, standing just inside the gate, looking round, I think I understood why. Even from a distance, the ruined church and long-neglected grounds were unappealing; close up, there was something about the place that made me feel decidedly uncomfortable.

As I walked forward, the skeleton remains of the medieval building – crumbling stone arches and blackened beams – soared above me. I could see tiny flickers of movement among the old rafters and knew the building had a resident bat colony; and that it was awake for the evening.

An avenue of old limes lined the path, leaves dark and greasy, trunks knotted with age and carved with obscenities by generations of local youths. At one time, the church had boasted two massive wooden doors. One was missing, the other swung loose on its frame. In a strong wind it would sway and creak, and I felt a moment's gratitude that I'd visited on a still night.

A high, blackened stone wall, crawling with ivy and lichen, rimmed the perimeter of the churchyard and, along its length, ancient yew trees grew. Just outside the wall, much larger trees had been planted; mostly beech with a few walnuts. They made the churchyard darker than it would otherwise have been, even so late in the evening, and obscured all views of the surrounding hills. It was like being inside a cocoon of wood and leaves, cut off from the outside world.

Rooks were nesting in most of the bigger trees; they should have been settling down for the night but my arrival had disturbed them. They were circling the church, crying out in the harsh caw that is so distinctive to the species. Wondering, briefly, whether I should come back in daylight, but knowing I would never find the time, I set off in search of newer headstones.

Edeline Witcher's funeral had been held in a neighbouring village, but her body had been brought here for interment. I hadn't attended that part of the service, I'd been needed at work, and had never seen her grave. Quite why I had the urge to see it this particular evening, I don't know. Maybe I thought being physically near her might help me remember what exactly she'd said about her husband's death. Perhaps I was hoping I might find Walter here after all.

After a few minutes the rooks settled down and silence fell as I walked through the churchyard looking for members of the Witcher family. Twice, on stones carved in the early nineteenth century, I found references to people I assumed must be Walter's ancestors, but it was nearly twenty minutes (I was about to give up, the light was all but gone) until I found a small wooden tablet bearing Edeline's name and her dates of birth and death. There was nothing else – no fond message from loved ones, no tribute to her character. I hadn't liked Edeline, but it still seemed terribly sad that her passing should be so little regarded.

There was no sign of a grave bearing Walter's name. I was about to head back to the gate when I spotted the Witcher name again on a small stone three yards away from Edeline's. 'Harry Witcher', it read, '1930–1982'. 1930. Harry had been a contemporary of Walter; a younger brother, possibly a cousin. And Violet had mentioned a Harry, hadn't she? Harry who had been killed in a train crash. She'd talked about someone else too – Alfred? Arthur?

I started moving again, but away from the gate, towards the rear of the churchyard, peering at headstones as I went. As I reached the furthest corner of the grounds I found a last, small batch to check: a group of four headstones, small and insignificant in themselves, but detached from the rest of the churchyard by a ring of straggly elder bushes. I pushed my way through and began reading.

The four stones all marked the graves of young men who had died in 1958. Two of them on the same night, 15 June; the third two days later on 17 June and the last on 18 June.

My interest growing, I remembered that Violet had talked about 1958. Archie. That had been the name.

She'd said something about Archie taking services in the church, until 1958. I'd assumed she was confused and hadn't taken much notice. Until she'd mentioned snakes. What had she said? They all died in the English winter?

For a moment I wondered if someone had brought taipans to England in 1958. But they'd barely been discovered in Australia then. It didn't seem feasible. And even if they had, was it remotely possible that some had survived; that there was a naturalized colony of taipans living and breeding in rural Dorset?

'Tropical snakes can't live in a cold climate,' I muttered to myself, wondering if I were really as certain as I was trying to sound.

I bent to look again at the four headstones. 'Reverend Joel Morgan Fain,' said the first, 'taken by fire on 15 June 1958. "And he will come unto us as the latter rain that watereth the earth."' I glanced back at the fire-stricken church, then turned to the second stone. 'Larry Hodges,' it said, '17 April 1919–15 June 1958. "And these signs shall follow them that believe."' Had Larry, too, been taken by fire? The third stone marked the resting place of Peter Morfet, who died on 17 June aged thirty-two, and the fourth lay on the grave of Raymond Gillard, who'd died the following day.

The rooks started cawing again, making me jump. I realized just how edgy I'd been since I entered the church grounds. Setting aside my adventure the previous night, I have never believed in ghosts or any sort of malevolent supernatural entity, but I defy anyone to feel entirely comfortable in a graveyard as night falls.

Besides, I was getting that feeling – you know the one I mean, the one that makes you want to glance over your shoulder. You know there's nothing there, of course there isn't, but even so, just a quick look.

I turned. A black-clad figure was standing not ten yards away, watching me.

'Good evening, Clara,' it said, stepping forward.

19

'HELLO, REVEREND PERCY,' I ANSWERED. 'YOU'RE out late.'

'Likewise,' he said, in a voice as old and small as the rest of his person as he stepped lightly round the elder bushes to join me.

Reverend Percy is my local vicar and, given my background, one of the few people in the area with whom I can't avoid being on speaking terms. There really is no getting away from the Church when your father is an archdeacon.

Of course, children of clergymen invariably rebel at some time during growing up. Vanessa, at fifteen, had gone predictably off the rails, refusing to go anywhere near a church except for midnight mass at Christmas, when most of her friends rolled up after late parties. At university, though, she'd fallen in with a crowd others called 'The God Squad'. Fifteen years later, she's chairman of the Parochial Church Council, runs the weekly Sunday school and edits the church magazine. I think even Dad sometimes gets a bit embarrassed by her sheer enthusiasm.

My own falling off had been much less dramatic. I'd never refused to attend church and still did, every couple of weeks. But I'd eventually been forced to accept that I was never going to share the unwavering faith of my father. I don't actually disbelieve; I still find a strong sense of peace in the rituals of a church service; I just don't have the unthinking, unquestioning belief in my heart.

But old habits are hard to break. So I'd met Reverend Percival Stancey shortly after moving to the village. I took communion from him once a month and resisted, as politely as I could, his attempts to press-gang me into the choir.

'Can I help you with something, dear?' he asked, as he stepped into the little circle formed by the four headstones and the churchyard wall.

'Were you here in 1958, Reverend?' I asked.

'Goodness me, dear, how old do you think I am?' Reverend Stancey chuckled back at me. Well into his seventies was the honest answer, but not one I was about to articulate. In any event, I knew the chances of his being in one parish for over fifty years were pretty slim.

Reverend Stancey was reading the headstones for himself, with an appearance of great interest.

'I came here in 1970,' he said. 'I never actually led services in this church.'

'Do you know when the fire happened?'

He looked up over my shoulder at the church, now completely black against a purple sky.

'Some time before I arrived,' he said. 'There was talk

193

of raising the money to rebuild it, but nobody in the village seemed interested. After a while the weather took its toll.'

He put out a hand, touched my arm. 'It's getting cold, dear. Can I walk you to your car?'

The idea of my needing the escort of a frail old man was amusing but sweet. I thanked him and agreed. We started towards the gate. Creatures were flying around us as we walked and, several times, I saw the reverend flinch.

'Vicar, I've been thinking about Walter. Walter Witcher. I've been trying to remember when he died. Can you help?'

Reverend Percy stumbled, and I put out an arm to steady him. 'Hmm, let me see . . . Thank you, my dear.' He regained his balance, and we were off again. 'There wasn't a funeral, was there? I offered, of course, but Edeline told me there was to be a very simple service at the hospital and that the chaplain there would conduct it.'

'Yes, that's what I heard too. But I can't remember when it was.'

'Let me see. September, wasn't it? Yes, definitely September, some time around the middle, because when I got back from visiting Edeline, Mrs Roberts wanted me to inspect the church. They'd just finished decorating it for the harvest festival. So, that would be the middle of September.'

I'd thought so. So why no record of his death?

'Did you visit him in hospital?'

'I didn't know he'd been admitted, dear,' he said.

194

'None of the Witchers attended church, in all the years I've been here. I had to rely upon others for news of their comings and goings.'

'Of course, I understand.' Then I remembered something. 'I found Harry Witcher's grave. Did you know him?'

'Harry, yes, poor Harry. Terrible business.'

'Was he a relative?'

'You're very interested in the Witchers, my dear. Ah, here's your car. And mine.'

I said good night to Reverend Percy and promised to see him in church very soon. We climbed into our cars and set off. I followed him up the hill that led out of the village and, as I turned into Bourne Lane, he drove on, round the corner and out of sight.

I parked in my driveway and glanced over at Sally's house. It was in darkness, and her car was nowhere to be seen. On my way home I'd stopped off at a hardware store and bought four heavy-duty bolts. Before I went to sleep that night they were going to be attached, top and bottom, to both my doors. Even if someone did have a key to my house, they weren't coming in again while I was sleeping. Of course, when I was out, it would be a different matter. I really had to get the locks changed.

I was hungry and tired. I fed the owl chicks and watched them settle down for the night. My fridge was packed full of salad vegetables, but I couldn't face all the washing and chopping. I poured a bowl of cereal and sat down at the table, watching the chicks squirm and snuggle into each other. I managed about half the bowl before giving up.

On a sudden impulse I picked up the phone. I found the number I needed in the directory and waited until a familiar woman's voice answered.

'It's Clara Benning, from down the road. I hope I'm not—'

'Clara, hi! How are you? I'm just about to put Sophia down. Did you want to come up and see her?'

'Thank you. I've got . . . can I just ask you something? About the morning you found the adder?'

'Of course.' Lynsey Huston's voice, so alert and friendly a second ago, had lowered, become more cautious. But I guess a mother finds it difficult to be reminded of how her child nearly died.

'When I came into your house that morning, I thought I saw damp footprints in the hallway.'

'Really?' Alert again, but edgy now.

'And I just . . . I don't want to alarm you and I'm sure it's nothing, but . . .' I stopped, already regretting having made the call.

'I saw them too,' said Lynsey. 'I just assumed they were yours. Or the ambulance men's.'

'Look, it's nothing. I shouldn't have mentioned it.'

'Daniel went downstairs early that morning. He said something woke him up.'

'Did he see anything?'

'I don't remember him coming back to bed, I'd fallen asleep. But I'm sure he'd have told me if there'd been anything to worry about.'

'Of course he would. I'm being stupid. I'm sorry. I'll let you put Sophia to bed.'

'We'd love to have you up for dinner some time. Maybe get a few of the neighbours round. How about—'

'Oh, I have another call coming in. Might be an emergency. Thank you. Good night.'

I replaced the receiver and started pacing the house again. I switched on the TV and spent ten minutes flicking from one channel to another. I picked up a book, but put it down again when I realized I hadn't turned a page in fifteen minutes. I thought, briefly, about going to bed. The clock said 9.30. Would I sleep? Out of the last three nights, two had been pretty eventful, but even so I didn't think so. I put running shoes on and pulled a fleece over my sweater.

Pretty dark outside now. The moon was up, but it was little more than a quarter full and there was plenty of cloud cover. I jogged down the hill, crossed the green and ran down the Bottom Lane.

I'm not sure what I was planning. I hadn't actually said to myself, *Go to the Witcher house and . . .* because I wouldn't have known what to add at that point. All I knew was that something in the natural order of English village life had been thrown completely out of kilter. People didn't die of snake bite in quiet English villages. They didn't wake up to find poisonous tropical snakes in their houses. And they certainly didn't come back from the dead.

I reached the end of the Bottom Lane and stopped.

Whoever said an Englishman's home is his castle could have had Walter in mind. I'd run past many times but never really thought before how impenetrable the place was. A low stone wall ran around the garden. On top of it, Walter had fixed a trellis and had then planted thick, thorny hedging. He'd chosen plants known for density of growth and proliferation of spines. The hedge stood over eight feet high. Armed with a sturdy pair of hedge clippers, it might be possible to cut your way through, but it would take time. The only gate was over five feet tall, with spikes along the top. Scaling it might be possible, but not for a man in his early eighties. If Walter was still around and living in this house, he wasn't getting in and out through the gate. I decided to follow the hedge round the boundary of the property, see if there was a back way in.

I hadn't brought a torch, but I didn't think I'd need one. I can see quite well in the dark. My colleagues and I are called out to night rescues on a regular basis and have become quite adept at making our way, swiftly but silently, through the dark countryside. We've passed by fishermen, stepped within yards of them, without them having any clue of our presence. Keeping upwind of badgers, we've watched them play and been close enough to join their games. We'd even seen roe deer nursing their young and caused them no disquiet.

The trick is complete concentration; to be totally in the moment, aware of and receptive to everything around you: the flap of wings approaching over your left shoulder; the tiny scurrying form at your feet; the scent of a dog fox. Try it some time. Clear your mind and let your senses do their thing. It's wonderfully exciting and, at the same time, quite calming, to become a creature of the night.

I blew it that evening, because my mind wasn't clear. I wasn't concentrating on what was going on all around me, I was thinking about other things and watching the Witcher hedge for any sign of a way through. Otherwise, I'm sure I would have heard sooner the faint sounds coming from the field on the other side of the path. I'd have had a sense of danger, of an imminent threat, of being stalked. I did, though, hear the soft swishing noise that told me something – probably a large mammal – was moving through long grass behind the other hedge. I stopped. Total silence.

I resumed walking, aware that I was moving further from the village, from any possibility of help, if that wasn't a deer, fox or badger I'd heard. I walked another ten yards.

Another sound. A small stone clattering against a larger one. Definitely something there. Something that had moved down the hill with me. Would an animal do that? Put curiosity above fear? Not any that I had regular dealings with. I stood listening and knew that, just feet away, behind a thin hedge of hazel trees and elder bushes, something else was doing exactly the same thing: standing still and listening. I could hear nothing, but every tiny hair on my body was standing to attention and I wouldn't have been surprised to look down and see my ribcage reverberating, so loudly and fiercely my heart seemed to be beating.

I took two steps backwards, half expecting something

to burst through the hedge at me. Another step, and I stumbled. I turned and started walking again, taking the largest strides I could and looking back over my shoulder every few seconds. I thought I could still hear movement in the field but I was hardly quiet myself now and it was impossible to be sure. I was still a good distance from the main part of the village and well out of earshot if I needed to yell for help.

I started to run. A dark figure stepped into the path in front of me. And another. I stopped. I heard a noise behind me and turned. Someone was squeezing through the hedge on to the path. A fourth followed, then a fifth. Five against one. Not good odds.

20

NOWHERE TO RUN. I STRODE FORWARD, CONSCIOUS of movement behind me, of them closing in, but knowing I had a second or two before they could catch up.

'Excuse me!' I said, relieved to hear my voice sounding cross. The two figures in front of me didn't move. I hadn't really expected they would; but I'd been in situations like this before. I dug my right hand into my pocket, found what I knew was there, wrapped my fingers around it. I stopped, two yards away from them, and turned slightly so I could see the other three approach.

The very worst thing I could do was show fear. Let them see I was afraid and I'd lost. They were young, which was a good thing; and almost certainly local – they looked barely old enough to drive, and there was no other village within walking distance. Local was also good. It made them accountable. They'd be the gang Sally had talked about, the ones who'd been hanging round the Witcher property. Probably the gang responsible for all the petty vandalism we'd been suffering.

'Ugly cow!' called a voice from behind me. A girl's voice.

I took a step forward, came close enough almost to touch them, and stared straight into the eyes of the one I took to be the leader. He was tall, over six foot, with bright ginger hair and an acne-scarred complexion. He couldn't be more than seventeen, but he'd be strong. He held eye contact with me, but there was something not quite certain in his eyes that gave me hope. The boy at his side, hair hidden beneath a hood, was looking at his friend, not at me. There was a lot of bravado holding this gang together. I just had to find the weak point and push.

'Got a paper bag, Nathe?' called one of the boys from behind me.

Nathe and his hooded friend sniggered. Nathe took a step forward. I could smell his sweat, stale cigarette smoke and something feral. His eyes raked down my body.

'Show us your tits,' he snapped, watching my eyes, hungry to see the panic in them.

'Fuck you,' I spat back, digging deep into the store of profanities I reserve for occasions such as these.

He sprang at me. I jumped back and raised my right hand above my head. He stopped and looked upwards, suffering just a second's loss of confidence as he wondered what the hell I'd got in my hand.

It was a heavy bunch of keys. House keys, car keys, hospital keys: a lot of them. I'd twisted my fingers through the keyring, and several of the thickest stood at right angles from my clenched palm. It was as handy a knuckle-duster as you could hope to see.

'Not sure what you idiots have in mind, but lay one finger on me and one of you is going to lose his eyesight.' I glared from one group to the other, daring them to come closer.

The girl nudged the boy at her side, egging him on.

'I am perfectly serious,' I went on. 'I am medically trained. I know exactly where to stab an eyeball so it comes clean out of its socket.'

None of them moved, but Nathe's eyes were gleaming. They weren't buying it.

'There might be five of you,' I said. 'And you might get me in the end. But one of you is not going to see the sun come up tomorrow morning. One out of five. Who fancies their chances?'

'I think what the lady is saying is, Do you feel lucky?'

As one, we spun round to look at the newcomer at the top of the path. Matt Hoare was leaning against Walter's gate.

'Well, do you?' he repeated.

'Shit,' muttered a voice behind me. There was a scuffle, and the girl darted towards the hedge.

'Hold it, Kimberly!' snapped Matt. She froze. Matt stepped down the lane towards us, the two boys stepped aside to let him past, watching him sullenly but not daring to move. 'Jason Short, Kenny Brown, Nathan Keech, Robbie Keech and Kimberly Aplin. There, you see, we're all friends together.' He glanced at me, gave a small nod and then turned back to the gang, who had huddled themselves together, pushing ginger-haired Nathan to the front. 'Now, this is what we're going to do, guys,' continued Matt. 'You're all going to go home while I write up a full report on this evening's little adventure. While Miss Benning here is deciding whether or not to press charges.' He turned to me. 'I think you should, by the way,' then, back to the others, 'While she's doing that, I'll be taking my report down to the station. So, even if Miss Benning decides you're not worth wasting her time over, someone might just decide there's an incident here needs looking into. At the very least, this is going to be on all of your files, so I recommend a period of very good behaviour. Now, get out of here before I let her loose on you.'

They turned and started to walk up the lane.

'Get a move on,' yelled Matt, stepping after them.

They picked up their pace and jogged around the corner, the girl and one of the fatter boys trailing behind the rest. Matt walked backwards down the hill towards me. He turned and, over his shoulder, I thought I saw a sixth figure step out of the hedge and follow the kids. A man, bigger and older than the rest of the gang. Allan Keech, I thought, instantly, but he was gone too quickly for me to be sure. Matt, walking back towards me, hadn't seen him. The moon had gone behind a cloud again, and he was just silhouette and eyes. I hadn't moved. Wasn't sure I was able to.

' "Fuck you" ?' he said. 'What sort of language is that for an archdeacon's daughter?'

I hit him. I couldn't help it. Not with the hand carrying the keys, thankfully, but with my left fist, a sharp, clumsy blow against his lower jaw. Not nearly hard enough to do any damage, but it can't have been pleasant. He didn't flinch.

'I'm so sorry,' I gasped, pressing my hand to my face because I was sure I was going to start crying, and I really, really didn't want to cry in front of Matt Hoare.

He stepped forward, put his hands on my shoulders and pulled me towards him. And I almost went. I almost allowed him to pull me into his arms and . . . what? What exactly was he thinking of? I never found out because, in the nick of time, I came to my senses and pulled back. He let go.

'Are you OK?' he asked. I nodded. 'Damn bunch of toe-rags,' he said. 'Nathan Keech has spent the last two years in and out of young offenders' institutions, and his brother looks set to follow the same way. Kimberly Aplin has been expelled from two schools for bullying and substance abuse. Kenny Brown and Jason Short both have convictions for shoplifting. I'm sure they're responsible for all the trouble we've been having lately, I just can't prove it. I've told them a dozen times to keep away from here.'

'Just kids looking for ghosts,' I muttered under my breath, not expecting him to hear me. I wondered if he'd offer to walk me home. I couldn't possibly ask, but I really, really wanted him to. When had I turned into such a wimp?

'Is that what you're doing?' he asked.

I looked up.

'I met Sally for lunch today,' he said. 'She mentioned your intruder's resemblance to Walter. Don't you think you should have brought that up last night?'

Sally had had lunch with Matt. Why did knowing that make me feel so uncomfortable? And what else had she told him? What had he told her?

'You don't believe me,' I said. I meant it as a question but it came out like an accusation.

'I don't disbelieve you. But Walter was a thoroughly decent bloke. I just can't see him faking his own death, hiding away from the world and then breaking into people's houses at night.'

'No,' I admitted.

Matt had turned to look through the gate towards the house. 'We really need to find out what's going on with this house,' he said. 'I'll send an email round to all the local law firms in the morning, try and find out who's acting for the estate. But if Walter and Edeline didn't make a will and there are no close relatives, it could drag on for years.'

'I should be getting back.' I took a step up the hill, hoping he'd follow, knowing he probably wouldn't. Then I stopped and turned back. Matt hadn't moved. He was just watching me.

'Did Walter have any brothers?' I asked.

He smiled. 'I was wondering when you'd think of that. He did actually. Three of them. Walter was the eldest.'

'There was a Harry. I saw his grave just now in the churchyard.'

He nodded. 'And Archie. He left years ago. Became a preacher somewhere in the States.'

'And the third?'

206

'That would be Saul. The black sheep of the family, by all accounts.'

'What happened to Saul?' I asked, not remotely tired any more.

'He left the village too. Driven out, according to the stories. Quite why, I've never been able to find out.'

'He could have come back. He could have heard about Walter and Edeline's deaths and come back to live in their house. He'd even have a legal claim.' Thoroughly excited now, I told Matt about the face I'd seen at the window several days ago, about the striking resemblance my intruder of the previous night had borne to Walter. When I'd finished, Matt continued to look at me for a few seconds, then he turned to the house.

'This house is built on the edge of a small chalk escarpment, did you know that?' he said, peering through the bars of the gate. 'At the back of the house, there's a sharp drop of about twenty feet.'

'I didn't know that.' I'd never seen the back of the Witcher house. The path I ran up from the river was flanked by dense woodland on both sides. You couldn't see the Witcher house until you were almost upon it. 'So you can't get in the back way?'

'Not unless you're a mountaineer. This hedge goes all the way round to the drop on both sides. I've walked round the perimeter a couple of times since the village idiots started telling their ghost stories. No way in or out apart from this gate.'

'I did see someone,' I said, bristling under his

comment about village idiots, wondering whether it was intended to include me.

'Want to check it out?'

'What?'

'Only one way to be sure old Saul Witcher isn't holed up in there getting all snaky and malevolent.'

'You just said there's no way in or out.'

Matt grinned at me and took a small bunch of keys from his jacket pocket. He sorted through them until he found a thin, rectangular-headed, silver key. He slipped it into the padlock. It turned, and the lock sprang open.

'There is now,' he said.

21

FAR FROM SURE, BUT MORE INTRIGUED THAN I WOULD have wanted to admit, I followed Matt down the path, which was about fifty yards long. He stopped halfway along and I caught up.

'I grew up in this village,' he said. 'I used to come and chat to Walter when I was a kid. I'd forgotten how beautiful this garden is.'

I'd never been in the garden at all, had only admired it from the gate, but he was right. It was a classic English cottage garden, with plants of every colour and description tumbling over each other, fighting for space in a plot that was by no means tiny. Early roses bloomed everywhere, scrambling up hedges, covering trellis screens, even clinging like parasites to trees.

In one corner, someone had built a grotto from local stone. Lanterns and small statues stood in nooks and crannies and, in its centre, a small spring rose up before meandering down the sloping ground. The stream twisted its way around ancient yew trees and huge old juniper bushes that stood proudly around the lawns.

The old flagstones of the path were overgrown with tiny creeping plants which we crushed as we walked over them. I thought I caught the sweet, lemony scent of thyme. Matt crouched low and brushed his hand over something at the side of the path and then held it to his nose, breathing in deeply. Then he swept his hand over it again and held it out to me.

'I used to do this as a child,' he said. 'Every time I came in here. Best smell in the world.'

I put my face against his hand and breathed in. Something sweet and light, tantalizingly familiar. 'Camomile,' I said after a second. I could also smell citrus on Matt's skin – he'd peeled an orange earlier in the evening – but I didn't mention that.

Closer to the house was a small orchard. Winds had shaken most of the late blossom from the trees and it lay, like wedding confetti, on the ground.

'Did you put that chain on the gate?' I asked. 'Is that why you had a key?'

'Let's just say I know the man who did. Walter was a gardener, you know,' said Matt. 'Worked at the local National Trust property for most of his life.'

We walked on and reached the house. All the lower windows had been boarded. Two of the four front doors had been bricked up; the other two looked sturdy enough. I was tempted to repeat 'No way in or out' but didn't trust how Matt might react. He was looking at the house, at the old stone walls with the crumbling whitewash, at the ancient wisteria drooping its blooms around the upper storey, at the thatched roof in sorry need of repair. He looked like a mountaineer preparing to scale a height.

'I read this story the other day,' he said, 'about how a couple were driving through the bush in Tanzania when they ran over a black mamba. Its mate gave chase, outran the car and killed both driver and passenger.'

From long experience, I know when I'm being wound up. But I've only ever learned one way of dealing with it. I ignored him and turned away. On the left side of the cottage, Walter had grown vegetables. The bed had a neglected air, but he must have had time to do some planting before being taken into hospital, because there were still some small plants, growing in neat rows.

'So, is it true?' said Matt. 'Can a black mamba outrun a car?'

'No.' I didn't look at him.

'Racehorse? I found another story about one chasing a man on a horse and killing him and the horse.'

'No.'

'Are you sure, because there're just so many stories of mambas having incredible speed. Not to mention pure bloody vindictiveness.'

I sighed. 'They are fast snakes. They are probably one of the fastest snakes in the world. But no snake, not even a mamba, can outrun a healthy, adult human, let alone a horse.' I turned back. 'What are we doing here?'

'Breaking and entering.'

'It's boarded up. We can't . . . hey!'

Matt had produced a Swiss army knife from his pocket and was using one of the tools to pry loose the nails that held the wooden board against the window closest to the left outside wall of the cottage. It was off in seconds. A broken and jagged pane of glass lay behind it. Pulling his jacket sleeve over his hand, Matt started to push the broken pieces to the inside. They crashed on to the hard floor, sounding disproportionately loud against the quiet of the night.

As I watched in disbelief, he reached into his pocket and pulled out a pair of gloves, like the surgical gloves I wear when I'm operating, only sturdier. He pulled them on to his hands and, from inside the house, I was sure I heard something moving. I looked up, saw the black windows of the upper floor, wondered what might be behind them. I glanced at Matt, but he didn't seem to have heard anything.

'Look, I really don't think this is a good idea. I have an early start and . . .'

'You can't leave now.' He turned back to face me.

'Why not?'

'I'm scared of ghosts.' And with that, he put both gloved hands on the window ledge and pushed himself up. He crouched on the ledge for a second and then jumped inside. He looked round the interior then turned back to me.

'You coming in or are you going to keep look-out?'

I grabbed hold of his hand, as if by sheer force I could stop him doing something stupid. 'This is really not a good idea. Even you can't just break into private property without a warrant or . . . or something.'

He sighed. 'Actually, I can. The Police and Criminal Evidence Act gives a police officer powers to enter private property without a warrant if he believes there's an imminent danger to life or limb,' he said, as though reading off a card. 'In my view, if Walter or Saul

212

Witcher or any elderly man is living in this house, possibly with a whole load of venomous snakes, he will be at personal risk,' he went on. 'The force is seriously overstretched at the moment, and I came down here tonight to have a quick look round myself before getting any of the men involved. It was just my bad luck to come across you and the village idiots having a get-to-know-you session.'

For a second Matt and I stared at each other. Then he spoke again, and I suspected he was reaching the end of his patience.

'You can either come in with me, if you promise to do exactly what I say, or you can wait outside, if you promise to stay exactly where you are. What I would really rather not do,' he continued, 'is escort you all the way home and then come back again, because, having made a racket getting in, and alerted anyone who might be in residence to our presence, I want to get this over with. Now, which is it to be?'

I'd already decided. If there were venomous snakes in the Witcher house, Matt Hoare was going to need me. I found an old plant pot, put it beneath the window, took the hand he offered me and was inside a second later.

Old labourers' cottages typically have two rooms on the ground floor and two on the first. Four cottages had been knocked together here, meaning we had sixteen rooms to explore. A prospect I didn't relish, given the state of the one we were in.

The walls were damp, bare stone. Great chunks of the ceiling plaster had fallen to the floor. A solitary light bulb swung on a thick electric cord. We stood in silence and I realized I was listening. For what, exactly? The smallest sound that might indicate Matt and I weren't alone. A light flickered on, revealing ash scattered around the room. I turned to look at Matt. He was holding a small pocket torch with a surprisingly powerful beam.

'I only brought one pair of gloves,' he said. 'Don't touch anything.' His flippant demeanour of minutes earlier had disappeared completely. I might have been in the house with a different man. A man that was an assistant chief constable.

The floor was covered in plastic linoleum. As I stepped on the only rug it squelched beneath my feet. There was a wooden-framed armchair against one wall, mould growing on its cushions.

Matt started moving, and I followed him through a doorway and into a kitchen.

'I can't believe people lived here,' he muttered. The kitchen had a stone sink and a fireplace containing a tiny, old-fashioned cooker. Straw tumbled from the open oven door, and I guessed a rodent had set up home.

The whole place stank of the damp that I guessed was everywhere: rotting the remaining pieces of furniture, the tattered curtains that barely still hung at the windows, and the rugs that lay like puddles on the floors. I also thought I could smell decomposing flesh.

The kitchen had the tiniest of windows. Peering through filthy glass, I could just about make out where the ground fell away, not three yards from the back of the house. There was no rear door.

A curtained archway led through to the second cottage along. Shuddering as the slimy fabric brushed my face, I followed Matt through to a very basic bathroom with white steel bath, basin and lavatory. Knowing the smell from the lavatory was about to make me gag, I led the way into the fourth room: a workshop. An old Formica counter rimmed two walls, and under the window sat a cracked and dirty glass case, the kind you might keep fish, turtles, mice or gerbils in. Or snakes. A narrow, closed door led to what I guessed must be another staircase. A few rusty tools were scattered around, but I was looking at the dried husk of a tiny snake, curled in the corner where the worktop met the wall. Matt saw me staring at it.

'Anything we need to worry about?' he asked.

I shook my head. 'Looks native to me. And long since dead. What did you mean about Saul Witcher being a black sheep? About him being driven out?'

Matt had moved away again into the third cottage. I followed him into another small room, remarkable only in its squalor. I could see the brickwork where the front door had once been. And the brickwork where the door to the kitchen had been.

'Why would anyone block off a doorway to a kitchen?' I said, more to myself than Matt as I walked over. From across the room, Matt shone his torch all around the door frame. The bricks looked old, crumbling in places and irregular, the mortar black with age.

'Maybe that part of the cottage is unsafe,' he offered. 'Too close to the escarpment even for the Witcher family's comfort.'

I didn't reply. I reached out, bracing myself for the rough chill of old brickwork. And didn't feel it. The bricks, ever so slightly, felt warm.

'Although, personally, I'd say the whole place needs a demolition notice on it.' And with that, Matt was gone, into the fourth and last cottage along.

Meaning to bring him back, to see if he agreed the bricks felt warmer than they should, I had time to notice the third cottage had no stairwell. Maybe it had been in the blocked-up kitchen.

From what I could see of the fourth cottage it was an exact twin to the first: a small, squalid sitting room, an equally poorly equipped and furnished kitchen. I didn't have much time to look, though, because Matt had opened the door leading to yet another stairway and was climbing up. Taking the light with him.

The staircase was narrow and steep. A door at the top was closed, denying us any real light. I climbed two bare wooden steps. Matt was only just in front of me, shining the torch at his feet. He looked back over his shoulder, and I saw a flicker of alarm on his face, a second before a loud bang sounded just behind me and we were plunged into darkness.

22

I DIDN'T SCREAM. EVEN REELING WITH SHOCK I KNEW I needed to listen. A split second before the door had slammed I'd heard something in the downstairs room. Something had moved. The door hadn't slammed shut by itself. Just one really pressing question now: the thing I'd heard – which side of the door was it on?

'Keep still.' Matt's voice sounded loud in the confined space and too calm. He couldn't have heard what I had. 'Don't move,' he went on. 'I've dropped the bloody torch and I really don't trust this staircase.'

I stood in absolute darkness, trying to rid my head of the horrible thought that whoever had slammed the door was in the stairwell with us. That any second now he would reach out and I would feel a strong clammy hand grab me. And I couldn't help remembering the last time a hand had taken hold of me, just hours earlier. I knew it was impossible, of course – Matt had been facing the door when it slammed, he would have seen anyone who . . .

I forced myself to keep quiet and still whilst Matt

fumbled around for the torch. Once he touched my ankle, but I bit my lip and began counting in my head. At fifty I would scream. I could hold it together till then.

Then a small beam of light appeared at our feet and began to dart around. Reassured there were no gaping holes immediately in our path and – more importantly – that there were only the two of us in the stairwell, we began to climb again.

'Keep to the edges,' he instructed. 'One foot on either side. And stay a few steps behind me. A breeze must have blown the bottom door closed.'

The evening, I remembered, had been exceptionally still, but it didn't seem a good time to mention it. Breathing a sigh of relief, I watched Matt reach the door at the top and twist open the handle. A little more light shone down the staircase, and I joined him. Only then did I risk looking back at the rotting wooden door that had slammed shut just behind me.

We looked briefly into two bedrooms, sparsely furnished and filthy. Matt pulled open the door of a wardrobe, and we peered inside. Dresses, cotton-flowered and shapeless, hung there. Matt pulled open the second door and we could see three men's suits. Several pairs of shoes lay neatly on the floor of the wardrobe.

The second room had two heavily stained mattresses on the floor but no other furniture. The floorboards were bare and unpainted; in places they'd rotted away to reveal the ceiling plaster of the room below. On the wall, directly in between the two mattresses, hung a black and white photograph in a black plastic frame. I wandered over, treading carefully.

When I drew closer, I saw the photograph was actually a framed newspaper cutting. The date in the top right-hand corner was 17 June 1956, and the picture showed a group of men, resplendent in cricket whites, standing in front of a Tudor house. At the end of the back row, slightly behind the men, were three women.

I looked at the man in the centre, holding a modest pewter cup. He was young, with a pleasant, open face. He had rather large features: big eyes, large nose, full lips on a wide mouth. His hair, a mid-brown in colour, I judged, was cut short in the fashion of the time.

'That's Walter,' said Matt, making me jump; I hadn't realized he was standing so close. 'He was still cricket team captain when I was a child.'

At the bottom of the picture the newspaper had named the players. I ran my finger along the list, matching names to faces. All the Witcher brothers had played cricket. Archie, who had long since gone to America, had been the tallest and the best-looking, darker than his siblings, with a narrow, slightly hooked nose and slanted dark eyes. He looked vaguely familiar, but I couldn't think who he reminded me of; someone on TV maybe. I tried to picture him in ministerial robes and couldn't. He looked nothing like any minister I'd ever met.

Harry, the drinker who'd met with a violent death, had looked a little like Walter but had been shorter, plump and quite fair. Saul, the black sheep, had been most like the eldest brother: same height, similar features. It was certainly possible that the man in my house the previous night had been Saul. Also possible that Saul was in the Witcher house right now. I couldn't resist a quick look round the room.

'That's the manor house,' said Matt, staring at the photograph. 'There's a field at the back that a previous owner levelled out and turned into a cricket pitch. Clive Ventry has mentioned restoring it. If he's ever in the country long enough.'

I had no interest in the manor-house cricket pitch. 'Strong family resemblance,' I said, flicking my finger from Saul Witcher to Walter. 'Did you know him? Saul Witcher, I mean.'

Matt shook his head. 'He left before I was born.'

'He could still be alive. He could be living in this house.'

'No sign of that so far.'

I couldn't exactly disagree. And yet, there was something about the house that just didn't feel empty.

'Why was he driven out?' I asked again.

'No one really knows,' Matt said. 'Or, at least, if they do, no one will talk about it. You've hit upon the local village mystery, Clara. I got curious myself a few years ago and went back through old records down at the station. Whatever happened, it was round about 1958, when the church burned down. Saul was in and out of trouble all his adult life but the offences all stopped in the summer of 1958. As far as the local nick is concerned, he ceased to be a problem that year. Harry and Archie Witcher both left that year as well – although Harry came back, a decade or so later.'

1958. So the church *had* burned down in that year.

What had Violet said? She never really knew what happened that night? Matt was still talking.

'There was something odd about that fire,' he went on. 'It's all documented, if you know where to look. The fire brigade wasn't called out till the early hours of the morning, by which time the fire had pretty much burned itself out. The police weren't called at all, although obviously they got involved once they heard about it. There were telephones in the village back then, of course, but even though people were trapped and died in the fire, no one called for help.'

'Two men died in the fire,' I said, remembering the graves I'd found earlier. 'At least two. One of them was the priest.'

Matt was nodding. It was no news to him. 'Captain going down with his ship,' he agreed. 'And two more a couple of days later.'

'Did Saul start the fire? Is that why he was driven out?'

'Not according to the reports. The police at the time interviewed several villagers who'd been at evening service that night. None of them claimed to have seen anything. They all assumed a candle had been left burning, that the reverend and the other chap who died had seen the flames and tried to put them out but had been overcome by smoke.'

'All of them just assumed that?'

'Yup. Six or seven identical stories. No one saw anything, but each had a pretty clear idea of what must have happened.'

'And the police just accepted this?'

He shrugged. 'Nothing on the records to suggest otherwise.'

'But some of these people must still be alive. Somebody must know what happened. I was talking to Violet Buckler earlier. She mentioned the church burning down. Although, come to think of it, she said she hadn't been there herself.'

'The plot thickens. You should join the police yourself, Clara. Investigation makes you quite chatty.'

There was no immediate answer to that one. Matt seemed to lose interest in the photograph and crossed the room. He pulled open a painted wooden door and disappeared. Not wanting to follow him around like a puppy, I walked over to the rear window. There was a tiny crack in the pane and I could smell the night air, scented and wonderful after the rank interior of the house.

Outside, the clouds must have shifted at exactly that moment, because the landscape below me was suddenly illuminated. I could see the narrow patch of rocky ground at the rear of the cottage, partly covered in a tangle of gorse and elder bushes, and then the incline which fell steeply for about twenty feet before sloping more gradually for another quarter of a mile or so. I wondered what it must be like, living so close to the edge of a cliff. A chalk cliff at that – not the most stable of rocks.

Then, from somewhere below me, came a sound, familiar in itself, but totally out of place in that context. There it was again, coming from behind the hedge that rimmed the garden, probably just below the escarpment. A gull-like cry, 'Ga-oh, ga-oh'. The call of a mute swan.

People sometimes imagine mute swans are exactly that, but they are only so named because of the relatively little noise they make compared to other swans. Mute swans will hiss to defend themselves, make an 'heeor'-like snort and also the ga-oh cry. I'd heard them many times over the years and felt sure that a large, adult mute swan was near by. And yet we were over a quarter of a mile from the river.

I could think of no reason why a mute swan would be so far from water in nesting season, but it didn't seem to be in distress and I stepped back from the window.

I was about to turn away, when I spotted the fingerprints. Someone had laid hands on the narrow, almost rotten window ledge and several prints were clear in the dust. And from somewhere near by I heard the faintest sigh.

I spun round, unable to resist the certainty that someone was watching me. I couldn't even hear Matt, and I had a horrible fancy that I'd been left alone in the house. Refusing to give way to panic, reluctant even to call Matt's name, I walked through the door and found myself in a dark corridor.

Which I really hadn't expected. Eight small bedrooms is what I thought I'd see on the upper floor of the house, each leading through to the next. I'd already been in two, and now I was above the third of the original cottages; the one that, on the ground floor, had a bricked-off kitchen. I had a choice. Turn left and head to the front of the house. Two doors led off from the corridor that way. Or go straight ahead. The floor-boards started creaking, and footsteps were heading my way. I stepped back, unsure, but Matt appeared at the far end of the corridor.

'Four more bedrooms,' he said. 'Not much in them and no prints in the dust.'

I told him about the prints I'd seen on the window and he nodded. 'Yes, I saw those too. I can have them checked properly in the morning.'

'They looked quite recent,' I continued. 'If Saul was the black sheep you seem to think, he'd have a criminal record. His fingerprints would be on police files, wouldn't they?'

Matt nodded his head slowly. 'Even if someone was in here lately, doesn't mean it was Saul,' he said. 'Could have been local kids. A vagrant.'

'How did they get in here?'

'The upper-floor windows aren't boarded. Which makes it more likely to be kids than an elderly Witcher brother. You won't touch anything, will you?' I shook my head and he squeezed past me. 'We're almost done,' he said. 'I just want to check these last two rooms. This cottage – number three, is it? – has an odd layout.'

He'd reached the first of the two open doors. He glanced inside and stopped dead. I caught up with him. There were no windows in the tiny room. We had to rely on the thin beam of Matt's torch to examine the solitary object standing in the middle of the floor. An old casket, fashioned from dark-coloured hardwood and with leather straps. It was large, over four feet long and a good eighteen inches deep. It looked very solidly made and had been intricately decorated. Carved roses and ivy leaves were strewn across it.

'Toss you for it,' said Matt.

'What?'

'One of us has to open it. I vote you.'

'I'm not touching anything. You were very clear on that.'

His face twitched in a fraction of his usual grin and he walked over to the casket. I found myself hoping it was locked. Matt crouched down. He flicked up first one catch and then the other. He looked at me over the lid and made a mock-fear face. I rolled my eyes but I was actually quite nervous. Matt raised the lid an inch and peered inside. A look of complete revulsion swept over his features as he started back, dropped the lid, stumbled to his feet and turned away, retching.

I took a step towards him, hand up to my own mouth to stop the whimper leaking out. He turned back, eyes gleaming, hands held out in a surrender gesture. He was perfectly, completely OK.

'Kidding,' he offered, with what I can only imagine was supposed to be a cute look on his face.

'Are you nuts?'

'Sorry.'

'You don't look sorry.' I was smarting with humiliation. Why, oh why, did I keep letting this man wind me up? 'So what is in there?'

'Blankets. Old ones. Stink to high heaven.'

I'd had enough. I was going home. Even if I had to make the journey by myself. I shot him the filthiest look

I could muster and turned away. He caught me before I'd reached the end of the corridor.

'I'd really like to leave now,' I said.

'I know, I'm sorry. We're almost done.'

And then he was holding my hand, and leading me back down the corridor and into the final room we had to explore. A long, narrow room, with built-in cupboards lining one wall.

At that moment the air shifted, I felt a sudden draught from somewhere and caught a new scent. A fresh smell, but still slightly nauseating for all that. It was the smell of warm food, something cheap like baked beans or tinned stew. I waited for a moment, sniffing the air like a hound, but it was gone.

Matt was trying all the cupboard doors. Without any success. All of them were either locked, or the wood had warped over the years and stuck.

'OK, we're done,' he said. 'I don't think anyone's been in here for a while, but I'll have some officers look it over in the next couple of days. They can check those fingerprints. There might be more to see in daylight.'

I think I started to sigh with relief but barely had time to open my mouth before we heard a loud crash below us and a low groaning sound; whether human or animal I couldn't tell. Our eyes met for a split second, and then he was moving, across the room. At the door he glanced back without stopping.

'Wait here,' he ordered, and he was gone. I could hear his footsteps, irregular and stumbling, hurrying along the corridor.

Wait? Alone, in the darkness? In this house? I didn't

think so. I strode across the room and out into the corridor. Without Matt's torch it was pitch black. Arms outstretched, ignoring the slimy damp of the walls, I retraced my footsteps, trying to remember where the doors were. I made it back into the bedrooms and could hear Matt on the main staircase. As he jumped down the final few steps, I was hot on his heels. I reached the ground floor just in time to see him disappearing into the second cottage.

When I got there Matt was standing beside the workshop counter looking out of the window. The glass cage we'd seen earlier lay in several pieces on the flagged floor. The board that had covered the window was swinging loose, and there was no glass in the frame. The room was open to the night.

'I need to check outside,' he said, over his shoulder. He reached for the worktop, ready to push himself up, just as I heard a sudden noise from close behind and spun round to see a huge shape hurtling towards me.

23

STRAIGHT AT MY FACE IT SHOT, BLACK EYES GLEAMING. I staggered backwards, felt the air move around me and a sharp flash of pain. Then it was gone, and I was clinging to Matt, my face pressed against his jacket. I could smell leather and the warm, slightly herbal fragrance of his skin; and I could feel the heat radiating off his body.

'Jesus wept,' he said. 'What the fucking hell was that?'

I wanted to laugh and cry at the same time. I knew exactly what it was, had known even as it came towards me, but my body was still trembling with shock.

'Fucking thing must have been three feet wide. Holy fucking shit!'

Well, someone had to take charge of the situation. I wriggled and took a small step back. He got the message and let me go.

'Nice language to use to an archdeacon's daughter,' I said.

He didn't reply. I wasn't sure he was capable of uttering anything other than profanities.

'It was a tawny owl,' I continued. 'Commonest owl you'll find in England. They usually nest in trees but . . .'

I didn't finish; it was neither the time nor the place for a lesson in ornithology. By this stage, I was pretty much recovered and thoroughly enjoying the look of shame on Matt's face. From somewhere close by the mute swan cried out again.

'I suppose there could have been two of them,' he said after a moment. 'The noise we heard could have been the first. It heard us upstairs, panicked and knocked over the glass tank.'

And pulled out the nails holding the board to the window, I thought, but didn't say. He could be right. It was nesting season and perfectly feasible that two owls would be in the property. And the wooden board could have been rotting around the nails. It wasn't impossible that the first owl had crashed into the board and dislodged it.

The truth was, I'd had more than enough of the spooky stuff. I needed a rational explanation and was quite happy to go along with the two-owls theory. Besides, I'd just been held against a man's body. My thought processes weren't exactly crystal clear.

'Tell me something,' said Matt, sounding a little more like himself. 'Did you jump into my arms or was it the other way round?'

Time to move on. I was about to leave the room, when I caught sight of something in the fireplace. I walked towards it.

'Come on, Clara, I think we've done enough. Let's get out of here.'

I bent down. Ignoring Matt's instruction not to touch anything, I reached out and picked up the crumpled, translucent thing that I might have thought was tissue paper if I hadn't looked more carefully. It was dry, crisp and soft, delicate and beautiful in its way, covered in regular, familiar markings. I stood up and held it out, trying to guess at its length. Five, maybe six feet.

'Oh shit,' said Matt.

I was holding up a snakeskin. A snake's skin cannot grow the way ours does and so, every couple of months or so, it will shed. The snake will stop eating and grow a little sluggish, start to look milky around the eyes. And it will wriggle out of its skin, leaving it behind like worn clothes on a bedroom floor.

'Do grass snakes grow that big?' Matt asked. I didn't bother to reply. It was clear from his tone that he already knew the answer.

'It wasn't here earlier,' I said.

'It must have been, we just didn't notice it.'

'I would have noticed this.'

He didn't argue any more. 'Is it from the taipan?'

'I can't tell. It's possible, but I'm just not familiar enough with their scale patterns. Besides . . .'

He gave a heavy sigh. 'Besides what?'

'It looks bigger.'

We were outside. Oh, the relief of fresh, sweet-scented air. Using a rock as a hammer, Matt had fastened both boards back to their respective windows. After he'd re-locked the padlock on the gate, the Witcher house was secure again.

I looked at my watch as we walked towards the village green, amazed to see it was nearing midnight. We'd been in the house for longer than I'd thought. I was still carrying the snakeskin. I'd asked if I could hang on to it for a day or so, have an expert look at it, and Matt had reluctantly agreed on the condition that I was not, under any circumstances, to let it out of my sight.

We passed the narrow drive that led to Matt's house – I realized I had no idea what it looked like – and reached the end of Bourne Lane. The scent of old roses hit me, making me think of old times, of Mum at her best, of days that would never come again. Feeling an overwhelming need to be on my own, I paused and turned to Matt.

'I'll be fine now, thanks. Please don't—'

'You're bleeding.' He reached out and touched my right temple. I'm sure it was the pain – the tiniest of pricklings – that made me jump as he did so. He withdrew his hand and looked at it. I could see a faint stain on his fingers, my blood from where the owl had caught me. Another scar. And on the good side of my face. As I say, I was tired. It would normally take a lot more than a scratch from a wild bird to cause tears to roll down my face. They must have been shining in the moonlight because I could see, from the narrowing of Matt's eyes, that he'd noticed them.

'I'm sorry about your mother,' he said, softly. I caught my breath and bit the inside of my lip. Tears were one thing, to start sobbing in front of someone I barely knew was quite another. I had to get away, back inside my own space. Instead, I just stood there.

'How do you know so much about me?' I asked.

'It's a small village, Clara. We make it our business to know as much as we can about each other.'

And I thought I'd moved here for privacy. 'I don't,' I said, sounding sullen.

'No, you don't.' He put his hand on my shoulder and ushered me gently down the lane.

I walked in silence, not arguing any more, but wondering what any of our neighbours would think were they to peer out and see the two of us, out at this hour, Matt with his arm – almost – around my shoulders.

We reached the end of my driveway and he carried on walking. We trudged over gravel, I fumbled in my pocket and found my keys, all the while thinking: *Now, surely now, he'll go.* I slid the key into the door and turned to him, not sure what to say next.

'Well, thanks,' I managed in the end, and realized immediately that that couldn't be right. What exactly was I thanking him for? Scaring me out of my wits? Getting me attacked by a panic-stricken owl?

'We need to have a look at that cut,' he said, gesturing that I should precede him inside. 'Unless you want me to wake Sally up.'

'No, no, I'll be fine. I get cuts and scratches like this all the time.'

He made no move to leave, so I turned my back on him and walked through to the kitchen, knowing he was right behind me. Walking straight to the sink – best to get it over with – I ran the hot tap until it steamed and found some antiseptic liquid in a cupboard. He took it from me, filled a bowl and made me sit down at the kitchen table. He pulled another chair close and sat down facing me.

'I'm first-aid trained,' he said, folding up kitchen roll, wetting it and pouring Dettol over it. 'Been on more courses than you can shake a stick at. We have to be able to patch up suspects after we've beaten them up. This might sting, by the way.'

'Ow!'

'Now you know how the badgers feel. Stitched up any more of them today?'

'No, today I rescued a swan,' I said, wondering if he knew everything about me, including what I did at work every day.

'Keep still,' he said, putting a warm hand on the side of my neck to make sure I did. 'A swan can break your arm, you know,' he went on.

'Don't be so ridiculous, of course it can't.'

'It's well known. A blow from a large swan's wing can break a human arm.'

I sighed. If I had a £10 note for every time . . . 'If a frail, elderly person suffering from severe osteoporosis was standing upright with one arm stretched out horizontally, and if a large swan were to take a dive, from a very great height, and hit the arm at speed, it is just possible the arm would break. In most other circumstances, well, you might as well say a robin can break your neck because it could, in theory, fly out at you from a hedge, startle you into falling backwards down some steps and . . . I'm sure you get my drift.'

'Absolutely.' Matt was frowning at me, but in an amused sort of way. 'And thanks, that's good to know, I won't be so jumpy next time I meet a swan. Are you cold?'

'No, there's water running down my neck.' There was too, but that wasn't why I was shivering. I was simply not used to being touched that way: by anyone, let alone a man.

Matt got up, found a towel and, instead of handing it to me, sat back down and wrapped it round my neck himself, tucking it into the top of my sweater. It brought him unusually, painfully close. Well into personal space that I normally guard fiercely. Oblivious to my unease, he carried on dabbing at the wound, although I was sure it must have been spotless by this stage.

'Is it true that most snake-handlers in the Appalachian mountains die of snake bite?' he said.

'Oh for heaven's sake! What did you do, buy a book? *101 Completely Implausible Stories about Snakes*?'

He stopped dabbing. His eyes dropped to the bowl; he was trying to keep a straight face but not quite managing it.

'It's called *Snakes: Fact and Fiction*,' he confessed, peering back up at me. 'Got it from the library.'

I couldn't think of anything to say. He'd taken a book out of the library. For no other purpose than to wind me up?

'I also got *Venomous Snakes of the World, Common British Reptiles* and *The Art of Keeping Snakes*. I'm becoming quite the reptile specialist.'

A sudden, inexplicable pang of disappointment. His

getting books from the library had had nothing to do with me; he was just trying to get a handle on the village's snake problem. As I sat there, staring at the table, feeling stupid, he stood up.

'I should go,' he said, heading for the door. 'Who will you talk to about the snakeskin we found tonight?'

'Oh, a chap called Sean North. He lives close by. He's—'

'I know who he is.'

I waited. Something in Matt's face had stiffened. 'Does he have the taipan?' he asked.

'Yes,' I said, feeling just a prickling of nerves, the sort you get at school when the headmaster invites you into his office. 'Is that a problem?'

He seemed to think about it. 'Probably not,' he said after a moment. 'Have you known him long?' he said, looking at me rather more intently than seemed necessary.

I shook my head. 'I met him on Saturday,' I said. 'But I really can't think of anyone better qualified.'

Matt was standing in the doorway, one hand on the handle of the open door. It was ridiculous, I really wasn't myself, but I discovered I didn't want him to leave.

'Thanks for your company in the scary house,' he said. 'You'll get back to me right away about the snake-skin, won't you?' And then he was gone.

24

THE ALARM WENT OFF AT ITS USUAL TIME, DRAGGING me out of a dreamless sleep into a fog of unprecedented sadness. I lay in bed, something I never normally do once I'm awake, half listening to the birds outside and feeling a totally inexplicable sense of loss. It went way beyond grief for my mother. I stayed there for fifteen, maybe twenty minutes, and wondered if I could possibly get out of bed that day. Or ever.

But get up I did – old habits and all that – and walked downstairs, aware that something was different, something wrong, but unable to put my finger on exactly what. Then I knew. The house was far too quiet.

The barn-owl chicks' cage was on the kitchen counter as usual. The lid lay next to it, not on top as it should have been. I could hear no sounds coming from it. For the past ten days I'd woken to the clamour of chicks eager for breakfast. This morning they were silent. I glanced round at the back door. The bolts I'd installed the evening before were all pulled tight. I walked to the front door. Locked and bolted. Returning to the kitchen, and not really wanting to see what was in the cage, I stepped towards it until I could peer over the brim.

It was almost a relief to see it empty. I stepped back, looking around the kitchen for perches, as though the chicks, way ahead of schedule, had learned to fly, but there was nothing. I walked quickly through the house. The doors and all the windows were closed and locked.

Who on earth steals owl chicks? And how had they managed it? The chicks had been in their cage when I'd gone to bed and again at 3 a.m. when I'd got up to feed them. All the doors and windows in my house had been locked. Yet someone had found their way in – again. I really, absolutely, did not believe in ghosts. But some time in the night my owl chicks had disappeared.

Of course, I reported their disappearance to the police, but the officer who took my call, whilst polite, clearly didn't attach any particular importance to the incident. There had certainly been no enthusiasm for investigating a second break-in-that-never-was.

I hadn't called Matt. I didn't need to be an expert in human psychology to know that the depression I'd woken up with was in some way connected to him. Spending time with Matt Hoare, even in the strange circumstances that seemed to mark all of our encounters, just wasn't good for me.

A rush of new arrivals at the hospital had kept me busy till after seven in the evening. When I was able to get away, I drove straight to Violet's house. I'd called in to check on her and Bennie earlier on my way to work. She'd had no recollection of meeting me the previous evening, but she was welcoming enough, especially when I made a fuss of Bennie. I'd brought her fresh bread, telling her I'd bought too much to use myself, had made her tea and toast and turned up the fire.

I'd reminded her about not taking Bennie out and, with no confidence she'd remember, taped a short reminder-note to her front door. Promising to be back in the evening with medication, I'd left her to her sad, cold day.

And now I was back. I had a medicine that would treat Bennie's chronic heart failure. I also had some inordinately expensive food for older dogs and some dietary supplements. I'd almost certainly wasted my money; I just felt the need to do something for that poor little dog and his owner.

I knocked on the door and was surprised, but actually quite pleased, to see it opened by Sally: district nurse, next-door neighbour and supplier of the best bacon sandwiches in the West Country.

'Hi, come in,' she said, leading the way along the narrow corridor. 'Violet's been talking about you. You're quite the flavour of the month. She says she's got something to tell you.'

'She remembers me?'

'Oh, her memory comes and goes. Although you can never predict exactly what you're going to get.'

Seeing me, Violet tried to stand, but the effort proved too much. I waved at her not to bother and bent down to look at Bennie, who lay panting on the rug.

'How's he been today, Violet?' I asked.

'Better, I think, a bit better.'

As a diagnosis it had more optimism than accuracy. Bennie was still very ill. It didn't take long to give him his injection. I picked up his food bowl, intending to carry it to the sink and wash it before trying to feed him.

'You were quite wrong, dear,' said Violet, reaching a hand out to me when I returned. 'Walter isn't dead. I remembered this morning, after you'd gone. He's just gone into hospital for a while, for a few check-ups. He'll be home soon. He told me himself.'

I put Bennie's food down and allowed Violet to take my hand, even found myself stroking hers. Her skin was soft like a baby's, only falling loose, with no substance between it and her bones.

'Violet, I'm sorry, but . . .' I stopped and looked at Sally. Surely this was more her field than mine. Distressed animals were my thing.

Sally looked quickly at Violet, but didn't seem to know what to say.

'Well, actually,' she began, then stopped. Violet turned to her.

'You must know, dear. You must see him, at the hospital.'

'Walter isn't at the hospital any more, Violet,' said Sally. She was looking at me. 'Unfortunately, we're not sure where he is.'

I raised my eyebrows at her, then glanced at Violet, like Sally unsure how much we should say in front of her.

'I was a married woman, you know, girls,' Violet snapped. 'You won't shock me.'

Sally half smiled and seemed to decide. 'I did some sniffing around today,' she said, her eyes flicking from me to Violet. 'Walter was definitely admitted on 28 August last year. I could even tell you which ward and how he was treated, although I probably shouldn't. And he was making a gradual but slow recovery right up until 6 September.'

'What happened then?' I asked. Sitting between us, Violet looked every bit as interested as I was. Her eyes seemed a brighter shade of blue than I remembered.

'Nobody can tell me,' said Sally. 'The hospital had a computer crash last week, the system went down for an hour. A whole chunk of data has been lost, including all geriatric patient records from early September till the end of the month. They can be found, of course, the hospital has back-up records, but they're stored off-site and I'm told there's no hurry to get them. Could be weeks before we know.'

'Does no one remember him?' I asked. 'None of the staff?'

'No one that I've found. They had a lot of temporary staff through in the last six months, so the nurses who treated him have moved on. Of course, I haven't had that much time to ask around.'

'What about records at the surgery?' I asked. 'Isn't the GP informed when a patient dies in hospital?'

'Those I *have* checked. I looked at July through to the end of the year. I found the notification of Edeline's death, on 17 November, but that's all. There is absolutely no mention of Walter. Until we see the hospital's back-ups, I think we have to assume

Violet could be right. Walter may not be dead.'

An unspoken question hovered in the room. *If he wasn't dead, where on earth was he?*

'Edeline told me herself that he'd died,' I said, still not wanting to believe it. 'She said the same thing to the vicar. To a number of people. Why would she do that if it wasn't true?'

'Lying came as naturally to Edeline as breathing,' said Violet, her voice sounding different; younger than usual, and something else: considerably less pleasant. Sally and I exchanged glances.

'Walter had brothers,' I said, still not wanting to think that Walter had broken into my house – twice. I turned to Violet. 'You were telling me about them last night, weren't you? I just didn't realize. There was Harry, Archie and Saul.'

'And Ulfred,' said Violet, as her tiny body seemed to shudder. 'He was the really odd one. I never liked to be too near Ulfred.'

Sally and I turned as one to look at each other and then back to Violet.

'Who was Ulfred?' I asked.

Violet looked from Sally to me. 'The youngest,' she said, tapping the side of her head. 'Not quite right up here, you know. He lived with Walter and Edeline, in their part of the house. Edeline took care of him, supposedly. He couldn't talk. Just used to make those horrible moaning sounds. Oh, and the snakes. Don't ask me why or how, but Ulfred always had a snake in his hand.'

25

VIOLET SHUDDERED AGAIN. 'I CAN'T BEAR THEM, dears,' she said. 'Horrid slimy things.'

I could barely keep still in the chair, and one glance at Sally told me she was feeling the same.

'Five Witcher brothers,' I said quietly.

'And they all lived together in a little crooked house,' added Sally.

'And you say he was . . . disturbed?' I sat there, looking at Violet, willing her not to drift off into forgetfulness again. Her eyes held mine, and I thought I saw something gleam in their blue depths. She knew something. She glanced at Sally, then back at me again. Whatever it was, she wasn't sure about mentioning it.

'I was looking at a photograph last night,' I offered, trying to find an unthreatening way of coaxing her to say more. 'Taken from a newspaper. It was a cricket team. I saw Walter, Harry, Saul and Archie but I don't remember . . .'

Violet was struggling to her feet. She swayed, and Sally jumped up to help her. Once out of her chair, she

242

crossed slowly to the dresser and pulled open the second of four drawers. She took what seemed to be an old scrapbook from it and began leafing through the pages. When she found what she was looking for she moved back, Sally supporting her. When both women were seated again the open page of the scrapbook was passed over and Sally and I held it between us.

'Was this the one?' asked Violet.

'Yes,' I said. I was looking at exactly the same newspaper cutting I'd seen in the Witcher house the previous night. I scanned the list of names again and spotted Jim Buckler, Violet's husband, although they hadn't been married when the photograph was taken. The tall, angular boy in the back row looked very young. And I thought perhaps he might have had bright ginger hair and freckles, although it was difficult to be sure. Sally, meanwhile, was doing just what I had the previous night, matching names of the Witcher brothers to faces.

'No sign of an Ulfred,' she muttered. 'Archie was a bit of a stunner, wasn't he? Reminds me of someone actually. Can't quite . . . did he have a family?'

'I think he emigrated. Who were the women?' I asked, looking at Violet.

'My friend Ruby and me,' she answered. 'And Edeline. Although Edeline never actually did much in the tea room. Just used to come along to chat to the men.'

Looking at the three women, it was obvious who each of them were. Violet had been small and slim as a young woman; and pretty, in a soft, quiet sort of way. Her friend Ruby had been larger and plainer, but

Edeline easily eclipsed both women. A good four inches taller than either, she wore the tight, cropped trousers which I think were called 'pedal-pushers'. She had the hourglass figure of a 1950s movie star, and her tight-fitting, low-cut blouse left little to the imagination.

'Was Ruby the friend who was in church the night it burned down?' I asked, taking a wild guess.

Violet's look of agitation had returned.

'I never knew much about it,' she said. 'My dad didn't like me to go to that church, not after the new minister arrived. But I heard a few things, from Ruby. And from Jim. He attended for a while. Until . . .'

'Until the fire?' I suggested. Violet nodded.

'What fire?' asked Sally, to my irritation.

'I wasn't there,' said Violet, looking agitated.

'I know, I know, you told me. So you knew Ulfred? How was he disturbed?'

Violet was silent for a minute that stretched into two. I was just about to give up, when she looked around the room, as though someone might have entered, unseen and unheard. I fought the temptation to do the same thing. Then . . .

'They said he was possessed,' she whispered.

Sally gave a quiet laugh and leaned back in her chair. I, on the other hand, felt something cold press against the back of my neck.

'By demons?' I asked. Violet nodded.

'Oh, Clara, come on,' protested Sally. I held up one hand.

'The Catholic Church has around two hundred practising exorcists,' I said quickly. 'Even the Anglicans

244

have people trained in that sort of thing.' I looked at Violet. 'I don't believe in demons,' I said truthfully. 'And I'm sure you don't either,' I added, because I didn't like how scared Violet was looking. 'But I know there are people who do. Fifty years ago, people were a lot more superstitious. Is that right?'

Ignoring Sally, Violet leaned towards me. 'They said it was the demon that made him the way he was.'

'Unable to speak, you mean?'

'Oh, not just that. There were times when . . . when he'd just go crazy. We'd hear him yelling, screaming. But never with words. Just those horrible sounds. And he'd throw things, break things. Just go mad.'

'And who took care of him? When he was like that?' asked Sally, still looking wary.

'Walter, the other brothers,' said Violet. She glanced down at her lap, then up again, but not quite meeting my eyes. 'We used to go down to the house,' she said, 'when it happened. Even at the end of the garden you could hear him.' Her eyes flicked up. 'I know we shouldn't have,' she said, 'but we were young. We didn't really think.'

'I understand,' I said.

'And afterwards, you'd see Walter, or one of the others, looking like they'd been in a fight. Black eyes, bruises. And it wasn't just the violence. He'd do other things. Dirty things.'

I looked at Sally. She gave a small, almost invisible shrug. Violet, by this time, seemed distinctly uncomfortable. I decided there was no point pressing her further on that one. I had a pretty good idea what 'dirty things' meant.

'And what did they do for him? Did they get him help?' I asked, knowing that help for people genuinely believed to be possessed usually only took one form.

'I didn't really know. I just heard bits and pieces.'

'I understand. What did you hear?'

'People said they strapped him up and starved him. For days on end, even weeks.'

'Oh, surely not,' said Sally, who looked like she'd heard enough.

I glanced at her, then turned back to Violet. 'I can understand him being restrained,' I said, 'especially if he was violent. But why starve him? What could that possibly achieve?'

'It helped them pray, they said,' replied Violet. 'They'd all go into the house, or sometimes they'd take him to the church – the reverend and several of the others. None of them would eat either, and they'd pray with him, for hours and hours, trying to cast out the demon. But it never seemed to work because, days later, you'd see Ulfred, still the same, but with his wrists bruised and bleeding, limping around.'

'Oh, this is ridiculous, complete nonsense.' Sally had come to the end of her patience. 'He wasn't possessed, he was ill. He should have been in hospital.'

'I know, dear,' said Violet. 'It didn't seem right. But the reverend, and so many men, so much older than me . . . they all seemed so sure. What could someone like me do?'

'And Walter went along with this?' asked Sally.

'I don't know. They say he and the reverend quarrelled. But his brothers and his wife were on the reverend's side. So were a lot of the other villagers. What could he do?'

'That reverend wants shooting.'

'He died in the fire. His grave's in the churchyard. Violet, this is really important.' I leaned towards her. 'Can you remember where Ulfred is now?'

Violet sighed and shook her head at me. 'He's dead, dear. A long time ago. Drowned, I think, they said. Drowned in the river. I couldn't help feeling relieved when I heard. Relieved for us, but mostly for him. Poor man.'

I felt all the air go out of me. A prime suspect had reared his head – and it had been shot right off. Suddenly conscious of the time, I glanced at my watch. Even if I drove like a maniac I would be late. I made my excuses to Violet and promised to look in on her and Bennie the next day. Sally walked to the door with me.

'Matt told me about your mother, Clara. I'm so sorry. I hope it wasn't sudden.'

'Thank you,' I muttered. 'She'd been ill for a long time.'

Great. Just when I was starting to feel relaxed around Sally, she now had an excuse for feeling she knew me. She'd start coming round, asking how I was, inviting me for supper, expecting me to share confidences. I'd come across so many Sallys before now. Right on cue, she said, 'Why don't you pop round for something to eat later?'

'That's really kind,' I muttered, pulling at the door.

'But I'm going to be late back.' I tugged the door open and went out, striding to my car and climbing in without looking back. As I pulled away, I felt a moment's regret for being so rude. Sally really hadn't deserved it. But it was probably for the best in the long run.

Besides, I had to see a man about a snake.

26

I TURNED THE CORNER, AND THE ROAD BEGAN ITS descent into Lyme Regis. It was a little before nine in the evening and the sun was low in the sky. I drove into the town, almost to the sea, and pulled over to check directions. I must have stopped too quickly because a small silver hatchback almost ran into the back of me. I turned to give an apologetic wave, but the driver revved up the engine and it shot round me and away down the hill. Checking the road more carefully, I pulled away again and turned right. At the end of the public highway I had to climb out of the car, lift an old wooden barrier and drive along a private road that was little more than a farm track. I was now on the Lyme Undercliff, a national nature reserve that is home to rare orchids, insects found nowhere else in the British Isles and internationally renowned herpetologist and TV star Sean North.

I came to the end of the track and parked next to the familiar, battered and filthy Land Rover. I climbed out, slipped the thin, light package under one arm and walked down to the single-storey, wooden-framed cottage nestling among young ash trees. It was painted blue and looked like a beach hut. I'd seen the house many times before, had even gone so far as wondering who might live in such a place, but had never got close to guessing the truth.

Feeling nerves jumping like crickets in my stomach, I walked up to the front door. There was no need to knock.

'C', said the note pinned to the wood, 'U R late.' Several exclamation marks. 'Gone to look at a nest,' it continued. 'If you do show, hang around. I'll be back. S.'

For a second, I considered leaving the package on his doorstep and phoning him in the morning. A week ago, I'd probably have done exactly that – even in spite of my promise not to let it out of my sight. But I had no desire to rush home, to the village creeping with snakes and mysteries.

So I walked back to the coastal path and started to follow its winding trail, deeper into the Undercliff, waiting for a sea breeze to rustle the treetops, knowing that when it did tiny circles of light would dance among the undergrowth like coins scattered from a giant's hand.

Formed from the landslips that are so common on this stretch of the coast, the famous Lyme Undercliff has been evolving for centuries. And it will never stop.

The most significant landfall of recent years, which largely created the Undercliff we see today, happened at Christmas 1839. Over two days, around 16 acres of land, including wheat and turnip fields and comprising some 8 million tonnes of rock, split off from the cliffs and slid towards the sea, opening up a chasm 40 metres deep and nearly a mile long. Since then, its steep sides have been eroded further by weather and by smaller landslips and have become densely overgrown, almost jungle-like.

Over the years, geologists, botanists and palaeontologists have found their own sources of fascination within the Undercliff, and I have mine too. I am intrigued that centuries of devastation can result in a place of such peace; and that its beauty can hide such peril. Never underestimate the Undercliff, my dad would say, on just about every walk we'd taken here. You might be only a mile or so from the town, but stray from the path, meet with a mishap – any number of concealed fissures and chasms could oblige – and you might not be found for days.

Reaching a wooden bench, I sat down. The sun was about to disappear, and it wasn't going quietly. Great beams of light were shooting out across the ocean, turning the dancing surf into a shining, silvery-white mass.

I sat there, staring out across the sea, and wondered what on earth I was going to do once I'd confirmed, one way or another, the origin of the skin in the brown envelope under my left arm. Nothing, of course, was the only sensible answer. I was a wildlife vet. I fixed up rabbits and hedgehogs. And yet . . .

The elderly man I'd seen twice bore a strong resemblance to Walter Witcher. And he'd had four brothers. I was sure that whatever was going on in my village had something to do with them and their house.

Could I track any of them down? Two out of five were dead: Harry was in the churchyard, Ulfred had drowned a long time ago. That left Walter, Archie and Saul.

Archie had moved to America. He'd be almost impossible to find, even if he were still alive. But Saul had been driven out of the village. He had to have done something pretty bad. And bad things, as a general rule, were remembered.

I could look through old newspapers. Crimes were usually reported, even fifty years ago. I might find some record of what Saul had done and where he'd gone. I could start with the time the church burned down and go from there.

And what about Walter? Assuming he wasn't dead (and not holed up in his old house), he had to be living somewhere. Could I find a list of old people's homes in the area, see if he was in one of them? If Walter had been successfully treated in hospital but had been still incapable of going home, a hospice or nursing home was the logical place for him to go. I could do all that over the phone.

Look through a few newspapers, make a few phone calls. I could do that, couldn't I?

The day was drawing to a close on the Undercliff. Clouds, which had been absent for most of the afternoon, were gathering now in the west, soaking up the last of the light, creating a palette of colour that would have been breathtaking had it not been so entirely commonplace in this part of the world. People grumble about our dreary British skies but, without our cloud, we would never see our sunsets. All things come with a price.

Behind me, a twig snapped. For a second I could hear nothing but the breeze shimmying through the young leaves; then the faint but unmistakable sound of tall grass being rustled.

The sun had sunk lower; a few more minutes and it would be rising on other shores. Its light was richer, and that golden, shimmering path it leaves in its wake reached across the waves towards me like an invitation to a better land. For the moment, though, I was stuck with this one.

'Sorry to be late,' I said, to the point on the horizon where the golden path began – or ended – I was never sure.

The man behind me laughed. 'And there I was, thinking I could steal through the gathering dusk like a shadow.'

'Heard you coming two minutes ago,' I said, without turning round. 'There's a lot of dry wood around. You should avoid it if you want to move quietly.'

He didn't reply. *Well done, Clara*, I thought. *This man is world-famous for tracking down rare creatures, and here's you trying to teach him how to move through forests silently. And, had you forgotten you've come here for his help?*

'You live in a beautiful place,' I said, in what I hoped was a placatory manner.

'I fell in love with the Undercliff when I was a boy,' he replied. 'I spent just about every free waking moment in it. Caught my first snake here.'

'Adder?' I queried, thinking it hadn't taken long to get round to poisonous snakes.

'Slow worm,' he said. 'Took me two weeks to work out my new prize pet wasn't actually a snake at all.'

He walked round the bench and, still without looking up, I shifted myself over to the left so that he could sit down on my right side. My good side.

'Thank you for . . .' I began.

'It's good to . . .' he said, at the same time.

I looked up, saw a flash of bright hazel, and dropped my eyes again.

'Would you like to come to the house for a drink?' he asked, after a second.

God, no! I could feel my hands shaking at the very thought of being alone with this man. In his house.

'I really need to get back,' I managed, knowing I sounded cold, even rude, but unable to make it any other way. 'I'd have sent this by courier, except I promised someone I wouldn't let it out of my sight.' Now I was rambling. And Sean North was giving me no help whatsoever. From the corner of my eye I could only see boots, jeans and a few inches of shirt. Considerably cleaner but otherwise very similar to the clothes he'd been wearing the day we'd met. I could feel him looking at me. I was being stupid. I risked giving him the half-profile and met his eyes.

'Hi,' he said.

I felt myself blushing, and only with an effort did I avoid looking away again. Now I was acting like a teenager who'd just been introduced to her favourite rock star. I pulled the envelope from under my arm and held it out. After a second's pause, he took it. He pulled open the flap and reached inside.

'Where did you find it?' he asked, pulling out the skin and holding it up to the fading light.

'An old house in our village,' I said. 'It's 125 centimetres long. I measured it three times, to be absolutely sure. I was wondering if . . .'

'It's not.'

'Not what? Not a taipan skin?'

'Not from our taipan. Our friend – I'm calling her Clara, by the way, hope that's OK – measures 117 centimetres. Remember, you were there when Roger measured her. So, unless she's shrunk – which I've never come across before – this isn't one of her sheddings.'

The sun had dropped below the horizon, leaving just a golden pool on the surface of the ocean. It was shrinking, even as I watched, along with my forlorn hope that we didn't have another lethal killer on the loose. Sean, I'm pretty certain, was still looking at me.

'I'd really appreciate your telling me this skin is from a different species,' I said at last. 'Something harmless. And preferably that it's several years old.'

'This is quite a new shedding. And, if you found it in an old house, it's probably very new. If it had been lying around for any length of time, it would have been eaten.'

He was right. I felt drained; as though words alone had the power to exhaust me.

'I can't tell you, off the top of my head and in this light, whether it is from a taipan. I'd need to look at it properly, take my time. All I can say for now is, it could

255

be. If you can't leave it, why don't you come back when you've more time.'

'No, of course I can leave it. I'd really appreciate your looking at it.' We sat for a second, watching the golden light on the horizon shiver and disappear. Sunsets always have the power to move me, but there was something about this one that seemed almost unbearably sad.

'How long could a taipan stay alive, in this climate? How long would it be dangerous for?' I asked.

Sean seemed to be thinking about it. 'Ordinarily, not long at all,' he replied eventually. 'I'd expect an escaped tropical snake to fall asleep within twenty-four hours and then just not wake up again. Even before it keels over, it probably wouldn't have the energy to hunt. It would be too cold.'

'So even if there is another one loose around the village we needn't be too worried?'

'Well, I'd like to say so.'

'But . . .'

'This spring's been a lot warmer than normal. A snake could stay alert for a few days. And even a sleepy, cold snake will defend itself. It'll still be dangerous.'

For a moment we fell silent, whilst I tried not to think about small chubby legs running through undergrowth, a tiny foot stepping on a sleepy – but very deadly – snake.

Then a warm hand lay on my shoulder, the knuckle of a little finger just grazing the skin of my neck, and Sean was pointing across me, to a headland a mile or so to the east of us.

'See that rock formation up there, the one that looks a bit mushroom-shaped?'

I nodded my head, conscious of his body leaning towards mine, of his familiar outdoor smell.

'That's the site of the famous Lyme volcano.'

I turned my head to look at him properly.

He smiled. 'What? You've never heard of the Lyme volcano?'

'Oh, I've heard of it. I just filed it in the same place as the Cornish pixie and the Irish leprechaun.'

'Your mistake. The Lyme volcano was absolutely real. I'll tell you a story.'

He leaned back against the bench, much to my relief, until I realized his left arm was lying along the top beam of wood and was less than an inch away from being around my shoulders.

'When I was about fourteen, I was poking around in the undergrowth when I saw what looked to be smoke coming from under a bush. My first thought was someone had thrown a fag-end away. I went up to investigate, only to find the smoke wasn't coming from a bush at all, it was coming out of a crack in the rocks – about six inches wide and too deep for me to see the bottom.'

'Smoke coming out of rocks?' I asked, interested in spite of myself. 'How is that possible?'

'Spontaneous combustion in a subterranean oil shale.'

'Excuse me?'

'Dorset's rich in underground oil reserves. So is Hampshire. Quite a lot of the south of England actually. Nothing to compare with the North Sea, but still significant amounts.'

'Really? I thought you needed special geographic conditions for oil.'

'Not really. Just an organic-rich sediment, like shale. If it's buried deep enough, the surrounding environment acts like a pressure cooker, turning it into oil. This all takes millions of years, you understand.'

'Oh, quite,' I said, realizing that we were nowhere near the subject I'd come to discuss but that I was nevertheless quite enjoying listening to him. A thought struck me. Was I chatting?

'Then it all depends on the combination of rocks,' Sean went on. 'The oil migrates from its source rock until it finds another rock, like limestone or sandstone, that can contain it in an underground pool. You have an oil reservoir.'

'How do you know so much about it?'

'I've served on a couple of committees looking at the environmental impact of drilling. People always get their knickers in a twist when anyone suggests drilling for oil in their back gardens. The impact's usually pretty low, but people envisage great Texas-style oil fields. Several prospective drillings around here have been stopped by local pressure.'

'But we still have oil fields? Here in Dorset?'

'Yep. Wytch Farm is very close. Largest onshore site in Western Europe. There's also been prospecting at West Chaldon.'

'And the spontaneous-combustion business?'

'Sorry, geology's a bit of a thing of mine. Well, the clay round here has a lot of iron pyrite in it. After rock movement – which happens all the time on this coast –

the iron pyrite can get exposed to air. It starts to oxidize and gets hot, triggering a spontaneous combustion. If fuel is present too, in the oil shales for example, you can get quite a substantial burning.'

'White cliffs of Dover, burning cliffs of Lyme,' I said.

'So, anyway, round about the beginning of the twentieth century, there was a combustion that became known as the Lyme volcano. Burned for days. I live in permanent fear there'll be another one, right under my house. My insurance premiums are sky-high. But it does come in handy as a chat-up line.'

I froze. He couldn't have realized what he'd just said. 'What happened to your volcano?' I managed.

'By the time I got back with my dad, two brothers and three neighbours, there was no trace of it. Had the piss ripped out of me mercilessly. So I spent the next few evenings in the local library until I'd proved that, on these cliffs, the rocks do burn.'

I realized I was smiling. It was a nice thought. Burning cliffs. A volcano on the Dorset coast. What happened next wiped the smile clean away.

'Did you bring a friend with you?' asked Sean, his voice dropping until it was almost a whisper.

'What?' Instinctively, I lowered my own voice.

'Someone's been listening to us for the last five minutes,' said Sean, his voice still soft. 'He's about twenty yards away. Eight o'clock. Don't turn round.'

I managed not to, but I couldn't help my eyes creeping to the side. Eight o'clock? That meant behind, slightly to the left, didn't it?

'And that, my dear, was the famous Lyme sunset,'

said Sean, in his normal voice. 'Quite something, huh?'

'Beautiful,' I managed. With the sun gone, darkness was falling fast, and I was feeling horribly exposed to whatever Sean believed was behind us. I'd heard nothing. But I hadn't exactly been listening. So far from the village, I'd felt safe. Had somebody followed me out here? It wasn't possible, was it?

Sean was getting to his feet. 'Now, I think it's time I poured you a drink and showed you my private collection,' he said, in the same unnecessarily loud voice. In most circumstances, it was a line that would have sent me sprinting for cover. But Sean wasn't even looking at me. He was scanning the ash trees that grew thickly together at the place he'd described as eight o'clock. Without speaking, we walked back to the path and, as we reached it, I saw a definite movement among the densely growing shrubs. Something that looked like dark clothing moving away.

'Stay here,' he muttered, and set off, at a slow jog, towards the place where he too must have seen movement. 'Steady on, mate,' he called as he approached the thicket. 'There's a hidden drop just by there. Stay where you are.' He ran in among the trees and disappeared from view, leaving me alone on the Undercliff path. The temperature had dropped sharply and a wind was getting up. I hadn't brought a jacket with me. I waited for Sean to reappear, wondering what I'd do if he didn't. Then, within a couple of minutes, he was back, walking quickly through the trees.

'Sorry,' he muttered, as he got close. 'False alarm.'

'Nobody there?' I queried.

'Amateur botanist,' he replied. 'Elderly American chap. Looking for green-winged orchids. I think I gave him a bit of a fright.'

'You gave me a bit of a fright.'

'Sorry, sorry. It's just, when I'm working, which I am most of the time, I have to rely completely on my instincts. Just occasionally, they let me down.'

He looked so embarrassed I couldn't help but take pity on him. 'Sounds like you spend too much time in the jungle,' I said.

'Maybe I do,' he admitted. 'Now, will you have that drink?'

I turned down, but less rudely, I think, the second invitation into Sean's house, but as I drove home I found myself feeling less anxious than I had for days. Something about the Undercliff, or maybe even the man who lived on the Undercliff, had calmed me. I was genuinely and deeply tired and was sure that, tonight at least, I would sleep. Surely the nasty surprises had come to an end for a while.

The roads were quiet, and it didn't take long to reach the turn-off for the village. As I slowed down and began indicating I caught a glimpse of a vehicle in my rear-view mirror. A small silver car. I turned and began the descent that led home. And another car followed me down. I didn't see it, even though I slowed right down several times, but I could see its headlights lighting up the road behind me as I made my way down the hill. After turning into Bourne Lane, I pulled over, switched off my headlights and sat waiting. I waited for five, maybe ten minutes, but the car didn't appear. There were no other roads it could have taken but it hadn't driven past me. In the end I gave up and drove home. But I couldn't help wondering if Sean's instincts had been sounder than he'd realized.

And when I climbed out of the car my front door looked decidedly different. The body of a dead adder was nailed above my letter-box, and someone had left me a message in white paint which, on a purely intellectual level, I couldn't exactly argue with.

'Ugly cunt,' it read.

27

SO, INSTEAD OF TAKING A LONG HOT SHOWER AND falling straight into bed, I had to find my can of white spirit and clean the front door. Whoever had paid me a visit that evening hadn't long left; the paint was still damp.

A carpentry nail had pinned the snake to the wood. It was dead, and I really hoped it had been before three inches of steel had been driven through it. Both snake and nail went in the outside bin. This was one incident I would not be reporting to the local police. Even if they didn't already have me filed as an attention-seeking time-waster, did I really want to tell some young constable what someone had thought appropriate to write on my front door?

Like many women, I cry when I'm angry. And I was very angry as I scrubbed the blue-painted oak of my door that night. I'd felt safe here. Safe from prying eyes and curious stares, from officious kindness and patronizing overtures of friendship. But events of the last few days had made me realize I wasn't safe at all. It really didn't matter how low a profile I kept, how well I hid my face away from the world, someone always thought they could judge me on how I look.

'Funny time of day to be spring-cleaning.'

I doubt I could have looked more guilty if I, myself, had been caught in the act of vandalism. I jumped and spun round, before glancing back at the door. It was streaked with white paint, but the words had been wiped away.

'I wouldn't have thought a man in your position would work the night shift.' It was the first thing that came into my head and sounded a lot more aggressive than I'd intended. But Matt was staring at my front door, about to ask me why I was cleaning white paint off it at a quarter past eleven in the evening. I really didn't want him to do that.

'Excuse me?'

He wasn't alone. At his feet sat a young, sweet-faced cocker spaniel, its fur a rich glossy black. Matt stepped forward, reached out a finger and touched the white streak that I hadn't quite managed to get rid of. Another two minutes and it would have been gone.

'Insomnia?' I tried again. 'I only ever see you in the small hours.'

'I've been having a drink with Clive Ventry. And Molly enjoys the moonlight. I was crossing the top of the lane when I saw you scrubbing furiously. What happened here?'

'Nothing.' I wiped the last trace away and picked up the can of white spirit. Leaving Matt and Molly on the doorstep, I went inside. Hurrying into the kitchen, I

rinsed out the rag and washed my hands. I felt something gently pushing at my calf and looked down to see
Molly nuzzling my leg. Which meant her owner had
also followed me into the house. I turned.

'You can't see my house from the top of the lane,' I
said.

'Did the owls turn up?'

'How do you know about that?'

'I've asked to be informed about anything that comes
in concerning the village. So did they?'

I crossed to the cage still on the counter-top and
feigned looking inside. 'Nope,' I said. 'Still AWOL.'

He turned and walked over to the back door to
examine the bolts I'd fitted.

'Did you draw these last night?' he asked.

'No, they're purely for decorative purposes,' I
snapped.

'Did you yell at the chicks too? Is that why they left
home?'

'You don't need to check up on me,' I said. 'I'm
perfectly OK, and I'm sure you have far more important
things to do.'

Matt slowly shook his head. 'You really don't do the
human race, do you?' he said.

I dropped my eyes back down to the empty cage. He
was perfectly right, of course, but I can't deal with
people thinking they know me. I can just about, if I have
to, deal with people on a professional level, but the
minute the conversation turns personal, something
inside starts tightening up.

It wasn't far off midnight, but Matt was showing no

signs of leaving and Molly had settled herself down on the kitchen rug. There were any number of hints I could have dropped, even without the rudeness that comes all too easily. Instead I found myself crossing to the counter and filling the kettle.

Matt settled himself down on one of the kitchen chairs. 'Black with two sugars, please,' he said.

'How's Clive?' I asked, because I needed something to say. I had no real interest in Clive Ventry.

'Tense.'

'Is he developing a snake phobia like the rest of us?'

'Oh, I think it would take a lot more than a few snakes to scare Clive. He mentioned something about having family to stay, and I got the impression said relatives weren't too welcome. I guess when you have a great deal of money you have to expect a certain amount of unwanted attention from the folks.'

As I reached for the coffee jar I remembered the village meeting at Clive Ventry's house, the tall man whom only Clive and I appeared to have seen in the upstairs gallery.

'Is that decaffeinated?' Matt asked, in the sort of tone you might use if you suspected someone of spiking your drink.

'Yes. Sorry, do you have a few hours of red tape to get through? Is that why you're up so late?'

'Lord, no, I'm a strict nine-to-five man. Most evenings I work on my novel.'

I think I almost did a double take. 'Your what?'

Two grey eyes were shining at me, and I didn't think I could look at them for more than a second. I turned my back on him and focused on the kettle switch instead.

'Historical romantic fiction,' said Matt. 'Set against the background of the Boer War. Two young girls from Shropshire volunteer to be nurses.'

'You're winding me up,' I muttered over my shoulder.

'Want to read it?'

The kettle had boiled. I poured water into two mugs and risked looking at him. 'You're a very strange man,' I found myself saying.

He laughed, still looking me straight in the eyes. 'Best men always are. And look who's talking.'

It was like a pain, the sudden shock of reality. I'd almost forgotten. Almost allowed myself to believe that I wasn't . . . I looked away, felt my teeth clenching, lips pursing.

'Oh, don't get pissy on me,' said Matt. 'I'm not talking about your face.'

I so much wanted to zone him out, not just ignore him but wipe him completely off the radar screen, the way I've done so many times in the past when people haven't been able to respect the boundary. I couldn't do it. I even found myself looking back at him.

'What, then?'

'Well, if you want to talk about strange, how about the bravest woman I've ever met who blushes bright scarlet and starts like an overbred whippet the minute someone speaks to her? Who's got the body of an Olympic athlete but wears clothes my Aunt Mildred wouldn't be seen dead in? Are we drinking that coffee or just cleansing our pores in the steam?'

I held out a cup. He stepped towards me and took it, but didn't move away. I fixed my eyes on the third button of his shirt.

'You've lived here for four years, and I bet you don't know the names of more than half a dozen of your neighbours. Any one of them would be happy to be your friend but you're more interested in hedgehogs. Yet, today you spent nearly fifty quid on drugs and food for a dog that's likely to die within the month.'

He leaned against the counter, still an awful lot closer than felt comfortable. How did he know all these things about me? Sally again?

'You should give your own species a chance, you know,' he said.

Still looking at the button.

'Now you're annoyed at me.'

'No.' Truthfully, I was amazed. It was the first time I could remember that someone – especially a man – had seen beyond my face. And at some point in the last few seconds I'd looked up.

'And you have eyes the colour of beech leaves in October. Yet no one is ever allowed to look into them.'

Back to the face. Why did it always come back to the face? Eyes back down, so much safer to look at the button on his shirt.

'It's late,' he said. He looked round the kitchen, found pen and paper and scribbled something down. 'These are my numbers,' he said. 'Home, mobile and direct line at work. If anything else happens, ring me straight away. Not the local police station, me. OK?'

I nodded, although I knew I never would.

Sometimes – not so much in recent years (I've learned to be very strict with myself) – I sit in front of a mirror; I keep the lights low, and I turn my head to the angle at which the badly scarred left side of my face can hardly be seen.

And I imagine what my life might have been if the events of that day, nearly thirty years ago now, had unfolded just slightly differently. If Mum had drunk a little less, if Vanessa had screamed a minute sooner, if Dad had been in his study instead of strolling in the garden. I might have been found – been rescued – before it happened.

I look at the good side of my face: at the smooth olive skin, the almond-shaped brown eye, tiny nose and high cheekbone; and I think about what could have been.

I see the friends I might have had, if I hadn't been so afraid of people and their endless supply of cruelty. I wouldn't shrink from the moment when strangers see me properly for the first time, or pretend not to notice how successfully (or not) they hide their shudders. I might not know what it's like to be pointed out, whispered over.

I might even have had boyfriends, seen the glimmer of attraction in a man's eyes, waited in agonies for phone calls, been sick with nerves before an important first date. I would not be nearly thirty and still . . .

So many people have tried to encourage me with hopes of a normal future. *Not every man is obsessed with looks, Clara,* they'd say. *You'll meet someone who will see the beautiful person you are on the inside.* As though being badly disfigured automatically makes you a better person. Like what's inside, by default, has to make up for what's gone wrong on the surface.

These kind people are wrong. I'm not beautiful on the inside. How can I be when people shy away from me, when drunken men crack crude jokes at my expense and teenagers follow me in the street, cat-calling and taunting? How can I even be normal when I am afraid to buy clothes from a shop because no one will willingly serve me? How could a beautiful soul survive a lifetime of that sort of treatment? So I am not beautiful, inside or out. I have a chip on my shoulder the size of a boulder, as my sister frequently and accurately reminds me. I am painfully shy, permanently short-tempered and totally self-obsessed.

I sat at my mirror for a long time that night, long after Matt must have fallen fast asleep. I sat there and made-believe that my face was whole and perfect, and that Matt could see me – not as the amusing curiosity I clearly was to him – but as someone whom he might just . . .

28

WEDNESDAY WAS OFFICIALLY MY DAY OFF. OF course, this was the first time in four years I'd ever taken the day off, and so I had to run the gauntlet of surprised and concerned staff before I'd been allowed to put the phone down and get on with what I had planned for the day.

First on my list was to track down Walter. After my early-morning run (on time and uneventful, just by way of a change), and a visit to Violet and Bennie, I settled myself down with tea, the telephone and several versions of the local telephone directories. I looked up Nursing Homes, Long-Term Care Homes, Sheltered Accommodation, Hospices and Geriatric Hospitals, and soon had a list of nearly twenty possibilities.

After two hours, I'd spoken to or left messages with just about every potential new residence for Walter within an eighty-mile radius of the village. Talking to a private nursing home just outside Axminster, I had a brief moment of excitement when the nurse in charge confirmed the residence of a patient named Witcher.

Five minutes later, I learned the patient was a woman and that her name was, in fact, Whittaker.

By eleven in the morning, I knew if I sat at my desk any longer I'd go stir-crazy. There were three places I still hadn't managed to speak to but I'd left messages at each and, with luck, they'd get back to me soon. I got into the car and headed for my local library.

Once there, I was taken to the basement, shown the shelf containing old copies of newspapers and left to my own devices. For nearly an hour, I struggled to read under a fading fluorescent light. I found the account of the 1958 fire at St Birinus quickly enough. The paper reported that the county fire brigade had been called out at 3 a.m. on 16 June 1958, to find that the fire had been burning for several hours and that the villagers had tried to deal with it themselves before calling for help. When the flames were finally extinguished, some time before dawn, two badly burned bodies had been discovered. They were later identified as Reverend Fain and Larry Hodges. Reverend Fain had been a single man, Larry Hodges left a wife and two teenage children.

The cause of the fire, according to several villagers, was believed to be a candle left burning after evensong.

The article finished with a short obituary of Reverend Fain. Born in 1933 in Alabama, Joel Morgan Fain had been the youngest son of a wealthy farming family. In his late teens, he became a member of the Pentecostal Church and, after studying classics at university, was ordained as a minister. Despite his youth, the article said, he'd been a leading figure in the emergence of the Latter Rain movement in the years after the Second World War. He'd come to England in 1957 to spread the word of God's new church and had been acting minister at St Birinus for just over eight months when he lost his life. The obituary had been written by Reverend Fain's close friend and fellow minister, Archibald Witcher. I sat back for a moment, trying to remember what I must surely have been taught about the Pentecostal Church.

Pentecost is an important Christian festival in late May which celebrates the descent of the Holy Spirit on the disciples of Jesus. The Pentecostal Church, though . . . hadn't it started in the United States at the beginning of the twentieth century, as a sort of break-away movement from the main Protestant Church? Yes, that was it. Over the years since, new branches had sprung up, some quite orthodox and respectable; others less so. As far as I could remember, what the various factions have in common is the emphasis on personal experience of the Holy Spirit and a very literal inter-pretation of the Bible.

So far, my trip to the library had taught me nothing I didn't already know.

In the following week's issue of the *West Dorset Chronicle*, I found four lines: 'Raymond Henry Gillard, aged 30, died on Wednesday, just hours after the pass-ing of his close friend and fellow villager Peter Morfet, age 32. Both men died, in their homes, of cardiac failure. Neither family was available for comment.'

Two men in their early thirties both die of cardiac failure within days of each other?

After that, I went further back through the dusty old papers, looking for any references to the Witcher family and to Saul and Ulfred in particular. The *Chronicle* had been a weekly publication, just eight pages an issue. Even so, it seemed to take for ever, and I couldn't be sure I hadn't missed something.

I went back to 1950 and found several stories of drownings, but all of them at sea or in the estuary, and no mention of Ulfred. At 1.30 I took a short break, climbed back up to the surface of the planet for fresh air and food and then, twenty minutes later, went back to work.

Harry, the youngest but one of the Witcher brothers, had been born in 1930. Just supposing Ulfred had been born in 1931, he would have reached his mid-teens by 1944. I picked up the box containing 1944's issues, meaning to work my way forward in time, and in the second paper I checked I found the story I hadn't even known I was looking for.

In July of that year a land girl from London, working and living on a nearby farm, had been gang-raped by five young men from my village. Four of them had been convicted at Exeter Crown Court and sentenced to between ten and fifteen years in prison. The youngest of the gang, Saul Witcher, had escaped imprisonment by virtue of being only fifteen years old, despite several of the older gang members naming him as ringleader. The jury had chosen to believe Saul when he claimed he'd taken no part in the rape.

At four o'clock the librarian came to warn me about the library's imminent closure. There must have been something about the way I was slumped over the desk, red-eyed and despondent, that plucked at her sympathy. 'Are you looking for anything in particular?' she asked, glancing at her watch.

As I gathered up my things, I explained briefly what had brought me to the library.

'Well, you know,' she said, gesturing me to the stairs. 'A lot of villages in the old days had their own parish newsletters. Where did you say you lived again?'

I named my village and saw her frown. She looked at her watch again, then turned away from the stairs. 'Just a minute,' she said, crossing the room to a large filing system. She opened a drawer and fumbled through it. 'Ah yes,' she said, straightening up and pushing her glasses back against her nose. 'The *St Birinus Gazette*. Published monthly from 1895 till 1972. We don't keep it here, I'm afraid, we just don't have the room, but a lady called Ruby Mottram has every copy ever printed. She was the editor for a long time. I'm sure she'd be happy to let you look through them.'

The last thing I wanted to do was look through more dusty old newspapers, but the woman was being kind, and I took the address she scribbled down for me.

Back in the car, I got ready to drive home, and just glanced down at the small piece of paper the librarian had insisted I take. The address was a residential home for the elderly, not three miles away. Even that wouldn't have tempted me. But I was remembering something else Violet had said.

People who were there didn't talk about it. Even Ruby, and she was my best friend.

A girl called Ruby had been in church the night it burned down. The Ruby on my piece of paper lived in an old people's home, she could easily be Violet's friend. Archie, Saul and Harry Witcher had all left the village shortly after the fire. Four young men had died, on or soon after that night. I decided to pay Ruby a visit.

The Copper Beech Residential Home smelled of urine, synthetic lavender and, for a reason I couldn't fathom, sawdust. It had been purpose-built, some time in the 1970s, and the moment I stepped over its threshold, at a little before 4.30 that afternoon, I knew I'd rather slit my own throat than ever end up in such a place.

As we walked further down the corridor, the smell of lavender gave way to one of thick, industrial bleach. But dust lined the corners where the tiled floor met the skirting boards, and around every light switch was a thin circle of grime.

We passed a lounge. Several women and one old man sat in uncomfortable-looking chairs around the perimeter. None of them was talking, no one was reading, nobody was watching TV or listening to the radio. One or two had their eyes closed, the rest just stared at some point a few feet in front of them; and I wondered what they were seeing, if anything. I had a sense of their bodies decaying, even as they sat there, hearts still beating, lungs continuing to pump.

'They have their tea in twenty minutes,' said the woman in the nurse's uniform who'd met me at reception. 'We prefer all visitors to go by then. It helps to get them settled.'

She stopped in front of a door that had been painted a pale, eggshell blue. Scuff marks scarred the lower inches, whilst grease stains around the handle confirmed the view I'd already formed about standards of hygiene at the Copper Beech. The nurse pushed the door open.

'Visitor for you, Ruby,' she called out, gesturing me inside, and I felt a stab of pity for Ruby, who hadn't been warned about my visit, who might have been sleeping, and who hadn't even been asked whether she'd like to see me or not.

Had she been given a choice, I realized as I walked in, she almost certainly would have declined the pleasure.

Because, at the sight of me, Ruby's eyes opened wide, like those of a wild animal caught crossing a country road at night. Then they darted to the unmade bed on her left, to the right where a wall was lined with bookshelves, down to the brown, flower-patterned carpet and then up to my face again. She shuddered – on her old, frail body it almost seemed like a convulsion – and seemed to shrink into the chair. Her short, fleshless fingers grasped its wooden arms as she looked up at me with what could only be described as disgust.

Seen it all before, Ruby.

She was sitting in front of French windows. The view of the small garden was hardly inspiring – weed-ridden lawn, a few tired shrubs – but beyond she could see the sea. On the horizon, the white sails of a yacht were slowly moving from east to west.

Looking round the room, I found a small, embroidered footstool and pulled it towards – but not too close to – Ruby's chair. Allowing my hair to fall over the left side of my face and twisting slightly in my seat to give her the half-profile, I introduced myself, told her I lived in her former village, knew her old friend Violet and was interested in looking through the parish newsletters.

She didn't reply, but I knew she'd understood because her eyes shot to the bookshelf behind me. I'd already noticed, on one of the shelves, several cardboard boxes, stacked neatly, individually labelled and dated.

'Miss Mottram, I'm trying to find out a little more about a family that lived in the village, the Witchers. Do you mind if I look through some of your old issues?'

Ruby's eyes hadn't focused on one object for more than a second since I'd entered the room. By this time they were darting around a small coffee table that lay to her right. Her hand shot out and grasped a TV remote. She pressed a button and a TV in the corner of the room flicked into life.

'Ruby?'

In response she pressed another button, and the volume increased. She was simply going to pretend I wasn't there.

Telling myself not to let it get to me – she was old, probably had no real dealings with people any more and could be suffering from any one of a number of degenerative ageing diseases – I walked over to the shelves. If she asked me to stop or leave I would, but until then . . .

I scanned the shelf. The sixth box along contained issues from 1950 to 1960. I turned back to Ruby.

'Ruby, do you mind if I . . .' I gestured to the box. She ignored me. I took it down and knelt on the carpet as I examined its contents. I quickly found the issue for July 1958 and flicked through its pages. There was nothing about the church fire, even though the newsletter must have been printed only a week or so after it happened.

Nor was there anything about the Witchers. I looked through the August issue and September's. I found, in October, the notice of the wedding of Violet Neasden to Jim Buckler in the nearby church of St Nicholas, the church I attended myself, but nothing about the fire at St Birinus, nothing about the Witcher brothers.

A glance at my watch told me I had ten minutes before teatime. I reached into the box at random, picked out a copy and flicked through it. Nothing. I tried again; and then again. What I really needed was to take them away with me, study them in my own time at home, but I doubted Ruby was going to agree to that. Every time I looked up, she seemed engrossed in the TV, but I was pretty certain her eyes strayed in my direction whenever I looked down.

I was about to give up, when I found something. In September 1957 a team led by Saul Witcher had won the annual village tug-of-war competition across the river Liffin. His new wife, Alice, had presented the trophy. Saul had been married: to Alice.

Five minutes left. I replaced the newsletters and the box. By this time I was pretty angry with Ruby. Old or not, degenerative disease or not, her behaviour really wasn't on. Think it's difficult to look at my face? Try doing it in the mirror. I walked back across the room, knelt down beside the TV and removed the plug from its socket. That got her attention.

'Hello,' I said.

She looked away again quickly, and I felt a moment's guilt that I might be bullying an old and vulnerable woman.

'Ruby, do you remember Saul Witcher?' I said, making an effort to keep my voice low. 'Married to Alice? Do you remember why he left the village? Where he went?'

Ruby's eyes were fixed on her lap. Her fingers were still gripping the remote, twisting it round and round.

'What about Ulfred? Saul's brother?'

No response. It was hopeless. I got up and made for the door.

'Ulfred drowned,' said a small voice behind me, so low I could barely make it out. 'They drowned him.'

I turned round, allowed a moment to check she'd really said what I thought she'd said.

'What did you say? Who drowned him? Ruby?'

I strode back across the room and knelt down beside Ruby's chair. She wouldn't look at me. As I watched, uncertain what to do next, she started rocking herself forward and back in the chair. We both jumped as a bell rang out through the building.

'Tea bell,' said Ruby to herself, and started to push against the arms of the chair. I offered to help, but she ignored my outstretched hand and struggled to her feet. Turning her back on me, she walked slowly towards the door.

'I'll tell Violet you said hello,' I muttered. Then thought of something.

'Ruby,' I called out, quite loudly, unsure how good her hearing was. She didn't acknowledge me, but I thought I saw a momentary pause. 'Ruby, did you know the snakes had come back?'

No response, and for a second I thought she was just going to walk out of the door. Then I heard a sound, like water being poured from a height, and a sour, acrid smell seeped across the room. I glanced down to see a dark wet stain on the carpet between Ruby's feet.

29

A FEW HOURS LATER I WAS BACK IN THE graveyard.

If Ulfred was here I hadn't found him yet. I'd started in the oldest corner and worked my way towards the group behind the elder bushes. I walked in straight lines, crossing and recrossing the churchyard, checking the names on each stone as I passed. I found a couple of Witchers – male and female – but they'd died too long ago to be directly connected to Walter and his brothers.

The wind had been increasing in strength for most of the day and the trees that circled the perimeter of the churchyard were swaying deeply. Their dark branches, heavy with spring leaves, were blocking light from the moon, causing weird and constantly changing shadows to dart across the ground, like tiny creatures scurrying among the stones. I had to steel myself not to shudder, to tell myself it was only the brush of long grass I could feel around my ankles.

After half an hour of searching, I had to switch on a

small torch to see names carved on the stones. After an hour, I was as certain as I could be that Ulfred was not resting in peace in this particular plot of holy ground.

I didn't relish the thought, but knew I had to check inside the church for some sort of memorial stone. If Ulfred's body had never been recovered, then a stone plaque in the church might be the only record remaining.

I walked back through the stones and arrived at the front door of the church. The one remaining door was slamming furiously against its casing. I stepped inside.

Was this really a house of God I'd just entered? Standing at the back of the nave, with the dark walls soaring high above me, watching the clouds race across the sky where parts of the ceiling had fallen in, I doubted it had ever felt like a place of peace. Now, so many years after worship had ceased, it seemed a place of old, bad memories and dark secrets.

And so much larger than its outer shell had led me to expect. The stone archways stretched up, just about supporting the blackened, fire-eaten ceiling beams. Ahead of me, lining up in the nave like the remains of a long-forgotten army, the charcoal-black pews stood empty and crumbling.

Inside the church walls, there was nothing to protect me from the foul stench of the bat colony, and the combination of rotting flesh and faeces was sickening. The wind howled, bats screamed and dry leaves hissed and rattled.

I hadn't wanted to dwell on what Violet had told me,

but in the place where much of it had happened, it was impossible not to. Looking ahead, to where the chancel rails separated the altar from the rest of the church, it was as though Ulfred were still there: tethered, weak with hunger, bewildered and terrified. I could almost see the congregation gathered around him, praying for the release of his soul, the minister muttering the age-old incantations of the exorcism.

Poor Ulfred.

Commemorative plaques are usually fastened to walls. I walked to the side, shining the torch carefully. At one time the church had boasted stained-glass windows. The heat from the flames had melted the glass, causing streams of colour – still vivid so many years later – to run across the carved window ledges and down the lichen-damp walls. In the moonlight, the colour that stood out most vividly was the red. The remains of the once-molten crimson stream flowed down the stones and across the flagged floor and, that night, in my keyed-up state, the old church seemed awash with blood.

I left the nave and climbed the chancel steps. Here at the front, it was easier to see how the building must have looked. To either side of me, three rows of choir stalls were still intact. Music had soared from them once, but now they stood, sullen and purposeless, their elaborate carving black with age. The lectern lay toppled over in front of the organ seat. The organ was still imposing, still beautiful.

My mother had played the church organ regularly, until her 'health' could no longer be relied upon. She'd particularly liked to play for weddings, and I remembered sitting by her side, well out of sight of the congregation, turning the pages for her and stealing glances at the magnificent dresses (to my childish eyes at least) of the bridal party.

From my privileged seat beneath the pipes I'd been able to see what had been denied to just about everyone else in the congregation: the intimate moments of the marriage vows. I would wait, barely able to contain myself, for the first shining of tears in the bride's eyes, for the tremor in the groom's voice, for their relief when the rings were safely past the knuckles and the difficult part was over. I soon knew those words by heart, even found myself mouthing along with the bride, and, I think, had a bride ever forgotten what she was supposed to repeat, the congregation might have been surprised by the small voice prompting from the wings.

But there was one part of the marriage I could never watch, one point at which I invariably turned away, checked my place on the page, even sought a squeeze of my mother's hand for comfort: the moment when the veil was lifted from the bride's face.

I had nothing to match my mother's talent, but I could play a few, very simple pieces on a church organ and, standing there that night, lost in memories, I had the ridiculous urge to pick up the stool and set it right, to sit down and touch the keys. What sound would the instrument make, after all this time? Would it be heard in the village, would people come running to see who was responsible?

Stupid idea, but something was pushing me forward,

lifting my left foot to press a pedal, taking my right middle finger and placing it down firmly on one of the keys.

The organ responded instantly, crying out with a sound like pain. As the harsh note rang out around the ruin, a flurry of bats soared up, drowning out the fading tone with their high-pitched screams. The creatures were almost powerless against the fast-moving air currents. They were being tossed, screeching, around the ruined eaves like litter in a whirlwind. Outside, rooks began circling again. I found I was trembling. It hadn't been a good idea. Those days were gone.

I passed the front windows of the church: three great stone arches, facing east, the largest stretching some twenty feet above me. Broken pebbles of coloured glass lay like unpolished jewels around the tiled floor.

Candlesticks, dull and dark, stood on the altar. Against the south wall hung a large tapestry. For a second, I tried to make out the scene it depicted but it was too discoloured with mould and damp. There was nothing left for me to do now but walk back along the south wall, looking for words carved in stone, feeling despondency seep into me like the chill atmosphere of the church.

Because what had I achieved after so many hours of sleuthing?

Walter was still missing. I'd learned a little more about Saul Witcher but had made no real progress in tracking him down. Nor had I found any real trace of Ulfred, just the testimony of two of his contemporaries – Violet and Ruby – that he'd drowned. Ruby, of course, had gone one further. *They drowned him*, she'd said. If she was right . . . well, that was quite a can of worms waiting to be opened up.

I was on the threshold of the church, about to step into the porch, when I saw movement. It was a corner-of-the-eye thing, over in a split second, but I was sure I'd seen a tall, dark figure behind the altar. I spun round, heart thudding in my chest, and felt my foot slide beneath me. As I tried to regain balance, I dropped the torch.

It fell heavy and loud on the stone floor, and a flurry of rooks, like pellets from a shotgun, scattered across the sky. I saw debris fall from above, heard it clattering on the stones and splashing into water.

At the front of the church the shadows were all still. I picked up the torch and turned once more to leave. My nerves were shredded to ribbons and I wanted nothing more than to be out of there. I stepped through the doorway and into the porch.

Splashing into water?

And yet again, I turned, making myself walk back up the aisle, keeping a wary eye on the shadows. I was nearing the communion rail. I could see what appeared to be a large wooden cellar-door built into the floor directly in front of the chancel steps. I'd missed it earlier; memories of my mother and her church music had been a powerful lure. It had once been one of a pair. The other door was missing, and in its place the stone tiles gave way to a soft, shimmering blackness. I moved closer, stepping into the stench of stagnant water that hovered like fine mist around it. Round the pool's perimeter, moss crept out like a slow-moving creature stealing its escape. I picked up a stone from the floor and dropped it.

Plop!

All creatures in the church held their breath. It seemed to be deep water, in a rectangular pool, about ten feet long and six feet wide. The ripples from the stone soon died away, but the water continued moving. It could have been a breeze, whispering softly across its gleaming, oil-like surface; it could have been tiny creatures breathing in its depths. I wasn't about to find out. There was something about the pool, about the way it reflected the stone arches of the church, that was slightly hypnotic. I couldn't help feeling that if I stood there much longer, staring down, I might just tumble in.

With an effort I looked up. And saw the tapestry on the south wall of the church moving, swaying gently, as if disturbed by a soft breath of wind. Had I seen someone, seconds earlier? For a fraction of time, I'd been sure the dark outline of a tall man was standing in front of the great arched windows. But nothing was moving at the front of the church. And the tapestry had fallen still. It was time to go, surely?

I made my way round the pool and climbed the three chancel steps. Nothing to see. Nothing to hear but the wind outside and the tiny creatures still pirouetting above me. I stepped forward again, checking right and left, wary of something springing out at me from behind the choir stalls. A quick glance behind the altar – nothing – and then I reached for the tapestry.

It concealed a door. Strongly fashioned of iron and

wood, set deep within a carved stone outline, it would be the door to the vestry, possibly also to the tower, and I wondered that I hadn't thought to look for it before.

The vestry is a room within a church, used to store vestments, or religious clothing, and other paraphernalia of worship. It's often used for parish-council meetings; lots of vicars use them as offices. I reached out for the circular iron handle, knowing I was about to do something that was, arguably, very stupid. I took a firm hold and turned. It moved in my hand.

Had I really seen someone by the altar? And if I had, where was he now?

The handle twisted a quarter-turn to the right and no further. If the door were unlocked, I would only need to push forward and it would open into the room beyond.

Had I seen my elderly intruder from the other night? Much as the thought set my heart beating even faster, I really didn't think so. The impression I'd had in that split second was of someone taller. I raised my head and sniffed the air. I was getting used to the stench of the bat colony by this stage. Was there anything else? The smell of male tramp that had stolen through my home like creeping floodwater the other night? No. Not that. But something all the same. Just faintly. Just possibly . . . pipe smoke?

I pushed the door forward and met with firm resistance. I tried again. Same thing. The door was locked. There was no sign of a keyhole, which meant it had to be bolted from the inside. Frustration getting the better of nerves, I found myself wanting to know what lay beyond that door. And vestries often had external doors; offering an easier way in for the vicar, saving him the trouble of always opening the large, heavy doors at the front of the church.

I left the church, walking swiftly down the aisle and out of the front door. Then, switching off the torch, I made my way round the south side of the building. Keeping close to the walls, knowing that if there were anyone around, he'd be very well aware of my presence, I moved slowly.

The outline of a church's walls are rarely straight. Which worked in my favour that night, because there were several nooks and corners to wait in, listen in, before being sure it was safe to move again. It probably only took five minutes to work my way from the main door of the church to the smaller vestry door, towards the front of the south wall, which I'd known must be there, but it felt like much longer.

This door had a latch.

I wasn't going in. I would just try the door, open it if I could and then stand well back – see if anything came out. I took hold of the latch and pressed my thumb down on the catch. It didn't move. Another locked door. I bent and risked shining the torch into the large key-hole. It was completely clear of the debris you might expect to see if it hadn't been turned in fifty years. I stepped back, looking all round the doorway, wondering if I really had the courage to do what had just occurred to me.

At one time, churches in England were rarely locked, the governing principle of sanctuary being a strong one. The Church believed that its buildings should be open at all times to those in need of prayer and solitude. Yet over the years, vandalism and theft has made such a notion impossible in all but the most rural of churches. Even small village churches had experienced problems, and sometimes an odd compromise had been reached. Church buildings were locked, but the key would be left where those in the know – the regular parishioners – would be able to find it. Fifty years ago, what had the parishioners of St Birinus done with their church key?

The doorway was arched, and a decorative stone lintel had been fixed above it, about seven feet off the ground. At the apex of the arched lintel leered the demonic face of a carved gargoyle, its stone eyes bulging. It was too high for me to reach, but a narrow ledge ran around the church a foot from the ground, and ivy, untrimmed for years, was growing up the old stone. I stepped on to the ledge, held on to the ivy with one hand for balance, and with the other felt around the lintel. Plenty of dry leaves, a few loose stones, nothing else. That left just the gargoyle.

Which, technically, wasn't a gargoyle at all, I realized, when I was practically face to face with it. Gargoyles (hideous though they may be) are functioning pieces of architecture; rain spouts, in fact. The rainwater falls on to the church roof, collects in drainpipes that run around its perimeter, and escapes through the gaping hole in a gargoyle's mouth. This carving had a wide-open mouth behind its obscenely protruding tongue but wasn't attached to a drainpipe. Strictly, it was a chimera, a stone decoration.

And its mouth was stuffed full of fifty years of

291

nature's debris. I pulled out a handful of rotting leaves, several more of mud, the remains of a bird's nest, and still there was more to come. After two minutes of digging around, my hand had disappeared completely inside the creature's mouth. Something ran across my fingers, and I couldn't help shivering. There was nothing in there. I was about to give up, when my little finger touched cold metal. I grabbed it and pulled my hand out.

Jumping down, I shone the flashlight on what I'd found. A large, brass key – stained with age, covered in mud but, as I could see once I'd wiped it clean on my jeans, completely free of rust. Knowing it would fit, certain it would open the door, I held it to the lock and paused.

A man had died, a tiny baby had been put in danger, people were being frightened out of their wits by snakes. And a man who smelled like humanity at its worst, who moved around the village like a shadow, was responsible. We'd found no definite trace of him in the Witcher house, but he had to be hiding somewhere. Had I found that place? And if I had, what should I do now? Did I really expect the police to investigate an old church tower because I'd seen a shadow? Unlikely. Could I bring myself to phone Matt? I knew the answer to that. Anyone else I could confide in? Knew the answer to that one too. I turned the key and pushed open the door to the old church tower.

30

ARKNESS LAY BEYOND, BUT THE BEAM OF THE torch picked out, one by one, all the usual fixtures and fittings of a vestry: vicar's desk, marriage register, cupboards, bookshelf, wardrobe for the various vestments he would need, even a small sink with a rusty kettle sitting on the draining board. Nothing I wouldn't have expected to see. I slipped the key into my pocket and closed the door behind me. To my left was another archway, which led to the spiral staircase. If this church were the Norman one I believed it to be, it would have been built some time around the eleventh or twelfth centuries. The original tower would have been smaller, just one storey above the main church building. Later, round about the 1500s, when bell ringing became popular, towers were built up further, to house a bell chamber. Two more rooms lay above the one I was standing in.

The stairs were narrow, hardly more than eighteen inches wide, and very steep. In places, centuries of foot-steps had worn away the soft stone, and I hoped I wouldn't need to run down them in a hurry. I climbed slowly, treading on the remains of jackdaw nests, brushing past cobwebs and listening hard all the time, until I reached the first storey of the tower: the ringing chamber.

The room was empty except for the eight bell ropes which hung from the ceiling and were gathered in a central point like a giant spider's web. Hand-bells stood on shelves around the chamber, and wooden trays held faded sheet music. Looking up, I could see small holes in the rough boarding of the ceiling through which the ropes hung.

I carried on up.

Eight great bronze bells, their powerful sound muffled for decades, hung motionless in the last and highest of the tower's rooms. Each was covered in the fine, white chalkdust that blows across the countryside here in strong winds. But I hardly gave them a glance. From the second I turned the last bend and stood in the archway of the bell chamber, my eyes had been fixed on something in the small area of floorspace that wasn't taken up by bells.

Not wanting to go any closer, I let the torchbeam wander round the outline of the heavy wooden chair. It had been crudely made, the parts roughly hammered together with thick iron nails, but it looked strong. The arms were wide and thick, the legs sturdy. Four leather restraints with thick, steel buckles had been hammered into the arms and legs.

People said they strapped him up and starved him. For days on end, even weeks.

Until that moment, I'd have dismissed as ridiculous the idea that inanimate objects could be possessed of any sort of malevolence but, as I looked at that chair, horrifying images flashed through my head: a tethered prisoner, screaming his fury to the heavens; a young man, starved and close to death, slumped in despair as blood seeped from the sores on his wrists and ankles; and dry old bones, flesh long since rotted away, still held tight by the leather straps. I think, for those few seconds, I was more scared than I'd ever been.

Sometimes they'd take him to the church, and they'd pray with him, trying to cast out the demon. Days later, you'd see Ulfred, still the same, but bruised and bleeding.

'Long time ago, Clara,' I murmured to myself.

It was hard to carry on looking at the chair. Harder still to turn away from it. So I stayed where I was and shone the torch slowly around the bell chamber, around the bare boards beneath my feet, along walls, up towards the cobweb-strewn ceiling. I think I must have groaned out loud at that point, and the soft sound seemed to echo from the old bells. More chimera, four in all, at each corner of the chamber where the walls met the sloping roof. A hideous creature, nearly two feet high, with the torso of an ape and the claws and tail of a cat, stared at me from the wall opposite the chamber. That was near-human intelligence I could see in its glaring eyes. It looked ready to spring. To my left sat a lion with wings unfurled, ready for flight; to my right a horned beast, brooding, chin resting sullenly on its near-human arms. Behind me, too close, hunched something else. I couldn't see it properly but, instinctively, I moved forward, away from it. All four statues seemed alert, hungry.

Had Ulfred really been left here? I tried to imagine what it would feel like, to watch darkness fall, see the shadows lengthen, and know these hideous stone effigies were to be your only companions through the long night. And I wondered how long it had been before the carvings had appeared to move, to speak to him. How long before the already disturbed Ulfred had lost his grip on reality entirely?

My torchbeam caught something and I stepped forward again. Lying against the skirting board, almost in the corner of the chamber, was a simple wooden shape, two pieces of wood fixed together at right angles. One of the simplest, most recognizable symbols in the world: the crucifix.

The cross of Christ had hung over my cradle when I was a baby. For me, it represented everything that was good and secure in my life. To see it there, in that chamber, with that dreadful piece of furniture . . . it felt disgusting.

I couldn't stay. As I left the room I saw that the chair was almost clear of the fine white dust that covered the rest of the chamber. As though someone, not too long ago, had sat upon it. And looking down, I could see the dust on the floor had been disturbed, by footsteps other than mine.

Back on the stairway, I started to descend but, on a sudden impulse, climbed the remaining five steps and pushed open the tiny, unlocked door that led to the tower's parapet. The wind hit me full in the face, pushing back the door, trying to send me back inside again, but I pressed forward and found myself sixty feet above the village.

Dark clouds sped across the sky and, far below me, their shadows raced to keep pace. Miles in the distance I could see the orange trail of streetlights, and car headlights winding their way between them. The village lay in darkness, other than the occasional porch lamp, or the soft glow behind curtained windows. All was quiet, all was still – apart from the thin beam of light moving slowly through a field close to the village green.

I locked the tower, putting the key back where I'd found it. As I left the church porch and stepped into the lane, I stopped quickly. Three figures – I recognized them instantly as members of the Keech gang – stood at the end of the lane, blocking my way home. They hadn't seen me, but it was only a matter of seconds. I backtracked, running across the churchyard and scrambling over its stone wall into the field beyond. I was very close to Clive Ventry's manor, almost certainly on his land, but I thought I could make my way round the rear of his garden, cut across a lower field and approach the green from a different direction. By that time, the gang might have moved on. Or I might be able to slip past them.

Heading downhill, I was able to move fast, and was soon in the field below the manor. Keeping close to the hedge, I made my way across it. When I reached the other side, I would squeeze through on to Carters Lane and head for home.

I'd gone about fifty yards when I heard voices again. Had I been spotted? Had they followed me down here? I stopped moving and sank to the ground. The hedge that ran down the field, at right angles to the one I was hiding behind, rustled and moved. A bird, startled from its nest, flew away without protest. A large figure pushed his way through the hedge; then another, shorter and stockier.

They were too far away for me to be sure who they were. It could easily be two of the Keech brothers. Given that I'd just seen three other members of the gang, it seemed likely.

They started moving down the field, along the line of the hedge. I let them get a good way ahead and then followed, knowing the chances of their seeing me were slim. I was wearing dark clothes, as I always do for field-trips at night, and tracking creatures through the nocturnal landscape was something I'd done many times before.

The Keech boys, if that's who they were, were about fifty yards ahead of me when I saw one of them turn to the other and speak. I couldn't hear any words, but there was something about the movement of their bodies, the gesticulating arms of the taller man, that made me think they were arguing. Then the taller one leaned over and grasped the other on the shoulder, and the shorter of the two seemed to sink a little. I found I was no longer certain it was the Keech brothers. Neither seemed to move exactly like young men do.

Then they crouched low in the field, and I did the same. They were gazing uphill, towards the manor house, by this time about a quarter of a mile away. The wind was still high, blowing steadily in a south-westerly direction, and around me trees were shivering and whispering to each other. The long grass of the field bent towards me, rippling like fast-flowing water.

How best to describe what happened next? It was as though I were in the midst of a wide, swift river. Water was rushing towards me, ebbing and swirling occasionally but, for the most part, flowing relentlessly onwards in the same direction. That's how it felt that night to be in the field of wind-blown grass. Then I noticed a current in the river, some distance away but getting closer all the time. Not more than a couple of yards wide, it still had formidable power, because the water it was controlling was moving at right angles to the flow of the stream.

I watched that flow of – water . . . grass . . . what on earth was it? – coming towards me, and knew that, fifty yards away, the two men were watching it too.

It could only be water, a stream diverted from somewhere. Except, it wasn't water, I was pretty sure of that. I realized I was trembling. I thought I'd seen everything the English nightscape has to offer, but this was totally new. And, like every other animal on the planet, I am unnerved by the unknown.

What was it? Half of me wanted to run, the other half was fascinated. I risked crawling forward a few feet. The current, unless it changed direction, was going to pass by me but hit the two men directly. They were watching avidly, crouched down, ready for action of some sort, but they didn't appear afraid. It was ten yards away . . . eight . . . moving at the speed an adult might walk . . . five yards.

Snakes . . . dozens of them . . . maybe hundreds. They were rippling through the long grass like ribbons flowing from a child's streamer. Their bodies gleamed slick and wet, shining in the moonlight. They moved over the land with a collective purpose, a common goal, driven by an instinct I could never begin to understand.

It was a grass-snake swarm. Young snakes, slim as pencils, moved alongside adults over five feet long. I saw dark snakes, pale snakes, could even make out the markings on their backs. They would be heading for water, possibly the river. I'd heard of such things happening, had even met an old man who claimed to have seen a swarm, but I don't think I'd ever truly believed in them until now.

It was beautiful; extraordinary; quite wonderful. I felt so immensely privileged and yet, at the same time, experienced a pang of sadness that caught me totally unawares. Why was there no one with me to see it too?

Except there was. I was sharing the experience with two men, who might, or might not, be the Keech brothers. Whoever they were, I somehow doubted they were here to admire the wonders of nature.

The swarm passed me, and I watched it continue down the hill towards the dark figures who were lying in wait. As the leaders reached them, the taller man called something and both stood up. The ripple of snakes exploded apart like water from a spray hose. Snakes fled in all directions, but the two men were ready for them. They were carrying sacks. They held them against the ground and swept them forward.

They'd done this before. They were fast and very efficient. Silently and swiftly they moved, sweeping up the poor bewildered creatures until the sacks they carried were bulging with wriggling, squirming life.

I wanted more than anything to stop them, but I didn't dare move. I was too close. And what could I do anyway? Reason with them? I couldn't even get away until they went. If I moved now, they would see me.

One snake, fleeing the commotion, came towards me. I kept totally still. Snakes cannot hear. They sense vibrations, partly through the air, mainly through the ground. They can see, but their vision isn't good. They do, though, have a powerful sense of smell – through their tongues. As the snake approached me, it slowed down, its tongue flickered like minuscule flashes of lightning, sensing another possible foe.

It stopped and rose up before me in a defensive pose. I found myself wanting to reach out and stroke its soft, strong length, to reassure it. Stupid really – a tame reptile will tolerate being handled, but the idea that this wild creature might need comfort from me was . . . well, maybe I was the one in need of comfort. I remained still, and the snake dropped down, tasted the air once more, and then slid away through the hedge.

At last, all the snakes had either escaped or been captured. The two men walked back towards the hedge. They squeezed through and disappeared from sight, but I was pretty certain they had moved downhill – towards the Witcher house.

I had to get home and call the police. The two men –

I was far from sure now that it had been the Keech boys – had committed a criminal offence. It is illegal to capture a wild British snake, and they must have bagged lots. I had no idea what they were planning, but I was willing to lay bets the snakes wouldn't enjoy it. I started to walk back up the hill too, keeping my ears open for voices on the other side of the hedge. About halfway up I startled another bird, and jumped as it shot into the air in front of me. I reached the top of the field and crouched in the hedge. Pushing my head through, I looked up and down the road.

Empty. My two friends had disappeared with their booty. I squeezed through the hedge, straightened up and walked quickly up the rest of the track. As I turned the corner, I heard a faint scuffle before my hair was yanked backwards and someone's arms wrapped themselves around me.

31

ALLAN KEECH WAS HOLDING ME TIGHT, ROUND THE waist and at the throat; his brother Nathan was coming straight for me. No time to think. I swung one leg up and connected with his crotch. He staggered backwards, and I felt Allan's hold on me relax. I drove one elbow back, felt the softness of stomach muscles he hadn't had time to brace, and then kicked back hard against his shin. He gave a pig-like grunt as he let me go.

I shot forward. Speed was what I needed now. I'd been lucky, they hadn't expected me to fight, but now I'd made them very angry. I could not let them catch me. I raced round the corner into Carter's Lane and carried on upwards. Soon, I'd be at the village green, close to houses, to help.

I could hear rapid footsteps behind me. Nathan was young and tall. He'd be fit; boys of that age nearly always are. Allan was heavier built, maybe fifteen years older than his brother. He was stronger but would be slower. Nathan was the one I had to outrun.

I run up this lane every day, and by the time I reached the top I knew I'd gained a few seconds. Still no time to waste, though. I had to cross the green and turn into the main road that led out of the village, run up it for five hundred yards and bear left into Bourne Lane. That was the home straight.

Which I wasn't destined to reach just yet: two more figures, a boy and a girl from Nathan's gang, sat on a bench at the point where the main road met the green. A third figure was loitering by the lane that went to the church and the manor. Allan and Nathan were coming up fast behind.

None of the others was showing any sign of having seen me. The wind was drowning out footsteps, and the couple were intent only on each other. The other boy was trying to light a cigarette. I jogged across the green and reached the bridge. I ran down three steps to the river's edge and ducked beneath the stone archway – and realized my mistake.

I'd panicked. If I'd thought this through, I'd have stayed in the open and yelled blue murder when any of them came close. Someone would surely have heard me; the houses weren't too far away. In any event, would they really have dared try anything, right in the middle of their own village? I should have braved it out, called their bluff.

Instead, I'd made myself their quarry. They would hunt me down now. With every exit from the green blocked, they'd soon guess where I'd gone. They'd come down here, trapping me beneath the bridge. I couldn't let that happen.

OK, think now, think. Only one option really: stay hidden for a minute or two, get my breath back, wait for the right moment to sprint. But as I pressed myself into the shadows under the bridge, I discovered something. Built into one of the bridge's arches – on the opposite bank to where I was standing – was a narrow tunnel. It was circular, brick-lined, about four feet in diameter, and it carried one of the numerous tiny streams through the village. Of course it was also dark, slime-drenched and full of swift-flowing water, but it stretched away before me, to where it would meet the culvert that took the stream down the side of the main road. The tunnel was fifteen, maybe twenty yards long. If I went through it, I would come out very close to where Kimberly and her friend were sitting. They wouldn't be expecting me to pop up out of the ground. The tunnel, uninviting though it was, might just give me a head start. And I had a torch.

I wade through streams and rivers a lot. I'm used to the assault of cold water rushing past my limbs, to weed that tangles itself around me. But, usually, I'm a lot more appropriately dressed. Within three strides, my trousers were soaked up to mid-thigh and clinging to me. I walked on across the river, wary of loose stones and sudden drops in depth.

At the entrance to the tunnel I shone the torch in, taking care that no flicker of its beam would be seen from above the bridge. I would have to bend over almost double to get through, and if I slipped I could be in serious trouble. It wasn't a good idea.

Footsteps above me. Someone was standing on the bridge.

'Where the fuck did she go? You lot, what the fuck were you doing?'

'Bitch didn't get past us, no way.'

Bad idea or not, it was the only one I had. I started forward, crouched low, shuddering as the water surged up around my hips. Weed hung from the roof, brushing my face as I made my way slowly through. A narrow ledge ran along both sides of the tunnel and I held on to it with both hands as I moved forward. It felt damp, spongy, quite disgusting, but it helped me balance. I stepped on something that squished beneath my feet, and almost moaned out loud.

Footsteps, echoing under the bridge. I flicked off the torch and pressed myself against the damp bricks. Looking back, I could see a dark shape moving around at the entrance to the tunnel. Once they saw me, one of them could be at the other end of this tunnel in seconds. They'd move a lot faster above ground than I could below it. Where had I left my brains?

I heard a faint scratching sound to my left and spun round. Tiny eyes stared at me before minuscule feet darted away. I could cope with a rat. What I wasn't sure I could cope with was the dark figure standing at the entrance to my tunnel, crouched down, peering in. I didn't move. I think I even stopped breathing. His head was moving around as he peered into the darkness. He hadn't seen me. A beam of light flicked on and shone directly into my eyes.

The figure behind the torch laughed softly. It was Nathan. No point hanging around.

I rushed forward, knowing I had seconds. No, I

didn't. A second figure was blocking the way out. Staggering backwards, I shot both hands out to grasp the tunnel wall and steady myself. My right hand connected, the other didn't. My left arm was gaping in space where the tunnel wall should have been. I switched the torch back on.

The bricks lining the tunnel-sides had fallen away at this point, to reveal another tunnel, smaller than the one I was in but also part-filled with flowing water. This new tunnel was no brick-lined river aqueduct but a much cruder passageway that had been hacked out of the rock. The beam gave up before the tunnel finished, and I had no idea how long it was.

OK, what was the worst they could do to me? Were they really likely to murder or seriously injure me – in the village we all lived in, little more than a few hundred yards from houses? Logically, I couldn't believe it. It was ridiculous to be hiding the way I was, skulking in the dark like a sewer-rat.

Humiliation, surely, was the worst I had to fear once they caught me. And I could deal with that. Heaven knows, when it came to surviving humiliation, I could write the book. It would soon be over, and they'd let me go. They couldn't do anything to me that I hadn't faced many times before.

'Oh, Clara,' called a voice from under the bridge, in a false, high-pitched tone, stringing out the final syllable so it bounced around in the tunnel. From the other entrance, someone else took up the cry.

'Claraaaa. Claraaaa.'

A boy howled, like a dog. Then began panting.

Someone else took up the chant of my name, low and insistent, like a drumbeat. I watched one figure take a step into the tunnel. At the other end, my one-time escape route, his partner did the same. They weren't waiting for me to give myself up; they were coming in to get me. Whatever they were planning was going to happen here, beneath the ground. Suddenly, it looked like humiliation wasn't the worst I had to fear. Driven only by the instinct to stay hidden, I bent lower and stepped into the second tunnel.

I heard, with a small measure of satisfaction, the mutters of astonishment I left in my wake. The gang might have known about the culvert, they hadn't known about this tunnel. But I had to go further in, get out of sight before they reached its entrance. I kept one hand on my head to protect it from the very uneven roof and held the torch-bearing hand in front of me. And then hurried forward into the darkness, as fast as was possible, given that I was bent over almost double and wading through water.

I had time to notice, even as panic grew, that this was no natural rock fissure I was scurrying through. As the torchbeam struck the sides, I saw pick marks and scratches where the rock had been hewed. My hand scraped continually against the ceiling, and fine, powdery dust scattered down around me. I was in one of the old chalk mines. Quite where I was heading, though, was another matter entirely. Just how far would I have to run before they gave up? How long would I have to skulk underground before I dared crawl back out again?

I could hear voices behind me, unnaturally loud in the enclosed space. I turned, dreading to see the beam of a pursuing torch; and ran straight into a wall of chalk rock. I dropped my own torch, and its light went out. I'd come to a dead end, I'd lost my light and the gang would be upon me any second. The situation really could not get any worse than this. Except . . . not three feet away from me . . . I could almost feel the warm, soft movement of air against my face . . . someone was breathing.

32

I FROZE, LISTENING AS HARD AS I'D EVER LISTENED IN MY life before.

Heavy, laboured – faster than normal, but too slow to be the breath of an animal – it was coming from somewhere to my right. And so was the smell of sour milk and stale sweat. A very human smell. There had to be another tunnel, maybe just a small culvert, that I'd missed in my panic.

Who was I most afraid of – Nathan and his gang or the barely human creature that had clawed at my flesh the last time I'd smelled anything that bad? Not too difficult a question. I started to edge backwards, and the stench followed me. I heard low whispers, even a giggle, and knew that Nathan and his gang were close. Then someone yelled, and it echoed, harsh and unnaturally loud, in the confined space.

'You lot! Stop pissing around. He wants us.' It was Allan's voice.

Someone tried to argue but was cut short.

'Leave her. If she gets lost in there, it's her own look-out.'

Grumbles, some more giggles and then the sound of legs striding through water. And, suddenly, they were just kids after all. High-spirited, a bit mean, but only after some fun at my expense. What lay close behind me, though, was another matter entirely. The gang was leaving the tunnel. And I was hot on their trail. I didn't care if they heard me. I only just managed to stop myself crying out. *Don't leave me! There's something in here.*

I carried on, pausing just for a second when I turned the last corner and saw the pale light at the end of the narrow tunnel. I watched the last of the kids climb back into the culvert and disappear from sight. And then I went too, into the culvert, checking quickly to make sure they really had gone, but far more concerned about what might be following me, telling myself that this positively was it. If I got out of this mess in one piece, I was having nothing else to do with the weird stuff going on in the village. Whatever it was, it could play itself out without me. I had had enough.

Four yards away from the culvert entrance. A quick glance back to see if anything had emerged from the tunnel. Two yards, one. I pushed through the thick stalks and hairy leaves of a large water-lily and was above ground once again.

The relief at being able to stand upright. I looked round to see stars, playing peek-a-boo with me as clouds sped across them; trees, bending and swaying; old houses, creaking in the wind but otherwise solid and familiar. I was alone on the village green.

* * *

Five minutes later I was outside my own house, staring at the large flower tub that stood above the cellar trap-door. It had been moved.

Just four inches to the right, but there was no mistaking it. The damp patch where it normally stood was quite clear, even in the moonlight. Someone had slid the tub away from its usual home above the trap-door and then, possibly in their haste to get away, hadn't put it back properly.

Why would they do that?

So when all I really wanted to do was batten down the hatches and take a very long bath, I found myself pushing with all my might against a heavy wooden flower tub. It took a few minutes but, eventually, I'd managed to push it away from the trap-door. What would be the point in anyone else doing it, though? The coal door was padlocked and bolted below. Not really expecting anything to happen, I took hold of the iron ring that would have served to lift the door and tugged hard.

I nearly fell over backwards, pulling the door with me. The whole thing had come clean away, and my cellar was open to the night. I checked quickly. The bolts and padlock were holding firm – but the wooden frame in which the door sat had rotted away from its concrete base. Down in the cellar, with the planter hold-ing everything in place, all had looked normal. Up here, it was as plain as the scar on my face that getting access to my cellar – and to my house – had been child's play.

At least I know, I muttered to myself, before realizing

the significance of the out-of-place planter. Someone had been in again. Suddenly freezing cold, I replaced the coal door and the planter and went inside – through the front door.

I bolted the cellar door, pulled the kitchen table up against it and looked for heavy things to put on the table. I carried over the microwave and a cast-iron casserole dish and felt foolish. So I searched the house, in case someone was lying in wait for me somewhere, checking and double-checking the locks on all the windows and doors. I didn't dare shower: not being able to hear anyone creeping up on me was just about unthinkable. I ran a bath and, when I'd washed away the smell of the river, I took my mobile phone into my bedroom and even a sharp knife from the kitchen drawer. Both went under my pillow. Even then I couldn't sleep. I checked the house again.

As I was walking through the dark, downstairs rooms I thought I heard movement outside, someone squeezing through the shrubs that grow close to the wall at the back of the property, but no one knocked on the door, no one tapped at the window, or called my name.

Upstairs again, I dozed off, only to wake suddenly when a branch scraped against the window. I lay, watching the moon-reflected leaves make patterns on the wall and knew that sleep wasn't likely to come again that night. Because when the sun rose it would be on the day I had to say goodbye to my mother.

It was Mum who taught me to sing. She realized when I was still very young that she would never make a musician of me, but she revelled in the promise of my voice. We sang for hours on end, and it was always just the two of us in our music room. Dad had just enough of a voice to lead his congregation, Vanessa was completely tone-deaf and had been banished from the age of six for being too destructive with the percussion instruments. Sometimes, as Mum and I sang together, it felt as if we were the only two people in the world, and I liked that just fine.

As our lessons continued, as my voice grew in strength and tone, Mum's one great desire became that I would sing in public; just in a small way, at school or maybe in church. She wanted me to stand in front of people and give them a reason to look at me that was to her credit, not to her shame. I think she would have seen it as evidence of my healing; of her redemption. I have never done so.

And that night, watching shadows play across the room like the ghosts of missed opportunities, I realized why. If I'd given her what she wanted more than anything else, I would have lost the power I had over her.

Oh, I'd been ruthless over the years, in exploiting the influence I knew I had over my mother. I discovered, by instinct, when I was little more than a toddler, that Mum would do anything to protect me from further harm. And I took a perverse delight in torturing her. Mum was the reason I became a vet. I'd always been drawn to animals, but I sensed her fear of them at a very young age. The tug of war between us when we'd meet a dog became almost comical, Mum trying to pull me away, I struggling to get closer. I stopped when Vanessa, a spiteful ten-year-old, jealous of the attention lavished on the damaged child, told me exactly why I looked the way I did.

But by that time, my petty, instinctive acts of revenge had become a genuine interest. I'd learned to love the animal kingdom: the infinite, surprising variety of it, for its own sake. I spent a summer at a nearby riding school and learned the names of every bone and muscle in the equine body. I got to know the local farm vet and, once he knew of my interest, he was happy to let me go on his rounds with him. In a rare spirit of camaraderie, Vanessa and I set up a wildlife hospital in our garden shed. We advertised in the local paper and, that summer, we nursed a constant stream of injured rodents and abandoned baby birds back to health. By the time I was ready to apply to vet school, I had so much knowledge and practical experience, I got offers from every course I applied to.

And I owed it all to my mother, who in a careless moment had destroyed my life; only to spend the rest of hers trying to rebuild it.

My eyes closed again. When they opened next, the light outside the window was silver and a song thrush was announcing to all who cared to listen that my garden was his territory and that everybody else had better just back off. It was 4.45 a.m. on Thursday morning: almost dawn.

33

IFOUND VIOLET'S NAKED BODY ON THE DOUBLE BED IN the centre of the room. A faded pink nightdress lay on the worn carpet at the foot of the bed. I didn't really look at it but I thought, perhaps, it had been torn. I stood in the doorway, unable to take my eyes off the still figure on the bed.

I'd had no idea she was so small. She looked almost like a child lying there, a child whose skin, threaded like marble with lilac veins, had stretched and sagged and was falling around her bones like the folds of a shroud.

Even from the doorway I could tell her last moments hadn't been easy. The flesh above her left breast had swollen and begun to discolour, the pastry-coloured skin taking on shades of red and purple. The swelling had had time to spread: the upper part of her left arm looked larger than her right. A thin trail of blood pointed the way back to the wound just under her collarbone. A pillow lay beside her head, stained with blood and with the vomit that still streaked the side of her face. Had someone, afraid the poison in her veins wasn't acting quickly enough, held the pillow against her face to speed the process along?

Her thin, white hair had soaked dark with sweat, and her bluebell-coloured eyes were open. I didn't want to think about the last thing they'd seen. I walked over, feeling as if I were passing through fog, the bed seemed so far away. I knew the rules, of course: touch nothing, call the police – but I didn't care. I was going to close her eyes and find something to cover her. Pink froth circled her mouth; she'd coughed up blood. I reached out, remembering how soft her skin was and bracing myself for how cold it was going to feel. I brushed my fingers over her temples, felt her eyelashes prickling my skin.

Warm!

The fog was gone and I was moving faster than I'd ever done, scanning her body for the tiniest glimmer of life. My right hand shot to her neck to feel for the carotid pulse whilst my left was tilting back her jaw, my head bent down to listen for even the faintest breath.

Nothing.

I found my mobile, punched in the three-digit number and answered the questions that I knew were necessary but seemed to take for ever. At last, with hands clenched together, fingers interlocked, I started pumping at her chest, directly above the sternum . . . twelve, thirteen, fourteen . . . When I reached thirty I stopped, pulled back her head, opened her mouth and checked the airway. Two breaths and I went back to pumping the chest. Thirty compressions, then more air.

Don't give up, I told myself, as I went from one simple action to the other. That's the mistake people make, they give up too soon. People can be brought back after five, ten minutes of clinical death, you just have to keep the circulation going, keep the body alive until help arrives, until the heart can be shocked back into life and the lungs forcibly reminded of what they're supposed to do. So don't stop. Bully them into carrying on, bloody well carrying on. For God's sake, Violet, don't give up.

Let me go, dear.

No, Violet, no. Come on, just one more minute. They'll be here soon.

It's over. Stop now, dear. Stop.

No, Violet, you can't die. If you do, it'll be my fault. Don't die, Violet, please.

I don't know how long I administered CPR to Violet, but I honestly believe, even now, that I didn't give up too soon. Violet hadn't been long dead when I found her, but she was deeply dead. If paramedics with defibrillators ready primed had followed me through the front door it would have been no use. She wasn't coming back. And there came a point when I knew I had to let go.

I found myself walking to the cupboard in the corner of the room, taking out a blanket and laying it gently over her still form. Downstairs I could hear movement, heavy footsteps and voices calling softly. I sat down beside Violet, telling myself it would take them a few more seconds to find us. Just long enough to say a proper goodbye. We had a little time.

I was wrong. For me, as well as for Violet, time had run out.

Part Two

34

'AND THAT'S IT, MISS BENNING?'

'Yes,' I managed, through a throat that felt like someone had taken a hold of it. 'That's it.'

Detective Inspector Robert Tasker stared at me for a second, his eyebrows high, brow crinkled. Then he dropped his forehead on to his hand and, with forefinger and thumb, he massaged his temples. Under the canopy formed by his other fingers he peered at me with brown, bloodshot eyes. It was a gesture I'd seen several times already. I waited.

'When the police arrived,' he said, 'they found you sitting by Mrs Buckler's body. They didn't see any sign of you trying to resuscitate her.'

'I'd just that moment stopped,' I replied.

'Just that moment?' Tasker gave an exaggerated sigh and glanced down at papers on the table in front of him. 'We got a phone call from Mrs Buckler's next-door neighbour, just after five o'clock this morning, reporting a disturbance.' He looked up. 'We have a witness who saw you crossing the green, heading for Mrs Buckler's house, at around that time. Yet when we arrive, twenty minutes later, she's dead – only just dead, mind you – and you're sitting by her side like the angel of death. How long did you administer CPR, exactly?'

High on the wall behind Tasker, the clock told me it was nearly noon. Six hours earlier, under arrest on suspicion of murder, I'd been driven straight from Violet's house to the police station. Once there, I'd been informed of my rights and asked to submit to a medical examination. I'd been offered a solicitor, which I'd declined, and then been locked in a cell. Just before 10.30 a.m. they'd collected me and brought me to an interview room. I'd been talking non-stop for well over an hour and wanted nothing more than to curl up and sleep. At least in the cell I'd been alone.

'For the benefit of the tape, the suspect is refusing to answer the question put to her,' said the man at Tasker's side, Detective Constable Stephen Knowles. Knowles was older, shorter and plumper than Tasker. There wasn't much hair left on his head, but a whole load on his body, judging by the dark curls clambering out over the top of his shirt and around his cuffs.

'She was dead,' I managed, after a few seconds. 'I tried to save her and I couldn't. I have no idea what time I started or when I stopped.'

Tasker and Knowles shared a look. I reached out, took hold of the water jug and found I barely had strength to lift it. I emptied it into my glass and drank it in one go. When the interview had started the jug had been full, but I was the only one drinking; the only one who seemed affected by the oppressive conditions of the place. The room we were in had neither air-conditioning nor windows and was getting hotter by the hour. The electric lights were too bright, the furniture too plastic and the room smelled of cold sweat and stale smoke. No-smoking signs hung on every wall, but the two officers had brought the smell in with them, clinging to their clothes like an uninvited guest.

'You seem to have made friends with a lot of the older people in your village, Miss Benning, would that be fair to say?' asked Tasker.

'I'm not sure I've really made friends with anyone in the village, young or old,' I answered, truthfully.

'What about Mrs Buckler?'

'I'd only just met her.'

'So you say. And yet you spent all that money on her dog.'

I had a moment to wonder how he knew about Bennie. Had Sally told him? Or Matt? Neither possibility held much appeal. 'She was old and frail,' I said. 'I couldn't do much for her, but at least I could help her dog.'

'Old and vulnerable, I'd say,' Tasker was saying. 'How much do you think her house is worth, Miss Benning?'

'I'm sorry, what?' The question took me totally by surprise.

'It's in pretty bad nick now but, renovated, it might fetch £200k. Maybe more. What do you think?'

'I really have no idea.'

'Oh, come on. From what I hear, you and the other residents get regular letters from a property company making offers.'

'They never mention value.'

'Still, must be worth something, mustn't it? Unlikely to have a mortgage, woman of that age.'

It was on the tip of my tongue to ask what all this had to do with me, but I couldn't help feeling Tasker would be happy to spell out precisely what it had to do with me.

'Mrs Buckler didn't have a family,' said Knowles. 'Did you know that?'

'I guessed. I think that's why her dog was so important.'

'Mr and Mrs Witcher didn't have close family either, did they?'

I realized I was sitting very still, almost bracing myself for a blow. 'I don't believe so,' I said.

'You were quite friendly with them as well, weren't you?'

'I spoke to Walter occasionally as I ran past his house. I barely knew Edeline. They weren't my friends.'

'And yet we have people who say they saw you talking to both of them regularly. A Mrs Stringer says most mornings she'd see you and Edeline chatting at her front gate.'

The unfairness of it. The conversations I'd dreaded, had forced myself to endure, were coming back to haunt me. 'After Walter died, she'd wait for me,' I said. 'I didn't have much choice.'

'It's always a bit of a mess, when people die intestate.

Always a good idea to make a will. Did Mrs Buckler make a will?'

'How on earth would I know? I'd only just met her.'

Tasker was leaning back in his chair. 'I'll tell you my problem, Clara,' he said. 'In my line of work we get cynical. We hear about young people making friends with vulnerable older folk and we ask ourselves why.'

I closed my eyes and shook my head at the irony of it. I, of all people, accused of inappropriate friendliness.

'What about John Allington?' continued Tasker. 'The man who died last Friday from an adder bite. How well did you know him?'

'I never met him.'

'Are you sure?'

'Of course I'm sure.' I hadn't met John Allington. At least, until after he'd taken up residence in the hospital morgue. Did it count as a meeting, if one party was a corpse?

'Ah, but Mr Allington did have family, didn't he? He wasn't all alone in the world like the Witchers. Like Mrs Buckler.'

I slammed my hands down on to the tabletop. Just loud enough to make both men blink. 'What on earth are you getting at?' I demanded, unable to cope with their clumsy insinuations any longer. 'Walter was a sweet man but he was shy. I hardly knew him. Edeline, I didn't like at all and avoided as much as possible. Violet seemed nice, but I only met her days ago. What in God's name is all this about?'

It was like watching electricity leap between the two men. One sat up, the other leaned forward, their eyes met, excitement gleaming as they realized they'd done it: after nearly two hours of questioning, they'd riled me, they were getting somewhere.

'Let's talk about last night, shall we?' said Knowles. 'Secret passages and old chalk mines. We will check they're there, you know.'

'You'll find them,' I said, feeling a moment's relief that the conversation was moving on. 'Chalk's been mined in this area since Neolithic times. Most of the early workings were barely below the surface. And very rarely recorded. These days, no one knows where half of them are.'

'I think you might be right, at that,' said Tasker, stretching his arms back over his head, as though the three of us were just chatting in a café. 'There was a case back in the sixties. In Kent. A shaft of an old mine opened up in the high street completely out of the blue one day. A mother and child fell into it. Bodies never recovered.'

Knowles had been listening, sullenly. Now he leaned forward again.

'Yes, yes, fascinating. So, quite an evening you had, Miss Benning.'

I didn't reply.

'For the benefit of the tape—'

Oh, for heaven's sake! 'Where, exactly, was the question in that last sentence of yours, Constable Knowles? I must have missed it.'

Knowles was smirking again – as though annoying a suspect constituted a considerable step forward.

'Thing is, Miss Benning,' he said. 'We've spoken to

326

the three Keech brothers about last night. And to Jason Short, Kenny Brown and Kimberly Aplin. Very cooperative witnesses. And what they say leads me to have some serious doubts about your story.'

I didn't like 'your story', but I didn't rise.

'Don't tell me, they were all tucked up in bed at nine o'clock.'

'Oh no. They freely admit being out last night. Apparently they have permission to shoot rabbits on Clive Ventry's land.'

'They were catching grass snakes,' I insisted.

'Now, *that* they emphatically deny.'

'Well, they would, given that it's illegal,' I snapped, wondering if I were really as sure as I sounded. In the end, the two men I'd watched in the field the previous night hadn't looked much like teenagers.

'Trouble is, with no evidence, it's your word against theirs. And there're six of them.'

'They assaulted me, threatened me and chased me. I already know there were six of them. It made it a very frightening experience.'

'Yes, yes. But, you see, they tell it differently.'

'Oh, this I have to hear.'

Knowles was reading from his notes again. 'All six witnesses report that, as they walked back towards the village, you appeared suddenly from the hedge. They expressed surprise and you reacted violently. You kicked Nathan Keech in the genitals, causing him considerable pain, elbowed his elder brother in the stomach and then kicked him hard on the shins. Then you ran off.'

'They grabbed me by the hair. And they chased me.'

'They say they were worried about you. Seems you have a reputation for being a bit odd. They saw you disappear beneath the bridge and became concerned. They looked for you, but you'd disappeared. After searching for a while, they went home.'

He wants us, they'd said, as they left the tunnel. But who was *he*? Clive Ventry? Walter's long-lost brother, Saul Witcher? Or someone else entirely?

'Not the first time you've threatened violence to these youngsters, is it, Miss Benning?'

'What?'

Another glance at his notes. He turned a page. And another.

' "I am medically trained," ' he read. ' "I know exactly where to stick an eyeball so it comes clean out of its socket." '

He looked up at me. 'Did you say that, Miss Benning? On 25 May, last Monday night?'

'They were threatening me.'

'Threatening you how, exactly?'

'They wouldn't let me get past them. They made verbal threats.'

'What kind of threat?'

Squirming with embarrassment, praying none of it showed on my face, I told them. Tasker looked away, Knowles back up at me.

'Well, they didn't mention that. They told us they saw you hanging round the Witcher house and were curious. They say you do it a lot. Hang round the Witcher house.'

Silence.

'Miss Benning?'

'Sorry. That question escaped me too.'

'Being uncooperative won't help you, Miss Benning.'

Tasker leaned forward and put his hand on the table. It seemed to act as a calming gesture, making Knowles back off.

'Let's talk about the dog, shall we?' said Tasker. 'Mrs Buckler's dog. Bertie, was he called?'

'Bennie,' I corrected, shutting my eyes to get rid of the sudden vision that was swimming before me. Bennie, dead and soaking, tumbling from the hessian sack.

'Pretty sick thing to do, don't you think? Put a dog in a sack with a snake. Throw them both into the river. Who'd do such a thing?'

'The Ancient Romans,' I suggested, for want of anything else.

Tasker raised his head; stared at me down his nose.

'It was a form of execution,' I explained. 'Convicted criminals would be tied in a sack. A leather sack, I think. And animals would be put in too. A dog, a snake and something else. Possibly a monkey. Maybe a cockerel. I think they each represented something, but I'm not sure.' I was thinking hard, but Roman-history lessons had been a long time ago. 'And a couple of other things,' I said, as more came back to me. 'Wolfskin or bearskin was tied over the condemned man's head, and wooden sandals strapped to his feet. It was all highly symbolic.' As I was speaking, I had a sudden flashback to Dr Amblin's bedroom. The dead adder, the toy monkey.

329

'And what had he done, this poor bugger?' asked Knowles. 'Must have been something pretty serious.'

'I'm sorry. I really can't remember.'

At that moment we all heard a sharp click from the room's recording equipment. We'd reached the end of our fourth thirty-minute tape. Tasker stretched back in his chair. 'OK, we'll take a break.'

Fifteen minutes later we were back, the two officers invigorated by a fresh intake of tobacco and coffee. Knowles switched on the recording equipment and sat down opposite me. Tasker remained standing. 'This snake business,' he said, leaning against one wall of the interview room. 'I really can't get my head around that.'

You and me both, I thought, waiting for him to go on. Knowles picked up the cue.

'Snakes turning up all over the place. People's bed-rooms, babies' cots. We even found one in your cellar this morning, Miss Benning. Wriggling around in one of those boxes of yours. Pet, is he?'

'There are no snakes in my house to my knowledge,' I said.

'So how did it get there?'

'Somebody is breaking into houses in the village and leaving snakes behind,' I said. 'I saw him in my house. I think it could be a man called Saul Witcher. I think he has a grudge against the village and I think he's living in the old family—'

'Yes, yes,' said Tasker, 'but where are they coming from, all these snakes? Most of them are wild British specimens, from what I understand. You can't just buy them in a shop.'

'Someone is catching them,' I said. 'Someone who knows a lot about their habits, probably someone who knows the village quite well. Someone like that would know where and when grass snakes swarm, the best places to catch adders.'

'We found another adder in your dustbin,' said Knowles. 'A dead one. Did you put it there?'

In all fairness, the police had been thorough. 'It was nailed to my front door a couple of nights ago,' I said. 'I thought it was a prank. We've been having problems with petty vandalism, practical jokes. It didn't seem worth reporting.'

'With everything that's been going on in your village, you didn't think another incident with a snake was worth reporting?'

Was I going to tell these two men the real reason I hadn't reported the incident? What someone had written in white paint on my front door? No, I wasn't. 'This is something to do with the Witcher family,' I tried again. 'One of the brothers, Ulfred, was supposed to have some sort of gift with snakes. Maybe Saul had it too. You really should be trying to track him . . .'

'And this other snake. The tropical one. What do you call it?'

'It's a Papuan taipan.'

'Yes, you've come across them before, according to Assistant Chief Constable Hoare. You've studied them.'

'I came across the Australian species a few years ago, but I understand the Papuan snakes are quite similar.'

'So you know about handling them?'

I shook my head. 'People don't handle taipans. Not if they have any sense.'

Tasker didn't seem to have heard me. 'My problem is, Miss Benning,' he said, 'the only person we know of who would know where to find snakes, how to keep them and how to handle them safely, is you.'

Silence fell. Both men stared at me. I fixed my eyes on a spot on the wall, directly behind Tasker's head; and knew things were about to get a whole lot worse.

'What happened to your face, Miss Benning?' said Tasker, quietly.

And there it was, the one I'd been waiting for. Deep breath.

'An accident,' I said. 'A long time ago.' It was my well-practised, time-honoured response. Normally it was enough. Today, it wasn't going to be.

'What sort of accident?'

'I don't remember it,' I said, telling myself I had to stay calm. 'I was a baby.'

A moment's pause, while the two regrouped their thoughts. Tasker was the first.

'As you got older,' he said, 'realized you were different, you must have asked what caused it. A burn? Car accident? What was it?'

'My parents never talked about it. And I never asked.' Both statements were perfectly true. I hadn't needed to ask. Vanessa had told me, before it even occurred to me that anyone might be to blame. Long before I realized how a particular arrangement of skin and flesh could have such a devastating impact upon a life, before I'd even realized I was different, Vanessa had told me all about it.

'You were never curious?' said Tasker, leaning forward, his eyes fixed on the left side of my face. 'A couple of old buggers like Knowles and me – it doesn't really matter how we look. But a young girl. From the way my daughters carry on, you'd think looks are everything to young women. So if a girl isn't just plain, if she's – I'm going to have to tell it like it is now – seriously disfigured; well, I can see that having a pretty devastating effect on a young woman.'

'Could really play with your head,' added Knowles.

I felt my hand creeping up the left side of my neck. It was an unconscious gesture, one I'd been making for years. I would take hold of the hair on that side of my head and draw it forward. I made myself put my hand down. *Hold it together, it can't last long.*

'I wonder why you didn't try plastic surgery,' said Tasker. 'They can do wonders these days.'

'For the benefit of the tape, the suspect isn't responding,' said Knowles.

'Did you have plastic surgery?' asked Tasker.

'I've had several operations,' I said, knowing I couldn't avoid a direct question. 'The first when I wasn't a year old, the last when I was sixteen. The doctors don't believe any more surgery would be beneficial.' I was staring down at my hands. All the blood seemed to have drained from them. They could have been made of wax.

'So . . .' Tasker's voice came from somewhere above my head. 'So this is as good as it's going to get?'

My hands were tensing, turning into claws. I had to get a grip. 'Unless there's a significant breakthrough in the technology, the doctors don't believe the potential benefits of further surgery would outweigh the risks involved.' I recited, pretty much word for word, what the last doctor had told me. I suppose it was a fancy way of saying, yes, this was as good as it was going to get.

'Have you seen anyone? Counsellor? Psychiatrist? Someone to help you come to terms with it?' Tasker's voice had lowered, he was leaning forward towards me, trying for a sympathetic look. But when I glanced up, his eyes gave him away. He was having far too much fun.

'My mother took me to see some people when I was younger,' I said. 'I forget the details.' I remembered the details only too well. Two psychiatrists, five counsellors and a behavioural therapist. Not until I left home did I escape the relentless barrage of professional, guilt-driven help. Had it helped? I honestly wasn't sure. I had no way of knowing what state my head would be in without the surfeit of therapy.

'I remember reading somewhere that very ugly people – excuse me, Miss Benning, I'm not trying to be rude – that they start to feel invisible after a while,' said Tasker. 'Once people have got over the initial staring, they don't look at all.'

Tasker paused for a moment to look at Knowles. As though taking up a cue, Knowles carried on.

'People tell us you don't mix much, Miss Benning,' he said. 'That you never seem to have friends of your own

334

age, you don't go out, don't have visitors. No boy-friends, obviously.'

And on they went. When one paused for breath, the other chipped in. With every fresh insult they hurled at me, they apologized – *sorry to be so blunt, Miss Benning, but you have to understand we're only doing our jobs* – and a person with half a brain might have been fooled that they were trying to empathize, to understand, instead of beating me up as viciously and relentlessly as ever rotten cops physically thrashed a suspect. But years of fending off similar blows came to my aid, and I don't think anything showed on my face. If it had, I think they might have stopped their barrage earlier; sooner reached the point at which they'd been driving all along.

'So, if I'd had a lifetime of that sort of treatment, I might be tempted to make the world pay me back some.'

'Just even up the balance a little.'

'Why shouldn't you have a bit of luck for a change?'

'It's not actually illegal, to be left money in someone's will. It's not strictly illegal to ask someone to leave you money, as long as there's no coercion involved – you see what I'm saying?'

They stopped. They were going to let me talk again. I wasn't sure my voice would still work.

'I . . . I never asked Violet . . .' I began. Who were the others? I'd forgotten. Oh, yes. 'Or Walter or Edeline for money.' I went on. 'We never talked about money, it never occurred to me that they might have any. Money is really not something I think about all that much.'

'Did you force Mrs Buckler to write a will in your favour?'

'No.'

'Did you suggest it to her? Perhaps in return for taking care of her, of her dog?'

'No.'

'Did you do the same thing with the Witchers? Is there a will in the house somewhere? Is that what you've been trying to find, on all your trips back?'

'I've been in that house once. With Mr Hoare. We were looking for Saul Witcher, not pieces of paper.'

'I think you were looking for a will. A will you persuaded Mr and Mrs Witcher to make. And when you didn't find it, I think you had another go – with Mrs Buckler. I think she changed her mind, that the two of you argued. I'm guessing you killed her dog to frighten her. And then you tried to force her hand. I think she struggled and I think you killed her.'

I had absolutely nothing to say. It wasn't happening. They didn't really, genuinely think . . .

Tasker slowly opened the folder that lay on the desk in front of him. From inside, he drew a single sheet of paper that had been encased within a clear, plastic wallet. He glanced at it, then turned it round to face me. The paper was distinctive, good quality, a yellowy-cream in colour, and I recognized it immediately. I buy it in Somerset, at a paper mill. As far as I know, you can't buy it anywhere else and I have two reams of it in my study.

It was a crude, simple document that took me five seconds to read, a last will and testament phrased in quasi-legal language, maybe composed by someone with just a vague idea of how the law worked. It wasn't legal – even in those first five seconds, I could see that. For one thing, it wasn't witnessed, just signed in a trembling, spidery scrawl by Violet Buckler, as she left everything she owned in the world to me.

35

I WAS OUTSIDE. THERE WAS SALT IN THE AIR AND A bakery not too far away. For a few minutes, all I could do was stand still and breathe in the clean air.

I hadn't been charged. A few minutes after producing the fake will, the interview had been called to a halt, and DI Tasker, to my utter amazement, had announced that I was to be released on police bail. Thirty minutes later I'd walked out of the front door into the station car park.

With no idea of where I was going to go, I walked towards the car-park entrance. I heard the sound of an engine starting up and, a second later, a car drew up alongside me.

'Get in,' said a voice I knew.

The dark-haired, grey-eyed, bespectacled man in the driver's seat was dressed as I'd never seen him before, in black trousers and tie and a white shirt with distinctive epaulettes on the shoulders. He leaned over and opened the passenger door. 'I'll drive you home,' he said.

I shook my head. What did I feel at that moment? I

couldn't possibly say. Shame? Anger? A little of both those and yet something else entirely. Something that felt like the last drop of hope trickling away.

Matt sighed, looking tired, and older than I'd previously thought him. 'Clara,' he said, 'I don't want to sound harsh, but in less than three hours, they are burying your mother. You need to get home. Now get in.'

He had a point. I climbed into the passenger seat of Matt's car and closed the door. He pulled out into the road and set off for home.

'Why did they let me go?' I asked, as we stopped at traffic lights on our way out of town. 'Why didn't they charge me?'

We set off again. 'Tasker hasn't enough evidence to charge you,' Matt said, his eyes fixed on the road ahead. 'He was pushing his luck this morning. Trying to find out exactly what you know. It's standard procedure.'

'They told me I have to go back in eight weeks,' I said, wondering if Matt had been listening to Tasker and Knowles interview me. If he'd heard everything they'd said to me.

'That's a formality. They'll have you back in like a shot if anything else turns up.'

'I didn't kill Violet.' I stopped. I sounded like I was begging. *Please let me not sink that far.* Matt's eyes hadn't left the road, even though we weren't travelling particularly fast. Every previous time I'd been with him, I'd found it difficult to look him directly in the eyes. Now, it seemed, he was the one who couldn't bring himself to look at me.

'Do you think I killed Violet?' I asked. 'Are you the reason I was arrested?' Before the words were out of my mouth I knew I'd never be ready for the answer.

'No,' he said, at last. 'But I can't ignore DI Tasker's case. You have a reputation for being a real recluse but you've been seen socializing with older people in the village. Violet, Edeline, Walter. People who have since died.'

'Walter might not be dead,' I said, knowing I was clutching at straws.

'If he isn't, we'll find him. I've got people looking.'

'I contacted around twenty nursing homes and residential—'

Matt raised one finger away from the steering wheel. 'We know how to trace missing people,' he said. 'In the second place, you know a lot about snakes. You have the expertise to catch and handle them. Most people wouldn't know where to start. It doesn't help that you conveniently had a live adder in your cellar, a dead one in your dustbin and ViperaTAb in your fridge . . . Yeah, I know it's standard practice to keep it at wildlife hospitals, we checked.'

'None of that's enough,' I replied, hearing my voice getting louder but unable to control it. I'd held myself together so well while Tasker and Knowles had been bullying me. Now, I was losing it. 'Even I know that. I know about snakes and I've been seen talking to two old ladies.'

'He also has a will, apparently made out by Violet, making you her beneficiary.'

'That document is an obvious and pathetic forgery.

Anyone could have stolen that paper from my house. This is about how I look. Tasker thinks I'm psychotic because I'm scarred. He thinks I'm on a mission to avenge myself on the whole human race.'

'Take it easy.'

'No. He's made his mind up. He won't even look for anyone else. Why isn't he looking for Saul Witcher? Why isn't he looking for Ulfred?'

'Saul Witcher is dead.'

'What? How do you know?'

'We checked. I had someone look into it the morning after you and I went round the house. He died in 1976, in Kingston Prison. He was committed seven years earlier for murdering his wife.'

'Alice,' I said. Matt raised his eyebrows and glanced sideways. 'She was called Alice,' I explained, ready to tell Matt about the story I'd found. Then found I hadn't the heart to. Saul was dead. I'd been so sure. 'What about Ulfred?' I asked without much hope. 'Did you . . .'

'Never existed.'

'He must have. Violet remembered him. So did Ruby Mottram.'

'We checked parish records and the General Register Office. No one called Ulfred Witcher was born in or near the parish for three decades. Violet and this Ruby must have been getting confused.'

'Will you talk to Ruby?'

'There's a red folder by your feet. Can you get it?'

I reached down and found the folder on the floor of the car.

'Open it.'

I did what I was told and found myself looking at a large portrait photograph. 'Do you recognize that man?' he asked.

I looked down at the colour photograph of a man in his late sixties, maybe early seventies. His thick hair was white, cut short at the back but falling over his forehead. His blue eyes were slanted and heavy lidded. Mouth generous. He'd been a good-looking man. Still was.

'Is this the man who broke into your house last Monday morning?' said Matt.

I knew it wasn't, but I took my time. Checked the face again, studied the information printed in the corner. Approximate height: six foot, two inches.

'No,' I said reluctantly. The picture was nothing like the man I'd seen in my house, or the face at the window of the Witcher house. 'Why . . .'

'That's Archie Witcher,' said Matt. 'We found him. Well, almost. He's been living in South Carolina for thirty years, running a church there. We got this photograph off the church's website.'

'You *almost* found him?'

'Haven't quite managed to pin him down yet. We did find news coverage of a scandal at his church, though. Apparently, prolonged fasting is an important part of worship in this particular congregation. He encourages people to go without food for weeks on end. Anyway, a young girl died, and there were rumours she'd been kept tied up. Her parents are in custody, and there's a warrant out for Archie's arrest. His current whereabouts are unclear. It is just possible he's come home. Are you sure this isn't the man you saw?'

I looked down once more, but the answer remained the same. 'No,' I said. 'The man I saw was nowhere near six feet tall. And he looked like Walter.'

'OK, well, we're talking to the state police out there and checking with Immigration. If Archie Witcher has come home, we'll find him. But I really don't think the Witcher trail is going anywhere.'

He was right. 'Allan Keech and his gang,' I said. 'They were out last night. It could have been them I saw catching snakes. Why would they do that if . . .'

'Why didn't you phone me? I told you: if anything happens, phone me. Didn't being chased through underground rivers and abandoned chalk mines count as something happening?'

'It was late.' *And talking to you hurts, a little bit more every time I do it.*

'We've already established I'm nocturnal.' Matt half smiled. I tried to respond but couldn't quite manage it.

We were back in the village, turning into Bourne Lane. We drove down in silence, and Matt pulled up in front of my house.

'Thanks,' I muttered, as I reached to open the door. I felt a hand touch my arm. Matt didn't speak, and so I turned to look at him.

'I'm going to give you some advice,' he said. 'Strictly off the record.'

I waited.

'First of all, you should go and stay with your family for a few days. Take some leave from work and make

343

sure we know where to find you but, otherwise, keep away from the village. Give us time to sort this out.'

'OK.' It seemed reasonable enough, even sensible.

'Second, and this is very important, stay well clear of Sean North.' That was so totally out of the blue I needed a second or so to take it in.

'Sean North has been out of the country for six months,' I said. 'He only arrived back on Saturday. He can't possibly . . .'

'No, he didn't.'

'Yes, he drove straight from the airport to meet me and identify the taipan.'

'North passed through Heathrow Immigration a week last Wednesday. He's been in the UK ever since. And he didn't come from Indonesia, he came on a flight from Singapore.'

'So what's the—'

'Singapore was a transfer. His flight originated in Port Moresby.' Matt looked at me for a reaction, but the name didn't mean anything.

'It's the capital of Papua New Guinea,' he said.

36

THE DAY WAS GETTING HOTTER. OUTSIDE, THE SKY was cloudless, the pure china-blue of early summer. Weather forecasters were talking about thunderstorms later in the day, but there was no sign of them yet. Even the breeze had dropped, and the sun seemed higher in the sky than it had any business to be so early in the year. It was a relief to step inside the cool, incense-scented interior of our old church.

'*We receive the body of our sister Marion*,' declared Andrew, Bishop of Winchester, welcoming us from the chancel steps, '*with confidence in God, the giver of life, who raised the Lord Jesus from the dead*.'

The nave was packed – they don't bury archdeacons' wives every day – and heads turned as the elegant, flower-strewn coffin was wheeled slowly up the aisle. She came to a halt at the chancel steps, and we took our seats. Only then did I realize that nearly two hundred pairs of eyes would have been watching me follow my mother's coffin down the aisle.

'*Now is Christ risen from the dead*,' recited the

bishop, '*and become the first fruits of them that slept. For since by man came death, by man came also the resurrection of the dead.*'

The service was long; beautiful and moving, I'm sure, but I heard very little of it. I was staring at the floor tiles. Old, square, some were a rich terracotta-red, others a deeper brown. Into every sixth or seventh tile a simple but distinctive pattern had been carved: a circle with four sword-like points stemming from it, each equidistant from the others.

Four divergent points, converging on a common centre. Four people who touched my world had recently lost their lives or come very close to doing so. John Allington; Violet Buckler; tiny Sophia Huston; and a resident of the Dorset longhouse. Two of them had been old, villagers all their lives; but Sophia was a baby, her family new to the area. In the Poulson house, the taipan had been found in a child's bedroom. If there was a connection, a real-life equivalent of the circle at the centre, I simply couldn't see it; the victims, the manner in which they'd been attacked, appeared completely random.

And the more I thought about it, the more disorganized it all seemed. John Allington's death had been both deliberate and calculated. If Sean's surmise was right, he'd been whacked over the head, injected with adder venom and then left to drown. In baby Sophia's case the adder had just been left in her cot; she might have died, might not have. Quite arbitrary. A dead adder had been found in the Poulson house, and the elderly Dr Amblin had suffered a head injury. Had he been intended to die the same way as John Allington?

Hit over the head to immobilize him, before being injected with a lethal dose of adder venom? Had the killer been disturbed in the middle of the act, been forced to flee? And yet the taipan had been found in a child's bedroom. Which could have been tragic but thankfully hadn't been. Arbitrary. Disorganized.

But, with Violet, the killer had become calculating again. I was pretty certain she'd been bitten by a snake; the wound and the swelling on her body told me that. What I'd seen on her corpse squared more with what I knew about adder poisoning than with how Sean had described the taipan's toxicity. Had Violet too been injected with concentrated venom? I guessed the post-mortem would tell us that. On the other hand, Violet, older and more frail than John Allington, might not have needed such a high dose. And then there were the traces of blood and vomit on the pillow beside her head, the pillow that had probably snuffed out any lingering trace of life. There was nothing arbitrary about Violet's death that I could see. Her killer had made sure.

But, taking all the attacks together, it all seemed so . . . disjointed, chaotic even; no discernible pattern: the action of a confused, disordered mind.

If I'd wanted to kill four people, Matt Hoare, I'd have been a lot more bloody organized than that!

The church had fallen silent. And, for a split second, I wondered if I'd yelled out loud. But no one was paying any attention to me, and after a moment the organ struck up. The congregation stood to sing. The hymn was Vanessa's choice, one of Mum's favourites. I couldn't join in. I couldn't take my eyes off the floor tiles.

Four sword hilts. Four suspects. One: Allan Keech, aided and abetted by his brother's gang. They'd lied about me, been seen hanging round the Witcher house. They were a nasty bunch and I had little doubt they were responsible for the dead adder on my front door. But did I really believe them capable of murder?

Two: the old man, seen properly by nobody but me. He'd broken into my house and left a snake behind. It wasn't unreasonable to suppose he'd done the same in other homes. I'd assumed he was one of the Witcher brothers, because of his age, the physical resemblance and my sighting of him in the Witcher house. He couldn't be Saul or Harry – both were indisputably dead. He'd looked nothing like Archie. Ulfred had never existed. That left only Walter.

Three: Sean North had become Matt's favoured suspect. Matt didn't want me to be the killer; to my huge relief. But Matt was wrong about Sean. In my heart I knew it. Whatever Sean had been doing in PNG, he wouldn't treat snakes in the way they'd been abused in my village. People he might not care about one way or another, but Sean North would never be cruel to an animal.

And the fourth suspect? Well, that would be me. According to Tasker and Knowles, I was public enemy number one. I was psychotic, getting revenge for the damage inflicted upon me as a child; I was doing it for the attention I craved; I was a parasite, preying on the vulnerable elderly, exchanging comfort and companionship for their worldly goods. And there was evidence against me: the adders, both alive and dead, found on my property, my DNA all over Violet's body; not to mention the fake will.

The whole business was a weird combination of the disorganized and the calculated. The ability to milk adders and inject their venom using a hypodermic syringe suggested a certain degree of sophistication, not to mention handling the most venomous snake known to man. And yet the attacks at the Huston house, at the Poulson home, had been left to chance. Was I looking for a clever killer? Or the opposite?

And poor Bennie, left to fight with a venomous snake as both drowned. What on earth was that about? And why was anyone bothering with adders when they had a taipan or two at their disposal? Were they saving the Papuan snakes for the big finish?

By this time I think I was almost mesmerized by the pattern at my feet. Four sword hilts: four suspects, four victims. The circle at the heart of the pattern could represent the violence they'd all been subjected to. But the sword hilts, reaching out to each other, almost formed a second, outer circle. Was there a connection between the victims that I wasn't seeing? And would it point to the true culprit?

We stood again. My brother-in-law and five men from the parish lifted Mum on to their shoulders and carried her back down the aisle, out into the sunshine and then a few yards across the churchyard. A short, slow walk. Her last.

'. . . *ashes to ashes, dust to dust; in sure and certain hope of the resurrection to eternal life.*'

Dad read the prayers as his wife's body was lowered

into the ground. Vanessa threw a single white rose in full bloom on to the coffin. At a nod from their mother, Jessica and Abigail did the same, only theirs were roses in bud. It was the sort of detail that was important to Vanessa. I had nothing to give, so I crouched at her graveside and dug my hands into the soft, loamy pile of earth that lay ready.

'Clara, we've got these for you.'

Vanessa was kneeling at my side, the black silk of her new dress getting filthy. She was holding something out to me, and I could hardly see what . . .

'The girls picked them this morning,' she said. 'They're your favourites, aren't they? They always used to . . .'

I blinked and then reached out for the home-tied bouquet. Vanessa pulled me to my feet and, somehow, I managed to stretch out my arm, to open my hand. I didn't see the tiny, china-blue flowers fall.

Around me, people began following my example, getting their hands dirty with the sweet-smelling earth that would warm my mother's final home. Over and over again, as I sobbed without restraint on my big sister's shoulder, people stooped to grasp and throw the soil, and it seemed each of them was leaving a little something of themselves behind, to comfort Mum in her long and lonely sleep.

And when it was almost over, when the forget-me-nots could no longer be seen, I realized I did have something for Mum, after all. I could forgive her.

37

THE GUESTS HAD ALL GONE – EVEN VANESSA AND HER
family had returned home – leaving Dad and me
with a fridge stocked with leftovers and a house-
ful of regrets. After a late dinner that neither of us
wanted, Dad disappeared to write thank-you letters.
His study was at the rear of the house, overlooking the
garden. From there, he wouldn't see the police car
parked directly opposite the house. In spite of what
Matt had said, I knew I was still Tasker's prime suspect.

I went upstairs to my old room. On Matt's advice I'd
taken a week's leave from work, and already I was
wondering what I'd do with my time. Work, sleep and
run. It was all I knew how to do. I opened up my
laptop, found the Google search engine and typed in
Roman executions. As Matt had said, the Witcher trail
really wasn't going anywhere. There had to be another
way forward.

A lot of entries came up, but none that looked helpful. So I went back to the search facility and typed in
dog, snake, monkey. Without much hope, I pressed *Go*.

And saw the Latin phrase that I remembered immediately, even though it had been years since I'd last heard or seen it. *Poena cullei*: punishment by leather sack. Just as I'd remembered, the animals involved – snake, dog, monkey and cockerel – held a symbolic significance: the snake, typically a viper, was one of the most dreaded beasts in Ancient Rome, chosen because its birth often signalled the death of its own mother; the dog was a despised animal at the time, and *less than a dog* one of the worst insults any Roman could hurl at another; the cockerel, supposedly, was devoid of all filial affection; whilst the monkey symbolized the human in his most degraded condition. Despised? Degraded? Causing the death of one's own mother? It made a gruesome sort of sense; because *poena cullei* was the punishment inflicted upon those convicted of parricide: the unforgivable sin of murdering an immediate blood relative.

Not the most comforting thing to read, the evening of my mother's funeral.

But what possible relevance could it have to Violet? Did someone believe she'd killed a close relative? And how did it square with all the other stuff that had been going on? John Allington had been found in water; half in, half out of his garden pond. He'd been bitten by a snake (or not) then almost drowned. But . . .

I sat racking my brains for what felt like a long time, but any available answer was eluding me. The Witcher trail might not be going anywhere, but *poena cullei* wasn't leaving the starting block.

Two victims, plus two intended victims. Baby Sophia, I had to push to one side for the time being; I had no idea how she fitted into all this. But I couldn't help feeling that, setting the whereabouts of the taipan to one side, Ernest Amblin, the oldest member of the Poulson family, had been the real target of the killer that night.

I remembered screams breaking through silence, a family staggering from its home, children crying, father barely able to walk, grandfather deeply shocked. Just hours earlier, Ernest Amblin had been at Clive Ventry's house, one of five older people sitting together at the far end of the room, looking wary. No – not wary – scared.

Were old people the key to this after all? Tasker and Knowles had wondered if I was preying on the elderly, worming my way into their affections. What if they were right about old people being targeted, just wrong about the motive?

There had been four snake attacks – John Allington, Violet and Ernest Amblin were all old people. I remembered the tiles in church, the four sword-like shapes connected by a circle. Something had happened in these people's early past that linked them together.

It's no good asking me about that night, dear. I never really knew what happened.

There was something odd about that fire.

I was back to the fire of 1958, which had directly and indirectly killed four people and caused three of the Witcher brothers to leave the village. What had been going on that night that was still having repercussions fifty years later? I fumbled in my handbag and found my notepad. Days ago, at the library, I'd summarized the newspaper coverage of the fire and the deaths of Joel Morgan Fain and Larry Hodges. I checked what I'd written, then went downstairs, crossed the house, which felt too silent, and tapped on the door of Dad's study before pushing it open. He half turned towards me and tried to smile. Notepaper lay in front of him. He didn't appear to have written a word.

'Hi.'

'Hello, sweetheart. I'm sorry, I shouldn't have left you on your own, not tonight.'

My father's grief was bearing down on him, a huge weight pressing on his shoulders. It felt wrong to be thinking about, talking about, anything other than Mum, but what choice did I have? I too had a weight hanging over me.

'Can I ask you something?' I said, sitting down beside him. 'It's nothing to do with . . . family, but it could be important.'

He nodded, even seemed to brighten a little, as though he might welcome the distraction. I explained about the fire, about the men being killed, and then asked my father exactly what an American Pentecostal preacher might be doing in rural Dorset in the fifties.

'There was a lot going on in the United States round about the turn of the twentieth century,' Dad said, not quite meeting my eyes and with a slight frown on his face, as though digging up a long-buried memory. 'Break-away groups, splinter groups, revival meetings. A lot of the charismatic churches first made an appearance – certainly the Pentecostal movement dates from back then.'

'But this was fifty years later.'

He held up one hand, his time-honoured method of

shutting me up. 'It all died down after a while,' he said. 'Some of the groups were actively persecuted and then, round about 1945, we started seeing the various groups revive. Without doubt, the scale of the Second World War had something to do with the re-emergence. Some of them took different forms, but what they all had in common was, well, enthusiasm verging on fanaticism, a very close and literal interpretation of the Bible and a belief that God passed on some of his own supernatural abilities to mankind. Do you know what the charismata are?'

'Gifts, is that right? The heavenly gifts.'

Dad was nodding. 'These sects all believed in gifts given by God to man. Some groups called them signs, but they amount to the same thing.'

'And these gifts, signs, what are they exactly?'

Dad shrugged. 'Healing the sick, that sort of thing. Mostly pretty harmless. And speaking in strange tongues, that's always a popular one.'

'So when people in a church service jump up and start spouting what sounds like complete gibberish – that's one of the charismata, the signs?'

Dad smiled. 'There've been reams written about tongues. On the one hand, people argue that what St Paul really meant when he talked about the disciples speaking in strange tongues was they'd be able to speak in different languages and more easily spread the word of Christ.'

'That makes sense.'

Dad nodded. 'That school of thought believes the charismata were only given to mankind for a short period, in the years immediately after Christ's death; that it's nonsense to talk about them having relevance today. On the other hand, some people believe the charismata, the signs, were meant to be eternal and that what you call gibberish is actually the language of angels.'

'You know, that word "signs", it's ringing a bell.' I reached out and took back my notebook. I flicked through till I found the inscriptions from the graves of the four dead men. 'Look, on Larry Hodges' grave. *And these signs shall follow them that believe.*'

'That's the Gospel according to Mark, if memory serves. Yes, it certainly points to a charismatic sect operating in your village back then.'

'Was that unusual?'

'Unusual – certainly. But not unheard of. Whose headstone was this on?'

I leaned forward. Dad was looking at the inscription I'd copied from the stone on Reverend Fain's grave: *And he will come unto us as the latter rain that watereth the earth.* 'Oh, I remember now,' I said, 'the newspaper referred to that too, something about him being a member of the Church of the Latter Rain. Why, what does . . .' I stopped. I didn't like the look on my father's face. As I watched, he removed his reading glasses and sat back in his chair.

'Let's just say it's a name that rings warning bells,' he said at last. He picked up his glasses from the table and reached into his trouser pocket. I sat, waiting for him to go on. 'The Latter Rain Church started somewhere in Canada in the forties, so the timing seems right,' he said, retrieving a pocket handkerchief. 'This Reverend Fain could have been one of its early ministers.'

'I've never heard of Latter Rain. What does it mean?'

' "Latter rain" refers to the late-summer rain that brings a harvest to fruition,' my father explained, as he polished first one lens then the other. 'In this context, it means the final days before God brings the earth to an end. The people who founded the movement believed that in the last days of God's earth there would be a great outpouring of the signs, the charismata. And that's still a belief that underpins the work of the movement today.'

'It still exists?'

'Very much so. Over time, the original doctrine was moderated somewhat. Some of the more sensible members distanced themselves from it, rejected its more controversial aspects and went on to found new movements. It's generally accepted that these people had a fairly positive effect on the Charismatic and Pentecostal churches. The Church of the Latter Rain is alive and well. For the most part, I'd say it's run by godly, well-meaning people who hold firm beliefs and do a great deal of good work.'

'So if Reverend Fain was part of the Latter Rain Church, it wouldn't necessarily be a problem?'

Dad shook his head. 'What I've just told you relates to the Church as it exists today. Back in the forties, early fifties, the Church was in its infancy. Very different story.'

'Go on.'

'The movement attracted some very unstable types.

People who genuinely believed, or pretended to, that the end of the world was imminent. Its leaders called themselves the Elijah Company, supposedly God's chosen saints, sent to lead the righteous to glory at the end of days. They believed the normal rules of existence didn't apply any more.'

'It was an end-of-the-world cult?'

Dad replaced his glasses. ' "Cult" isn't a word I normally like to apply to any church but, in this case, I think your Reverend Fain could have been a dangerous man. The movement was known to indulge in some very odd, occult-like practices.'

He stood up. For a moment I wondered if he'd lost interest, if he'd decided that we'd had enough talk for the evening that wasn't about Mum, but he crossed his study and pulled open the double doors of one of the walk-in cupboards that line the south wall. Shelves were piled high with box files. After a couple of minutes he pulled a box from a pile and carried it back to the desk, blowing off dust as he did so.

'Haven't opened this in twenty years,' he said. 'I taught a course in the late seventies on the charismatic churches. Gathered some weird and wonderful literature together. One chap in particular stood out. Ah, here we go. What do you make of that?'

Dad handed me a black and orange pamphlet. The front cover, about the size of a hardback book, showed a crude drawing of a fire; the whole thing was just fifty pages long. It had been written by a Reverend Franklin Hall. I looked at the title on the cover, then up at Dad.

'Formula for Raising the Dead?' I queried. Dad was

half smiling. 'Probably one of the more extreme examples,' he said, 'but not untypical of the stuff that came out of the Latter Rain in its early days. We also have accounts of healing through fasting, a fascination with the zodiac, levitation, the sudden manifestation of supernatural fire and smoke. Oh, and driving out demons.'

I looked up. 'Exorcism?' I queried, remembering Violet's story of what had happened to Ulfred. And yet Ulfred, if Matt were to be believed, had never existed.

'According to Reverend Hall. He talked about a series of meetings in San Diego in 1946. Thousands of people went on long fasts, up to sixty days in some cases. According to Hall, demons were cast out, lunatics healed, cancers disappeared, cripples walked and the dead came back to life.'

'That's quite a claim to make.'

'Oh, he wasn't the first. A man called William Branham is generally considered the founder of the movement. His biography describes how he raised a child from the dead in Finland in the forties. The boy had been killed in a road accident. Branham brought him back.'

Brought him back. How could three simple, innocuous words make me feel so cold? If I had the power to bring someone back from the dead, would I do it?

I looked down at the pamphlet Dad had given me and began flicking through the pages again. 'So, how is it done?' I asked, wondering if I really wanted to know.

'Oh, there's no secret satanic formula,' said Dad.

'Anyone hoping to go down to the crypt and throw a party would be pretty disappointed. From what I can remember the central idea is that when Christ was talking about resurrection, he didn't mean a sort of spiritual resurrection but a physical one.'

' "I believe in the resurrection of the body," ' I said, automatically.

'Exactly,' nodded Dad. 'You have to see the argument. I say precisely that in church several times a week. Anyway, Reverend Hall takes it one step further and argues that, with sufficient faith and after undergoing a series of tests, we can bring about resurrection of the dead here on earth. We don't need to wait for the second coming.'

'And does he say how?'

'Well, he's a little vague on the details but, from what I can remember, the key seems to revolve around sufficient prayer and fasting prayer.'

'Fasting prayer?'

'A substantial period of time, sometimes several weeks, with no food, and prolonged prayer. Can't say I fancy it much myself.'

I was remembering what Matt had told me about Archie Witcher encouraging excessive fasting in his church in South Carolina, about the young girl who'd died. It seemed the legacy of the more extreme Latter Rain practices lived on.

'You look tired, sweetheart,' said Dad.

I smiled at him. I doubted I looked as tired as he did. 'One more thing, and I'll leave you in peace,' I said, pushing my notebook so it was directly under his nose.

'The other inscriptions, do they mean anything? Are they all part of this Latter Rain thing too?'

Dad glanced down for a few seconds. 'Pass me the big black book, will you?' he said. I leaned across the desk and picked up the large, leather-bound Bible that had sat in exactly the same place on Dad's desk for as long as I could remember. He began flicking through pages. 'Ah yes, I thought so. This one's from Mark. The two verses read, *And these signs shall follow them that believe; in my name shall they cast out devils; they shall speak with new tongues; They shall take up serpents; and if they drink any deadly thing, it shall not hurt them; they shall lay hands on the sick, and they shall recov*— What?' Dad broke off. He'd seen the look on my face. 'What's the matter, Clara?' he asked.

'What about the other one? The one on Peter Morfet's stone? *Behold, I give you the power.* Do you recognize it?'

'I think it's from Luke.' Dad started flicking through pages again. Here we are, 10:19: *Behold, I give unto you power to tread on serpents and scorpions, and over all the power of the enemy: and nothing shall by any means hurt you.* Now, are you going to tell me what all this is about?'

'Reverend Fain was a snake handler.'

Dad looked troubled. 'Snakes again?'

'There was an old lady, Violet, she talked about snakes in connection with the church. I had no idea what she meant, but now it's obvious. Fain could have brought venomous snakes with him from the States. Back in the fifties customs controls wouldn't have been anything like as strict as they are now. Something went wrong, and people died. Two men supposedly died of heart failure. I'll bet that's a cover-up. I'll bet they were bitten.'

'There's no record of the Latter Rain Church handling snakes. The people who do that belong to a different church entirely.'

'But they're both break-away movements from the Pentecostal Church. And it's one of the signs, isn't it? The power to take up serpents. If these people believed in an outpouring of the signs, then why not?'

'Clara, this was fifty years ago. What can it possibly have to do with—'

'Some people have long memories.' I stood up. 'Thanks, Dad, you're a star. I'm going to have a look on the internet, see what I can dig up.'

Dad sighed. 'The official name for snake-handling sects is the Church of God with Signs Following,' he said. 'Clara, are you sure this is what should be exercising your mind right now? We all need time to grieve.' He stopped for a second. 'Is there anything you want to tell me?'

I was desperate to get out of the room, but Dad's face was full of concern. 'I think I've been grieving for Mum for a long time,' I said. 'And I don't believe it's over yet. But just now, I need to think about something else. And no, there's nothing I need to tell you.'

Dad was far from happy but, short of physically restraining me, there was nothing more he could do. Back upstairs, my first internet search brought up hundreds of references to the Church of God with Signs

362

Following. The movement had sprung up, independently, in two distinct areas of the US. In the first decade of the twentieth century, the Reverend George Hensley, during a Sunday service in rural Tennessee, had taken up a live rattlesnake, and the practice had caught on.

At the same time, in Alabama, a preacher called James Miller had done much the same thing. The movement spread throughout the southern states of the US. George Hensley had died in 1955, of poisoning following a rattlesnake bite.

I remembered then Matt's quip about snake handlers dying of snake bite. And Dr Amblin's frantic questioning of Sean and me about where the taipan had come from. Could it have come from North America, he'd asked, before relaxing a little when we'd assured him it couldn't. Maybe I should have guessed before now what had been going on back in 1958.

Snake handling, casting out demons? Then I remembered something else. I grabbed my notebook and flicked through until I found the page with Reverend Joel Fain's biography. He'd studied classics at university. He would have known about the *poena cullei*. Fain had died fifty years ago, but his influence, it seemed, lived on.

It was nine o'clock in the evening. I knew Dad would go to bed some time within the next hour and then spend several hours reading. I walked to the window. The unmarked police car hadn't moved. Wandering the room, feeling the need to get out and yet trapped, I picked up my mobile and checked messages at home.

Unusually, there were several, all of which had been left early that morning. Two from Vanessa, one from Dad and one from the wildlife hospital, hoping my mother's service had gone well and looking forward to having me back at work, but not till I felt ready. The next was from Sally.

'Hi, Clara,' she said. 'I know you'll have a lot on your mind right now, but I just thought this was important. Ernest Amblin was discharged today, and I popped round to see him. We got to talking about Edeline, and Ernest said she used to clean for most of the wealthier families in the village and that she always stayed for hours longer than she was paid for. Seemed to crave company. But then there were weeks on end when she didn't show up for work, wasn't seen around the village at all. He had suspicions she had a serious mental disorder, but he could never persuade her into the surgery to talk about it. And, of course, in those days, people knew relatively little about mental illness. Anyway, Walter could have been trying to deal with her condition himself. Maybe even keeping her locked up. Perhaps there was a side to Walter most people didn't see.'

Sally's voice on the tape paused to take a breath.

'Anyway,' she went on, 'I hope it all goes well today. I bumped into Matt, and he said you'd be away for a few days. Let me know if I can do anything.'

Sally almost seemed ready to hang up, then, 'You know I said Edeline cleaned for people?' she went on. 'Apparently, she'd been heard to boast she had keys for most houses in the village. So, if people didn't change their locks, and if those keys are still in the Witcher property, it might explain how someone is getting in and out of houses.'

Sally said goodbye again and hung up. There were two more messages. A familiar and very distinctive voice rang out from the tape. 'Clara, Sean North here. It's eight o'clock Thursday morning . . .'

At eight o'clock that morning I'd already been arrested. I wondered when Sean had learned that he, too, was a suspect. 'Can you give me a call?' he went on. 'There's something I want to talk to you about. Or just drop by. I'll be home all day and most of tomorrow. See you.'

I pressed the button for the last message.

'Miss Benning, this is Denise Thompson here, from the Paddocks Hospice. So sorry not to have got back to you before, but we've had a few emergencies here and I'm afraid your message got lost under some files. Anyway, you were enquiring about a patient, Walter Witcher. Our visiting hours are between ten and twelve, and two and four. Walter hasn't been well for some time, though. I don't want to alarm you but, if you'd like to see him, I think you should come soon.'

38

FROM A HOOK IN THE KITCHEN, I TOOK KEYS TO mum's old car and to the garage, a quarter of a mile away, where it was kept. Parking on our busy street had always been difficult; once all four of us had cars, it had become impossible, hence the extra garage. I jogged down through the garden, opened the gate and then walked along the narrow riverbank until I could step into the next garden. Crossing our neighbour's lawn, I slipped through a small gate and out on to the street. I could see no movement in the police car. I ducked down a sidestreet and reached the garage.

Just over an hour later, I parked. The tide was in and I could hear waves crashing against rocks fifty yards below me. The small house seemed to be in darkness, but I thought I could see light flickering at the back. I walked round, my footsteps sharp on the gravel path. A wooden table and two chairs stood on the grass at the rear of the property. On the table a sheltered candle burned. It was a small garden, about twenty yards of lawn, a low fence and then the cliff edge. The tall man sitting at the table watched me approach. When I was close enough to see the moonlight glinting in the black of his eyes, he spoke.

'I'm not supposed to talk to you.' He raised a small bottle to his lips and drank.

'They told me that too,' I confessed.

He held up his bottle. 'Drink?' he asked.

'You didn't fly in from Indonesia on Saturday morning,' I said. 'You came from Papua New Guinea. The police know that's where the taipan came from.'

Sean leaned back further in his chair. 'They only know that because I identified it. Not that it makes any odds where I flew in from. You can't smuggle a live reptile on a plane any more.'

If Sean was a guilty man, he was incredibly adept at hiding it.

'So were you in Papua New Guinea?' I asked.

'Yes. I spent ten days there with my director, planning my next series. Six programmes in total, all based on the islands.'

'So why say you were in Indonesia?'

Sean sighed. 'There's a chap in the States, another herpetologist, who's been sniffing around after me for years. Every time he gets wind of a project I'm planning, he tries to get in first. Of course, he does everything on the cheap, so he can marshal his troops much faster than I can. He makes crap programmes but, once he's covered a subject, there's not much point in me doing it. Hence the fake Indonesian trip. Just trying to throw him off the scent.'

'Oh.'

'Trust me, Clara, when you look like I do, you can't smuggle a pair of nail scissors through customs, let alone a deadly snake. Casually dressed men with long hair get stopped and searched every trip. It's a standing joke with the film crew; they allow extra time to get me through airport security.'

He raised the bottle to his lips again, his eyes not leaving mine. The police would be able to check what he'd told them, speak to his director, find out if the rival herpetologist really existed. I didn't need to. I knew he was telling the truth.

'Drink?' he repeated.

I thought about it. For a split second. 'Yes, please.'

He stood, gestured me to sit and disappeared inside the house. A light flicked on, and through the half-open back door I could see a very small, neat kitchen. I turned to look out over the ocean as I heard the fridge door open and close. Gulls were flying north, away out to sea, casting dark shadows over the lawn as they passed.

The air was cool after the heat of the day, and very still. I heard Sean come back and sit down. He held out a glass and passed me the bottle of amber-coloured liquid. I put the glass down and drank straight from the bottle, as I'd seen him doing. The sharp, dry, almost insubstantial taste hit the back of my throat, taking me by surprise. I'd expected something richer, stronger somehow.

'I have wine in the fridge, if you prefer,' said Sean.

'This is fine. I like it,' I replied, truthfully. After a second I added, 'My first drink.'

'Of the evening?' Sean had pulled his chair round so that he was sitting directly opposite me. I carried on watching the dark sky, although the gulls had disappeared.

'Of my life,' I replied.

Sean remained silent, but when I turned to him he was watching me. 'My mother drank,' I said. 'For years, since before I was born. She gave up a career as a professional musician to marry a country clergyman twenty years her senior. Then found she couldn't cope with clerical life.'

Still Sean said nothing, but his eyes didn't leave my face. It must have been the ever-deepening darkness that stopped me minding.

'She tried very hard,' I said, wanting to be fair to Mum. 'She had treatment, was in and out of clinics for years. Sometimes she'd go for months without a drink, but sooner or later she'd always feel a need that was overwhelming.'

Sean's hand settled over my own, and I jumped at the suddenness of the touch. 'It's getting cold,' he said, misinterpreting my shivering. 'We should go in.'

'No, no, I'm fine,' I said, quickly. 'I have to go in a minute. There was just something I wanted to ask you.'

Reluctantly, it seemed, he peeled his hand away from mine. 'Ask away,' he said.

I explained my theory that an American preacher had been practising snake handling in my village church back in the late fifties and that something had gone badly wrong one night, leading to the destruction of the church and the deaths of four men.

'It's a long shot, I know,' I told him, 'but I think what's been going on recently might somehow be linked to what happened back then. It's the older people, who would have been around in 1958, who seem to be the targets.'

'And if you can find out more, it might point to who's responsible now?'

'I saw a programme you made once on snake handling,' I said. 'And I wondered whether you knew anything important.'

'Such as?'

'Well, how it's done, for one thing. How do these people handle rattlesnakes and not get bitten all the time?'

'They do get bitten. Deaths are quite common.'

'Yes, but not as often as you'd expect. And there's all sorts of speculation, about whether the rattlesnakes have their venom glands removed, whether they're milked of venom just before the service, whether they're drugged. Did you consider that when you were filming?'

'Of course. At one church they let us examine the snakes before the service. Ten full-size rattlesnakes, everything intact, not interfered with in any way. All quite deadly. We watched them being held high, strung around necks, passed from one worshipper to the other. I'm sure some of the churches fake their stunts, but not all of them. This one didn't.'

'How? How do they do it?'

Sean smiled. 'Well, I've got a theory. Want to hear it?'

I'd almost smiled back before I stopped myself. 'Yes, please.'

'Ever heard of the Ophites?'

'The what?'

'Ophites. Also known as the Serpent People. They were a Gnostic sect in North Africa round about AD 1000.'

'Gnostic ... as in the early heretics who wanted greater spiritual knowledge than the established church thought good for them?'

'Clergyman's daughter, huh? Well, there were umpteen of these sects around at the time, but what they all had in common was the importance they attached to the serpent in the Adam and Eve story. For them, the biblical Tree of Knowledge in the Garden of Eden directly symbolized gnosis, or knowledge. And the serpent was the guardian of the Tree; guardian of knowledge, if you like. For them, the serpent symbolized understanding and enlightenment.'

'OK, I think I'm following. This is completely opposite to the biblical version, which has the serpent representing the devil.'

'Indeed. The Ophites saw the serpent as the hero of the story and the God-figure as the evil one, trying to deny Adam and Eve access to knowledge.' He leaned back in his chair, balancing on two legs. 'If you think about it in an abstract sense,' he went on, 'you can see their point. On the one hand, you're being offered understanding, wisdom. On the other, you're kept in ignorance like a child. Which sounds evil to you?'

'You need to have this conversation with my father.'

'I look forward to it. Anyway, these sects venerated the serpent, even worshipped it. As far as they're concerned, the snake taught Adam and Eve the truth in Eden. And, according to a number of accounts, snake handling played a part in their rituals – snakes wrapped around the sacramental bread, that sort of thing.'

I opened my mouth to interrupt. It was interesting, but I couldn't see where Sean was going.

'Another reason why the Ophites weren't popular with the orthodoxy,' said Sean, not giving me a chance to speak, 'was their rather licentious behaviour. It's not hard to see the symbolic significance of the snake in that sort of activity. Do you want to come inside? It's really quite cold.'

Once again, Sean tried to stand, but I held up a hand to stop him.

'How is this relevant? Modern snake-handling sects don't venerate the snake. For them, it's a symbol of the devil, which they can overcome if their belief is strong enough.'

'Yes, and that's where they're fundamentally mis-guided. But even though their motives are confused, when they handle snakes, they're tapping into some-thing primitive.'

'Huh?'

'The tradition of snake handling within a religious setting goes back thousands of years. Long before George Hensley picked up a rattler, the Hopi people in North America were performing annual snake-handling rituals to guarantee healthy crops. You find references to snake handling in many parts of Africa and Asia. And Olympias, the mother of Alexander the Great, was reputed to be a snake handler.'

372

I thought for a second.

'OK, I get that. But my question is how? How do they do it without being harmed?'

'We're back to Gnosticism. Modern Gnostic churches – the spiritual descendants of the Ophites, if you like – don't handle snakes themselves, but I think they've come closest to understanding how it's done.'

'Go on.'

'Gnostic churches emphasize learning through personal experience. And they place great importance on connecting to something they call the Pleroma.'

'Sean, you're losing me.'

I could hardly see his face by this stage, but a glint in his eyes told me he was smiling again. 'Hang on in there,' he said. 'The Pleroma represents everything divine in our universe; a sort of inner core at the heart of everything. If you've tapped into the Pleroma, you can see and experience the divine in all things. My theory is that these snake handlers, the successful ones, are experiencing the divinity within the snake. And in doing so, they become as one with the snake. Just as countless other cultures around the world have done. That's why they're not harmed.'

'Oh my.'

He was grinning at me now. 'Take your time,' he said.

'I'm beginning to wish I hadn't asked. So, what you're telling me is that snake handlers, without knowing it, are tapping into some form of cosmic, divine energy that exists within snakes?'

'I knew you'd get there in the end.'

'Oh, come on . . .'

373

'Clara, it's only Western civilizations, dominated by the Judaeo-Christian religions, that see the serpent as evil. Name me any other culture – Hindu, Greek, Norse, Native North American – and the snake will make its appearance in the mythology more frequently than just about any other animal on the planet and nearly always as a positive force. It represents wisdom, immortality, life, fertility, knowledge.'

My brain couldn't absorb much more. 'They're just snakes, Sean. Reptiles without legs.'

Sean was shaking his head. 'So why do cultures all over the world incorporate a serpent into their creation myths? There are umpteen gods depicted in serpent form, Quetzalcoatl in Central America, Aidophedo in West Africa; in Cambodia, you see stone sculptures of snakes guarding temples. Oh, and there's a Greek myth that talks about Asclepius, who had his snake familiars crawl across the bodies of sick people at night and lick them back to health.'

'That's gross.'

'That same myth talks about people getting second hearing and second sight if their ears or eyes are licked by a snake. Why do you think a snake is one of the symbols of modern medicine?'

I sighed. 'Fascinating though this is, it's not helping me find out how our village church burned down.'

'Ah, glad you mentioned it. Because, in spite of what you might have read in Genesis, the snake as a positive symbol can be found throughout Christian teachings.'

'Where?'

'Gospel according to John. *Just as Moses lifted up the*

374

serpent in the desert, so must the Son of Man be lifted up.'

'That's a bit nebulous.'

'Book of Numbers. *And the Lord said to Moses, make thee a fiery serpent, and set it upon a pole: and it shall come to pass, that everyone that is bitten, when he looketh upon it, he shall live.*'

'Still not—'

'Gospel according to Matthew. *Be ye therefore wise as serpents, and harmless as doves.* That's Christ himself speaking, by the way.'

'OK, OK, you made your point.'

'You've heard of Gematria, the practice of assigning numbers to letters and working out a word's numerical value?'

'Hmm,' I said. I hadn't, but there was a limit to how ignorant I wanted to sound.

'If you use the Hebrew Gematria, the numerical value of the word for serpent is 358. Guess what the value of the word for messiah is.'

No point delaying the inevitable. 'It's 358, isn't it?'

'Yup. Ever been to Milan?'

'No.'

He stood up. 'Come inside. I've got something to show you.'

Totally bemused now, I waited until Sean had picked up both beer bottles and then followed him into the house. We walked though the kitchen and turned right. At the end of the corridor he pushed open a door and gestured me inside. It was his bedroom.

I stood, on the threshold, staring at the huge picture

above his bed. I stepped into the room and moved closer. It was a reproduction of a stained-glass window; an image of Calvary hill. A huge cross took up most of the centre; prone figures lay at its feet, but no Christ figure hung from the cross. Instead, entwined around it was a massive serpent.

'I think the original window is in a museum now, but it was made for the Duomo itself,' said Sean, sounding pleased with himself. 'Behold . . . the Crucified Serpent.'

39

ICOULDN'T TAKE MY EYES OFF THE IMAGE ABOVE THE
bed. The snake as a symbol for Christ? I'd had more
Christian teachings than most people, but I'd never
heard of such a thing before.

'It's astonishing,' I said.

'Does it help?

'I'm not sure.'

I moved closer to the picture, sensing Sean following
me. Even without his lecture, I'd known something
already of the immense impact of the snake or serpent
upon worldwide mythology, but I'd had no idea its
reach had gone so far. The snake curled around Christ's
cross. It was almost blasphemous. And yet the window
had been created for one of the most famous churches
in Europe.

'The Sistine Chapel has a fresco featuring the serpent
on a staff,' said Sean. 'So does a famous painting by
Rubens. Strictly, those depict the Brazen Serpent,
the idol Moses made in the desert, but the images
are very similar. Serpent on a staff, serpent on a cross.

It's easy to see how one could have led to the other.'

'And there are people who can do what you said, become one with snakes?' I asked.

'I've seen it many times.'

I took my eyes away from the picture for a second. 'Can you do it?'

'Nope. Been bitten more than I can count. But I've seen a tribal leader string three Papuan blacksnakes around the half-naked body of a young girl the night before her wedding. She was in some sort of drug-induced trance, but he wasn't. The snakes didn't touch her or him. I've watched young Indian kids carry deadly cobras around for hours on end while the medicine men do their thing. These snake handlers you're talking about are probably one of the best examples. Entire congregations pass these snakes from one to the other. People do get bitten, usually when they're distracted or have an attack of nerves, but even then not nearly as often as they should. I doubt I'll ever be able to explain it fully, but in some circumstances – particularly within a religious context – a connection can be made between man and serpent.'

It would be a powerful thing to witness, I acknowledged. Even more powerful to experience. If Reverend Joel Fain had had the sort of ability to connect with snakes that Sean was describing, if he'd been able to transmit it to his congregation, it would have given him a pretty powerful hold over them. Big question now: what else might he have persuaded them to do?

Behind me, Sean moved, and I stepped back from the picture. Only then did I really look around. The room we were standing in wasn't large. The floor was polished oak, the bed the only piece of furniture. One wall was glass and, in daylight, would give a fabulous view over the ocean. Quite something to wake up to.

I turned abruptly and almost stepped into Sean, who was still looking at the picture. He turned too and walked back through the house. I followed, feeling my heartbeat slow a fraction as we left the bedroom behind.

Along the corridor we went, past the kitchen. Sean opened a door, stood back and allowed me to pass through into the main room of the house. I paused on the threshold and turned back to look at him. He was trying not to look smug but not quite managing it. He reached up and pressed a wall switch. At once the lighting changed from soft, white light to the deep crimson shadows of infra-red. I moved into the centre of the room and stood, just taking it all in.

'Wow,' I said, turning round slowly. 'It's fabulous.'

The room was large, stretching the full width of the house and taking up most of its length. I realized that the other rooms – kitchen, bedroom, bathroom – had deliberately been kept as small as possible and purely functional in layout. This room was what the house was all about.

As in the bedroom, one wall was glass and looked out towards the sea. Covering completely the three remaining walls and stretching from floor to ceiling were huge, glass-fronted vivaria. Their floors were strewn with deep red sand, brightly coloured rocks and sun-bleached driftwood. Intricate fronds and the broad, velvet leaves of tropical plants reached everywhere. Concealed lighting lent shades of emerald, gold, yellow to the numerous greens of the foliage, and along the rear walls were reproductions of ancient cave paintings.

The cages, with their tropical planting, their rock formations and driftwood sculptures, would have been fascinating even without the long, elegant creatures that hovered, hung on branches, coiled around rocks, watching us.

I walked towards the largest of the cages. The snake inside, which must have been nearly three metres long, rose off the ground until its head was almost on a level with mine. We held eye contact. The snake's scales were gold, unusually large on the back of its head; an inverted white chevron pattern ran down its back. Without taking its eyes off mine, the snake swayed an inch or so to the right, then back to the left. I had to fight an urge to sway with him. I realized my eyes were stinging and that I hadn't blinked for several seconds.

'Is this a cobra?' I asked, in a low voice.

'This is Taka. He's a four-year-old king cobra,' Sean confirmed. 'He was captured by Customs and Excise when he was just a baby. He'd been badly injured in the journey, and none of the zoos who might have taken him felt they could nurse him. I think he likes you.'

'How can you tell?'

'He's not hooding.'

I walked on, circling the room, past a slender, bright-green snake that Sean explained was a white-lipped pitviper from the tropical forests and bamboo groves of Asia. In a cage that contained a lot of water, I saw an

African rhinoceros viper, a metre and a half long, brightly coloured with blue, yellow and scarlet scales, and with two horn-like protuberances on the tip of its snout. In the infra-red light the snakes were more active than I'd ever seen in reptile houses; as I walked I was conscious of slow, graceful movement all around me.

When I'd seen and admired and been introduced to all seven snakes that shared Sean's living area, I turned to him. For the first time since I'd arrived, he'd stopped looking at me, apparently as mesmerized as I was, even though he saw the snakes every day.

'Why do you like snakes so much?' I asked him. At the question he turned back to me.

'They're the most compellingly beautiful creatures on earth,' he said, as though it were obvious.

'Yes, they're pretty but—'

'Pretty?' He put his arm around my shoulders and gently walked me over to the rhinoceros viper. 'They're like diamonds,' he said. 'The closer you get, the more stunning they become.' We stood watching the snake slide slowly around a log.

'Beautiful but cold,' I said, moving on to the next cage, forcing his arm to fall to his side. 'They have no facial expressions, they're solitary, exhibit no responsiveness to their owners and they get stressed when handled.' I was playing devil's advocate – privately I was in complete agreement that the snakes were fabulous, I just liked hearing Sean talk about them. 'They've never really done it for me,' I finished.

'That's a gender thing. Only a man can really appreciate a snake.'

I took a sideways glance at him, wary of a leer or a crude Freudian joke. He was perfectly serious, his eyes fixed on a tiny harlequin snake that had half buried itself in some deep sand.

'Snake keepers are invariably male,' he went on. 'I think we're in awe of their power.'

Sean seemed almost hypnotized by the curling and coiling of the small snake. If he hadn't carried on talking, I'd have thought he'd forgotten me.

'And they're such awesome hunters,' he went on. 'Such speed and power. There's nothing short of miraculous about it. The prey just disappears, flesh, bones, fur and all. They almost seem to personify death. And then they shed their own skins and emerge all shiny and new. Like reincarnation. Life and death. It's as fundamental as that.'

He turned to me then. 'And you prefer lizards.' He was teasing me, but gently – he didn't really seem to mind that I preferred other, less strange, reptiles.

'In the wild,' he said, glancing back at the striped tail-tip peeking out of the sand, 'even in the places where I go, it's incredibly difficult to spot a snake. They're so fast, so shy. Only in captivity can we truly appreciate them. But they're never ours.'

'You're attracted to the mysterious,' I said.

He looked back. 'Every time,' he said.

I felt my face glow warm. 'Where's the taipan?' I asked, glancing round, as though I might have missed it.

'Hissy Clara's in an annexe I have at the back. Funnily enough, someone tried to break in there last night.'

What?

'Oh, don't worry,' he went on, seeing my shocked face. 'I'm very well alarmed. Whoever it was scarpered before I'd even got out of bed.'

'Thank you,' I said. 'For showing me.'

'Pleasure. Have a seat.'

There were only two chairs, directly in the middle of the room, both large, covered in leather, on swivel bases. A small table stood between them. I imagined Sean sitting here, as night fell, watching the ocean and then turning to look at the even more amazing view inside the room. I found myself wondering who usually sat in the other chair. I lowered myself on to the soft leather and discovered that it's possible to be nervous in the presence of a man and yet not want to leave. Then a document on the coffee table caught my eye. I picked it up.

'What's this?'

Sean swung round on the other chair to face me. 'That would be your CV,' he replied.

'I know what it is,' I snapped, unreasonably. 'What's it doing here?'

'Roger emailed it to me,' he said. 'Although that's not quite what you asked me, is it?'

I waited, knowing I was glaring at him and not even trying to stop.

'Before we both got hauled up to account for ourselves to the local constabulary, I left a message for you to contact me. I don't know if—'

'I got it,' I interrupted. 'Just this evening. Why do you have my CV?'

'I always check people's background and

qualifications before I offer them a job. I understand it's normal practice in recruiting circles.'

It took a moment to sink in. 'What sort of job?' I asked, thinking I must have misunderstood. 'Do you need a researcher?'

'Well, that's part of it certainly. But what I really need is a co-presenter. The director wants a young female, and a qualified vet would be ideal. One thing the taipans in PNG are doing is attacking livestock, cattle, sheep, goats. If they can be treated, it will save the islanders a fortune. You'll have to do some screen tests, of course . . .'

I'd lowered my eyes to the document in my hand. I wasn't listening any more. Something very cold had formed in the pit of my stomach. 'You want me to appear on television?' I interrupted.

'Well, let's be very clear, I'd still be the star, but, yes, there would be a bit of on-camera work.'

'Are your ratings falling?' I said, quietly, without looking up.

'Sorry?'

'Venomous snakes losing their ability to shock, are they?'

'Clara . . .'

I turned to face him, saw his eyes open wider with alarm and was glad of it.

'I've got a better idea,' I spat at him. 'Why not employ a burn victim? Someone who's had a serious frying. They could look really gross on camera.' I was on my feet. I couldn't remember standing up, but the coffee table was lying on its side between us. Sean had risen too and taken a step back, looking as though a favourite dog had just turned vicious.

'Or – I've got it – someone with no arms and legs,' I went on, hearing my voice rise. 'They can slither around on the ground – just like a snake. Or what about—' Around me, the snakes were reacting to the sudden, unusual amount of movement, seeking hiding places.

Without my seeing him move, Sean had crossed the distance between us and taken hold of my upper arms. 'Stop it,' he said, quietly.

I tugged first one arm free and then the next. 'Thank you for the drink and the information,' I said. 'I won't be bothering you again.' I pulled away and set off for the door. I managed two steps before he'd got hold of me again.

'No, you bloody well don't. Just calm down and listen to me.'

'I want to leave.'

'And I don't give a fuck. You're being stupid and offensive. And you're going to hear me out if I have to keep you here all night.'

I took a deep breath. 'How the hell can someone who looks like me appear on television?' I yelled at him, all control gone. 'I spend my entire life trying to avoid being stared at, and you want to beam me on to people's television screens, so perfect strangers can be made to feel ill just by looking at me. What the hell were you thinking of? How can you . . .'

And that was it. Battery empty. I don't think I knew what exhaustion was until that moment.

'Are you done?' asked Sean.

I didn't answer. Hadn't the energy. I was done.

'My ratings are absolutely fine,' he continued. Throughout my tantrum Sean had remained annoyingly, humiliatingly calm. 'We just all think another presenter will broaden the show's appeal. If you're sensitive about your scar – because that's all it is, you know, a scar – we can shoot you to avoid it ever showing. We can film over your shoulder, from the right side, in half-profile. We'd let you see footage and approve it before we edit to the final cut.'

I wasn't struggling any more, but he wasn't taking any chances. He had me in a firm grip.

'I think, after a while, you'd get much more relaxed about it, but that would be up to you. I'm offering you this chance because you're a qualified vet and because you've experience of working with tropical reptiles. And, yes, partly because of how you look. I can't be the only man in the world who thinks you're gorgeous.'

Complete silence in the room. I think even the snakes were listening.

. . . that's all it is, you know, a scar. I can't be the only . . .

It was ridiculous. He was taunting me for some unfathomable, cruel reason of his own. There was simply no point arguing further. I should just turn and leave. His grip on my shoulders loosened, and that was the moment. For the last glare, the spin on the heels, the walk out of the house. His left hand reached out and, with one finger, he traced the line of my cheek down the right side of my face.

'You're beautiful,' he said. He was whispering by this

386

time. Then the finger was moving again, down under my chin, and up the crumpled, puckered flesh of the left side. 'And you're flawed. That makes you very intriguing.'

The room became dark, and the only sound in my ears was the roar of the ocean, fifty yards below us. It wasn't until later, when he pulled back a fraction, that I realized he'd kissed me.

Trembling with shock, I had no idea what to do or say. I didn't even know what to think. His arms were around me, his body just inches from mine, our cheeks still touching. I'd forgotten he smelled of tropical forests at dawn. 'Will you stay?' he whispered.

'Why?' I managed, through a throat that felt as if it had been sewn up. And my stupid question shattered the moment like a hammer through crystal.

Sean laughed, and his arms fell to his sides. He took a small step backwards, shaking his head. 'Well, I was hoping we'd make love, but if you have something else in mind . . .'

My hands flew to my face. What kind of an idiot must he think me?

'Another time maybe?' suggested Sean.

'I'm sorry. I have to go. I shouldn't have . . .' I turned, and this time nothing stopped me. I half ran through the room and into the kitchen. My hand was on the back door when he called out.

'Hold up. There's something I need to give you.'

I stopped, hardly daring to face him, but I could hear him opening the fridge door. Out of the corner of my eye, I saw him holding something out to me. It was a small box containing several tiny vials. I took it, read the label and looked up at him for confirmation.

'This is the recognized anti-venom for taipan bites,' he said. 'I got it unofficially from a mate at London Zoo. If you are bitten, you need to get to hospital. If you can't – well, I suppose you can administer it yourself if you have to – you have syringes and stuff?'

I nodded.

'This is all we can rely on for the time being,' Sean continued. 'I've been in touch with London and Liverpool poison centres, but they don't keep it in stock. They've sent for some, now they know there are un-authorized taipans in the country, but it could be days before it arrives. Keep this cold and keep it close to you. If you get bitten, you have hours – you know that, don't you?'

'Sean, you need this. You're the one looking after the taipan.'

'Hissy Clara is perfectly safe. I can handle a snake in a cage. But I've had time to check the skin you gave me. It's definitely from a taipan, but not from Clara. It's quite a bit bigger and the scale patterns are different. There could easily be another taipan somewhere in your village. Please be very careful.'

I left the house and walked slowly back to the car. Sean walked with me, not speaking, but, as he opened the door for me and I climbed inside, he put one hand over mine on the steering wheel.

'In Papua New Guinea, taipans are starting to be seen around houses,' he went on. 'They seem to have worked out that where there're people, there's food. It's one of the things we'll be investigating when we go out there.'

'But snakes avoid human contact.'

'Usually they do. But there are parts of Asia where snakes are seen a lot around villages. And now, in PNG, it's becoming quite a problem.'

'So if there is another one here, we can't just expect it will keep to the wilds.'

'Wouldn't count on it.'

I took a moment to think about the implications of deadly snakes haunting houses.

'Be careful,' he said again. I nodded, and he stepped back, closing the door. The window was open, though, and there was no mishearing his next words.

'The offer stands, by the way.'

'Which?' I replied, without thinking. 'The job or . . .'

Sean's eyebrows drew together, but his lips were smiling. 'I think you're flirting with me, Miss Benning. Now, that is definitely progress.' He turned and walked back towards the house. 'Both,' he called over his shoulder. 'Both offers remain open indefinitely.'

I drove for nearly an hour and then pulled into an old farm track where I knew I wouldn't be disturbed. I climbed on to the back seat and pulled my coat around me. I lay, listening to the sounds of the night and thinking, not about snakes or ghosts, but about something I'd filed away at the very back of my memory. Something that happened nearly seventeen years ago.

I'd been at secondary school, and had come out of the cubicle in the girls' lavatory to find six older boys waiting for me. Two of them held a struggling twelve-year-old. Tears were pouring down his face. As three of the boys came for me, I noticed one of the girls from my class keeping watch at the door. Another girl I knew came out of a cubicle, saw what was going on, dropped her eyes to the floor and scurried out. The boys dragged me back against the wall.

'Come on, kiss her and we'll let you go,' urged one of them.

The boy, tiny and feeble though he was, needed four bigger, stronger boys to be dragged close enough to me. Even then, one of them had to take hold of his head and force it towards me, press the tear-stained, snot-ridden face against mine. My own head was pinned tight, strong hands gripping my hair. I hadn't struggled; there had been no point. I'd closed my eyes and gone away to another place. When I opened them again, the cloak-room was empty. I washed my face and went back to class.

All the time I remained at that school, the twelve-year-old never looked in my direction again. Neither did any of the others treated in the same way. Ironically enough, I couldn't say I was bullied at school; I was the torture inflicted on other victims.

It went on for years, and I never once told a soul. But to this day, I only have to hear the word 'kiss' for that vile memory, and all the subsequent ones, to come racing back. Neither in real life nor on the TV screen can I bear to watch people kissing. I can hardly even bring myself to read the word in a book, because when those memories start banging on the cellar door, my entire body wants to curl up in shame.

My eyes were closing and the stars becoming blurred. As I drifted off to sleep I was remembering, but I wasn't in the girls' lavatory any more; I was back in the house on the Undercliff. My head was filled with the sound of waves breaking over rocks, the rough skin of a man's face was pressed against mine, and the bitterness of seventeen years was fading away.

When I woke the sun was high in the sky. Time to visit the man we'd all believed was dead.

40

PREPARING MYSELF FOR ANOTHER DEPRESSING OLD-folks' home with substandard hygiene and an ambience that sucked the spirit right out of you, I was pleasantly surprised by my first view of the Paddocks Hospice. It stood, high on the Downs, over-looking a river valley.

Just before turning into the driveway I passed a stud farm and, as I got out of the car, I saw that the land around the hospice had been fenced in and turned into paddocks for the animals. Four horses grazed in the field immediately below the garden. Another three were in the field to my right. A slender grey mare, who only needed a horn to be the perfect mythical unicorn, started cantering up towards me. The other horses joined in and, as they approached, I could feel the ground trembling beneath their weight.

I walked to the main entrance. A group of patients were sitting on a terrace, watching the horses and enjoy-ing the morning unfold before them.

Pulling open the large double doors, I went inside.

. . . that's all it is, you know, a scar.

The woman at the reception desk looked up and smiled.

I can't be the only man in the world who thinks you're gorgeous.

Concentrate!

Five minutes later a hospice nurse was leading me through a modern building filled with natural light. Most of the windows were open. I could smell fresh coffee and recently mown grass.

'This is a lovely place,' I said, as we turned a corner and walked along a short corridor.

'Thank you,' my guide replied. 'We've only been open six months. Walter was one of our first guests.'

'In your message, you hinted that he was very sick.'

She stopped in front of a white-painted door and touched the handle. 'He is, I'm afraid. When he arrived here he'd just recovered from a very severe bout of pneumonia. Frankly, we didn't expect him to last this long. You're not a relative, are you? He said he didn't have any family.'

I shook my head. 'Just a friend,' I said. 'From the same village.'

'Well, it will be nice for him to have a visitor at last. Six months, and you're the first.'

She sounded disapproving, but any defence I could have made would have taken far too long. Although, now that it came to it, I found myself very nervous about opening that door and walking inside.

'Do your patients ever leave the hospice?' I asked, not sure how to frame the question uppermost in my mind.

393

'For short visits. It's just that someone said they saw Walter in the village.'

Her head was shaking emphatically. 'Completely impossible, I'm afraid. Walter hasn't walked since he came here. He can't even stand unaided. He's quite *compos mentis*, though, you'll be able to have a chat. Right, then. Good morning, Walter, a young lady to see you.'

And there he was. My old friend. My ghost. My prime suspect in the terrible crimes being played out around my home. Oh, Walter, I should have known better.

His pale-blue eyes watched me approach the bed. He was just as I remembered. Plain, good-natured face with a rather large nose and chin, wispy strands of grey hair around his crown and ears. The same, but smaller somehow, maybe a little thinner; and fainter, as though his life essence were fading away, hour by hour.

'Hello,' I managed, feeling my throat fill up and my jaw start to ache. 'Do you remember me?'

I heard the sound of a door closing and knew that Walter and I were alone. His lips were moving. He was trying to speak, but the sounds were struggling to get out. I guessed his vocal chords were out of practice. I bent closer, until I was leaning over the bed.

'I think that rabbit you fixed up will have had its way with my lettuce by now,' he croaked.

A cry slipped out of me that was half laugh, half sob. I sat down in a chair at Walter's bedside and took hold of his hand. I remembered it being large, a gardener's hand. It was still large, but very weak.

'I was in your garden the other night,' I said. 'It's looking very beautiful. A lot of the roses are out. And you can smell them as you come down the lane. Especially the yellow one that grows round the gate.'

I carried on for a few moments, sensing that news of his precious garden would mean more to Walter than anything. His lips formed a faint smile and his head nodded a few times. When I'd run out of things to say about the garden, I apologized for not having visited him before.

'I had no idea you were here,' I said, knowing I could hardly tell him his own wife had spread the premature news of his death. 'I don't think anyone knows. I'm sure there are people who'd like to come and see you, if they did.'

'Edeline died, you know,' he said, and I wondered if he'd guessed what she'd done. 'Last November.'

'I know, I'm very sorry.' I tried to push my fury with Edeline to one side, to think back, remember exactly what she'd said to me. Had she actually used the word 'dead'? Had we all just got the wrong end of the stick?

'I saw her grave in the churchyard a few days ago,' I said, in a sudden fit of contrition for maybe misjudging Edeline. 'Would you like me to put some flowers on it for you? I remember her telling me she had some of the roses from the garden in her wedding bouquet. She'd like that, don't you think? Or, I could get them from a shop – whichever . . .'

Walter was nodding at me. 'Red ones,' he said. 'From near the fruit trees. She always liked red. So lovely with her dark hair.'

The Edeline I remembered had steel-grey hair, but I smiled and agreed that, yes, that must have been very striking.

'She was a very good-looking woman when I married her,' said Walter, who once again, it seemed, had guessed what I was thinking. 'Best-looking girl for miles around. A lot like Archie. Both tall, lots of dark hair, deep brown eyes. Those two got the good-looking genes of the family.'

But Edeline and Archie had been related by marriage, hadn't they? How could they share genes? Walter must have seen my puzzlement.

'Edeline was our cousin. Did you know that?'

I shook my head. I hadn't.

'Aye, first cousin. Her mother and our dad were brother and sister. Some people said we shouldn't marry on account of that, but it happened quite a lot in those days. We couldn't get about the way they do now. Couldn't meet so many people.'

'I understand,' I said. 'Cousins still do marry.'

'All I thought about was how bonny she was. And how I could get her to marry me and not Archie or any of the others that were after her.'

As he spoke, something in Walter's face darkened. He wasn't looking at me any more, but towards the open window.

'I think they were probably right, though,' he went on. He seemed lost in thought. Old thoughts; not pleasant ones. Then he looked back at me. 'We never had any children, so maybe . . .'

He left the thought hanging. I waited, in case he

wanted to carry on speaking, but he seemed content to hold my hand and stare out of the window. After a while, I thought it safe to risk a question.

'Walter, did any of your brothers have children? Do you have any nieces or nephews?' I wasn't quite sure where I was going with this. I still believed the intruder I'd seen had been old, not middle-aged. But his resemblance to Walter I was sure about. Somehow, I had to get to the bottom of that.

'Saul and Alice had a son,' replied Walter. 'They moved away, you know, after all the . . . after what happened.'

'Something happened?' I ventured, hardly daring to hope, but Walter was shaking his head.

'A long time ago, dear. Harry, Saul and Archie, all gone. It wasn't a good time.' He looked back at me, and I knew with absolute certainty that there was more he could tell me. And that he never would.

'What happened to Saul's son?' I asked. According to Matt, around ten years after fleeing the village, Saul had murdered Alice and been sentenced to life imprisonment. Any child they'd had would have been left alone in the world.

'Social workers came to see us, after his mother died. Wanted us to take him in. Said we were his only family.'

I listened, still holding Walter's hand, willing him to go on.

'I had to say no,' Walter continued. 'Edeline, by this time . . . she wasn't fit. We couldn't have done right by the lad. He went into an orphanage . . . no . . . a children's home, they called it, but I expect it came to

397

the same thing. Didn't seem right, but what else could I do?'

Walter's eyes were pleading with me, but I was a long way from understanding anything much. There was a great deal Walter wasn't telling me. *They moved away . . . after what happened.* He knew something about 1958. He was holding back about Edeline too. But he was so frail. How could I ask without distressing him?

'So did you ever hear about him? About what happened to him?' A child born in the early sixties would be approaching fifty by now. Still too young to be my intruder but . . .

'He came to see us a few years later. He'd be around seventeen, had just left the home and wanted some money to move abroad. I gave him what I could, but it wasn't much. I couldn't take to the lad, far too much like Saul for my taste. Told us stories about how they'd treated him in the children's home. Trying to make us feel guilty.'

'He'd been treated badly?'

'So he said, but I couldn't believe some of the stories he told us. I think his dad must have been turning his head.'

'He still saw his father?'

Walter nodded. 'The lad used to visit him in prison. They encouraged it, the staff of the children's home, thought it would be good for him to keep in touch with his father. But Saul told the lad stories, twisted stories, about how the village turned against him, drove him and his mother away. He claimed that was the real reason his mother died. It was rubbish, of course, Saul only got what he deserved, but you could tell the lad had fallen for it. He'd been taught to hate us, to hate the village for what he thought they'd done to his parents.'

'How long did he stay?'

'Not long. He went when he realized he wouldn't get anything else out of us. We never heard from him again.'

'Can you remember his name?'

'He was called Saul. Like his dad. Just like his dad.'

I couldn't help a shiver. Another Saul Witcher. With a grudge against the village.

The light in Walter's eyes, which had seemed quite bright when I'd arrived, was fading now. I was tiring him.

'Walter, someone in the village mentioned Ulfred. I was wondering if . . .'

The hand holding mine gripped tighter. I'd been wrong when I'd described it as having no strength. There was quite a lot left there after all.

'We did our best for Ulfred. Nobody could have done . . . He wasn't right, you know. Born wrong. It just got worse as he got older. Couldn't see, couldn't hear, couldn't talk. But so strong. I couldn't manage him. And he and Edeline. How could I have stopped them? I couldn't stop any of them.'

I'd gone too far. Walter was seriously distressed. I had to calm him down. I covered his hand in both of mine. 'It's OK, Walter, really. It was a long time ago. Don't get—'

'And after that . . . what they did to him . . .'

There were no monitors in Walter's room, but I was pretty sure his heartbeat was getting dangerously fast, and he was struggling to catch his breath. 'Walter, I'm sure it was an accident. Please . . .'

'I had to send him away. Dr Amblin helped us. And the curate. Found a place for him. He was all right. They had doctors and male nurses. They could look after him.'

'I'm sure he was fine. You did the right thing.'

Walter's breathing was slowing. I waited, gave him a moment, allowed the tight muscles in his face to relax.

'I expect you were able to visit him?' I asked, when I judged it safe.

Walter named a psychiatric hospital in a town not fifty miles away but over the border in Devon. I repeated it to myself several times to make sure I wouldn't forget. 'We went once or twice,' he said. 'We could see he was comfortable, being looked after. They even let him keep a pet snake. But he didn't seem to want to be with us. There was no point visiting, so we stopped.'

'And is he still there? Is he still alive?'

'I never heard that he died, love. I suppose he must be.'

41

IT WAS COMING UP FOR ELEVEN IN THE MORNING WHEN I drove up the lane that forms the back entrance to the Little Order of St Francis. A quarter of a mile along it, I drove through an open gate and tucked Mum's car close to the hedge. I got out, closed the gate and started jogging up the lane. I had another half-mile to go.

All around me was a sense of great stillness. The air pressure had dropped, birdsong had faded away and even the seabirds had found somewhere to shelter. Somewhere, just over the horizon, heavy clouds were mustering as nature braced itself for a storm.

I climbed the fence and made my way through the field where we keep our convalescent deer, wondering how my little team were getting on without me. I hardly ever took leave. Even when I did, I usually phoned in at least twice a day. I'd never been out of touch this long before. At this hour, the staff would be busy doing ward rounds and keeping on top of the feeding schedules. If I was lucky, I wouldn't be spotted. Keeping close to the hedge, I made my way towards the outbuildings at the back of the hospital where we keep two Land Rovers. Spare keys to both vehicles and to the garage were always on my own keyring.

I managed to open the garage without raising any shouts of alarm. I chose the Land Rover I was most familiar with and started the engine. Driving forward, I risked the time it took to jump down and lock the garage doors. Until the staff were called out on a rescue – which didn't happen every day – the missing vehicle wouldn't be noticed.

By this time, the police would know I was no longer at the family home. If Dad had been cooperative – and I was certain he would be – they'd know I'd taken Mum's car. By switching vehicles, my chances of being stopped by a cruising patrol car had lessened, but I still had to keep to the back roads. That meant everything was going to take much longer.

The old Victorian asylum building was massive: red brick, stretching ahead of me for almost a hundred yards. It stood in a small hollow, surrounded on all sides by low hills and dark, beech woods. Even the sunniest days would bring little light.

On the drive over, my thoughts had been churning like the contents of a tumble-dryer as I struggled to put everything I'd just learned into its proper place. Walter knew something about the night of the church fire. He'd probably never tell me voluntarily and I'd never have the heart to push for details, but he knew something. That meant there was more for me to learn, if only I could find the right source.

There had been something wrong with Edeline. More than the promiscuous behaviour Violet had hinted at. Walter had talked about a relationship between Edeline and Archie but, according to Violet, Edeline had been playing fast and loose with all the Witcher brothers. What had she said? *You never knew which cottage she was going to appear from in the morning.*

What a weird scenario. Four Witcher brothers: Walter, Archie, Harry and Saul, each living in one of the four small cottages that had been the Witcher property before the walls were knocked through. Edeline had been legally married to one of the brothers but had kept house for and provided other, more intimate, services to the others. Sexual appetites aside, what kind of woman would do that? Didn't it suggest a rather disturbed mind? Several rather disturbed minds?

Most important, though, I'd learned that Ulfred was real. Matt's investigation hadn't been thorough enough. Ulfred had slipped through Matt's net and was still out there.

I remembered the look on Walter's face when he'd said, *And after that . . . what they did to him . . .* and found myself shuddering again. But whatever had been done to Ulfred hadn't killed him. Walter, Ernest Amblin and the curate had had him committed to the hospital I was approaching. Walter had visited him. Had never been informed of his death. He might still be here. Or, then again, he might not be. He might be back in his old village, hanging around the old family home.

As I parked I had a sense of growing excitement. This was the answer, it had to be. Dangerous, disturbed

Ulfred, one of Walter's brothers, to whom something dreadful had happened long ago. I walked to the main entrance – double doors of heavy old wood, studded with iron. They were wide open. An NHS signboard told me that I'd arrived at the Two Counties Psychiatric Hospital, established in 1857. Stepping over the threshold, I pushed the internal glass doors and walked inside.

A man in overalls was washing the floor with a long-handled mop, singing to himself as he did so. As I walked past him, towards the reception desk, I noticed he was wearing slippers. And that there was no water in his bucket.

The reception desk was empty. I looked round, found a bell and pressed it. Nothing happened. I watched the man in slippers clean the floor for three, maybe four minutes and then pressed the bell again. A door in the office beyond the desk opened, and a woman in her mid-forties with startlingly black hair came in carrying a mug.

'So sorry,' she said. 'I'd just brewed tea. Can't stand it stewed. What can we do for you?'

'I'm enquiring about a patient,' I said.

'Are you family?' she asked, putting her mug down on the desk.

I hadn't thought this through. 'No, I'm not family,' I said, speaking off the top of my head. 'But I've just been with the patient's elder brother. He's really quite ill. It would be great to have just a quick chat with your administrator. Or maybe someone in medical records.'

The steam from the mug was making the woman's glasses mist over. 'Well, we normally—' she said.

'Can I help you?' said a voice from behind me. I turned to see another woman, thin and unusually tall, across the corridor. In spite of her offer, she didn't look remotely helpful. She stepped forward until she loomed over me, and I felt like a child again, looking up at an angry adult. I resisted the temptation to take a step backwards.

'I'm looking for a patient,' I said. 'Someone who's been with you for a number of years. I was with his brother just now. I don't need to see him.' Heaven knows I didn't want to see Ulfred. 'I just need to know if he's still alive.'

The woman was frowning. 'When patients die, we always inform the families.'

'That's what I expected. But no one has heard from this patient in a very long time. He'll be in his seventies. All I need is for you to confirm he's still here.'

'His name?'

'Ulfred Witcher.'

The woman's eyebrows rose, then she shook her head. 'Doesn't ring a bell,' she said.

I opened my mouth to speak, but she stepped back and beckoned me to follow her. She opened a door on the right of the corridor, and we passed through. The reception area we'd just left had been plastered and painted a soft yellow colour, but the corridor we were walking down now was the same dark-red brick of the outside. Doors were placed at intervals, to my right and left, but none were open. Fluorescent lights ran the length of the ceiling. Several flickered as we walked under them. In the distance, I could hear intermittent, discordant sound as people yelled and heavy objects clanged together.

We reached the end of the corridor and turned. Glass windows on my left revealed an office that was our destination. The tall woman opened the door, and we went inside. A man in navy-blue tunic and trousers slouched at a desk, drinking coffee and reading a tabloid newspaper. He looked up as we entered and stared. Another woman, shorter and plumper than my guide, sat at a computer. She too looked up.

'We need to check a patient record,' said the tall woman, speaking to no one in particular. 'Either of you remember an . . .' She paused and looked at me.

'Ulfred Witcher,' I prompted.

Plump woman began typing. 'How are you spelling that?' she asked after a few seconds. I told her, and she resumed her tapping. From somewhere deep within the building I heard the sound of a man crying out.

'Nothing,' said plump woman after a few more minutes. The tall one looked at me with something like satisfaction on her face.

'Didn't think so,' she said. 'I've been here ten years, and I remember most people who've passed through.'

'Let's try a few different spellings,' suggested Plump. 'Sometimes patient records get inputted wrong at the start and nobody bothers to correct them.'

'Thank you,' I said.

'We can't search by Christian name, unfortunately, the system doesn't allow it. Shame really, I don't suppose there are many Ulfreds.'

'It's an unusual name,' I agreed. 'I think he may have

been admitted in 1958, maybe 1959. Does that help?'

'We'll try that in a minute. I'm not getting anything here.'

'We had a Wishart a couple of years ago,' chipped in the orderly. 'Released into the community. Reg, his first name was. Man in his fifties.'

'Ulfred would be older than that,' I said, despair growing with every tap of the keyboard. Surely not another dead end?

'OK, I'm getting a list of 1958 admissions,' said the typist. She was staring at a list on the screen. 'The place was full back then; a lot of people came and went that year.' The rest of us grouped ourselves around her. She flicked down towards the end of the list, to where the names beginning with W would be. Waters, Williams, Wottren. No Witchers. Nothing that could even be a possible spelling mistake.

'OK, let's try 1959,' she said cheerfully. A few minutes later, we had no choice but to give up. The hospital had absolutely no record of an Ulfred Witcher. Ever.

'I'm sorry to have wasted your time,' I said. Walter had lied to me. What other explanation could there be?

'Are you sure it was this hospital?'

I turned and saw the tall woman was speaking to me. I managed to nod my head. 'I'm sure this was the one his brother named. Are there others in the area that you know of?'

My moment of hope was soon dashed. She shook her head. 'Not in this area. And certainly not at that time. The Victorian asylums were built very large, usually to

407

accommodate a whole county. Two counties, in our case. If a Dorset man was hospitalized in 1958, he'd have come here.'

'I won't take up any more of your time. Thank you very much for checking.'

The tall woman, whose manner had softened a little, escorted me back along the corridor. From somewhere above us I could hear laughter, which became louder and more insistent until it degenerated to shrieks. I couldn't help a shudder.

'It's disturbing if you're not used to it,' said the woman at my side.

'How many patients do you have now?' I asked, as we approached the door.

'Just under a hundred,' she replied, pulling it open for me and smiling at the cleaner in slippers. 'That looks lovely, Eric, well done.'

'They need to move to more modern facilities,' she went on, turning to me again, 'but the money never seems to be available. I'm sorry we couldn't be more help.'

'I do appreciate your trying.'

'My name's Rose Scott,' she said, holding out a card. 'Call me if you think of anything else.'

Back outside, I barely had the energy to walk to my car. Why would Walter lie? Had he played some part in Ulfred's death? Walter was a good man, but the best of us make mistakes. Maybe there'd been a terrible accident and, even now, Walter and others were trying to cover it up. Without much hope I dialled the number of the Paddocks Hospice.

'I'm so sorry,' the nurse in charge said, when I'd been

408

connected. 'I think I did warn you that Walter was very weak.'

'Has something happened?'

'He's still with us, but I'm afraid he slipped into unconsciousness shortly after you left. We're not expecting him to wake up.'

I couldn't speak, but the nurse seemed to know I was still on the line.

'You mustn't feel responsible in any way. We've been expecting this for days now. We're all just glad he was able to have a visitor, something nice, before the end.'

The end? Had I reached the end of the road too? It was nearly noon, and I was fast running out of options. I started to drive, without any clear idea of where I was going and, more out of habit than anything else, turned on the radio. I didn't hear music, I heard a nail being driven into my coffin.

'*And police have issued a description of the local woman they want to interview in connection with the death, early this morning, of a Dorset man. Clara Benning is described as being five foot three inches tall, of slight build, with long, dark-brown hair and severe scarring on the left side of her face. The public are warned not to approach Miss Benning, but to notify them immediately upon any sightings. The dead man, who has been named as Ernest Amblin, a retired GP in his late seventies, was found in the fields near his home early this morning. It's believed he was out on a late-night fishing trip and his death is being treated as suspicious. Police have issued a telephone number . . .*'

How I managed to keep driving I'll never know. I couldn't stop thinking about all the people I knew who would have heard the broadcast and who would now know I was wanted in connection with someone's death. My father, sister, the staff at work, Sally, Matt ... except ... it could only have been Matt who'd authorized the story, who'd turned me into a wanted criminal.

And Ernest Amblin, that nervous, grumpy old man, was dead. He'd been killed early this morning, when I'd disobeyed Matt's clear instructions to stay with my family and had spent the night in my car. With no alibi at all.

What, in God's name, was going on? Three old people were dead. Someone was picking them off, one by one. And the detectives in charge of the case probably weren't looking for whoever was responsible. Because they thought it was me.

My next journey took a little over twenty minutes. This time, though, I didn't announce myself at the front entrance. I had a feeling that if I sought admittance I'd be denied it. Instead I walked round the back of the building.

The hot stillness of the early morning had gone. The wind was getting up and the storm clouds had finally made their appearance. They hovered in the west: low and black; heading our way. I reached the part of the garden I remembered, and then slipped inside the open French window.

'Hello, Ruby,' I said, to the startled woman in the chair by the bed.

At the sight of me, Ruby began pushing herself up. Her eyes were fixed on the alarm buzzer by the bed. I crossed to it and put my hand over it.

'I'm sorry,' I said, as she sank back down into the chair. 'Not just yet, I'm afraid. I have some questions for you.'

She didn't respond, and I walked closer, until I was standing directly in front of her chair.

'Ruby, people are in danger. John Allington, Violet Buckler, Ernest Amblin – they're all dead. I don't want to scare you, but someone is harming elderly people who used to worship at St Birinus. You have to help me, for your own sake.'

Ruby, as before, wouldn't look me in the eye. She was shaking, darting frightened glances from under what was left of her eyelashes. I crouched down so I was directly in her line of sight, forcing her to look at me.

'You find me repulsive, don't you? Well, here's the thing. I don't care. We have more important things to talk about right now than how I look.'

Several times I saw Ruby's eyes flicker to the emergency switch, but she made no attempt to reach it.

'Let's talk about snake bites, shall we?' I said. 'Do you know what happens to flesh when it's been injected with snake venom? Do you? Because let me tell you, Ruby, this scar of mine looks like a scratch in comparison.'

Ruby was pressing herself into the back of the chair, shrinking away from me, but I couldn't afford to take pity on her.

'First thing that happens is the flesh starts to swell,' I

411

said. 'Have you seen a hand swollen as big as a balloon – swollen so much the skin, even the flesh, starts to crack and tear? And it discolours too – goes red, purple, eventually black. Quite often, even if the antidote is given in time and the patient lives, the flesh still dies. The limb has to be amputated. And what do you think happens if the person is bitten on the face? Can you imagine what it would feel like to have your face swell up like a black balloon? You can't amputate a face, Ruby, trust me on that one.'

I was trying to keep my voice low. I didn't want any passing staff to hear me and come to Ruby's rescue. Not till I'd finished with her.

'Now, someone in our village is keeping some extremely poisonous snakes and using them to hurt people. There is enough venom in a single bite of one of these snakes to kill fifty people. Fifty! A child would have no chance. Now, I know you can tell me something about what's going on. You can tell me what happened in 1958. And I'm not leaving here until you do.'

She glanced at the emergency button once more.

'Please, Ruby,' I added, softly.

She looked at me. I think it was the first time we'd made eye contact. Then she bent forwards. I heard the creaking of her joints as she leaned down, saw the pink, bare skin of her scalp where it shone through the sparse wisps of grey. And I watched as she drew up the front of her nightgown. Her legs were thin; papery skin looked ready to flake away, broken capillaries made a spider's web across her calves. Her knees were bruised.

Unsure now, I think I even backed away a fraction,

but the nightdress continued its slow, relentless journey over the shrivelled remains of her limbs.

When the middle of her thighs were bare she stopped. She looked up at me then, and I thought I could see a strange triumph in her eyes. Her right thigh was normal – for a woman of her years. Her left barely looked like a human limb.

The outline of the femur protruded through what was left of her skin. It looked like someone had grabbed huge handfuls of her flesh and wrenched them away. The remaining skin had been stretched over the wound and roughly sewn, like a child's attempt at patchwork. It was an old wound, but it glared red, even purple, in places. It was a hundred times worse than my own scar. Fortunately for Ruby, it was in a place easier to hide.

'What did this?' I asked, gently. We weren't enemies any more. I'm not sure we ever had been; we'd just needed to understand each other.

She shook her head. 'Never knew,' she said. 'There were a dozen of them. Mainly brown. Some grey. Markings down their backs, and they made a noise with their tails. A sort of . . .'

'Rattling sound?' I offered, thinking, *Of course, what else would it be?*

She nodded. 'Yes, that was it. A rattle. We all ran of course, when they got loose, but we must have panicked them. They were everywhere. This one got me by the door. I never knew there could be so much pain.'

I leaned closer. 'I'm sorry. Truly I am. But it means you know how important this is. You have to tell me what happened that night.'

She stared at me for a long time. 'I was starving,' she said, at last. 'Past starving, actually. The hunger pains had gone, but I had no strength left. I couldn't even think straight any more. It was a bit like falling asleep standing up.'

A church that starved its congregation. I remembered what Dad had told me about the Latter Rain Church encouraging weeks of fasting and prayer. About the young girl who'd died in South Carolina, a member of Archie Witcher's congregation.

'But I had such a hopeful feeling about that night,' continued Ruby. 'I thought it was going to happen for me at last. That I would speak in tongues, that I would take up a serpent.'

She rose, craning forward in her chair, and raised her voice.

'*And these signs shall follow them that believe*,' she said; '*in my name shall they cast out devils; they shall speak with new tongues; they shall take up serpents; and if they drink any deadly thing, it shall not hurt them; they shall lay hands . . .*'

'Ruby!'

Her attention snapped back, but for a second the look in her eyes had scared me. I was no longer sure I was dealing with someone entirely sane. But I remained still, and listened, as she told me the story of what had happened that Sunday night, fifty years ago.

42

Sunday, 15 June 1958

*T*HE LANE IS DARK BUT NOT SILENT. NO ONE IS *speaking, but low sounds fill the air: shoulders brush against the hedge, footsteps crunch over stones, wings flap overhead. From a tree near by a barn owl scolds. Several of the villagers carry lamps, but the light they cast seems feeble. More people join the crowd as slowly, steadily, the procession draws nearer the church.*

Through the avenue of lime trees they pass. The youngest, twenty-year-old Ruby Buckler, close to fainting after five days of self-imposed starvation, stumbles and almost falls. She is caught from behind by strong arms and steadied before being pushed gently on her way.

The stone church seems enormous. The colours of the stained glass are dull, like unpolished jewels, the faintest of lights flickering behind them. The path turns and so does the procession of villagers. The north doors of the church are already open.

One by one the silent members of the gathering congregation step over the threshold. The pews are soon full. A stranger might think the whole village present, but Ruby knows they are not. Some are unable to attend, like her friend Violet, who is at home looking after a younger brother and sister. Others, she knows, will not come. Even after everything they've seen and heard, some people still refuse to hear the true word of the Lord. Nor will they have anything to do with the Reverend Fain.

Ruby blinks, her eyes already stinging from the smoke. She can smell something in the air that isn't candle smoke: something rich, foreign, almost choking in its intensity. And at the front of the church stands a huge figure, clad in black. Excitement twirls in the pit of Ruby's empty stomach. It is the Reverend Joel Morgan Fain.

'He had such a way with him, the Reverend,' said Ruby. 'He made you feel – oh, I can't describe it – like electricity was running through you, like you could barely sit still in your seat, like you wanted to jump up and shout, or throw yourself to the ground and offer yourself to the Lord.'

'Was he handsome?' I asked.

Ruby reached out and took hold of my hand.

'Handsomest man you ever saw,' she agreed, her eyes glinting. 'Tall as an oak tree,' she went on, and her thumb began making circles around the palm of my hand. 'Thick black hair, eyes like the sky in winter.'

I tugged my hand, managed to pull it out of her grasp.

Even I can tell the difference between religious fervour and sexual arousal. Ruby was in the grip of one powerful fifty-year-old memory.

'He was waiting for us, as we went in,' she said. 'Standing just in front of the altar. He seemed like a spirit himself, floating above us, in the cloud.'

Ruby was losing it. Or else . . .

'Were the lights on in the church?' I asked.

She shook her head. 'Candles,' she said, her eyes gleaming. 'Candles everywhere. It was hard to breathe, the air was so thick with smoke. And I could smell something else too. Holy incense.'

I'd never heard of Pentecostal churches using incense. I wondered if some sort of hallucinatory drug had been burning in the church that night.

'Ruby,' I asked, 'were the Witchers in church?'

Ruby's face changed. 'Edeline was,' she spat at me. 'Right up the front, tossing her head, hair all over the place. I never believed it was real for her.' Ruby leaned forward towards me. I fought the temptation to pull back. 'Why would the Lord cause the buttons of her blouse to open every time?' she demanded of me. 'She was always the first to collapse, you know. Always right near the Reverend.'

The old folks seemed united in their opinion of Walter's wife. But it wasn't Edeline I was interested in. 'What about the others?' I asked. 'The Witcher men? Walter?'

'Walter never went,' she said, with the faintest shake of her head. 'Walter was a good man.'

I stared at her. 'And the others?' I urged, before she

could realize what she'd said. 'Saul, Archie, Harry, Ulfred?'

Her expression changed again, and I sensed her pulling back from me. She looked at the door. 'They bring tea round soon,' she said. 'Tea and a biscuit. Two if we've been good.'

'Ruby, please carry on.'

For a while the service follows familiar lines. The Reverend preaches, people pray. Every so often members of the congregation, moved by the Holy Spirit, will jump to their feet and shout their praise to the Lord. Behind Ruby, Florence Allington has fallen into a trance. Ruby wonders how soon she should time her own faint. She risks a brief glance down to check the prayer mats are covering the cold stone of the floor where she will fall.

I almost asked if Florence Allington had been related to John, but it seemed more important to keep Ruby on track.

'Did you faint?' I asked her. 'I mean, go into a trance?'

She nodded. 'It wasn't too hard,' she said. 'Especially when you hadn't eaten. You took deep breaths and then held your breath. The church would go black at the edges and you could fall down.'

I could hear movement in the corridor. It was some distance away, but I sensed I was running out of time. 'What about the snakes, Ruby? People got bitten, didn't they? Apart from you. People died that night?'

The rattlesnakes are in a large, wooden casket carved with roses and ivy leaves. From her position on the floor Ruby watches Harry Witcher carrying it from the vestry. She gets to her knees and resumes her seat, praying that this time – this night – she will receive the gift of the Holy Spirit and be able to touch the snakes.

Reverend Fain reaches into the chest and takes out a snake: five feet long, brown with black markings, thick around the middle. Holding it between his hands, he starts to move towards the congregation. 'Behold,' he is saying, 'I give unto you power to tread on serpents and scorpions, and over all the power of the enemy; and nothing shall by any means harm you.'

Ruby's voice had risen, far too loud. Someone would hear and put a stop to our nonsense with tea and two biscuits. 'Luke, chapter 10, verse 19,' she said proudly. 'That's what he'd say as he carried the snake around, inviting all who were blessed by the Spirit to touch the snake for themselves.'

I tried to imagine the collective delusion necessary for normal, rational people to allow a rattlesnake to be carried among them. 'And people did?' I asked.

Ruby nodded. 'Only those blessed. Those who weren't blessed kept their heads down and prayed.'

I'll bet, I thought. 'Who else touched the snakes?'

By this time, Reverend Fain has been among them for three months, and several villagers have received the gift of handling snakes. Ruby watches as John Dodds approaches the chest and reaches down. He lifts a snake, smaller than the one the Reverend is carrying, greyer in colour, and hangs it around his shoulders. He stands there, enjoying the congregation's eyes upon him, as the snake moves down his body, coiling itself around his right arm. Peter Morfet is approaching the chest too, closely followed by Raymond Gillard. Ruby wants to watch, but the Reverend is drawing close to her; it's now or never.

She stands, looks into those wintry eyes and feels a shock of electricity start in her groin and rush up through her whole body. It is the sign she has been waiting for. She reaches out with both arms, the Reverend bends forward, and she is holding the snake. Expecting something wet and slippery she is amazed to feel the warm, muscular body of the snake move through her fingers. Without thinking, she drops her gaze to just below the Reverend's belt and feels something stir deep within her own body. Face blazing scarlet, she hands the snake back to the Reverend. He smiles at her, mutters a blessing and moves on. Ruby falls to her knees.

'I don't think I've ever been happier,' said Ruby. 'I'd received the Holy Spirit, been blessed with one of the gifts. I just wanted to pray and pray and . . .'

'When did the snakes escape? When did people get bitten? Was the service over by then?'

She looked at me as if I were stupid. 'You haven't heard a word I've said, have you? This was no ordinary service. These were just the preliminaries. We were going to raise Ulfred.'

'Raise him?' I said, hoping I wasn't following Ruby

but at the same time very much afraid I was. I remembered Dad's study. The orange and black booklet written by the Reverend Franklin Hall. Formula for . . .

'Yes, raise him,' said Ruby. 'From the dead.'

The snakes are away now, the chest standing forgotten by the altar, and Peter Morfet and Raymond Gillard are unfastening the great wooden trap-doors at the front of the nave, just below the chancel steps. The congregation is silent again: all the praying, all the chanting, has stopped. Everyone watches as the padlocks are opened, the bolts drawn back, and the doors pulled apart. Ruby cranes forward in her seat to catch a glimpse of the still, black water shimmering in the candlelight.

One of the village's numerous underground streams feeds the newly dug baptism pool. Ruby has seen several villagers baptised in the last three months, and is waiting for news of her own. She can't help wondering, even though she knows it is unholy, how cold the water will be and whether there is anything living in its depths.

The door to the vestry opens, and a strange procession enters the church. Archie Witcher, tall and handsome, a little like Reverend Fain, especially in his ministerial robes, comes first. Behind him walks Saul Witcher, carrying two wooden poles, one tucked under each arm. Saul steps further into the chancel, and the congregation, as one, stretches forward to see. A wooden chair, old but stoutly made, is strapped to the two poles. Ruby can see Harry Witcher now, carrying the other ends of the poles. Between them, raised high like an ancient king taken captive in battle, sits Ulfred. Thick ropes bind him to the chair, beginning at his ankles and winding their way up to his neck. His mouth is bound with blue cloth and his eyes, though open, are dull and unfocused.

Ruby clasps her hands tightly together and makes herself carry on praying. Something that feels like panic is twisting about in her stomach.

Saul and Harry, with Archie leading the way, walk slowly down the chancel and reach the steps. Ulfred starts to struggle, to pull against ropes that are pinning him so tight he can barely move. Ruby finds herself wanting to flee, to run out of the church, not to have to witness what will happen next. She tries to pray harder but is having trouble remembering even the simplest prayer.

It's all been explained to her. Ulfred is possessed. That's why he can't speak or barely see, why he makes those strange, frightening sounds. It's also why he has such a strange power over snakes. It isn't the Lord's power that makes Ulfred able to handle snakes without being harmed, Reverend Fain has explained. Ulfred's power comes from the original serpent of the Garden of Eden. From the devil himself.

'Our Father,' prays Ruby, 'our Father.' If only she could remember more, maybe she wouldn't feel so afraid. Wouldn't have this terrible urge to yell at them all to stop it.

Since he first arrived among them, the Reverend has tried many times to exorcize Ulfred, but the demon inside him is too powerful. There is only one way to free their brother Ulfred, Reverend Fain explained to them last Sunday, and that is to release his mortal body. Without an earthly home, the demon will flee back to hell. Then, through the power of the Lord, Ulfred will be raised up, as Christ was raised up, and his spirit will be pure and free. He will be able to see and hear and speak. He will be repulsed by snakes as all good Christians are. They are doing this for Ulfred. Because they love him. When this was first explained, Ruby had been horrified, had looked round the church, waiting for the protests to start. But . . .

Saul and Harry set the chair down. The demon inside Ulfred is terrified now, seeing through Ulfred's cloudy, half-blind eyes. The Reverend, his voice soaring to drown out the terrible sounds Ulfred is making, leads them all in prayer. Ruby tries to join in, but she can't. Her voice just won't work any more. She looks round, and what she sees scares her more: so very few seem to be sharing her horror. Peter Morfet has dropped his head into his hands, Florence Allington has fallen to her knees and seems to be weeping; her husband, John, keeps glancing at the door. Curate Stancey has risen from his seat. Most of the others, though, are staring, glassy-eyed, their lips muttering words that she no longer believes are prayers as they watch the four men gathered around the prisoner at the baptism pool.

At a signal from the Reverend, Harry and Saul crouch. Harry seems to stumble, almost to fall. Then they take hold of the poles again. Ulfred is keening now, and Ruby wants to slam her hands over her ears to drown out the terrible sound. Except, it can't really be

Ulfred crying, it must be the demon inside him, knowing it is about to be driven out, because Ulfred, poor, mad Ulfred, would surely not understand what is going to happen.

Harry and Saul pull sharply upwards on the pole nearest the congregation and Ruby watches in horror as the makeshift sedan chair tilts over and Ulfred is pushed under the water.

They can no longer hear his cries, but a surge of bubbles shooting to the surface means he's still yelling. Ruby can't look any more. She takes her hands away from her ears and covers her face; finds the words to pray again, to pray that it will stop, that someone will stop it. They can't really mean it, can they? They're not actually going to . . .

She is peering through her fingers. She can't bear to watch and she can't bear not to. The chair starts to buck, the wooden poles to clatter against the flags. Saul and Harry press down harder, and she can see the veins standing out in their bare forearms. There aren't so many bubbles rising to the surface now. Archie lowers his Bible, steps forward, peers into the pool.

Ruby jumps up and opens her mouth.

'Stop it. For God's sake, get him out of there!'

It isn't Ruby's voice. Jim Buckler is striding down the aisle towards the pool. Ruby thinks she might faint with relief. Peter Morfet, scarlet-red in the face, stands up too and joins Jim. All around her faces register shock. Some look angry, some disappointed, others hugely relieved.

But Reverend Fain is blocking the aisle, and Ulfred's

two rescuers will have to get past him. And Saul and Harry are two of the strongest men in the village. The chair is still now and there are no more bubbles in the pool.

'For pity's sake, someone give us a hand,' shouts Peter, and Ruby thinks she sees another man stand up. Harry lets go of the poles. Saul yells something at him, but Harry shakes his head and falls back. Edeline takes Harry's place and starts screaming as Peter Morfet grabs hold of her and tries to pull her off. Jim Buckler and the Reverend Fain are grasped tightly together, pushing and shoving, but the Reverend is a much bigger man, and Jim can't get past him. The door to the church slams open, and Ruby turns round, hoping to see more help. But people are leaving, running out into the darkness.

Other men, even some of the women, are moving forward. Fights break out at the front of the church. Ruby is shocked to see the Reverend slam his fist into Jim's nose. Blood sprays in all directions before landing, like tiny rubies, on the stone floor of the church.

People are yelling, screaming. Some are even still praying. Ruby glances at the door and steps into the aisle. A high-pitched howling soars above the din, and Ruby can't help but glance back. Two men have caught hold of Edeline by her hair and are dragging her away from the pool. Edeline is bucking and kicking, howling all the while, shouting obscenities so dreadful Ruby is sure she will be struck down, because no one could say such words in church and be allowed to live.

Edeline has broken free. The men bar her path back

to the pool, and she is looking frantically around. Then she darts forward. The men run after her, but she has reached the casket of snakes. The padlock hasn't been locked. She reaches for it, even as she is pulled away herself and the chest falls forward. The lid opens, and the rattlesnakes pour out on to the flagstones. For a second they lie stunned, then start to move, to seek hiding places around the church. Fresh screaming breaks out. Ruby heads for the door again, but a fleeing woman knocks her to the ground.

Pain soars through Ruby's body. She has jarred her back badly and is lying on something sharp. And she can smell burning. She feels heat and realizes her own hair is alight. She jumps to her feet, swatting her head and screaming as loud as anyone. She sees that one of the hassocks has caught fire. As she watches, flames shoot up towards the wooden pew. Ruby turns and runs, along the back of the nave, knocking over another candle-stand on the way.

The snake is waiting for her in the porch. It rises up two feet in the air, forming a perfect S shape. Ruby has a second to think how beautiful it is before it strikes.

43

'THANK YOU,' I SAID. 'THANK YOU FOR TELLING me.'

I was sitting on Ruby's bed, close to her chair. Her right hand clutched the chair arm, her left lay in mine. I held it as tightly as I dared, hoping that simple human touch might slow the trembling.

'I thought I was going to burn,' said Ruby. 'The fire was everywhere. Everyone was screaming, rushing around. No one stopped to help. I was in agony, but I had to crawl out by myself.'

'You must have been terrified.' I was speaking automatically, thinking hard. Ulfred had drowned that night after all, had been murdered, with half the village colluding. It had been the final disaster in a tragic chain of events.

A charismatic but seriously disturbed man had arrived in the village, throwing the quiet, orderly life of rural England into uproar with his terrifying but totally compulsive way of preaching. The congregation – normal, decent people for the most part – had seen a temporary escape from the monotony of daily life and grabbed at it. They'd followed his lead along the path, which had seemed innocuous at first: services that were a little more thrilling; practices that might be unconventional but were surely harmless. And gradually, the path had darkened, taken twists that none of them could have anticipated.

On that last night, enforced starvation and, I was willing to bet, the use of hallucinogenic drugs had brought out the darkest recesses of their human natures. Even then, I'd been so thankful to hear, common humanity had won through for many of them. Several members of the congregation that night had tried to save Ulfred. Others, such as Ruby, who hadn't dared intervene, had been horrified in the end.

I no longer wondered why those who remembered 15 June 1958 wouldn't speak of it. If I'd been in church that night, I'd want to wipe it from my memory too. I knew why Walter had lied to me. Knowing what his brothers and his wife had done to the most vulnerable member of the family, it would be easier, by far, to pretend he'd simply been taken away for help.

Ruby's hand was still trembling, and the late-afternoon air coming through the open window was getting colder. 'Can I get you a cardigan?' I asked. She looked at me, and her eyes shifted. 'What was it?' she said. 'Was it a sn—' She stopped. It took me a second to realize what she meant.

'No,' I said. 'It wasn't a snake.'

Ruby reached out and touched the left side of my face. I made no attempt to stop her. 'I never married,' she said. 'Word got out around the village about how badly I was marked – down there. Nobody was interested. After the war, there were plenty of girls, not enough men. It was the bonny ones, like Violet and Edeline, who got the men.'

Ruby's hand left my face and fell down until it was touching mine.

'My mother drank,' I said. 'She was an archdeacon's wife but, even so – probably because of that – she drank. She stopped for a while, when she was pregnant with me, but then she just couldn't cope with being stuck at home with two young children. One afternoon, she and my sister and I were in the sitting room of our house. I was just a baby, not even a year old. She put me on the rug, in front of the fire. She'd been drinking since mid-morning and then . . . she just fell asleep.'

Ruby's eyes were fixed on mine. She looked calmer, but her hands hadn't stopped shaking.

'I think Vanessa must have played with me for a while and then got bored. She wandered off into the next room.'

Outside, the sky, so blue an hour ago, had taken on the strange yellowish cast that always precedes a storm.

'And then my mother's two Jack Russells got out of the kitchen – maybe my sister left the door open, I don't know. They hadn't been fed all day. They hadn't been out, either. They were hungry and restless. They came into the sitting room, heard me squeaking on the rug and got excited. They used to play with squeaking toys, you see, they thought I was a toy. They started pulling me around the room . . . I think the louder I screamed, the more excited they must have got.'

'They could have killed you,' whispered Ruby.

'My sister heard what was happening and came running in. She screamed, of course, and my father heard her. It was only a few minutes, but by the time he picked me up the dogs had eaten . . .'

I stopped. Less than two minutes, it had taken, finally to tell someone the story of how my life had been so completely changed. Twenty-nine years: and two minutes.

'And the thing is, I remember it. I know it must be a false memory – I was only nine months old, I couldn't possibly remember it really. I had a lot of nightmares when I was younger; maybe that's how it started. But it feels so real. I remember the dogs' breath, hot on my face; I can even feel their saliva, running down my chin. And the noises they made – the yipping and squealing as they got more and more worked up. And I remember hearing my mother too. That's the worst of it. I can remember her, lying on the sofa, half conscious. And she's talking to them, thinking they were just playing with something, urging them on. With no idea it was me they were . . .'

It was my hands that were trembling, not Ruby's.

'My sister had nightmares too,' I said. 'For a long time afterwards, I'd hear her screaming in the night. Even now she can't bear the sight of blood. There was so much blood, you see, in the sitting room that day.' Vanessa and I both carried scars, I realized. But the attention of the family had been focused entirely upon the obviously damaged child. Vanessa, at five years old, had been left to deal with it alone.

'And she's terrified of dogs,' I went on, realizing at last the significance of what had always seemed an irrational, hysterical fear. 'I'm not. I don't mind them at all, but she can't go anywhere near one. Poor Vanessa.'

'Did you ever wish they'd killed you?' asked Ruby. She looked at my scar again. 'Being damaged like that, if you're a woman, it ruins your life.'

I looked at Ruby, asking the same question I'd asked myself so many times: did I ever wish those dogs had killed me? And I swear, at that moment, I saw a door opening up before me; it was as though in Ruby's sad, small figure I was looking at my own future. For a minute, maybe more, I looked at the ghost of myself in fifty years: lonely, unfulfilled, eaten up with bitterness. And I made a decision.

'It's only a scar,' I said. 'It won't ruin mine.'

Outside, I leaned against the Land Rover and closed my eyes. Finally, I'd told someone the truth about what had happened to me, and I knew there'd come a time when I'd be glad I had. For now, though, I just felt weary. Especially as it seemed the more I learned, the less I knew. I'd found out, at last, the terrible story of the night the church burned. But it was so long ago. Even if someone had wanted to avenge the terrible wrong done to Ulfred, even if there was a good reason why they'd wait fifty years, who was left? His sister-in-law and two of his four brothers were dead, a third hadn't been heard of for years and the remaining brother was close to death himself.

There was no getting round it: I hadn't made the link between past and present; I was still the prime suspect.

I got back into the car and started driving again. With absolutely nowhere to go, I still had to keep moving. Staying on the B roads, taking short cuts across farmland whenever I could, I drove for an hour, trying to see some way clear to what I should do next but unable to drag my thoughts away from the terrible story Ruby had just told me.

We'd probably never know what had driven the Reverend Joel Fain to bring his message to a new part of the world, but his coming had had a devastating effect on the people who'd welcomed him. Even after fifty years the story had the power to anger me. I'd known charismatic ministers in my time – my own father was one; in many ways a minister's success in a parish will depend on his own personality. But I'd never before heard of one who used his gifts in such a destructive and dangerous manner.

Thanks to Ruby's detailed memory, I could picture Joel Fain so clearly: a young, handsome man, tall and striking with his cold blue eyes, dressed in ministerial robes, an imposing figure at the altar, his deep, lilting Alabama accent sounding so exotic to the Dorset folk of fifty years ago. And, I think, if I'm honest, my anger had more than a little to do with his physical presence. Joel Fain hadn't been tall and handsome for nothing; his looks had woven a dark spell around his gullible parishioners.

I'd become the chief suspect in a murder investigation, largely, I believed, because of how I looked. Joel Fain, on the other hand, had received only adulation and respect. Even Ruby, whose life had been so badly damaged as a result of Fain's actions, still remembered him fondly. And then there'd been Edeline, also dark and striking, who'd used her beauty to indulge excessive sexual appetites. And Archie, who'd shared with Edeline the attractive genes of the family. I'd tried so hard, my whole life, not to envy people whose looks make life easy for them but . . .

A sudden thought. Almost from nowhere.

I'd connected my intruder with the Witcher family largely because of how he looked: average height and build, large, plain features with loose, saggy jowls and pale eyes, wispy remains of hair around his crown. Walter, Harry and Saul had all resembled each other as young men and would be expected to age similarly. But that wasn't the only physical type that ran in the Witcher family. Archie and Edeline had been quite different: tall and athletically built, dark-eyed and handsome, even allowing for the very slightly hooked nose. And I knew someone else who looked like that. A man of just the right age.

I pulled over, checked the map and set off again.

What if Saul Witcher the younger, the boy who'd been abandoned when his mother was murdered and his father sent to prison, had come back? What if he'd come seeking revenge on the villagers who'd driven his parents from their home; who, in his mind at least, had set in motion the events that led to his being orphaned and condemned to a brutal, possibly abusive, children's home? Saul Witcher Junior could be both disturbed and dangerous. And I had a strong hunch who he was.

I drove into the nearest town and found the public library. Raindrops were falling as I got out of my car. The librarian was serving visitors when I walked past her desk and didn't seem to notice me. I found the public computers, connected to the internet and, in the search engine, typed the name that was on my mind. Several entries sprang up, including a number of references to the mining and oil-exploration companies owned by the man I was interested in. The South African-based group holding company wasn't exactly forthcoming with information, especially personal information about its principal shareholder, but I did find several newspaper stories expressing concern at the group's environmental record and about conditions for workers in its numerous companies.

I could find no trace of his early life. Just a brief reference to a marriage to a South African woman and his successful application for citizenship. I read that he had oil-exploration companies in Angola, Nigeria, Niger, Libya and South Africa. His company specialized in picking up data produced by previously unsuccessful companies and updating it using the latest technology. When the presence of oil was confirmed, he'd apply for a licence to drill, choosing either to exploit it himself or sell the exploration rights to larger oil companies. In addition to his oil-exploration companies, he owned a number of mines, in Australia, Tasmania and Papua New Guinea.

Papua New Guinea.

In more recent years, with a comfortable fortune behind him, he'd developed an interest in long-distance sailing. He'd made several solo, round-the-world trips, becoming something of a celebrity in yachting circles. Sean had been convinced the taipan eggs couldn't have been smuggled on a plane. *Check overland routes,* he'd said, *small commercial shipping lines or private yachts.*

According to Walter, Saul and Alice's son had emigrated. If the young Saul Witcher and the man I was investigating were one and the same, he'd come back with enough money and status to guarantee entry into the society he had good reason to hate.

I sat, thinking. His marriage to a South African woman had enabled him to apply for South African citizenship. After that, it would be a relatively simple matter to legally change his name. Years later, with his new name and nationality, with a new accent, who would connect the successful businessman with a boy who'd visited so briefly?

Another idea occurred to me, and I entered *marriage records* into the search engine. Several companies appeared, each offering to search records for me in return for a fee. I had my credit cards with me and, after a short delay while my details were registered, I typed in Witcher, Saul and 1957.

Ten seconds later I was looking at a page listing people with surnames beginning with Wit who had married in 1957. There was nothing on the first page, so I flicked through to the second. On the third I found it. On 13 April 1957, Saul Clive Witcher, of my village

435

in Dorset, had married Alice Olive Ventry, daughter of Graham Ventry.

Alice's maiden name had been Ventry, Saul's middle name was Clive. Clive Ventry, owner of our local manor, self-made millionaire and celebrity yachtsman, had been born Saul Witcher.

44

S AUL WITCHER HAD COME BACK, TO THE VILLAGE OF
his ancestors, under an assumed name, telling no
one of his origins. I printed off several pages, shut
down the computer and ran outside, into a torrent of
rain. The high street was noisy as cars sped through
puddles and people hurried along under umbrellas. I
needed a moment to calm down, to get my thoughts
together. I ran to the car and set off.

I drove a mile or so to the next small town. Perhaps
by instinct, maybe force of habit, I headed for a steeple
I could see above the buildings and found myself
driving through the town and out towards the coast. In
a small church car park close to the cliff edge, empty but
for an old blue Fiesta, I pulled up. I'd kept the radio on
the whole drive over, mainly to see if there'd been any
developments in the Ernest Amblin case; although I
didn't need telling the police hadn't yet found their chief
suspect.

There was nothing about me. Instead, the news
coverage concentrated on the severe weather warnings

in place across the south-west. The storms we'd expected all day had arrived with a vengeance. Already, a number of towns and villages had lost power, several rivers were predicted to overflow, roads were blocked by fallen trees and people were being advised to stay in their homes wherever possible.

The phone barely had time to ring before it was answered.

'Matt Hoare.'

'It's Clara.'

A sharp intake of breath. 'Do you have any bloody idea . . .' He stopped; I could hear him breathing. I waited. 'Where are you?' he said at last.

'Close by. Just listen to me, please. Give me five minutes.'

And Matt, to his credit, did exactly that. He listened, without interrupting, while I told him of my meeting with Walter, my failed attempt to track down Ulfred at the psychiatric hospital. I described, as well as I could remember it, Ruby's account of the night of 15 June 1958, the night of Ulfred's murder. I told him everything I'd learned about Clive Ventry, aka Saul Witcher, and about his apparent ill treatment in the children's home.

'He blames the village for driving his parents away,' I said. 'Dozens of people were in church that night but the rest of them seem to have turned on the three Witcher brothers, to have held them solely res—'

'Clara—'

'Clive Ventry has business ventures in Papua New Guinea. That snake we caught is around four months old. Normally a taipan takes two months to hatch.

438

Keeping eggs cold can extend that to around a hundred days. Go back seven months and I'll bet you'll find Clive paid a visit to one of his companies in Papua New Guinea.'

'Clara, stop!'

I stopped.

'I want to know exactly where you are.'

I told him.

'Right, I'm sending someone to pick you up. Don't you dare move.'

'Not Tasker. He thinks I killed Violet. I'll come back to the village. I'll give myself up to you.'

'Just listen to me. We've had the handwriting analysis on the will found in Violet's house. It isn't in Violet's handwriting and it isn't in yours either. Violet's fingerprints were on it, but not in the places you'd expect if she'd handled it normally. It seems like a pretty crude attempt to direct the blame at you. Although I can't see anyone thinking they'd get away with it for long.'

'What about my fingerprints?'

'Not a trace. Whoever took it from your house didn't get lucky. But we did lift a second set of prints from it. Someone handled the paper who wasn't you or Violet.'

I was finding it hard to breathe. Was it over, then?

'We've also had the results of the post-mortem on Violet,' continued Matt, in a softer voice. 'There was a strong concentration of adder venom in her system, but she died when someone held a pillow over her head and suffocated her.'

Silence. I could hear him breathing. I think he could probably have said the same about me.

'Are you OK?' said Matt.

'Yep.'

'There is more. Seems she put up a bit of a fight. There were traces of skin under the fingernails of her right hand. We'll be able to get DNA from it, but whoever killed her would have visible scratch marks.'

Shortly after I'd been arrested, I'd been examined by a police doctor and a WPC. I'd had plenty of scratches, I always have, but none that could have been made by human fingernails. The DNA results would clear me. Matt was still talking. I forced myself to concentrate.

'Ernest Amblin was found by his son-in-law on the riverbank just before midnight last night. He'd drowned, but the pathologist found bruising on his shoulders. He'd been held under by someone pretty strong.' Matt was silent for a moment and, when he spoke again, his voice had hardened. 'I understand you have an alibi for late yesterday evening.'

'Yes, I was with . . .' I stopped.

'Sean North. I know. He's been helping us with our enquiries since early this morning. Didn't I tell you to stay away from him?' Matt's voice had risen. He was pretty close to shouting at me.

'Is he a suspect?'

Another pause. And a heavy intake of breath. 'Unfortunately not. Before you arrived he spent nearly an hour on the phone to his TV director. After you left he phoned Australia. The phone-company records confirm he made both calls from his house. He couldn't have been anywhere near Amblin when he was attacked. Now, listen, I don't have a lot of time.'

Matt was on the move. I could hear his footsteps on gravel and the wind whistling though tall trees. A car door banged shut.

'I've been quietly keeping an eye on Clive Ventry for a while now,' said Matt. 'He owns an oil-exploration company that applied to the government twelve months ago to do test drilling in various sites around the village. Apparently, there was some initial work done years ago which his company has reanalysed. There could be up to 600 million barrels almost beneath where I'm standing, which would make it the largest onshore oil field in Europe.'

I could hear a car engine starting, wheels turning over small stones.

'His application's been turned down twice,' continued Matt, 'mainly due to strong local resistance, but Clive doesn't seem one to give up easily. He's been buying up a lot of land. His company is behind these offers-to-buy letters we've all been getting. We also think he may be running a campaign of intimidation. All the petty vandalism that's been going on, the phone lines cut, that sort of thing. We think he's trying to make it so uncomfortable for people here that they sell up and—'

'The opposition gradually erodes,' I finished for him. 'Allan Keech and his brother's gang are working for him, aren't they?'

'We think so. We found a sort of den in a garage. Seems to be the place where the gang hang out. We found some paint that looks very like the stuff you were cleaning off your front door the other night. There were a couple of grass snakes in a box, too. It looks like it was the kids who were leaving snakes in houses.'

Those kids had handled adders, not to mention a taipan, without being bitten? Had murdered three old people? Relieved as I was at finding I was no longer a suspect, it didn't seem terribly likely.

'I hadn't suspected any connection between Ventry and the Witcher family but, if you're right, it would add another dimension to the whole business. Right, I'm getting on the radio now. Someone will be with you in ten minutes.'

'Oh, please, just let me come home. I'll come straight back to the village, I promise.'

'It isn't possible. A bloody great oak tree came down across the main road about an hour ago. No one's getting in or out of the village tonight.'

'You're there now?'

'I am. I've just been up to see if it can be shifted. No chance. It needs heavy lifting gear. Ventry's here too, fortunately. And as his helicopter can't take off in this wind, he's stuck here for the duration. Now, I don't want any arguments. I'll leave orders that no one's to speak to you until I get to the station. You might have to spend the night in a cell, and I'm sorry about that, but it serves you bloody well right for running off.'

'OK,' I said, and realized I was smiling. It was just the relief, I told myself, of knowing I was no longer suspected. And, in any case, I was so tired, spending the night in a cell didn't seem like too much of a problem. I'd probably be asleep the minute the door clanged shut.

Another second's pause, when I felt myself holding

my breath. Then, 'I'm glad you're OK,' he said. 'I'll see you soon.'

The phone clicked, the line went dead and he was gone.

I sat in the car, unable to see out through windscreens that were being pelted with heavy rainfall, feeling the vehicle buffeted by strong winds every few seconds. Ten minutes went by, and no patrol car arrived to pick me up. My eyes were starting to close. It felt like it might all, at last, be over. There were loose ends, of course, but the police could tie them up. It wasn't my job, it had never been my responsibility. I could go back to the life I knew, fixing up wounded animals, hiding my face from my own kind.

That's all it is, you know, a scar.

I'm glad you're OK. I'll see you soon.

My eyes drifted open. I'd spent twenty-five years constructing a barrier around me that I'd thought as strong and impenetrable as a fortress. And the events of the last few days had blown it apart like dynamite under a sandcastle. Twenty-five years playing hide-and-seek with life and it had finally found me. No, it had done more than that. It had grabbed me by the scruff of the neck and dragged me, kicking and screaming, into the sunlight. And now . . . was I going to slip back into the shadows?

Twenty minutes had passed since Matt had put the phone down, but still no sign of the patrol car. I guessed the police had a lot on their plate with the storm. They'd get to me soon enough.

I pulled down the sun visor above the driver's seat and pushed back the slide to reveal the mirror that I'd never used before. And I took a good, long, hard look at my own face, probably the first time in my life I'd done so.

It wasn't too bad at all. I wasn't gorgeous (thanks all the same, Sean), nor was I pretty (although sweet of you to say so, Violet), but the reality honestly bore no relation to the deformed monster I'd constructed in my own head. It had been ten years since I'd last talked to a plastic surgeon, but the technology had moved on; there might be more they could do for me. And I would buy some decent clothes, that Matt's Aunt Mildred might consider being seen dead in. By this time I was definitely smiling at myself, something else I'd never done before. Perhaps I could buy some make-up. Damn it, I'd even do Sean's screen test.

A tapping on the car window made me jump. I turned, hoping to see a uniformed constable, dreading that it would be Tasker but knowing I could deal with him all the same. What I saw was a thin, elderly man with a wet blue anorak pulled over a damp black suit, thin wisps of hair plastered to his face. I leaned over and opened the passenger door.

'Clara!' he said, peering in at me. 'Do you realize half the county is looking for you?'

I turned to look again at the blue Fiesta parked close by. If I'd done more than glance at it when I'd arrived, I might have recognized it. I was in a church car park after all. Reverend Percival Stancey had no doubt been visiting one of his colleagues.

'Why did you lie to me?' I asked, pushing myself upright and staring directly into his eyes. I'd always thought of the small, black-clad man as kindly, old-fashioned, maybe a little self-centred, but basically a good man. I didn't any more. 'Why did you tell me you weren't in the village in 1958? You were in the church the night it burned down. Ruby just told me. She saw you, sitting at the back.'

Reverend Percival Stancey sighed. 'I think the rain's slackening,' he said. 'Could you bear to take a little walk, dear?'

I climbed out of the car and found my jacket. I didn't think the rain was slackening at all, quite the opposite, but I found I didn't mind it. Percy gestured me to precede him across the gravel towards the clifftop. Wondering if I had more to learn after all, I set off.

'I was still a curate back in 1958,' Reverend Percy said, as we approached the low wall that separated the car park from the much rougher land that ran along the clifftop. 'I think there's a gate just along here.'

We turned and followed the line of the wall. 'And I wasn't based in the village,' he continued. 'I was assigned to a parish about ten miles away. I heard about Reverend Fain, and I was curious. So I cycled over one night and attended an evening service.' We reached the gate. Percy opened it and gestured me through. I paused for a second. The cliff edge was very close and the ground far from even. It was really no place for a man in his seventies to be walking. Especially not in this weather. 'This was the fifteenth of June?' I asked.

'No, no, some weeks earlier. After you, my dear.'

I walked through the gate, intending to keep close to the wall. I might no longer be a wanted suspect but the last thing I needed was to explain how an elderly clergyman in my company had plummeted to his death.

'There was a lot of hysteria,' Percy was saying. 'People shouting out, waving their arms around, babbling and ranting. All nonsense, in my view. I reported back to my vicar, who asked me to keep an eye on it. So I started cycling over every couple of weeks, just so we knew what was going on.'

'What did you make of Reverend Fain?'

Percy had positioned himself next to the wall, with me on the outside, closest to the cliff edge. He took my arm, and we walked forward. The rain was running down my neck, and the wind made it difficult to hear what he was saying. Percy, though, seemed hardly to notice the weather.

'A very bright man. He had an imposing personality, great physical presence. I thought he could be a very powerful influence, for good or bad.'

'And which path did he choose?'

Reverend Percy sighed. 'Oh, the bad, of course. Men of that kind always do.'

'But he seems to have taken the whole village with him.'

Was it my imagination, or was Reverend Percy veering to the left, steering me closer to the cliff edge?

'No, no. Fewer than half, I'd say. And before you blame these people, you have to remember that they'd not long been through a long and very dreadful war. Two wars, in the case of some of the older ones. The sort of messages Fain was preaching, about signs presaging the end of the world, about our living in the last days of God's earth, they were very convincing at the time. Fain claimed he was a member of the Elijah Company, a sort of group of saints sent by God to bring all his true children home. That was his reason for being in England, he said, he was a living saint. I must say, he always looked the part.'

We'd stopped walking. A quick glance to the left told me I wasn't more than two feet from the cliff edge.

'When you've lived through the slaughter of millions,' Percy went on, 'it doesn't require a great leap of faith to see signs of the apocalypse.'

'I do understand that times were different then. But fasting for days on end? Handling poisonous snakes? How could the Church condone that sort of thing?'

'We didn't, but we had to tread carefully. He wasn't breaking any English laws. There was no incumbent vicar in the parish, and the people of the village had a right to conduct worship in the church building.'

The reverend was smiling, but sadly, and his eyes weren't focusing on mine. The wind was getting up, and I began to feel distinctly uncomfortable so close to a seventy-foot drop.

'So what did you do?' I asked, wondering how I could move without looking foolish. Stancey was very close to me now, leaning towards me.

'We wrote to people we knew in the United States, trying to find out what we could about Fain. Snake handling had been banned by this time in a number of states, and we wondered if maybe he'd broken the law, was possibly on the run.'

'You wrote letters,' I said, unable to help a glance back. A sudden gust hit me full in the face. 'And five people died.'

Stancey gripped my shoulder. 'We had no idea things would go as far as they did. It all got totally out of control that night.'

'I'll say,' I said, stepping to one side. 'Do you realize that everyone in the church that night could be considered an accessory to murder?'

Stancey froze. 'What on earth are you talking about?'

'Ulfred was murdered,' I said. 'No reasonable, sane person could seriously believe you'd be able to kill him and then bring him back to life.'

'I think you've—' He was moving again, stepping towards me. I moved too. I was getting back on the safe side of the wall.

'I know you and some of the others tried to stop it, but how on earth could you let it get that far?'

'Clara . . .'

I'd backed myself up against a gorse bush. 'You allowed a severely handicapped man to be tied up and drowned.'

'What exactly did Ruby tell—'

Stancey moved closer. To get round him and the gorse bush I had to step very close to the cliff edge.

'What did they do with the body?' I asked. 'Is he in the churchyard somewhere? In an unmarked grave?'

At that moment, the ground beneath my feet gave way. I felt a sickening lurch in my stomach as I slipped downwards. Far below me, I heard loose rocks clattering. My arms flew out and caught hold of Percy. With surprising strength for so elderly a man, he clung on and staggered backwards. For a second I thought all was lost, and then my feet found something solid to push against and we shot forward.

We both fell against the low stone wall. For a moment neither of us could speak as we struggled to get our breath back. I wasn't the first to recover. 'Perhaps this wasn't such a good idea,' Percy said. 'Let's go back to the cars.'

We walked back through the gate as my breathing slowed to normal.

'When the fire broke out, most people fled,' Percy said, breaking off as a fit of coughing caught up with him. 'Ernest Amblin and I managed to get to the front, to that baptism pool they'd dug. We pulled Ulfred up and cut him loose.'

I'd taken Percy's arm again. 'And was he—'

'He wasn't breathing. Ernest couldn't find any pulse.'

I was barely breathing either. I didn't dare interrupt.

'Ernest showed me how to massage his heart. And he gave him the kiss of life. I think you call it CPR these days. And all the time the church burned around us.'

I tried to picture it; the heat, the hiss of the fire, the screams. Percy's hand closed over mine.

'I sometimes think, dear, that if I do go to hell, it won't come as a surprise,' he said. 'I think I caught a glimpse of it that night.'

'Did you save him?' I managed after a moment.

'Oh yes. It took a few minutes, but he gave a gigantic

breath and water poured out of him. We managed to carry him out and get him home. So you see, Clara, in a manner of speaking, we did raise a man from the dead that night.'

'What happened then?'

'Walter took care of him, arranged for him to be taken somewhere, very discreetly. It was quietly but firmly suggested to Saul and Harry that they find somewhere else to live for a while. Archie had already fled; no one ever saw him again, although he did send money to pay for Reverend Fain's headstone. Edeline was allowed to stay out of respect for Walter. And then no one ever spoke of that night again. I think a lot of people assumed Ulfred really had died.'

We'd reached the cliff wall and I had to let go of Percy's arm.

'Shortly afterwards, we heard from the ministry we'd written to in the States,' Percy continued. 'Too late, of course, by this time.'

'What did they tell you?'

'Shocking story. Joel Fain stood trial in 1956 for murdering his father. Apparently Fain Senior found his son, an ordained minister by this time, in the churchyard. He and other members of his church had exhumed a new grave. It was clear, by that time, what they'd been planning to do. At least, try to do. The father went mad, attacked his son, locked him away in the family house. Then, the father went missing. He was found, after a week, trapped in a cabin in the middle of the woods.'

'Dead?' I asked.

'Oh yes. He'd been shut in the cabin with a rattlesnake. It took him several days to die.'

'And Fain stood trial?'

'He insisted on defending himself. It was quite a sensational trial in its day. He kept making references to Cicero, the famous Roman lawyer, and to his first trial, when he defended a young man accused of the same crime.'

'Killing his father?'

'Exactly. Fain thought himself quite the classics scholar, by all accounts. Anyway, Fain's mother employed lawyers of her own, trying to convince the court her son was insane. If he'd been found guilty, he'd have faced the death penalty. Perhaps she saw an insanity plea as the only way of saving him. She must have been successful, because he was transferred to a secure hospital and then he escaped. People thought she must have helped him; that she was hiding him somewhere. She wasn't, as we knew by then, although she may have helped him get to England.'

Fain had killed his own father. And such a man had held sway over an entire parish.

'If we'd only known sooner,' Percy was saying, 'we might have saved those three men who died with Fain. Although I can't help thinking it was all for the best in Ulfred's case. He needed specialist help.'

I was shaking my head. 'No, no. It still doesn't make sense.' We were back at the car park. I stopped and turned to face the old clergyman. 'Walter is still alive,' I said.

Percy looked at me in astonishment.

'He is,' I insisted. 'I saw him this morning. He told me Ulfred was sent to a psychiatric hospital – so I guess that fits with what you just told me – but I went there and they had no record of an Ulfred Witcher ever being admitted. They checked right back to 1958. They were very thorough. They found absolutely no trace of him.'

Percy was looking annoyingly calm. 'Well, they wouldn't. But he was there all the same. I visited him myself, in the early years.'

'I don't—'

'Ulfred's name was Dodwell. He wasn't Walter's brother. He was Edeline's.'

45

'DODWELL? FRED DODWELL? IS THAT WHO YOU mean?'

Fred? Ulfred? It had to be. It was no use, I simply couldn't concentrate and carry on driving. I turned off the main road and pulled over.

'Yes, I think so,' I said, switching off the engine. 'I'm so sorry I wasted your time this morning. I got my family connections completely mixed up. So, you do know Fred Dodwell?'

'Of course. I'd have known who you meant immediately if you'd had the correct name this morning, we all would have. Fred arrived here before any of us, in the early 1960s, I think, maybe even . . .'

'1958?' I said quietly.

'Could be,' she agreed.

'So, is he still with you? Is he still . . .' I could hardly bring myself to say the word. I found myself quietly praying she would tell me Ulfred had died, peacefully, some years earlier. And knew that she would not. The line had gone quiet. I sat, listening to the wind in the trees. It was getting stronger.

'Mrs Scott?' I prompted.

'You understand there are issues of confidentiality here. Normally, all I'd be allowed to tell you is that Mr Dodwell had been admitted and was currently a patient here. Then you'd have to submit an application to visit.'

'I understand.' I waited, sensing there was more to come.

'Can you tell me more about the nature of your interest?' she said eventually.

I thought for a second. Had I anything to lose by telling her the truth? Or, at least, part of it.

'Somebody's been seen around our village,' I said in the end. 'The village where Mr Dodwell used to live before he was committed. Someone has been breaking into houses, into my house. I saw him and thought I recognized him.'

'You know Fred?'

'No, no. I thought it was someone else, a man called Walter. But Walter and Fred are first cousins. I think there might be a resemblance.'

No response from Rose Scott.

'He's possibly living in the old family home,' I went on. 'He's been scaring people, even hurting them.' I paused for a second. 'This Ulfred – Fred, I mean – he may have a thing about snakes,' I said.

'Oh . . .'

I waited. For what felt like a long time. 'Mrs Scott,' I said in the end, 'are you still there?'

'Can you come back to see us?'

There wasn't time. It would take nearly an hour to get back to the hospital. If there was even the remotest possibility Ulfred was still alive, I had to let Matt know now.

'I'm sorry. There are people I need to speak to. Is there anything you can tell me? That might help?'

She was quiet again for a while. 'OK,' she said in the end. 'In the circumstances, I think we can probably stretch the rules a bit. Fred was brought here as a very young man. This hospital was just about the only world he'd ever really known. And, according to his records, when he arrived he was deeply traumatized. The doctors never really got to the bottom of that.'

'I understand,' I said, thinking it had taken me a while. 'I believe he was handicapped,' I went on, trying to ignore the dread in my stomach. 'People have told me he was blind, deaf and dumb. And that he was . . . well, they said retarded. I'm not sure . . .' My voice tailed off; I wasn't sure what the politically correct term for retarded was.

'Fred wasn't retarded. I'd say slightly below average intelligence. But he could be very cunning, especially when his own interests were at stake. He wasn't blind, either. When he arrived he had very serious cataracts in both eyes. He was operated on in the seventies. His vision was never great, but he could see well enough. He remained profoundly deaf, though.'

The man in my house hadn't heard me coming downstairs; hadn't reacted when I'd dropped and broken a glass.

'He could lip-read,' Rose Scott was saying. 'And we

taught him to talk a little, but when people have never heard sounds, their speech can't ever be completely normal. They can never quite get the tone and inflection right.'

I thought back to the strange, guttural noises that had come from my cellar that night, and the low moaning Matt and I had heard in the Witcher property. I also realized that Rose was talking about Ulfred in the past tense.

'He was never one of our easy patients,' Rose continued. 'Do you have a medical background, Miss Benning?'

'Well, yes, but . . . I'm a vet.'

'Oh, right. Well, Fred's case was reviewed many times over the years, as theories changed and we learned more about mental illness. Most recently, in the early 1990s I think, he was diagnosed as having two different forms of Impulse Control Disorder. He was a paraphiliac. He also had IED – Intermittent Explosive Disorder. I don't know if you're familiar with either of those terms?'

I was struggling. 'Paraphilia means inappropriate sexual behaviour, doesn't it?'

'Pretty much. Fred had symptoms of both exhibitionism and frotteurism. We'd find him . . . well, I'm sure you don't need the details. But it was the other disorder that was more of a concern. The IED. He was on medication, of course, a combination of anti-depressants and mood stabilizers. For months on end he'd be quiet, perfectly amenable to everything we asked of him, and then, for no apparent reason, he'd just break out into a rage. When that happened, he had to be restrained. He was very strong. And didn't seem to care how much damage he did.'

I waited, sensing she had more to tell me.

'We avoided letting him be alone with the women patients, even female members of staff.'

'Is he still with you?' I ventured, with a sudden flashback to the night I'd found myself alone with a man who had broken into my house; of the way he'd looked at me, touched me . . .

'This snake business . . .' Rose Scott didn't seem to have heard me. 'That was the strangest thing. He almost used to sense them. He'd go out in the woods, close to where he thought they'd be, and lie flat on the ground, almost as though he were listening for them. Except . . .'

'He couldn't hear,' I finished for her.

'Exactly. And he had such a way with them. He'd bring adders back, scare us all stupid, but they never bit him, not once.'

I wondered whether Sean would consider Ulfred to have been at one with the snakes, tapped into some sort of divine presence. I was pretty sure I thought it all nonsense, but I really didn't like the idea of someone handling venomous snakes with no fear of being harmed.

'And is he still . . .' The main doors of the psychiatric hospital had been wide open when I'd arrived earlier that day. There had been no perimeter fence that I'd noticed.

'His records state that he didn't have any family.' That time, Mrs Scott must have heard me. She was avoiding the question. 'When patients are with us for

457

any length of time,' she continued, 'we routinely keep in contact with close family but, in Fred's case, we didn't hear anything back, not for years. He only had one visitor in all the time I've been here. Quite recently, too. A tall, striking-looking man.'

Clive Ventry was a tall, striking man. He'd made contact with Ulfred. It was all I could do not to cut off Rose and get Matt on the phone now. I wanted to start driving again, to get back to the village. Hell, I'd even phone Tasker if I had to. I forced myself to stay calm. The more Rose could tell me, the better.

She was still talking. 'He said he wasn't from the UK. He had an accent.'

Of course he had an accent, he'd lived in South Africa for decades.

'He gave Ulfred some eggs.' Rose didn't seem put off by my lack of response. She must have sensed I was listening hard. 'Six of them,' she went on. 'About the size of duck eggs but with leathery shells. Snakes' eggs, he said they were, that he'd picked up on his travels. They were dead, of course, he was quite emphatic about that, or we couldn't have allowed Ulfred to keep them.'

I found myself looking round, scanning the road ahead and behind me. After spending the night and most of the day avoiding the police, I'd have given anything to be picked up right now. *Oh, come on, Rose, get on with it.*

'Ulfred already had a snake. A cornsnake, pretty little thing, totally harmless. We hoped it might stop him catching wild ones. He put the eggs in the cage with it, to keep them warm, he said. We indulged him, even though we knew they were dead.'

'When was this?'

'Not long ago. Last autumn sometime. We tried to trace this visitor afterwards, just in case he knew anything. But we got no reply from the address he gave us, and even the police couldn't find him.'

'The police?'

'Yes, of course we notified them straight away. Fred wasn't a criminal, you understand, but he would never have been recommended for discharge, even if he'd had family who could care for him.'

'Ulfred isn't with you any more, is he?'

A long pause this time.

'No, I'm afraid he isn't,' she said eventually. 'He went missing last November. You see, the majority of our patients remain here on a voluntary basis; there's really nothing to stop them coming and going as they please. Not that we've ever had a problem with unscheduled disappearances. But, one day, Fred went out into the grounds and just didn't come back. We searched for hours before we notified the authorities. He must have walked into town, caught a bus there. Because he'd just vanished. And so had the snake eggs.'

46

'DID THE POLICE LOOK FOR HIM?' I WAS DRIVING again, the phone clamped tight between my left shoulder and my ear. It was highly dangerous, given the state of the weather, not to mention illegal, but the roads were quiet. The storm had driven people indoors.

'Of course, he was still classed as a vulnerable and potentially dangerous patient. There was a massive police search.'

I thought quickly. The hospital was in Devon, out of Matt's area command. His staff wouldn't have been directly involved. They'd probably have been informed about the search for a missing patient, but there'd be no reason for them to make any connection between the long-incarcerated Fred Dodwell and the Witcher family.

'We wrote to his last known address, but the letter was returned by the post office with a "property empty" notice on it.'

'His sister died,' I said. 'His brother-in-law was in a hospice.'

'That would explain it,' she said. 'Fred is still listed as a missing person, but the police search was scaled down after a few months. Nothing had been heard of him, no sightings reported. The officer in charge of the case thought he must have died on the streets somewhere.'

If only. 'He isn't dead,' I said. 'He's living in his old family home. I think he may have killed three people.'

'Oh, my God.' Rose fell silent, trying to get her head around what I'd just told her, but I hadn't the time to help her out.

'I need to go. Mrs Scott, can you get on to the officer in charge of the search and tell him what I've just told you?'

'Of course, but he'll need to speak to you. Can't you come back here?'

'I have to get home. I'll give you an address where they can contact me.'

'But . . . you said you live in the same village. Miss Benning, Fred Dodwell won't have been taking his medication for months now. He could be a very dangerous man. Please tell me you're not—'

I pressed the button that would cut her off. I didn't need to hear from Rose Scott that Fred Dodwell was a dangerous man. I'd learned that myself. Nor had I time to waste listening to her well-meaning attempts to persuade me to stay away from him. I had no intention of going anywhere near Ulfred.

I found the paper Matt had given me, peered down at the mobile number and, with one hand still clutching the steering wheel, dialled it.

Some time last November Ulfred had left the

psychiatric hospital and made his way home. There was no answer on the mobile number I was ringing. I dialled Matt's home number.

Rose Scott's description of Ulfred's condition had made me remember Walter's dark hints. *I couldn't manage him. And he and Edeline. How could I have stopped them? I couldn't stop any of them.*

Edeline and Ulfred had been brother and sister. Sexual promiscuity was one thing, but all her husband's brothers and her own too? It was little wonder Walter hadn't wanted her to look after his brother's child. Edeline hadn't been the sort of woman you'd want around any child.

Within weeks of Ulfred leaving the psychiatric hospital, Edeline herself had been dead. Had her brother been responsible?

Continuous dial tone on Matt's line. I tried his mobile again.

John Allington had been in the church that night in 1958; Edeline had played an active part in his near-drowning. If Ulfred was seeking revenge for what had happened to him, those two would be obvious targets. Yet Violet hadn't been in church at all. Ernest Amblin had saved Ulfred's life. Why would he want to hurt them?

The more I thought about it, the less sense it all made. Ulfred was wreaking violence upon his contemporaries, people whom he associated with what had happened to him, whether they'd been genuinely involved or not. His was a disorganized and therefore very dangerous mind.

Could a disorganized mind have faked Violet's will? Injected adder venom into John Allington?

A man whom I was certain was Clive Ventry, aka Saul Witcher Junior, had visited Ulfred. Had he helped him leave shortly afterwards? Had Clive raked over old memories; blowing on the sparks of resentment, fanning them up until Ulfred's desire for revenge burned as brightly as his own? Was Clive using Ulfred as the instrument of his own vengeance? Or was it just about greed? Maybe Ulfred had been part of Clive's local nuisance campaign? Before it all got horribly out of hand?

Had Clive tried to pin the blame on me because he'd sensed that Matt and I were getting close to finding Ulfred? Was he taking me out of the picture to buy himself more time, until government authorization for his drilling project came through?

There was still no answer on the mobile. I tried Matt's home phone again. Same continuous dial tone. The storm must have brought the phone lines down in the village. If lines were coming down all over the area, everyone would be using their mobiles. I had no way of knowing when I might get through.

According to Matt, a massive tree had come down across the only official road into and out of our village. The road would be blocked for hours, probably all night. *No one's getting in or out of the village tonight.*

If Matt thought the village was cut off, he wouldn't be trying to get help. He'd wait till morning, till backup could arrive, before arresting Clive Ventry. But Matt didn't know about the other, infinitely more dangerous, threat in the village. He didn't know about Ulfred. What if Matt decided to take another look around the Witcher house?

OK, I had a choice. I could drive immediately to the nearest police station, give myself up to the desk sergeant and convince them that Ulfred was a real threat and that they had to get to the village right now.

But what if they didn't believe me? What if no one was available to talk to me? What if I were kept in a cell for hours?

No way in or out, Matt had said. He'd been brought up in the village, played around the fields as a boy. But he probably hadn't spent the last four years running daily around every road, track, footpath and bridlepath in existence. He hadn't spent his weekends poring over Ordnance Survey maps, trying to find new routes, where the possibility of human contact was minimal. Nor had he driven or trekked for hours every week over the fields, woods and valleys of the area in search of wounded creatures.

I knew all the old farm tracks, many of them disused now, the bridleways, cycle tracks and footpaths. I knew which rivers were navigable, where you could take an ordinary car, where you needed four-wheel drive and where a vehicle simply wouldn't go. I knew all the shortest routes for getting from A to B, I even knew As and Bs that nobody else dreamed existed. In spite of what Matt had told me, I knew I didn't need the main road to get back to the village.

* * *

When I was just under two miles away, I turned off the road and drove along an old track that leads to a disused chalk quarry. I was heading due north, along a route I knew well. I'd driven here just days ago, when Craig, Simon and I had rescued the mute swan.

Of course, there is a world of difference between driving across country in the daylight, in good weather, with two men to assist you, and doing it alone, in the midst of a bad storm, when the darkness is deepening with every passing second.

The quarry track stretched for about three quarters of a mile, the last two hundred yards of which were overgrown with heather and gorse. At the end of the track was a ramshackle collection of buildings that once stored equipment for the quarry workers – and the great gaping hole in the hillside that is all that remains of the old earth workings. I had no wish to linger here. To my left was a padlocked, solid-steel gate. Normally, when we came this way, we had a key, which I didn't have tonight, but I wasn't going to let a minor detail like that hold me back.

Three days ago, we'd noticed a rotten section of the fence, just yards away from the gate. The blackthorn on the other side was thin and spindly. I turned the vehicle so that I was directly opposite the weak point before dropping the Land Rover into first gear and making sure I had enough traction beneath the tyres.

And as I paused there, summoning up the nerve, I found myself remembering the night Matt and I had stood at the gate to the Witcher property. No way in or out, I'd reminded him. He'd grinned and produced a key that had the lock open in seconds. *There is now*, he'd said, with a grin. I pressed my foot down hard on the accelerator and the Land Rover shot forward. It hit the fence with an almighty crash. For a second, wooden palings were flung against the windscreen, I could hear undergrowth scraping the underside of the vehicle, then the palings fell away and I was on the other side. *There is now*, I said to myself, but I wasn't grinning.

The next mile took me through woodland. It was an ancient beech grove, and some of the trees reached nearly seventy feet in height. They swayed as if they were possessed that night, swooping down towards me with incredible force. People talk about trees rustling, of them whispering. That night they roared and screamed at me as the wind tore through their crowns, ripping away branches, pushing against trunks that had withstood the storms of decades. I wouldn't have put money on any of them lasting the night.

More than once, broken limbs hit the Land Rover, thudding against the roof, the side panels, even the front windscreen, which narrowly avoided shattering. At one point, I had to brake sharply to avoid driving into a fallen trunk. It was maybe three hundred years old, with a huge girth and a network of branches that spread out across the ground like a spider's web. I reversed up and found a way around it.

I made it through the beech grove, knowing the Land Rover had suffered serious damage and that I'd have a lot of explaining to do. But then again, trouble with the trust that ran the Little Order was likely to be the least of my worries. From this point on, the going was a little easier, but the rain was falling heavily again, hampering visibility further and softening the ground. If I got stuck now, it was all over.

But Land Rovers are designed for exactly this sort of terrain, and I didn't get stuck. I drove through another gate, this time not locked, and I was on Clive Ventry's land. At this point the track forked. If I turned left, I'd get to the river, as Simon, Craig and I had done days earlier to rescue the swan. That way, too, offered a possible way into the village, but I really hoped I wouldn't need it. So I switched off the vehicle's headlights and turned right, heading uphill. I drove through one four-acre field, then another larger one. By this time I was close enough to see the manor house. It was in complete darkness. Without driving across Clive's back lawn, I couldn't get much closer to the village roads, so I stopped the car and got out.

For a split second the countryside around me flashed into what almost seemed like daylight and I felt totally exposed. Then darkness fell again and thunder cracked. The storm was getting closer.

I ran round the back of the vehicle and lifted the tailgate. We never know when we might be called out on an emergency rescue so the Land Rovers are always equipped with rope, wire, torches, basic tools and medical supplies. I found the most powerful flashlight, my medical bag, a pair of binoculars, a sharp knife and a wrench. Then I set off up the hill towards the house, feeling the primitive urge common to all living creatures to hunker down and take shelter from the storm, but forcing myself to go on.

The rainfall was almost tropical in its intensity by this stage, hurtling itself out of the sky, and it occurred to me that the taipan, if it was on the loose, would feel perfectly at home in the downpour. I wondered where it was, sheltering in a building somewhere, or lurking in the undergrowth, and I found a moment to wish I was wearing stout boots, preferably thigh-high, instead of trainers.

There are no streetlights in our village and, after night falls, it is always dark. To see our way around, we rely upon our neighbours maintaining outdoor lights on their properties. Normally, that's just about enough, but none of them was alight now; the power failures across the county had affected us too. I stole past the manor and ran across the formal garden at the front. There was a thick yew hedge lining the garden, but I was pretty certain I could squeeze underneath it. On the other side, only dark shapes of buildings lay ahead of me. I set off running again, keeping a careful look-out all around me. This was one night I was not going to be ambushed by Allan Keech and his friends; or anyone else for that matter.

I ran across the village green, unable to keep from shuddering as I saw the darkness beneath the bridge and decided that no power on earth would get me under it again. No one was in sight as I ran up the hill that led home and, just before Bourne Lane, I turned and jogged down the narrow, laurel-lined drive that led to Matt's house. There was a car parked outside, a green hatchback. A small candle flickered in the window closest to the front door. I banged on the door and heard footsteps on a tiled floor. A bolt was being drawn back. The door began to move inwards.

'I couldn't get you on the . . .' I began. And stopped.

'Hello,' said the woman standing at Matt's threshold, like the beautiful gatekeeper of a place to which I would never be allowed admittance. 'Are you looking for Matt?'

Somehow I managed to nod.

'He had to go out,' she said. 'He should have been back by now. I've been keeping dinner.'

Something had sprung into life inside me: a snarling, creeping thing that I had to push down and ignore; I could not allow it room to breathe and grow or it just might swallow me whole.

'Did he say where?' I croaked.

'Look, come in for a sec, it's pouring.'

She stepped back, and I had no choice but to follow her. In the next few seconds I had time to notice that Matt's hallway was large, its walls lined with stone. A fire burned in the hearth, and the floor tiles were old and cracked. The pictures on the walls were strikingly modern. Mostly, though, I couldn't take my eyes off the woman, who smelled like sandalwood and Indian spices. She must have been close to six feet tall, slender as a willow sprig, with a wavy mass of bright-red hair.

'Is it urgent? Can I do anything?' she was asking me.

'Are you with the police?' I asked, knowing she wasn't.

'No. I'm Rachel, Matt's girlfriend.'

And I'd had to make her say it.

'Is something wrong?' she went on.

Was this what it felt like then, to know your heart was breaking? *Oh Christ, Clara, concentrate!*

'I'm not sure,' I started. How much could I tell her? 'Have you got any phones working?'

'No. The lines went down an hour ago. Just after Matt had a call. I haven't been able to get through on either of our mobiles. Matt has his radio, of course, but he took that with him.'

'Listen, this is really important. Do you have any idea who phoned him or where he's gone?'

She was frowning now, picking up on my anxiety, wondering if she'd done the right thing inviting me in. 'Yes,' she said slowly. 'I answered the phone. What was he called now – Chris, Colin . . .'

'Clive?' I offered. *No, please no . . .*

'Yes, that's it. Sounded very uptight about something. Wanted to see Matt right away. Matt spoke to him for a couple of minutes and then went out. He took his car, probably just because of the rain. He can't get out of the village, can he?'

'Not easily,' I muttered, thinking hard. 'And this was an hour ago?'

'Pretty much. Look, do I need to—'

'Keep trying the mobile. Try and get through to Matt's colleagues. Ask for DI Tasker. Tell him Clara Benning is back in the village. That should get him running.' Rachel stared at me for a second and then turned to a small table. There was a pen and message pad on it and she started to scribble. 'And tell him to talk to his colleagues in the Devon police about Ulfred Dodwell and the Two Counties

470

Psychiatric Hospital. Can you remember that?'

'Clara Benning, Ulfred Dodwell, Two Counties. I've got it.' Rachel was looking wary, wondering what kind of scary lunatic she'd invited into the house.

'Thanks. And tell him if he drives up to Rickstone quarry and follows my tracks north-east, he can get into the village.'

'OK.' She left the table and moved to the door. She wanted me out of there. But she'd probably do what I asked.

'And if anyone else comes to the door, don't open it till you're sure you know who they are.'

'Don't worry,' she said, shaking her head emphatically. 'I won't.'

Back down the hill, across the green and along Clive Ventry's drive, I ran like the hounds of hell were after me. Matt had been missing for an hour. He'd taken a call from a distressed-sounding Clive and had gone out. I reached the stone archway of the manor house and ran into the cobbled courtyard beyond. Then I forced myself to stop, get my breath back and take stock.

The medieval manor buildings encircled me. Ancient windows with nothing but blackness behind stared down from all sides. Any one of them could be concealing watching eyes. In the small garden, centuries-old yew trees had been sculpted into tall, mushroom-like shapes. Handy enough hiding places for anyone lurking. I counted four thick wooden doors, including the double pair at the centre-front of the manor. Any of them could open in a split second.

Three cars were parked by the front doors. A dark Jaguar that I thought I'd seen being driven around the village and which I guessed must belong to Clive Ventry, and a small silver hatchback, remarkably like the car that had been behind me the night I'd first visited Sean on the Undercliff. Had someone from this house followed me there? There was also a black Golf. The car Matt had driven me home in the previous day had been a dark-coloured Volkswagen. I strode across to the driver's door of the Golf and pulled it open. There was a car radio that didn't look as though it belonged in a civilian vehicle, and on the carpet was the red folder I remembered. It was Matt's car.

Walking quickly across the cobbles, I came to the house. I peered through one window, then another. The manor seemed to be in complete darkness; I couldn't even make out candlelight.

Go round the back, all my instincts were screaming at me. *You have no idea what's in there. If you have to go in, put it off for as long as you can.*

Ah, but that's all you'd be doing, said another voice; a calm, gentle voice that I thought I recognized but in my keyed-up state couldn't be sure about. *You'd be putting it off. If you're going to do that, you might as well go home.*

The front door was solid oak, with a huge, iron circular handle. It turned easily in my hand and the door opened. I stepped inside.

47

THE OLD HALL WAS SHIMMERING WITH MOVEMENT; caused not by the living creatures I'd been dreading but by light, flickering around the room. A few seconds went by before I could trace its source, then, through one of the tiny-paned windows, I saw the full moon had risen. And in a clearer part of the sky where there was no storm, clouds were speeding across it, causing the moonbeams to dart and shiver. A large mirror over the empty hearth and dozens of crooked windowpanes sent the beams scurrying in a hundred directions.

I stood there, checking each corner of the large room, making sure every movement was nothing more substantial than light; that none of the shadows contained something lurking. Directly ahead of me was the staircase where I'd been forced to stand just over a week ago.

To my left was the great oak table around which villagers had gathered. Various pewter items were placed on its surface but nothing coiled around any of them. I bent down, checked the floor, the chair legs, alert for any shape that might seem out of place. Only then did I allow myself to move away from the door.

I stood in the centre of the room, listening. No sound but the rain and the occasional protesting creak of an old house bullied by strong winds. Where to look first? The house was huge. For no reason other than I had to make a choice, I moved right, towards a carved oak door at the bottom of the staircase.

Pulling my sleeve down to cover my hand, I pulled gently on the handle. The door opened and I moved inside. I was in a sitting room filled with elaborately carved dark-wood furniture. Across the room was an old stone hearth. A draught coming through the open door made a small cloud of ash float into the air before drifting back down again. I circled my way across the room, afraid of who or what might creep up on me if I kept my back turned for more than a second or two. An open door at the far end led into complete darkness. Switching on the torch, I saw another large, oak-panelled room, this time furnished as a study. Bookshelves lined the walls. The curtains on the three windows were all drawn. Shining the torch everywhere, peering into every corner, I crossed the room until I stood before Clive Ventry's desk.

Several telephones, a state-of-the-art computer and a desk-top printer sat on the antique desk – as did a scattering of papers. I shone my torch across the desk, glancing at invoices, profit and loss statements, geological reports too technical for me to understand. None of it meant anything, and I was feeling distinctly uncomfortable being in one place for so long. I was just about to turn back when my torch beam flickered on a sheet of headed notepaper that rang a bell. It was an official letter from the Department for Business Enterprise and Regulatory Reform, BERR, formerly the DTI.

Using the edge of the torch, I pushed the letter until I could see all of it. It was short, just three paragraphs long, from the head of the energy exploration department. 'Dear Clive,' it began, before going on to give Clive the 'very good news' that the minister had finally approved his request to drill.

In spite of local opposition, Clive Ventry had been granted permission to explore the ground around the village for oil reserves. If the huge onshore oil field that Matt had speculated about lay beneath the village, Clive would probably make millions from it. To add to the millions he already had.

And then almost as if it were following my train of thought, my torchbeam picked out another letter, this time from a local solicitor, confirming Clive's appointment the following week to discuss revising his will. The second paragraph went on to explain that, as the situation currently stood, Clive's estate would pass to any surviving family members, the exact division to be decided during the probate process. His ex-wife, the letter explained, following her generous divorce settlement, would be unlikely to make a successful claim.

I'd covered the length of the house and had to turn back. I flicked off the torch and, as I walked back through the darkened rooms, I found myself wondering to whom Clive was planning to leave his many millions and whether his uncle Ulfred was in line for a bequest. And then I remembered his other uncle, and wondered whether the prospect of a legacy might be enough to bring Reverend Archie home.

Returning to the hall, I peered through the window. Matt's car was still outside.

I made my way past the huge oak table, past dressers filled with pewter and antique china, past the corner where five old people had huddled nervously. Two of the five, Violet and Ernest, were dead. How many more had to die before Ulfred would be satisfied?

In the room's far left corner, three small steps led through an archway. Only darkness and intermittent shadows lay beyond. I thought about switching on the torch, but knew it would make me a sitting duck for anyone watching. The middle stair creaked, but I didn't think anyone but I could have heard it.

I was in the back corridor of the house, the place where the servants would have scurried about in the old days. A wooden spiral staircase wound its way upwards. I couldn't see the end of the corridor, but coats and hats hung along the walls, wellington boots stood beneath them. I waited for a few seconds, just to make sure nothing solid lurked amidst the mass of coats, hats and boots. Then moved on.

The room ahead of me was a dining room. More heavy, dark-oak furniture; more china, glassware and silver. Did one man really live here alone? What delusions of grandeur could persuade someone from humble roots to buy and maintain such a property for his sole use?

There was nothing out of place in the dining room that I could see. I stepped back out and, very wary now – I really didn't like the ranks of coats – walked a few steps down the corridor. A doorway to the right led to a small kitchen. An enormous range cooker stood against one wall, a kitchen sink was directly opposite. There were large cupboards, and I knew I really should check them, but my heartbeat, already working on over-time, had accelerated. There was a smell in the kitchen; one that I knew all too well.

Take care now, Clara, you're very close, said the calm, familiar voice in my head.

A doorway on my left led to another kitchen. Someone familiar with manor-house design might recognize it as a butler's pantry, a scullery, whatever; it just looked like another kitchen to me. It had a sink, what appeared to be a large dishwasher and shelves stacked with glassware and cutlery. The smell was stronger. Another doorway, another room beyond.

I saw the slick, dark pool on the floor before I'd moved within two feet of the doorway and knew my senses hadn't let me down. There really is no mistaking the smell of fresh blood.

Steady, Clara, stay calm, said the voice, *just a few more steps*.

I don't remember taking those steps. I have no way of knowing how much time passed between my realizing what I was going to find and then standing in the third kitchen of the manor house, shining my torch down on what had once been a man.

48

I WAS OUTSIDE AGAIN. HOW I GOT THERE, I'LL NEVER know. I was leaning against Matt's car, the rain was a freezing torrent, pouring over my head, but I was glad of it. I looked up and saw the raindrops falling towards me from an infinite sky. I let them run over my face, wishing they could cleanse the inside of me as well, wash away the memory from my head, the smell from my nostrils. But I think I knew, even then, that nothing would ever be able to do that.

On legs that felt weaker than a toddler's I staggered through the manor garden and made my way round the back of the house. I thought I'd seen every manner of cruelty the human animal is capable of inflicting on others. I'd been so wrong.

The man lying on the kitchen floor had had no head; just a mass of chopped, glistening bone and flesh. Parts of him – pieces of his brain, his face, his hair – lay splattered around the floor. As though he'd just exploded apart.

A sudden vile taste and convulsion of muscles warned

me I was about to vomit. I stopped, bent over and began retching, but I hadn't eaten all day and nothing but bile came out. When I could stand again I raised my face once more to the skies, wishing that, for once in my adult life, I could find the words to pray and the heart to mean it. Because if ever I'd needed faith, it was now.

Steady, Clara. That voice again. So hauntingly, comfortingly familiar, making me want to curl myself into a tight ball, press against the warmth and safety I knew it represented. *Take it easy*, the voice went on, *you know what you have to do next.*

I was crossing the lawn at the back of the house.

You are going to be seen, Clara, get close to the hedge.

I turned to where the hedge lined the lawn. It was a million miles away. A sudden flashback: a human eye, knocked clean out of its socket, had rolled three feet from the body, to rest in the dust under the table. I'd fallen. I was kneeling on the wet grass, sinking into mud.

Clara, get moving.

I can't.

Yes, you can. The poor man you saw in there wasn't Matt.

I pushed myself up. There had been no black-rimmed, oblong spectacles anywhere among the carnage on the kitchen floor. A small gold chain around the neck of the victim had shone in the torchlight, a signet ring had gleamed on the little finger of his left hand. Matt didn't wear jewellery. Plus, the clothes were wrong and the body had been taller and of a heavier build than Matt.

479

I'd known instantly I was looking at the remains of Clive Ventry. If it had been Matt, I think I'd still have been standing there.

It wasn't Matt, it wasn't Matt. Muttering it to myself like a mantra, I made it to the bottom of the lawn and climbed the stone wall that separated Clive's gardens from the rest of his land. Only they weren't Clive's gardens any more. They belonged to his two uncles: the dangerous, long-incarcerated Ulfred and Archie, who'd once tried to kill his own cousin.

Kill a close relative. Archie, Saul Senior, Harry and Edeline had all been involved in Ulfred's attempted murder. He had been cousin to three of them, brother to the fourth. Was that close enough? If Ulfred was finally getting his revenge, did that explain the Roman symbolism I kept seeing in the attacks? But would a man of below-average intelligence, who'd had little formal education, have even heard of *poena cullei*? It didn't seem likely. Saul Junior, of course, was a different story. If he'd held the village responsible for the deaths of his parents, he might have seen some rough justice in the echoes of the ancient execution. But whether he'd been the orchestrator of the recent attacks or not, he wasn't someone I had to worry about any more.

The Land Rover was where I'd left it. No signal on the mobile phone. I had to hope Rachel was having more success than I. Pulling off my soaked jacket, I climbed into the drivers' seat.

Where am I going?

To the snake house, of course.

I fell forward, my head bouncing painfully against the

steering wheel. Why? Why in God's name do I have to go there?

Because that's where Matt went. He found Clive's body and has gone to track down Ulfred. That's why nothing's been heard of him for more than an hour.

I raised my head. Ulfred will be watching. He'll see me coming.

But there's another way in. You know there is. You've known about it for some time.

I can't.

Silence. But I'd recognized that voice; I knew exactly to whom it belonged, and I knew from long experience that if it and I got into an argument, I would never win.

So why was I wasting time?

It took another fifteen minutes to get to the river. Slurring in mud, I reversed until the vehicle's rear was almost touching the water's edge, then switched off the engine. I found and pulled on waders, waterproof trousers and a life-jacket. Even without the present storm, the river was flowing as fast as it had for months. Besides, it had been drummed into us for so long by the health and safety people, I think it was automatic. Working near water, wear the proper gear.

I pulled a light waterproof jacket around my shoulders and climbed out of the car. Pulling out the dinghy and launching it by myself wasn't easy, but I managed it. I put the equipment bag in the bottom, climbed in and shoved hard.

Some time over the last twenty-four hours, my subconscious had solved the puzzle that had been nagging at me for days. If someone was living in the old Witcher house, how was he getting in and out, how was he moving around the village without being seen? Now I knew. He was travelling via the waterways and the old chalk-mine workings. Tonight, so would I be.

There are probably more streams in our village than roads. I've no idea how many offshoots of the river Liffin there are, but just about every street has a small, brick-lined waterway running down it. They are all crossed by numerous tiny bridges; they frequently tunnel under roads. Someone could crawl through these ditches with very little risk of being seen, especially at night. And where the watercourses didn't go, the chalk workings probably did.

At first, I was travelling in the same direction as the river, its flow was carrying me along and I needed the paddle only to steer. Soon, though, I would have to turn upstream and paddle my way up an overgrown, fast-flowing backwater.

The night Matt and I had visited the Witcher property, I'd felt sure someone was still living there. Matt had put my instincts down to girlie jumpiness, but the stench in the lavatory, the warmth of the downstairs wall, the movement I'd heard: all had made me sure the property was not the abandoned one we'd thought it to be.

We searched it thoroughly, Matt had reminded me; no sign of anyone living there.

Except we hadn't searched it thoroughly. There was a downstairs room in the third cottage that we hadn't been able to access. The only doorway had been bricked up, but I'd felt warmth behind those bricks. A way inside there must be.

I'd reached the downstream tip of the island where we'd rescued the swan. It was time to find out how strong my arm muscles were. I turned the dinghy sharply and started to paddle back upstream, this time going behind the island.

The flow was powerful, but the backwater was sheltered and the tree canopy held back some of the rain. I put my head down and concentrated on maintaining the rhythm of the double paddle.

The narrow stream was awash with debris. Branches, litter, even a couple of drowned animals sped past. Several pieces collided with me, the larger ones sending the dinghy spinning, threatening to wash me back downstream before I could regain control. My arms were tiring long before I reached the point I was heading for, but I pressed on.

It was harder to spot the change in the water flow at night, but I remembered a tree stump that had tumbled into the water. I waited until I was just past it, then pulled the paddle into the dinghy and grasped hold of the willow branches in front of me.

The river began to tug me back, as though not liking the new direction I was taking. I clung on and risked grasping another branch a little further away. Holding on to one branch after another, I pulled myself, dinghy and all, under the thick screen of willows until I was through the tree line and into the darkness on the other side. I found the dinghy's painter, flung it round a trunk and tied it off.

Breathing heavily, I tried to get a feel for my surroundings, but it was impossible. The banks were steep, the pale glow of the chalk obscured by vegetation. Thick, unpollarded willows and rare black poplars grew so close to the edge they seemed about to tumble in. I had to get some idea of where I was. I found the light and shone it around.

I was in a swift, narrow river, roughly a hundred yards from the chalk escarpment on which the Witcher house stood. The land on either side of me, what I could see above the banks, was densely wooded with gorse, hazel, bramble. It would be almost impossible to walk through. Keeping to the river offered the only way up.

Which wasn't going to be easy. The land was sloping upwards now and the water was fast. Shining the torch on the bank, I could see scars on the rocks that looked as if they'd been made with primitive tools. I thought perhaps I was in one of the old chalk workings rather than a natural watercourse.

There was no possibility of paddling the dinghy upstream from this point. I would have to wade. I took hold of a tree root to steady myself and stepped out into water that was waist deep. I took the dinghy's painter from the trunk, passed it over my head and across one shoulder. If I needed a quick getaway, it would certainly help. Switching off the torch was the hardest thing I've ever done, but I needed to be invisible; and I had to be able to see in the dark.

I set off, keeping to the middle of the stream to lessen the risk of the dinghy catching against the banks; and shutting my mind to the chill of the water and to its relentless pull. Tortuous or not, this was my only way in.

Since the night I'd heard the mute swan call, so close to the Witcher property, I knew there had to be water close to it. Water that no one else seemed to know about. It had only been a matter of time before I made the connection with the unusually flowing water entering the backwater of the Liffin. I'd realized that another stream entered the Liffin at that point, one that ran through the village, going underground as so many of them did, only to emerge from the chalk escarpment beneath the Witcher house.

As I climbed the incline, I noticed trees growing from the almost vertical banks, branches spindly from lack of proper light, leaf cover almost non-existent. One of them had fallen across the stream to form a living canopy over the water.

Once past the fallen tree, the incline of the stream's bed became steeper. At the same time, I realized the banks were getting lower and allowing me more light. Not twenty yards ahead of me, perilously close to the chalk edge, sat the Witcher house. And from this angle, I could see what nobody else in the village knew existed: the great, yawning hole in the escarpment, about fifteen feet below the foundations of the house, from which the river, black and foaming, was pouring.

The place should have been condemned years ago, I thought, as I drew closer. Not only was the house precariously close to the edge of an unstable chalk escarpment but it sat directly above the old mine workings that seemed to riddle the village's foundations.

In the increasing amount of light, I could make out

the ferns that grew on the banks, avoid the loose branches that still came spinning towards me, spot the tiny eyes that peered fearfully at this strange intruder into their territory. To my right, rocks had tumbled away into the river and I could see what appeared to be a narrow path leading up from the water's edge, away into the undergrowth. I paused for a second and looked at the muddy track. Were those footprints, all but washed away by the rain? It was hard to be sure, and I had no time to waste worrying if this was yet another way into the property. I set off again and, with every step I took, the cavernous gap that reached up into the bowels of the house before me was growing larger.

The water had become shallower and the strain in my thighs told me I was climbing quite steeply. The darkness in front of me seemed to shimmer in expectation, and I had a sense that something, lying in wait just beyond the dark, was hungry. And that it knew I was getting closer.

For the first time since I'd left the manor, driven by the voice in my head, I allowed myself to think about what lay ahead. What might be waiting for me in the old Witcher property – the snake house, as I'd started calling it to myself?

Ulfred Dodwell had spent his formative years shunned and feared by his own kind. He'd been mocked and bullied, eventually abused in the most dreadful way. He'd entered an institution as a young man and had remained there for fifty years. Even after constant care restored much of his sight, enabled him to communicate with those around him, he'd continued to avoid people, seeking solace instead among wild animals. He'd deliberately sought out creatures as secretive, misunderstood and feared as he.

I had to believe that the man I was about to face had no concept of morality. That he'd learned to consider everyone in the village, me included, as his enemies. Nor could I allow myself to think of him as an old man. Men don't lose all their strength when they turn seventy. Ulfred would be both strong and wily. He'd been crawling around the old mine workings and the watercourses. He could move around silently, would be able to see well in the dark. He had a strange, unfathomable power over snakes. He was a creature of the night.

I reached the shadow of the escarpment. A few more steps would take me inside the manmade cave that lay beneath the house. I would be sheltered from the rain. I could climb out of the river, maybe lose some of this bone-chilling cold. But this close, the gloom under the rocks was impenetrable. Did I dare?

I tugged the dinghy's painter off my shoulder. If I jumped into the boat the stream would wash me back to safety. But I knew the voice in my head, silent for so long, was waiting to spring into life again the moment I hesitated. It would tell me that I could deal with Ulfred. That I was young and strong; I had good eyesight, a strong sense of smell, acute hearing. More than all that, I was used to the darkness; I knew how to remain unseen, how to track scared, hostile creatures. After all was said and done, I was a creature of the night too. I stepped into the shadow of the cave, and the darkness swallowed me whole.

49

FOR SECONDS THAT FELT LIKE DAYS, BLACKNESS AS solid as rock surrounded me. I could almost feel it, reaching out, stroking my face. Then, far too slowly, it began to shift in its intensity and melt into shapes. The cave, little more than a fissure in the rocks now that I was standing inside it, stretched ahead of me, reaching deep into the escarpment. Looking up, the rock ceiling was about three feet above my head, forming the narrow canopy of chalk that was holding up the house. To my right, a roughly flattened rock provided a crude landing stage and, beyond that, I could see a ladder. I climbed out of the water, still holding on to the painter, and noticed a small, iron ring hammered into the rock. Someone kept a boat here.

I made my way back along the rocks. The rain, falling as heavily as it had all evening, poured over the cave entrance like a waterfall. But at its edge, thick elder and brambles grew. I knelt down and found a branch strong enough to tie the dinghy to. Then I pulled brambles over it until it was almost covered. Someone arriving in the dark, amidst heavy rain, might not see it.

The ladder, leaning against the rock wall of the fissure, was a rusting and very old one made of iron. It looked as though it had once been used in a mine. There had been safety bars attached at two-feet intervals. They'd long since broken off, but their stubs remained. Two feet above me, a wooden trap-door had been built into the rock ceiling. Anxious not to make a sound, I picked up the ladder to see if I could wedge it against the door. Luckily, or maybe by someone's design, the hole was bigger than the trap-door, and the ladder's rim slid easily into the gap between rock and wood. I tested its strength and began to climb.

At the top, I stood with my face pressed against the wood, finding it dry, and far warmer than I would have expected. I could hear nothing. I slid my hand until I found a small iron catch, and twisted. The door fell towards me. I allowed it to swing down. Then went up.

Ignoring the stench, I pulled out the torch and switched it on. I shone it all round, checking every corner, every shadow, measuring the room, alert for hiding places, for sudden movement. There was plenty of life in the room, none of it human. I climbed up and stepped away from the trap-door.

The room was small, as I'd guessed it must be, and would have been, at one time, an ordinary part of the house. A few crumbling remains of plaster clung to the walls, and electrical wires poked out where lights might once have been fastened. Against one wall, a narrow, banister-less staircase led upwards. Opposite was a mattress and a pile of soiled blankets, which were responsible, in part, for the dreadful smell.

I walked forward, past rotting remains of tinned food and sour milk, still in bottles, which I guessed had been stolen from doorsteps. The heat in the room was coming from four Calor-gas burners, standing in the corners, each turned up to full. Spare gas canisters lined one wall. I couldn't believe Ulfred had brought them all here without help. They could have been here before his return, stored by the Witchers for heaven only knew what reason. A sudden, severe series of power cuts? The end of the world? Or they could offer further proof that Ulfred had been getting help from someone.

Ulfred, of course, was using the gas heaters to keep his menagerie alive. It was like being in Sean's house again, only in a nightmarish parallel world. Crude makeshift vivaria stood everywhere: a large fish tank with a plywood lid, plastic storage boxes, metal buckets, even shoeboxes. Gingerly, I lifted the lid of one, to find half a dozen young grass snakes wriggling around inside.

I made my way round the room, peering inside cages that were transparent, carefully lifting lids of those that weren't. In a bucket I found one dead adder and another that probably wouldn't last much longer. In a Tupperware box I found eight grass-snake eggs. It was far too early in the year for grass snakes to lay their eggs, but it was possible the heat of the room had thrown their breeding cycle into disarray.

None of the creatures was healthy. The conditions they were living in were cramped, unsanitary and unsuitable. The room was too hot for British snakes. I wondered when any of them had last been fed. I remembered my owl chicks and knew, finally, what had happened to them. I carried on checking the room until I was sure I'd seen inside every box, every tank. I found only British snakes, half of them dead or dying.

No sign of the taipan. None of Matt. I had no choice but to check the rest of the house.

Switching off the torch, I crossed to the staircase. Only gloom at the top. Halfway up, I thought I heard something that wasn't the weather outside. I stopped, but the sound didn't repeat itself and I carried on. I could no longer see the steps beneath my feet or anything that lay ahead. Feeling carefully with my toes, one arm out in front of me, the other clutching the wall, I made my way slowly upwards.

At the top, nervous about switching on the light again, I reached all around. Brick walls on two sides. I stepped forward, both arms outstretched. Wood. My fingers traced over its rough grain a second before it moved. I'd pushed open a door. Peering forward, I could see into a familiar room. The same one I'd been standing in with Matt, just seconds before the glass tank downstairs had crashed to the ground. One side of the room was lined with floor-to-ceiling cupboards. Matt had been unable to open any of them; he'd assumed they'd warped over the years. They hadn't. They'd been locked from the inside, and I was about to step out of them.

The noise again, louder this time, more distinct. Something heavy was sliding across wooden floors. A low, guttural grunt and then – oh Lord – the soft moan of a voice I was sure I recognized. Something was heading my way, was only in the next room. I could hear slow, heavy footsteps and the sound of a load being dragged, catching on corners, being tugged free.

There was nowhere to hide downstairs in Ulfred's rancid, snake-filled nest. Even if I made it back through the trap-door in time, I would have no way of knowing what was happening above me. I needed to see what – or whom – Ulfred was dragging. I stepped back into the cupboard, pulling the door almost closed, and then moved sideways. If I were really lucky, the cupboards lining the wall of the room would run into each other and I could retreat into the far darkness, well away from the doorway and the stairs.

I wasn't that lucky. I travelled a yard or two before coming up against a solid wooden wall. I fumbled in my pocket, knowing there was a knife in it somewhere. I'd never have dreamed I'd use a knife against another living creature, but I was not going to be caught like a rabbit, helpless in a trap. My hand froze before it could find what it was looking for. The door to my cupboard was opening.

I held my breath, pressed myself against the cupboard wall and watched as a formless shadow moved into view. I only knew it to be human because of the low mutterings coming from its mouth. It was repeating something that sounded like: 'Chazza ton man.' Whatever meaning it held in Ulfred's mind, I could make nothing of it. Then Ulfred bent forwards, I heard grunting as he took hold of something and pulled it through the cupboard and into the stairwell.

Whatever he was dragging was heavy, and Ulfred's breathing was becoming faster, more laboured. Every time he took a breath I could hear a soft whistling in his lungs. Seven months living alone in the Witcher house had done nothing for his health. He closed the door, and the darkness was complete. He stood absolutely still and breathed in deeply through his nose. Then silence. Ulfred was holding his breath.

We stood there, the two of us, in a world so black it could have been a void, and I knew that, somehow, he'd sensed the presence of another. Seconds ticked by and still he didn't move. What was he doing? Not listening. Ulfred couldn't hear. Hoping to see something? Knowing the flicker of eyes was the most likely to give me away, I forced myself to close them. Could he smell me? I could certainly smell him. Was he touching the walls, waiting for me to give myself away with the vibration of movement? I wouldn't now have time to find the knife, but I held on firm to the torch. If he moved towards me I would bring it down with all my might on his head. I couldn't bear to keep my eyes shut any longer and opened them a fraction. Still the outline of the most dangerous person I'd ever encountered was standing motionless, no more than three feet away.

When I knew that I would have to scream soon, when I was practically doing a countdown to it in my head, he moved again, and the tension snapped.

I heard him making his slow, heavy way down the stairs, dragging his prize with him. Something hard and heavy like bone thumped on each step and I realized I wasn't so terrified I couldn't feel fury. Was that Matt's skull being pounded repeatedly against the hard wood of the stairs? How many blows would it take to cause serious brain damage? To kill him?

I stepped forward, thinking only that I could launch myself from the top of the steps, land on him, gouge his eyes out . . .

Don't you dare!

I have to do something. I can't stand here while . . .

For God's sake, Clara. He's far too strong for you. Wait and think.

Trembling, I forced myself to remain still, just out of sight of the stairwell. Sounds from below told me Ulfred was moving more freely. He was no longer dragging whatever – whomever – he'd hauled down the stairs. Then a creaking sound on wood and a trembling in the wall I was leaning against told me Ulfred was, once more, coming up the stairs. I stepped back. Was he coming for me?

I closed my eyes, dropped my head and held my breath. I would fight like fury if he caught me. I still had the torch. In my pocket I still had a knife – why hadn't I got it out while I had the chance?

Ulfred reached the top of the steps. He paused for a moment to gather his breath, and I knew it was all over. I could feel him staring directly at me. I braced myself to leap forward. Then I heard the sliding sound of a wooden lock and the cupboard door opened again. In the very dim light from the room beyond I saw Ulfred step forward and close the cupboard door behind him.

I listened to footsteps fade away.

Well, now would be a good time to do something!

OK, OK! I stepped forward and switched on the torch. In a second I found the wooden slides that, when pulled into position, effectively locked the cupboards from the inside. I pulled them into place.

Knowing that locked doors weren't always too effective against Ulfred, I turned and ran down the steps. So much easier now that I dared use the light. At the bottom I ran straight to the prone figure lying against the far wall. I didn't need to see his face to tell me who it was. I'd worn that jacket myself.

I took hold of Matt's shoulder. As I pulled him round to face me he moaned softly. The tremendous relief at knowing he was still alive lasted a split second. Just until I saw his grey eyes, swimming with blood. And the same substance trickling from his mouth. A thin, croaking sound was coming from his lips and I knew he was fighting for breath.

'Matt!'

Talking, making any sort of sound was stupid, I knew that, but I couldn't help it. Matt's red eyes focused on mine. His lips moved again.

'Arm,' he gasped. And tried to turn his head to look at his right arm.

I pulled at the jacket and managed to get his arm free of it. His shirt was red with blood. Finding my knife at last, I slid it under the neck of his shirt and cut downwards, pulling apart the sodden fabric until I could see his flesh.

This was no adder bite. Even without the profuse bleeding, I'd have known that. The taipan had bitten him high on the shoulder, and already the skin around the wound was swelling, turning purple. His flesh was dying, even as I looked at it. Worse than that, the poison was rushing through his system, eating away at his organs, paralysing the functions he needed to keep him alive. In a short while, he wouldn't be able to breathe unaided. By morning, his internal organs would have dissolved. He'd be a rotting husk.

If you get bitten you have hours, you know that, don't you?

Just over an hour ago, Matt had left his house. There was still time. From one of the many pockets in my coat I found the box of vials Sean had given me and the syringe I'd taken from the Land Rover's equipment bag. Normally, I carried it for when I needed to inject tranquillizers into large mammals. I guessed Matt counted as a large mammal. I glanced at the writing on the box. Anti-venom needs to be administered slowly, preferably diluted in an intravenous drip. There was no time for that sort of nicety, but I still had to be careful. I filled the syringe, found a vein and then, agonizingly slowly, watching the second hand on my watch all the time, I injected Matt's arm with the only stuff in the world that could save him. I took another vial and did the same thing. And then had to stop.

I could not give Matt the full dose of anti-venom in one go; that would as likely kill him as the bite. I'd given him a fighting chance, but he needed to be in hospital. I found a small inside pocket in his jacket, meaning to tuck the rest of the vials into it, but had to pull out a folded document to get them in. I almost certainly wouldn't have looked at it, but I caught sight of Clive

Ventry's name and address in the top left-hand corner.

Knowing I might be wasting precious time, I smoothed it open and then flashed the torch on to a report from a genetics laboratory, addressed to Clive. It thanked him for the recent samples, informed him that the method used to test them had been Short Tandem Repeat, PCR DNA profiling and that it was the most up-to-date and reliable method currently in use. It went on to state, with 99.99 per cent accuracy apparently, that no biological relationship had been found between Subject A and Subject B.

Had this been what Clive had wanted to talk to Matt about? Quite probably, but I had no idea what it meant. Knowing I was running out of time, I tucked the paper into my own pocket, put the anti-venom vials in Matt's jacket and then, with a small ballpoint, wrote the word 'pocket' on his forehead. Without much hope, I checked my mobile for a signal. Not a chance.

Matt's breathing was shallow and laboured; far too fast. He was in a great deal of pain. Which was about to get a whole lot worse. Because he had to move.

I put the knife back in a trouser pocket and, taking hold under both arms, pulled him towards me. He was conscious, but only barely. 'Come on,' I said, as loudly as I dared. 'We have to get out of here. We have to get you to a hospital.' I was tugging at him, trying to lift him, but he was a dead weight. By the time I had him in a sitting position I was close to sobbing with the hopelessness of it all. I would never be able to get him down the ladder and out of the cave by myself. I took hold of his head, forcing him to look at me.

'Matt, Sean has given me anti-venom.' His face was inches from mine. I thought I saw a flicker of understanding in his eyes. 'If we can get you to a doctor you'll be fine. But if you stay here you're going to die. You have to get up.'

And bless his heart, he did get up. He made a massive effort – that poor heart, weakened already by the toxic cocktail it was being forced to pump round – and, leaning his entire weight on me, he managed almost to stand. At the last minute he fell forward on to hands and knees, but that was fine. He could crawl. I pushed him forward, urging him onwards all the time until we reached the trap-door.

How in the name of all that was holy was I going to get him down?

For heaven's sake, Clara, use your brain. How do you lift roe deer?

Rope! I'd seen rope, I was sure of it. I spun round and spotted it. Thin, nylon, a washing line most likely, but it would do. I grabbed it and passed it round Matt's chest under his arms and tied it in a bowline. Then I looked for something solid to take the weight. There was nothing obvious, but the ladder itself might work. I passed the line through the top rung and wrapped the rest round my waist. Then I pushed Matt's legs round until they dangled freely over the trap-door. His eyes met mine.

'Could use some help here,' I said.

His mouth twitched, he reached out and took hold of the top rung. Then he fell forwards, over the gap, and the nylon rope dug deep into my hands and waist.

Not quite ready, I felt Matt's weight pull me forwards, and I braced both feet against the top rungs of the ladder. Matt was now dangling in thin air and the rope was cutting me in half. I began to ease it down. Inch by inch, Matt dropped closer and closer to the rock beneath us. But, somewhere in the house, movement had begun again. Ulfred was on his way back.

I risked letting more rope go. The ladder slid sideways and Matt dropped like a stone, landing heavily. He almost dragged me with him, but at the last moment I let go of the rope.

Knowing the worst bit was over, I pulled the ladder straight and slid down in seconds. I cut the washing line off Matt, then, leaving him where he'd landed, I ran for the dinghy and pulled it free from its bramble shelter. Dragging it further into the cave, I tied it to the iron mooring ring and took a second to wonder how I was going to get him into it.

'Sorry, Matt,' I muttered, knowing there was only one way. Tugging roughly at his shoulders, then his back, then shoulders again, I rolled him across the stone landing stage until I could guard his head and tip him into the dinghy. I made sure his arms and legs were inside and that his head was protected.

It was going to be OK. All I had to do now was untie the painter, climb in with him and the water would carry us both to where I'd left the Land Rover. I'd drive to the nearest A&E, and doctors could administer the rest of the anti-venom. People survived taipan bites, just as long as they had the anti-venom and hospital treatment in time. Matt was going to be fine.

I had a split second to register the new smell – pipe smoke.

Clara, look out! screamed my mother's voice, loud in my head. I pulled the painter loose and shoved the dinghy hard. The river took hold and it sailed away from me, out of the cave and into the ravine. I turned, just as the stocky, familiar figure reached the bottom of the ladder and I realized it had been Ulfred that I'd seen catching snakes in Ventry's field a few nights earlier, not the Keech brothers at all. Ulfred switched on a torch and shone it directly at me. I had a moment to wonder if I could leap into the river and wade downstream after Matt's dinghy, whether there was the remotest chance I wouldn't be caught. I took a step backwards.

If Ulfred had been in the field that night, who had he been with? Clive Ventry? Or . . .

It could have been thunder I heard next. More likely it was the sound of a heavy rock being hammered against my skull. The world flickered like an old movie on a worn-out cine screen. Then it simply went away.

50

I DIDN'T WANT TO WAKE UP. HOW COULD I HURT SO
much and still be alive? The bones of my skull must
have been crushed; nothing else could account for
the crippling pain in my head. I wanted to vomit, knew
I was about to, but couldn't move a muscle. I would die
here, on this wet stone floor, choking on the expulsed
contents of my own stomach, and it would feel like a
blessed release.

I didn't throw up. There was nothing left inside me,
but a sudden fit of coughing forced my eyes open.
The rough chalk floor of the cave had changed. The
stone was smooth, cut into regular shapes, and
the dreadful screeching noise wasn't in my head after
all. It was coming from dozens of tiny creatures circling
high above me. I was in the old church.

The buckle of my life-jacket was pressing into
my chest. I tried to bring one hand forward, meaning
to push myself up a little, feel my head, get a
sense of how badly hurt I was, and found I couldn't.
My arms were bound to my sides with the nylon

washing line I'd used to lower Matt out of the house.

Pressed against the stone as I was, I could see very little. Even moving my eyes hurt. But I could tell I was towards the front of the nave. For one thing I could smell the stagnant water of the baptism pool, the one where Ulfred had almost drowned. And I could just about make out a few rows of pews, some overturned, some still upright. And I could see Ulfred himself, not three yards away, sitting quietly in the front row.

I blinked and he came into focus. Very like Walter. His eyes were perhaps a little smaller, his chin more pronounced. Ulfred had more hair than Walter and was of a slightly larger build. Other than that, they could have been brothers, not cousins. They would, in poor light and at some distance, easily be mistaken for each other. Except I couldn't imagine Walter as I was seeing Ulfred now, intent upon nothing but the slender form of the Papuan taipan lying across his lap. I saw gnarled fingers reach out and stroke the snake, run themselves down its length. And I watched the snake allow itself to be handled, with no thought of escape or defence.

Lie still, I told myself, closing my eyes again. As long as Ulfred thought I was unconscious, he might leave me alone. If Rachel had managed to get through to the police and give them an accurate message, they'd surely be on their way. They might even be in the village, doing what I'd done, tracking Matt to Clive Ventry's house. They'd find Clive's body. They'd look for Matt. And for me.

But the last time I'd tried, there had been no mobile-phone signal. And she might not have remembered about the route in.

Breathe steadily, don't let flickering eyelids give me away. I would be OK. After finding Clive's body, Matt would have radioed for help. Faced with another murder, the police would arrive on foot if they had to. But that was assuming Matt had seen Clive. If he'd just spotted Ulfred leaving the manor and decided to follow him, he might not have had a chance to call for help. Oh God . . .

Rose Scott, the administrator at the psychiatric hospital. She'd have raised the alarm, told the authorities that Ulfred had turned up in his home village. One way or another, help was on its way, it had to be. It was just a question of whether it would get to me in time.

Movement in the church. Footsteps. But Ulfred was still sitting in the front pew. Before I could remind myself to lie still I'd stiffened.

'I thought you were awake, my dear.'

Ulfred's lips hadn't moved, but I would never have taken the voice for his. There was nothing left of rural Dorset in the deep, educated voice addressing me now. Archie Witcher, speaking with all the nuances and cadences of his adoptive southern United States, had come home after all.

I curled up my legs, pushed hard and rocked myself into a kneeling position. As blood drained from my head it took with it some of the pain. I could focus on the man, still over six feet tall, standing before me.

Archie was as handsome as they'd all described: far better-looking than his photograph had led me to expect. He had a face that must once have been close

503

to beautiful, so perfect were its lines and proportions. The white skin had the wrinkles you would expect in a man of over seventy, but it remained an arresting, compelling face, especially his eyes – a soft, light turquoise, rimmed with black lashes. He was a perfect-looking man in the autumn of his life. And, after inheriting his nephew's fortune, his remaining years were set to be very pleasant indeed.

And I couldn't help feeling just the faintest glimmer of disappointment. Had it, after all, just been about money? Had Archie come home, fleeing scandal and possible prosecution in his adopted United States, only to covet the immense wealth he might inherit if his nephew were to pre-decease him?

'I'm so sorry you suffered the inconvenience of being moved, Miss Clara,' said Archie, speaking down at me from what seemed a great height. 'I have water, if you need it.'

I nodded, managed to croak a 'Yes, please' at him. Time was what I needed now. Escape was impossible, but rescue was on its way. I just had to give them time.

Archie turned and walked away, and I remembered the village meeting in Clive Ventry's house, exactly a week ago, when I'd seen a tall, dark-clad man disappear along an upstairs corridor. Rose Scott had told me about Ulfred receiving visits from a distinguished man with an accent. I'd assumed it had been Clive; it could just as easily have been Archie.

As Archie disappeared from view I found myself wondering whose hand had struck the blows that ended Clive's life. Ulfred, still absently stroking the snake, looked like nothing more than a sad, slightly puzzled old man. He'd certainly broken into my house and scared me witless, but . . .

Footsteps coming back.

Ulfred hadn't actually hurt me that night. He'd had another chance to do so days later, in the chalk mine. I'd stood within feet of him, had listened to him breathing, but he'd let me go. Had Ulfred really killed four people? Or had his cousin Archie used him, helped him escape from hospital, hidden him in the old family house, given him food and fuel? Was Ulfred's presence in the village nothing more than a smokescreen? Had Archie even engineered the snake incidents because they, more than anything, would point to Ulfred's being involved?

Archie drew close and crouched down until his face was almost on a level with mine. He was dressed in a black shirt and trousers, but I could see dozens of shiny, dark stains on his clothes. The hand holding the glass of water had a red tinge to it, like the hand of a butcher. I glanced over at Ulfred. His clothes were filthy but held no sign of blood that I could see. I was beginning to think I knew which of the two men had hammered Clive Ventry's head to a pulp.

But Ulfred was going to take the blame for everything. I could even see it making a sort of twisted sense. Ulfred, if found guilty, would simply go back to where he'd lived for the last fifty years. But why on earth had Archie killed three other people as well as his wealthy nephew? What could he possibly have to gain from the deaths of John Allington, Violet Buckler and Ernest Amblin?

Archie held the glass to my lips and I drank. The cold water helped a little.

'Thank you,' I said to the stone floor when the glass was taken from me. 'Ca— can I ask you something, Reverend Witcher? Please.' I kept my eyes down and my voice low. He must not think me a threat.

'Of course, my dear.' Archie's breath was sharp, acidic, like that of someone who hasn't eaten for some time. His voice was as low as mine. We were whispering to each other, in this long-forgotten church, while the storm raged on around us. What could I ask that wouldn't seem threatening? Then I had it. 'Why . . . why did Ulfred leave the snake in the baby's cot?' I asked, risking a quick glance up.

Archie shook his head, the picture of sorrowful concern. 'I thank the Lord you were there in time, Miss Clara,' he said. 'What a terrible accident that would have been. The dear, innocent babe.'

'But . . . accident . . . did he not mean to hurt her?'

'Of course not. But the dear baby's parents breed poultry. They had newborn chicks. Ulfred needed them to . . .' He looked uncertain, as though delicacy prevented him from being more explicit.

'Feed his snakes,' I offered, dropping my eyes once more.

'Yes, indeed. I think, from what he's told me, that the baby's parents might have been disturbed when Ulfred entered their property. The snake, a favourite of his, got left behind in his haste to get out. As indeed was the case with the taipan in Dr Amblin's house. Dear Ulfred has many talents but is not always – what shall we say? – entirely reliable.'

So baby Sophia and the Poulson children hadn't been intended victims after all. Just in the wrong place at the wrong time.

'How does Ulfred get into these houses?' I said, again asking the first thing that came into my head. I knew how he got into mine, but not about the others. 'Does he use Edeline's old keys?'

When I glanced up, I saw Archie smiling, gently shaking his head. 'Dear Ulfred is so resourceful,' he said. 'I hardly know how he achieves half of the things he does, Miss Clara. Edeline's old keys have certainly been useful, but Ulfred has a real gift for making his way into places. There's barely a house in the neighbourhood that he isn't familiar with. He was a boy in this village, you understand.'

But Archie too had been a boy in the village. And something about his accent was bothering me. Even after fifty years, would his voice be so thoroughly American? It wasn't just his pronunciation, he had completely absorbed the speech rhythms and phraseology of another nation.

He leaned towards me again. 'By the way, Miss Clara, what did you do with the other taipan? Ulfred is very attached to his snakes, you understand. Is it in that house on the Lyme Undercliff?'

Several nights ago on the Undercliff, Sean had surprised an elderly American tourist claiming to be looking for orchids. A couple of days later, someone had tried to break into his house. It was all making sense. Archie had been following me, looking for the taipan. He'd wanted his deadliest weapon back.

I turned my head a fraction to face Ulfred. He was watching us closely, his eyes, I noticed, fixed on my mouth.

'She's quite safe, your beautiful snake,' I said, speaking slowly and continuing to face Ulfred. 'She's being very well looked after.' Ulfred's small eyes narrowed, and his fingers, moving across the snake on his lap, seemed to tremble. 'That's why you came into my house, isn't it? You were looking for her. I can get her back for you.'

Archie rocked back on his heels, preparing to stand up. *Ask him something else. Keep him talking.*

'Why are we in church?' I asked, as Archie rose to his feet. 'Now that you're back, are you going to hold services here again?'

He didn't reply but walked up the chancel steps and knelt down behind the choir stalls.

Keep him talking!

'My father is an archdeacon,' I called in desperation, knowing that I was soon to find out exactly why we were in church. And that I wouldn't like it. 'He'd be interested in your church. About your work in America.'

I couldn't see what Archie was doing, but I heard a zip being pulled, the sound of something rustling.

'*And these signs shall follow them that believe,*' I called out. What came next? What the hell came next? '*In my name shall they cast out devils; they shall speak with new tongues; they shall take up serpents; and . . . and . . .*' It was hopeless, completely hopeless, he would come back, something hard would slam down on to my skull, and it would be my brains spraying through the air. Would he use water from that stinking pool to wash the floor clean? I opened my mouth to scream.

Hands grasped my shoulders from behind. 'Have you welcomed our Lord and Saviour Jesus Christ into your heart, Miss Clara?'

I found myself nodding vigorously.

'I'm so glad.' He was closer to me now. I could smell the pipe smoke that clung to his clothes, the acetone in his breath and the stench of blood that lurked beneath. His hands began to knead the flesh of my shoulders. 'In these last days of God's earth, when all the truly righteous will be saved and the sinners cast into the eternal pit of flames, I'm so glad you have found the Lord, Miss Clara.'

From beneath gut-churning terror, I felt fury rising up to take its place. I knew a man of God. A man who had welcomed Christ into his heart, and it wasn't the devil pawing at me now.

'Blessed be the Elijah Company, blessed be the fellowship of saints who work tirelessly against sin and corruption in these final days.' He leaned in further, the papery skin of his cheek touched mine and the weight of his body pressed against me. His hands left my shoulders and slid lower. And I was getting angrier by the second. I was not going to be touched that way, not by him.

'And the reason we are in church, my dear,' he said, dropping his voice to a whisper again, 'is that our friend Ulfred needs the shelter of his old home for a little while longer. If you were found there, Miss Clara, the dwelling would be thoroughly searched. They would find his resting place, his little collection. The time for that is not yet here.'

Archie was buying time. Just as he had when he'd tried to put the blame on me. When he'd put the adder in my cellar, created the fake will out of my stationery and left it in Violet's house. Buying time so he could – what was it, exactly, this monster still needed to do?

Inside me, anger and terror were jostling for position, but terror, I knew, would serve me best. Terror would keep me submissive, and that might keep me alive. Over in the front pew, still stroking the taipan, Ulfred sat watching us.

'I understand you have been speaking with Ruby Mottram,' said Archie. 'Where is she, Miss Clara?'

And fury won the day. Was that feeble old woman his next victim? My head shot up to face him. 'You can stay away . . .' I began. And stopped. I looked into those cold blue eyes and everything fell into place. *Eyes like the sky in winter.* Oh dear Christ! My own eyes must have opened wide with shock, maybe I made a small start backwards. Whatever it was, he saw and registered the change in me.

Clara, no. Say nothing. Don't make it worse.

His eyes locked on mine. I wasn't going to look away again. He opened his mouth to speak, but it was my turn.

'You're not Archie Witcher,' I said.

Blue eyes narrowed. 'But of course I am, Miss Clara.'

Clara, he's insane. Don't rile him.

I forced myself to speak slowly, not to scream at him.

'Archie Witcher is in the churchyard. He's been there for fifty years. In the grave that bears your name. You even paid for the headstone.'

'My dear . . .'

'You're not a Dorset man.' I was struggling to my feet and he was letting me. 'A man from the West Country would never speak the way you do, not if he'd lived in America for a hundred years.' Almost there, almost upright, he still hadn't tried to stop me, he was rising with me. 'And you know what?' I went on. 'Archie Witcher had brown eyes. Dark-brown eyes. Several people have mentioned them. I saw a photograph of you yesterday; a police photograph, in colour. I should have realized then. Brown eyes don't fade to blue, even after fifty years.'

At that, finally, he stepped forward; so tall, such a huge man. He caught hold of my shoulders and dragged me towards him.

'Archie Witcher burned to death in here that night,' I hissed into his face. 'The night you nearly killed Ulfred. Three people were bitten by your snakes. Two of them died. You knew there'd be a police investigation, that you'd face charges, so you fled back home. But you couldn't go back in your own name, you were a wanted man there too, for murdering your own father. So you stole Archie's life. You've been pretending to be another man for fifty years and now you've come back to steal his nephew's money.'

He started moving, taking me with him. I had to scramble to stay upright. We struggled round the baptism pool, getting perilously close. At the front

511

pew, still holding the taipan, Ulfred rose to his feet.

'That's why those people had to die,' I yelled. 'John Allington, Violet, Dr Amblin. They all knew you. Might have recognized you. You've been killing the people who know you're not Archie.'

And now you're one of them. Oh, Clara, will you never learn?

We stopped. Still holding tight to my upper arms, he bent lower, his face just inches from mine. From the corner of my eye, I thought I saw Ulfred take a step forward.

'And who am I, Clara?' he whispered. 'If I'm not Archie, who then?'

'Joel Fain,' I managed. 'You're the Reverend Joel Morgan Fain. You were the minister in this church fifty years ago. People trusted you, they believed in you, and you . . .'

I couldn't go on. Fain was changing. He released me, drew himself up and took a deep breath. His eyes closed, and then a tremor seemed to run through him. His eyes opened again and he was different, I swear it, as though I'd been looking at a photograph that had suddenly slipped into sharper focus. His eyes had gained colour; he seemed even taller. He opened his mouth and the voice that came out was young and strong.

'Thank you, Clara,' he said. 'It feels good to hear the sound of my own name.'

I took a step back, but I'd lost my bearings and came up against the chancel rail. Joel Fain strode forward with me. Behind him, Ulfred was moving too, stepping closer.

'I hear about you, Clara,' Fain crooned at me. 'Even tucked away inside Ventry's house these past months. The servants and villagers talk about the scarred beauty who hides herself from the world. They talk about your mother and what you've done to her. You killed your mother, Clara. She drank herself to death because she couldn't bear the sight of you. Isn't that right?'

Mum's voice in my head had fallen silent. The calm, wise words that had been guiding me had become twisted, were coming instead from Joel Fain's mouth. And yet they rang so true. Mum's death had been my fault. She'd needed a drink every time she looked at me. Fain reached out and stroked the scarred side of my face.

'Branded a sinner,' he whispered, 'carrying the mark of Cain.'

At the back of my mind, something was trying to break free.

'Do you know what happens to those who kill their parents, Clara?' He was still touching me.

'They get punished,' I whimpered, and felt my face become damp. Fain raised his hand and we both looked at the glimmer of tears on his bloodstained fingers. Then he leaned in, and the tip of his tongue was running across my cheek, into the corner of my eyes, along my hairline, licking away my tears as though he enjoyed the taste of pain. It was all I could do not to throw back my head and howl. Then he pulled away. His eyes were still staring into mine but I don't think he could see me any more.

'Punished, punished,' he repeated, 'as I have been

punished.' And then, almost faster than I could watch, he pulled open the front of his shirt and tugged it off. In places his skin hung a little loose on what had once been a well-defined torso; in others, it bore the livid, twisted scars of severe burns. He held out his arms for me to see. More scars, but not from burns.

'My father held my head under the water of the river, did you know that, Clara? Held me under until I thought my body would explode with pain, but I did not die. My body burned in this church, but I did not die.' He thrust both arms towards me. 'The serpents and the crawling things have many times taken hold of my flesh and poisoned it, but I did not die. The bringers of death cannot harm me, Clara. The blessed Lord gave me power over death. I am a true member of the Company of Elijah, and I herald the last days of God's earth.'

A sudden noise startled both of us. One of the bats had become trapped among the organ pipes; it was fluttering around, making a sound like wind through old bells. Was it loud enough for people in the village to hear? Probably not, but—

I turned and sped across the chancel. I fell against the pulpit, somehow managed to stay on my feet, and darted round the back of the choir stalls. Then I leapt and landed face down on the organ keyboard. The long-abandoned pipes burst into life and the sound rang around the church. Bats began screaming, a flurry of rooks dived through the nave. Then my hair was grabbed from behind and Fain's free hand wrapped itself around my neck. I was wrenched back again,

514

pulled across the floor, down the chancel steps, nearer to the baptism pool. Then we stopped and I was hoisted to my feet again.

'I have seen the dead walk, Clara,' said Fain, but his eyes could no longer meet mine. 'I can bring you back, if your faith is strong enough. Shall I do that? Shall the two of us raise your mother?'

'Stop it.'

Bubbles of saliva were forming in the corners of his mouth. 'Shall we bring back your handsome policeman?'

'He isn't dead!' Even as the words left my mouth I realized how stupid they were. Fain and Ulfred would look for Matt, as soon as they'd finished with me; they'd find him and they'd make sure.

'He will be. The taipan is the deadliest creature that crawls on God's earth. That fool, Ventry, had no idea what he'd brought back from his trip. He thought the eggs were dead. I took them to Ulfred. I knew, if anyone could hatch them, he could.'

We were at the side of the pool, just below the chancel steps. From what I'd been able to see, Ulfred had not once taken his eyes off us. I twisted my head, to make sure he could see my mouth. 'Ulfred will take the blame for everything you've done,' I said. 'That's been your plan all along, hasn't it? You helped him escape because you knew, sooner or later, that people would get suspicious about all the old folk dying. That they'll find my body, and Matt's, and Clive Ventry's. Everyone will assume it was Ulfred, he'll go back to hospital and you'll get all Clive's money.'

Fain was pushing me down, trying to get me to the floor. I pushed back, but I knew I couldn't stay upright for long. He was too strong, and he had the use of his arms.

'And his snakes will all die,' I yelled at Ulfred. 'They're dying now. And you won't take care of them, will you?'

'What in the . . .' Fain had lost patience. He struck me across the face. Then he kicked both my legs from under me. The pain in my back as I landed on the stone floor almost made me pass out again. But I held it together for long enough to realize I was lying on plastic. A large bag of tough black plastic with a zipper fastening up the middle. It was a body-bag, almost exactly the sort in which cadavers are kept in hospital morgues. Except it hadn't been made for human corpses. It was designed for the bodies of very large animals. Zoos keep them. We have them at the wildlife hospital for when large deer die. And I keep a stock in my cellar. I was going to die in one of my own bags.

I squirmed round, away from the pool. Fain kicked me hard in the stomach, and I stopped struggling.

With eyes that seemed to be growing dark, I watched Fain reach out and take hold of a large piece of stone that had fallen from the walls. He placed it by my feet and then walked back across the chancel. Ulfred had moved forward and was staring into the pool with something like terror on his face. Fain reached him and held out his hands for the snake. Ulfred took a step back and his hold on the taipan seemed to tighten.

I saw Fain's head move and knew he'd said something

to Ulfred, but a dark silence seemed to be growing around me. I thought I saw Ulfred blow softly across the snake's head, but I couldn't be sure. Then he handed the taipan over, and Fain walked back towards me.

It was only a few yards from where the two men passed the snake between them to where I lay, unable to move, but it seemed to take Fain a very long time to reach me. Because I had plenty of time to think the strangest of thoughts: that the snake that had bitten Matt was about to bite me too, which was weirdly intimate in a way, and that if Matt didn't drown out on the river, or die of exposure in the storm, if he reached a hospital in time, then he would remember me for always, because you don't easily forget someone who died the death that should have been yours.

And then I thought that this was the way I was always meant to die. It was fitting that I should suffer the *poena cullei*, because Fain was right. I had caused the death of a parent. Because of me, Mum had drunk herself to death.

And the last thought, as Fain knelt down and placed the slender, almost weightless body of the snake over mine, was that Sean was going to be really, really mad at me.

The heavy masonry stone was tucked inside the bag and the zipper pulled shut. I didn't move. Neither did the taipan. I could barely feel its weight, it was so light, but I knew its head was inches from mine. Then two strong hands were placed against me. They pushed hard, and I felt myself slide across the stone floor and into the water.

51

DOWN WE SANK, TWO CREATURES DESTINED TO DIE together, deeper and deeper into a place from which sight and sound had been banished. We went lower still, the pressure built in my ears, and I felt the world spinning away from me, saw everything I loved drifting upwards, as though life itself were floating away. And I wanted to reach up towards it, to drag it down with me, because the loneliness I felt then was more intense than anything I'd ever known.

And as I lay there, in a hell that was cold and all-consuming, I knew that I'd stopped sinking. Bare rock was hard beneath me. And my hell stank of industrial plastic.

I was still breathing.

The thick polyurethane bag in which Fain had trapped me wasn't watertight – cold trickles everywhere told me that – but it was keeping the bulk of the water out temporarily and creating a small bubble of air that was keeping me, and my serpent friend, alive.

Armed with a glimmer of hope, I still didn't dare

move. If the snake bit me, it was all over. The anti-venom had gone with Matt, and there had only been enough to treat one bite. Astonishingly, the snake was still. But if I started to move, it would panic and defend itself.

The weight of the water was pressing down on the bag, and I had no choice but to turn my head slowly to the side to keep breathing. Still the snake didn't move. I began to slide my right arm out from under me, aiming for the trouser pocket where I'd stored the knife.

My arm was at my side, my hand directly above the pocket. But the ropes were tight around me, and every movement seemed to drain me of energy.

Then the snake began to move.

I felt it glide upwards. It wouldn't like the wet, or the cold of my plastic jacket. It was heading for warmth. I felt it slide, so light, so very deadly, up over my chest and on to my shoulder.

Behold, I give you the power to tread on serpents and scorpions, and over the power of the enemy: and nothing by any means shall hurt you.

Was it my voice? Or my mother's? I had no idea. But it rang loud in my ears as my fingers crept into the confines of my pocket.

The silken skin of the taipan brushed my cheek, and I felt it pause. I braced myself for the shock of pain, for the fangs sinking into me, the realization that I'd lost. I could almost hear it breathing. Then something swept lightly across my face, and the snake resumed its journey.

My fingers touched the cold metal of the knife's

handle. A few more seconds and I would be able to take hold of it. But the bag was filling rapidly. And the world's most dangerous land-snake had wrapped its tail around my neck, whilst its head lay against mine.

And nothing by any means shall hurt you.

I took hold of the knife, carefully eased my hand free and sliced at the nearest rope coil. It doesn't take long to cut through a washing line. I sliced another coil and another, until I could bend my arm at the elbow and point the knife at the plastic directly above my face. I took the biggest breath I could – knowing it might be my last – and drew the knife down as far as I could reach. Water poured over me. I was still bound, I couldn't swim, but I found the tag of my life-jacket that Fain hadn't known I was wearing and pulled hard.

As the life-jacket filled with air I shot to the surface like a cork from a bottle, and thought my head might explode from the din ringing round the church. What the hell was making that ungodly sound? Was the building falling down? The rope coils had loosened. Shrugging myself free of them, I reached for the stone tiles surrounding the pool, kicked hard against the water and fell, once more, on the cold church floor. I pushed myself to my feet, ignoring the pain in my head and the cacophonous din reverberating around the ruin, wanting only to head for the door. And the deadliest snake in the world, which for a few minutes had shared my grave, came to the surface and swam lazily towards me. *And nothing by any means shall hurt you.*

I staggered backwards. And saw Ulfred, clinging to the pipes of the organ with one hand, hammering away at its keys with the other, while Fain's strong fingers closed around his throat.

I had no need to call for help. The loud, discordant notes of the church's instrument were doing it for me. And you know what? I think my mother had a hand in that racket as well. The taipan was sliding out of the pool, and its liquid, amber-coloured eyes seemed to look only at me. But no snake can outrun a human.

I turned and fled; past the dark water where Ulfred and I had both so nearly lost our lives; down the long aisle where the fire that killed Larry Hodges and the real Archie had started; into the porch where Ruby had been bitten. On I ran, into the night, along the avenue of old limes and out through the gate.

Straight into the arms of Detective Inspector Robert Tasker.

52

THE OLD WOOD BROKE APART LIKE BRITTLE GLASS. Three blows of the axe and the lock shattered; the door swung loose on its hinges. A uniformed constable stepped inside and wedged it open.

One by one, the forensic staff followed and fanned out through the old house, measuring, recording, photographing. We were the last in line, the least important, only there to take care of the living.

Stepping over the threshold was easy. But staying there, breathing the rancid air once more, was probably the hardest thing I've ever done.

'First time through the front door,' I managed, in a voice that sounded nothing like mine.

'Wait in the car,' said Sean. 'Craig and I can manage.'

'Your car's a health hazard,' I snapped back. I took a step, and the smell seemed to solidify around me.

'Whereas this place has a future for people taking rest cures,' muttered Craig, who was bringing up the rear.

'Which way, miss?' asked the constable who was to be our escort.

Avoiding the police teams, I led the way through the downstairs rooms, up stairs, along corridors that were no longer dark – floodlights had already been set up everywhere – and down the steps into Ulfred's lair. Everywhere, noise and artificial light surrounded us, cutting like knives through the atmosphere. Of course, the police teams could do nothing about the smell.

'Holy shit,' came Sean's voice from behind me as we stepped down into the hidden room. 'Excuse me, Clara.'

'Christ!' muttered Craig, getting his first glimpse. 'Sorry, boss.'

I opened my mouth to admit I'd said much the same thing myself the previous night and found I couldn't speak. A young woman in protective overalls was taking swabs from a stain on the floor. Matt's blood.

I turned away and watched Sean making his way slowly round the room, peering into containers and boxes, just as I'd done, hours earlier. I saw shock and compassion on his face. I watched him stifle a yawn and, seconds later, I did the same. He'd been awake most of the night. I hadn't slept at all.

After I'd fled the church and as soon as I'd been able to speak, I'd told DI Tasker where his boss could be found. A dozen constables were dispatched and, within the hour, Matt had arrived at the Dorset County Hospital. Only just in time. Ten minutes after his arrival, his respiratory system had closed down and he'd stopped breathing. He'd remain on a ventilator until the paralysis wore off – if indeed it did. On my insistence, Sean had been dragged from his bed at 2 a.m.

to supervise whilst local doctors administered the rest of the taipan anti-venom.

Sean had set up a phone link between the hospital and a specialist poison-research facility in Sydney. Australian doctors, experts in their field, were still guiding the Dorset team through Matt's treatment. Everything possible was being done, but it would be twenty-four hours at least before we'd know if he was going to live.

How I was going to get through that time, I had no idea. But for the next hour or so, I could do my job. I could take care of the snakes.

Sean and Craig had already transferred several of the grass snakes to the ventilated carry-boxes we use to transport small animals. Craig stacked three in his arms, our constable assistant did the same, and they climbed back up the stairs to load them into the waiting Land Rover. I bent, found another container, and held it out for Sean. Using a hook, he scooped a sick-looking adder from an old cardboard box and dropped it in. He looked at me, then down at the snake again.

'We won't save half of these,' he muttered, bending to examine another container. Then he straightened again. 'How did he do it?' he asked. 'This Fain character. How did he manage to control a man he'd once tortured and tried to kill?'

'I'm not sure he did, in the end,' I said. The last few hours, I'd thought of little else other than the strange influence Fain seemed to exercise over those around him. 'In the beginning,' I went on, 'it was probably a combination of fear and dependence. I think Ulfred was afraid of Joel Fain. I think he remembered the power Fain had over all the people around him when they were both younger. All the terrible things Fain made them do to Ulfred. How can we know what Fain threatened him with?'

'And he clearly depended on him for food,' said Sean, looking round at the remains of tinned food, of stale milk clinging to chipped bottles.

'For fuel too,' I agreed, nodding at the Calor-gas containers. 'You wouldn't want too many naked flames down here. And, of course, they shared an obsession with snakes.'

Footsteps told us Craig and the PC were coming back. In silence, we continued transferring snakes until all the living specimens had been put in carry-boxes. Then Craig and the policeman disappeared again. Sean looked at me.

'We're done,' he said. 'I need to have a look round that church, see if I can find Hissy Clara's big brother. I doubt he went far in that downpour last night. You should get some sleep.'

'I'll be lucky. DI Tasker wants to talk to me again, and my dad and sister have been leaving messages every half-hour since dawn.'

'Well, they can wait. I'll take you home.'

I shook my head. 'I'm going back to the hospital,' I said. 'I want to check on him.'

Sean's lips had tightened. 'They won't know anything till this evening at the earliest,' he said. 'You'll have a long wait.'

'I meant, check on Ulfred.'

The previous night, Fain had all but choked the life out of Ulfred, but Tasker's men had got to them just in time. Ulfred had been rushed to hospital and was currently in a room not far from the intensive-care ward where Matt was being treated. Fain was in a police cell.

'Ulfred has that power you told me about,' I said, as warm hands touched my shoulders, 'that power over snakes. He did something to the taipan last night, I'm sure of it. It sounds ridiculous, I know, but he's the reason it didn't bite me.'

'I've seen stranger things. Come on now, I think we've seen enough of this place.'

I started to climb the steps. At the top, I allowed Sean to steer me back along the corridor, down the stairs and out of the snake house.

Tail End

Three weeks later

THE SUNSHINE OF THE LAST FEW DAYS HAD OPENED the dahlias. I gathered seven, adding them to red roses that, long ago, a raven-haired girl had carried in her wedding bouquet. And I tried to think of her kindly, that beautiful, disturbed woman; to be glad she'd known the love of a good man.

Sadly, Walter never regained consciousness after my visit. His funeral service had just finished in the nearby church of St Nicholas, and I'd driven on ahead of the cortège to pay one last visit to his garden. In a few minutes, he'd be laid to rest beside Edeline.

It seemed something heavy had lifted from the Witcher house since I'd last been near it. The wisteria was fading, but a deep-pink climbing rose over the front elevation was at its best. The flowers, the sunshine, seemed to soften the house somehow. I could see the sweet home it might once have been. That it would never be again.

Because in the last few days, the Witcher house had been officially condemned as unsafe. It was to be demolished shortly and the land put up for sale. Another house, a little further from the escarpment edge, would be built. Children might play in this garden. And maybe the terrible story of the Witcher family could safely be forgotten.

'Thought I might find you in here.'

I turned. Dorset's Assistant Chief Constable was leaning on the gate. The full dress uniform hung loose on his shoulders and there was a stiffness about his body. He began to walk towards me, treading carefully over the uneven paving, and I felt the old shyness creeping over me again. The last time I'd seen him properly, he'd been spinning away down a fast-flowing river. Earlier, in church, I'd spent the better part of an hour looking at the back of his head. Face to face was a different matter.

'Nice suit,' I managed, although I was looking at his shoes.

'Look who's talking,' he replied. 'I like you in green.'

In the flowerbed at my feet, oriental poppies were starting to open, but I knew they'd droop the moment they were picked. Some flowers just won't be tamed.

'Sally took me shopping,' I confessed.

The black shoes stopped when they were three feet away from me, and I made myself look up. Above the crisp, white shirt Matt's face looked unnaturally grey.

'Are you back at work?' I asked, although I knew he wasn't. I had daily updates on his progress from Sally. It would be some weeks yet, maybe longer, before Matt was fit to return to active service.

'Lord, no. I can barely stand for an hour at a time. I probably shouldn't have walked this far.'

'Sit down for a minute,' I suggested, not really expecting him to agree, but he nodded and we set off towards a wooden seat tucked away within a rose arbour. As we sat, a tiny shower of peach-coloured petals fell around us. For a minute, maybe two, neither of us spoke.

'Ulfred has been released from hospital,' Matt said at last. 'Did you hear? He's gone back to the Two Counties.'

'Nobody tells me anything,' I replied, stirring the rose petals with my foot. 'I'm still practically a daily visitor to Lyme Regis police station, but the flow of information isn't exactly two-way.'

'Ask away,' he said, 'I'm in a chatty mood,' and it suddenly occurred to me that if I looked him fully in the face, he wouldn't see so much of my scar. Amazed I hadn't thought of that before, I turned to him. His eyes were shot through with red veins and the normally bright whites looked yellow and sore.

'What happened to you that night?' I asked.

A tiny light bounced in charcoal-grey eyes. 'Before you trussed me like a chicken and chucked me through that trap-door, breaking two ribs in the process, you mean?'

'Cracked, not broken. There's a difference.' I was still looking at him, and finding it wasn't so hard after all.

'Not in terms of pain. But, since you ask, Clive phoned not too long after I'd spoken to you and I went round. He wanted to talk about the man who'd been staying with him.'

'Fain?'

'Fain,' nodded Matt. 'Posing as Archie Witcher, the long-lost uncle. He'd turned up last October apparently; must have followed a circuitous overland route, because there's no trace of him coming through airport Immigration. Clive's housekeeper was just told he was a distant relative from the States, a clergyman over on some sort of spiritual retreat. She says he stayed in his room most of the time. Went out walking after dark, liked to visit the old church.'

'A wanted man lived among us for months, and nobody knew he was there,' I said. 'Call yourself a policeman.'

'I was too busy trying to get to know you better.'

Eye contact broken. I looked down at my watch to check the time. My left wrist was empty. 'But Clive was having doubts?' I said, examining a small scratch on the back of my hand.

'Big time. Although, he'd welcomed him initially. Apparently, when you're brought up in a children's home, you crave family. Then he got suspicious. So he stole his toothbrush and arranged a DNA test.'

'I saw the report,' I said, glancing up. 'It was in your pocket. So Subject A and Subject B were Clive and Fain?'

'That's right. And the test confirmed no possibility of a biological relationship. Clive knew he'd been had; he just wasn't sure what to do about it. He also admitted that night that he'd been born a Witcher, just as you'd guessed. He'd preferred to keep it quiet because he knew certain members of his family, especially his

530

father, probably weren't remembered with any great fondness. I couldn't draw him on the local vandalism issue, but we're still talking to the Keech gang.'

'Why didn't he just confront Fain himself, though?' I asked. 'Clive Ventry never struck me as the shy type.'

'No. But the taipan eggs had disappeared.'

'So it was Clive who—'

'Yeah. He found them on some land he had in New Guinea. Of course, when you charter your own planes, illegal smuggling becomes a whole lot easier. He claimed he genuinely believed they were dead, but when he heard about young tropical snakes being seen around the village and found the eggs had gone, he put two and two together. We should probably get going, by the way, they'll be here soon.'

We both remained on the bench. But Matt leaned forward, away from me.

'I told Clive I'd get some men out to the village, one way or another, and that he should stay where he was and keep the doors locked,' he said, addressing the petals at his feet. 'As it turns out, that was probably the biggest mistake of my career.'

I looked at the hand on the bench beside me, felt my own start to move towards it. 'Fain was still in the house?' I asked, gently.

Matt's hand moved before I could reach it. He gathered a handful of rose petals and started crushing them between his fingers. 'Almost certainly,' he said. 'Clive was alive when I left, dead when you arrived less than an hour later. I think Fain heard us talking and realized the game was up. He panicked.'

'But he would have killed him anyway, wouldn't he? For his money? Isn't that what this was all about?'

Matt shook his head. 'I'm not sure what he was really up to in the end, Clara. Maybe he just wanted to live out the rest of his life quietly and comfortably as Archie Witcher. Clive would probably have found him somewhere nice to live, given him a bit of a pension. Or he could have been planning an unfortunate accident, once the world had accepted him as Clive's closest living relative. Of course, for him to stand a chance of inheriting, the people who knew him fifty years ago had to be out of the picture.'

I gave myself a minute to think about it. John, Violet, Ernest. He'd been picking them off, one by one. Who had been next? Ruby? Reverend Percy?

'So how did you end up here?' I asked.

'I saw Walter.'

And even I had to think about that for a second. 'You mean Ulfred?'

'Just a glimpse. It was perishing dark and completely pissing it down. But I could have sworn it was Walter, standing against the hedge at the top of Bottom Lane. Then he disappeared.'

'He was good at that.'

'I ran down the lane, but there was no sign of him. I figured he'd gone into the house somehow. I got on the radio, told the control room where I was going and went in after him.' Matt leaned back against the seat, and I could feel the fabric of his jacket against my skin. 'That place is a lot spookier when you're on your own,' he said, looking towards the Witcher house.

'Tell me about it,' I agreed. Hearing Matt's version of events was taking me back, all too vividly, to the night both of us had nearly died.

'Rare old game of hide-and-seek you and I were playing that night,' said Matt, and he almost seemed on the verge of smiling again. 'But the house seemed empty,' he went on. 'I looked all round. I was just about to give up, was making my way back down . . .'

I wasn't sure I wanted to hear much more. If he decided he'd said enough I wouldn't argue. 'We should go,' I said.

'They got me on the stairs,' said Matt. 'I opened the door and saw Fain at the bottom, with that fucking snake hanging round his neck like a pet. He must have killed Clive and then followed me down.'

'It's OK. Don't—'

'I was about to yell at him to put his weapon . . . Christ, I'll laugh about it one day. I didn't get the chance to finish. There was a noise behind me. Ulfred must have taken the scenic route, the same way you got in. He swung something at me and I fell. It stunned me for a minute or two. And that was all the time our preacher friend needed. I guess you know the rest. And you're right. We need to get moving. Help an old man to his feet.'

Matt reached out an arm, and I took it, pulling gently. He came up far too easily; there was nothing of him.

'Where's Fain now?' I asked, as we set off back to the path.

'Custody. Still claiming he really is Archie Witcher and that Ulfred is responsible for the murders. He's wasting his time. Even without DNA evidence we have three people who picked him out of an identity parade.'

'After all this time?'

'Yup. Reverend Stancey, Janet Dodds and Margaret Rosing. Ironically, I think they'd have been his next three victims. Even after fifty years, they were all certain.'

'Not someone you forget in a hurry,' I said. 'What about Ruby?' I asked. 'Did she take part?'

'She couldn't identify him; became very distressed.'

'She's very frail,' I said, wanting to be fair to Ruby.

'She's written to him three times. And put in a request to visit.'

'You're kidding me?'

'We see it all the time.' Matt stopped, took off his glasses and rubbed both eyes. 'Unprincipled, charismatic men in prison inevitably attract a female following. It's nice guys like me who can't get a look-in.'

Another glance at my left wrist. Still no watch there. Had that been flirting? Then I remembered the red-haired Amazon I'd seen in Matt's house that night. *I'm Rachel, Matt's g—*

In the distance I thought I could hear the engines of several cars. We set off again. 'Was Fain the one who visited Ulfred?' I asked.

'He was. Rose Scott has identified him too. And those were Fain's fingerprints on that supposed will of Violet's. The case against him is pretty strong.'

'Will he stand trial?'

Matt drew a deep breath. 'Personally, I doubt it,' he said.

534

'Why?'

We'd almost reached the gate. We stopped and faced each other, across Walter's sweet-scented path. 'I think he'll be pronounced unfit to plead,' he said. 'The court will order a psychiatric evaluation, even if he won't agree to it himself. The man's completely insane.'

'You sound very sure about that.'

'I looked into his eyes when he put that snake on me.'

For a split second, the eyes looking down at me were no longer grey, bespectacled, a little bloodshot. They had the colour of hard-packed ice.

I could hear car doors slamming. Walter had arrived at St Birinus.

'How soon do you leave?' asked Matt, who must surely have heard them too.

'Next month.' We had to go. They would have lifted Walter out of the hearse, be carrying him up the church path.

'Just when we were getting close,' said Matt.

'I'll be back by Christmas,' I muttered, noticing that aphids had already appeared on the tiny rosebuds around the gate and thinking that Walter would have had a plan for dealing with them. 'A locum's covering my job. I haven't resigned.'

'Hmm,' he said.

'What?'

'I can understand a wildlife vet from rural Dorset becoming a TV star. I just can't see her making the return journey.'

We looked at each other, then I raised my left hand again and glanced down.

'There's no watch on that wrist,' said Matt. 'It's ten minutes past the hour, and we are officially in trouble with Reverend Percy.'

'I'm used to that.' I carried on examining my wrist, as though a watch might miraculously appear if I looked for long enough. 'He's on a personal mission to get me into the choir.'

'He tells me he's seen a lot of you recently.'

Somehow, we'd moved closer. I could smell the wool of Matt's jacket, warm in the sunshine, his skin, his hair.

'Are you OK?' he asked.

It was a question I really couldn't answer. I had found myself at St Nicholas' rather frequently over the last three weeks. My thoughts had a way of clearing, somehow, when I was in the old church building. The horrid, claustrophobic jumble of Fain, Ulfred, dark water and poisoned flesh would fade away and there'd be space in my head to mourn for Mum; to think about the future. And when I got scared, when I jumped at shadows and my breathing threatened to spiral out of control, sitting at the organ always managed to calm me.

A familiar scent was drifting up. I bent low and swept my hand over the camomile that crept across Walter's path before straightening and holding it up to Matt. He raised his own hand and pressed mine closer to his face. I could feel his breath on my fingers, his mouth against my palm, as the church bell began its toll for the dead.

Had I found the faith I'd been looking for my whole life? I honestly don't know. Was it my mother I heard that night, guiding and calming me as I stared death in the face, or just the better, stronger part of me? I'm still thinking about it. For now, all I can be certain of is that there came a night when I walked among serpents. And they did not harm me.

Epilogue

HISSY CLARA, THE SMALLER OF THE TWO PAPUAN taipans, was released on to a grassy hillside of her home island a few months later. Ultimately, over six million people around the world would watch the footage as Sean North unfastened the lock on her cage and gently coaxed her out. I'm in the shot too, smiling, as the gunmetal- and amber-coloured snake, grown to nearly three metres long, shimmered in the sunshine and sped towards freedom.

Her larger sibling was never seen again.

THE END

Author's Note

The portrayal of snakes in *Awakening*, their habits and the effects of their venom, is as accurate as I have been able to make it and I have to thank Richard Gibson, the curator of lower vertebrates and invertebrates at Chester Zoo, for correcting the silliest of my mistakes. Those that remain are my responsibility, not his. It wasn't always easy, balancing Richard's insistence on fairness and accuracy with my need to write a scary book, but I hope, in the end, he thinks I've done justice to these fascinating and beautiful creatures. I should also point out that I've found no proof that grass snake swarms, as described in *Awakening*, really do take place, but I know of people who swear they have seen them. Richard thinks these sightings will be cases of mistaken identity; I prefer to believe that even on this tiny island of ours, we still have a few things to learn about the world around us.

The Church of God with Signs Following and the Church of the Latter Rain are real organizations and the accounts in *Awakening* of their founding and their early work are based on documented evidence. Joel Morgan Fain is a fictional character but George Hensley, William Branham and Franklin Hall were real people. The publication *Formula for Raising the Dead* by Franklin Hall is also real – I own a copy myself.

Acknowledgements

The following reference books came in very handy: *Venomous Snakes of the World* by Mark O'Shea; *The Serpent's Tale: Snakes in Folklore and Literature* by Gregory McNamee; *Keeping and Breeding Snakes* by Chris Mattison; and *The Art of Keeping Snakes* by Philippe de Vosjoli. Thanks, once again, to the ladies at the library.

In addition, a number of people very generously gave their time and their expertise to help me write this book and I would like to thank them. For the ecclesiastical detail, I am indebted to Avril Neal and Andrew Haseldine; my medical and psychiatric friends are Bridget Davies, Denise Stott and Mary Weisters; Adrian Summons was a star when it came to police procedure; and for all matters veterinary and zoological I am sincerely grateful to Fiona Smith, Richard Gibson, Kevin Eatwell and the Yorkshire Swan Rescue Hospital.

I would like to thank the team at Transworld for their encouragement, their enthusiasm and their unfailing hard work; in particular, Sarah Turner, Patsy Irwin,

Nick Robinson and Kate Samano. In the US, my thanks are due to Kelley Ragland and Matthew Martz of Minotaur Books.

Team Buckman continue to work miracles, whilst Anne Marie Doulton is slowly making herself indispensable. My thanks and love to them.

Sacrifice

S. J. Bolton

Moving to remote Shetland has been unsettling enough for consultant surgeon Tora Hamilton; even before the gruesome discovery she makes one rain-drenched afternoon . . .

The corpse I could deal with. It was the context that threw me . . .

Deep in the peat soil of her field she uncovers the body of a young woman. Her heart has been removed, and the marks etched into the woman's skin bear an eerie resemblance to carvings Tora has seen in her own cellar.

And there I'd been, thinking the day couldn't possibly get any worse.

But as Tora begins to ask questions, terrifying threats start rolling in like the cold island mists . . .

'Splendidly crafted, deeply disturbing . . . This debut novel will deservedly be a bestseller'
THE TIMES

'A chilling, **mesmerising** debut thriller'
TESS GERRITSEN

'A **dazzling** debut in thriller-writing: fast paced, gripping and full of atmosphere'
CLASSIC FM

'Grabs from the very beginning and **holds on tight**'
LITERARY REVIEW

9780552156158